DESTINY

SKYE MALONE

Destiny
Book Nine of the Awakened Fate Series

Cover design by Karri Klawiter
www.artbykarri.com

Proofreading by Monica Bogza
www.trustedaccomplice.com

ISBN-10: 1-940617-62-6
ISBN-13: 978-1-940617-62-6

Library of Congress Control Number: 2019905985

Join Skye Malone's mailing list to hear about new releases!
www.skyemalone.com/mailinglist

PRONUNCIATION GUIDE

Dehaian (deh-HYE-an)
Driecara (dree-uh-KAR-uh)
Greliaran (greh-lee-AR-an)
Ivalaen (ih-val-AY-en)
Kreyus (KRAY-us)
Periantrea (per-ee-AHN-tree-uh)
Prijoran (prih-JOR-an)
Ruanir (ru-ahn-eer)
Sieranchine (see-EHR-ahn-cheen)
Strakirin (strah-KEE-rehn)
Teariad (tee-AR-ee-ad)
Venika (ven-EE-kuh)
Vetorian (vet-OR-ee-an)
Yvaria (ih-VAR-ee-uh)
Zekerian (zeh-KEHR-ee-en)

For Keri
My sister, my ally, my friend.
Love you.

PROLOGUE

OBLIVION

In the darkness, the creature floated, surrounded by silence, drifting into the void. There was nothing now. Nothing to see, to hear.

To fear.

There was only the silence. Dark. Empty.

Endless.

It wasn't afraid. It had been once, perhaps, but the past was gone and didn't matter anymore. Now, there was only peace, welcomed, craved, finally achieved.

It had searched so long for peace.

And then, in the darkness, there was a light.

∽ 1 ∽

ARI

"Gods of the ocean…" Damerion whispered. "We're too late."

The Vetorian city of Periantrea spread out below us, a wasteland of shredded tents beneath a magical veil that flickered in and out of existence like a spark from a dying fuse. Where once there'd been a market inside the hollowed-out shell of a crashed commercial plane, now there was a ragged confetti of tinfoil scattered as far as I could see. The sunken military ship that held Kreyus' throne room lay on its side, toppled from its resting place against boulders a hundred stories high. Even the rocks hadn't survived unscathed. Gravel and debris peppered the destruction, as if tossed around by a giant child.

Which described Logan well, all things considered.

My stomach churned. That would-be rapist jerk wasn't what he used to be: a strakirin, a ruanir, a *person*, albeit a sociopathic one. Where he'd once had green scales, glowing hair, and an eel tail like me, somehow the magic that had nearly killed us at the sunken ruins of the wizards' island had instead transformed him into an amorphous creature like the Beast. From the looks of it, he had powers like the Beast too.

I cast a half-hearted glance at the others around me. Soldiers and mercenaries, all of them. Whoever had survived the canyon where Logan had become what he was now. "Do you think they made it out?" I asked. "The Vetorians? Did they…"

I could read the expressions on their faces. Dehaian bodies collapsed into nothing when they died. Explained a lot about how humans had never come across one.

And why we possibly weren't seeing any now.

"They would have fled if they could." Ezio's voice was tight. These were his people. His tribe. God only knew how many friends and family he might have lost today.

Damerion glanced at him, his normally stoic face touched by sympathy. They loved each other, Damerion and Ezio. Being soldiers from different nations didn't change that.

"Where would they go?" I tried. "Is there a hideout or—"

Metal creaked in the eerie silence. A door on the ship inched open. Paused. Inched a bit wider.

Ezio darted down toward it. "Hello?" He said something in a language I didn't know.

Someone answered in what sounded like the same language.

"They've got wounded," Ezio called up to us.

The mercenaries took off immediately, flying down to join him.

"Go," Damerion ordered several of the soldiers behind us. "Help them."

The guards sped down toward Ezio as the door on the side of the ship opened fully.

"The rest of you, search the wreckage," Damerion continued. "Find any survivors you can."

Soldiers raced away.

"And look for any communications relays that are still active!" Damerion shouted after them.

I stuck close to Damerion, moving as fast as I could with a rib that was almost certainly fractured, if not broken. That's what the Yvarian field medic had said, anyway. The only medic left, with precious few supplies after the attack in the canyon and every attack before that. Even the glowing gel, sieranchine, that the dehaians used to heal wounds was gone now.

But I was in much better shape than the dehaians who emerged from the sunken ship.

I slowed, shocked. Swimming fitfully, dehaians kicked their way from the wreckage, many of them supported between those who were only in slightly better condition. Shredded fins met my eyes. Bloody cuts on skin and scales alike, too. Some of the wounded seemed barely conscious, and their companions struggled to lift them out from the toppled vessel.

My God…

"Is the Praelex there?" Ezio called. "Did he survive?"

"Here." Kreyus swam from the doorway. A ragged gash marred his forehead, and another showed on his cream-colored tail, long and deep. The only hint that it hurt him to move was the tightness around his eyes. Pausing at the door, he reached back to help someone else out.

Chloe.

A breath pressed from me. She was alive. Her cheek was

swollen, she had the beginnings of what looked like a black eye, and she cradled one of her pale arms against the cream scales on her chest. Kreyus said something to her, and she nodded, jerking her chin slightly as if to tell him to go on.

He didn't budge. Putting an arm around her, he kept her close while they both swam up toward us.

"What happened?" Damerion called.

"We could ask you the same thing, commander," Kreyus replied. "One moment, my daughter was debating our current Yvarian policy with me, and the next…" He glanced at Chloe. Despite his calm expression, I caught a flash of worry in his eyes.

"Noah," Chloe asked. "Is he, um…"

I wrapped my arms around myself protectively. I didn't want to answer that, because I knew what everyone around me believed. That Noah was dead. That he'd been killed in the canyon, destroyed by the old magic unleashed by Osias—the Driecaran spy who was still out there somewhere, hellbent on starting a war.

But I wouldn't believe he was really gone. I just wouldn't. I'd thought Noah was dead before, killed by the poison inside me, and I was wrong. Even if I couldn't feel a single trace of him through the empathic connection he'd restored between us moments before he… before he *didn't* die… that didn't mean a damn thing.

I'd see him again. I'd feel his arms around my body, supporting me, holding me, whenever he got out of the avalanche that had buried the island's ruins in the canyon. He had the power to shake the ground like an earthquake, after all. I couldn't go to him, because the magic there would hurt me, but he'd still get out. I just had to hang on till then.

"Gone, my lady," Damerion said. "He sacrificed himself to save us."

Chloe turned her face away, crushing her lips against each other as if to keep a sob inside. I looked anywhere but at her.

"Noble young man," Kreyus said quietly. "Sacrificing himself twice to save his… friends." His gaze flicked to me before returning in concern to his daughter. "She felt it, when the Beast came under attack and when he…" His hand tightened around Chloe's shoulder. "When he died."

My temper flared, driving a protest to the tip of my tongue, and I clamped my mouth shut against it. Arguing wouldn't help anyone right now, me included, because in the end, it wouldn't matter whether they said he was dead or not. Noah would still come back. He would prove them wrong.

He had to prove them wrong.

"However," Kreyus continued, "given that anything strong enough to kill the Beast would undoubtedly be a threat to us as well, I ordered my people to take defensive positions till we could evaluate the situation." He paused. "There was only enough time for some to reach safety."

"What stopped him?" I blurted out.

"Him?" Kreyus turned to me, an eyebrow rising.

"We didn't see," Chloe said. She wasn't looking at me either. Or at anyone. "Some of the Vetorians, they… they shouted something about darkness and then slammed the door. We heard them screaming outside, but they…" She seemed to run out of words to describe it.

"The throne room is the most heavily defended part of the city." Kreyus' grip on Chloe shifted, almost as if he was reassuring himself that she was still safely with him. "As many layers of magic protect it as those on your palace at Nyciena. The creature took the ship down around us, and then seemed to grow… amused." His jaw muscles clenched. "We heard laughter before it moved on."

"We have to warn Zeke." Chloe looked up. "Everyone in Teariad too. If that thing goes through there…"

"Our soldiers are searching for a functional relay now, my lady," Damerion said.

She nodded, the motion tight.

"Why did you say 'him'?" Kreyus asked, watching me intently.

I didn't know how to explain. "The, uh… the thing that attacked you was, um—"

"Commander!" A soldier raced toward us, her brown pony-tail whipping in the water with her speed. "We found working communication relays."

"Where?" Damerion replied.

She pulled to a sharp stop. "There's one in Lady Chloe's tent and another by the weapons storage." The woman paused. "We've made contact with a caravan that was headed to a nearby village, sir."

"And?" Kreyus demanded.

The soldier glanced toward him, suddenly looking like

she regretted not leaving more space between herself and the Praelex. "At least one village destroyed. No survivors."

Kreyus turned away. Chloe appeared nauseated. "Did you reach Nyciena?" she asked weakly.

"They're requesting the king's presence now, my lady."

Chloe drew a breath like she hadn't been breathing this entire time. Damerion gestured for the soldier to lead the way.

Chloe's tent was flattened, its contents scattered across the seafloor like everything else around it. Among the wreckage, the soldiers had propped a metal ring up on a stand. The water inside it seemed to shimmer oddly, glowing with a blue-green light and moving differently than anything else around us.

"—on his way." The voice seemed to come from nowhere. We drew closer, and the blur of blue-green light resolved into the face of a dehaian woman. "Is Lady Chloe—"

The woman cut off, glancing to her right and then moving out of view quickly.

Zeke appeared. "What is it? What's happened?"

The soldier backed away fast as Chloe swam up to the communications relay. "Zeke?"

"Are you—" Alarm and anger suffused his expression when he saw the swelling on her face and her swiftly darkening black eye. "Who did that to you?"

"You have to get out of Nyciena. There's a… a creature. It…" Chloe shook her head like she was fighting for the words. "Zeke, it killed Noah."

My fingers dug into my forearms at the words. They weren't real. They wouldn't be real. He'd show them.

Shock moved through Zeke's expression. He dropped his gaze away, processing her statement.

"It destroyed Periantrea and a village near here too," Chloe continued. "Killed… I don't know how many it killed."

Zeke looked back up sharply. "Your father?"

"He's alive. But this thing… It might be heading east, we think."

The king was silent for a moment and then turned to someone out of view. "Raise all defenses. Broadcast an alert to all of our allies and then evacuate the city. Send everyone to the southern and northern encampments. If this thing cuts a straight line through Nyciena, maybe it'll miss them."

"Zeke," Chloe said.

He turned back to her.

"Please go with them," she pleaded. "Right away. Please don't wait."

He hesitated. "I'll go as quickly as I can."

That wasn't a yes, and I could tell Chloe knew it. "Zeke—"

Kreyus put an arm around her shoulder again. "May your defenses hold, Highness."

Zeke nodded. His eyes went back to Chloe. "See you soon." He added something in a strange language, and a struggling smile pulled at Chloe's lips. She repeated it back to him.

The connection ended.

"How soon can we leave for Nyciena?" Chloe asked immediately, turning to the others.

"My lady," Damerion started.

Chloe pinned him with a look that spoke volumes, most of

them violent.

"You are safer where that creature is not," Kreyus said.

Chloe didn't respond.

"Your people need you here," Kreyus continued.

"Those are my people too." She didn't meet his eyes. "Chloe Kowalski, Lady of Yvaria, valya Praelex of the Ivalaen. We agreed to that. And if anything happens…" She struggled for words, unable to bring herself to continue.

Kreyus was silent for a moment. "Ezio!"

The Vetorian swam over to us quickly.

"I am reassigning you to the defense of the valya Praelex. That is your sole mission. Her life, your hands. Do I make myself clear?"

My stomach twisted, my gut telling me what was behind the stone-cold look in Kreyus' eyes. He'd kill Ezio if something happened to Chloe. He really would.

Ezio didn't even blink. "Yes, sir."

"Gather five others you trust. I want three guards around her at all times, in rotating shifts, understand?"

Ezio nodded.

"Dismissed."

Kreyus looked to Chloe as Ezio swam away. "I do not approve of this, daughter." His voice was so low, I could barely hear him.

"I know," she replied.

Chloe reached out, clasping Kreyus' hand. He looked at her a moment longer, something almost soft slipping into his eyes.

And then it was gone. "My people require medical

attention, commander, and I have not seen our doctors among the wounded."

Damerion regarded him briefly. "You will have our assistance." He turned, calling out orders for his soldiers to scavenge medical supplies and triage the wounded. Kreyus brought Chloe with him, heading for the nearest person who could help them.

I hovered, uncertain what to do. The dehaians were going to keep heading toward Nyciena, and I needed to get home—which, based on what Ezio had told me, was basically in the same direction.

But I also didn't want to leave.

My gaze drifted to the miles upon miles between me and the canyon where I'd last seen Noah. Inside my mind, I reached for the connection between us gingerly.

Silence. But he was back there, and the farther I got from him, the less I could do to help—because there had to be *something* I could do to help. Even if I couldn't feel him, even if the distance wasn't hurting like it always had in the past, that didn't mean anything about whether he was alive or—

"Ari?"

I flinched.

Damerion hesitated. "Any sign of strakirin?"

I shook my head.

He nodded, still studying me, but now a hint of sympathy crept into his eyes. He'd been kind to me on the way here, kinder than he'd been before the canyon. Gentler, in a way, as if he cared about more than just his target or his mission to stop the judges and the Driecarans. As if my pain at the fact Noah was still back there—not dead, because he wouldn't be dead—might matter to him.

Beneath the battle-hardened commander, I was finally catching glimpses of the person he seemed to be inside.

"The Vetorians will have medical supplies. You can get that rib treated." He twitched his head toward the Yvarian medic. "Follow him. He'll make sure you're taken care of."

"Thanks."

He started away, only to pause when I didn't move. "Your people still need you, Ari. We do as well. We can't tell whether that thing is coming if you leave."

I gave a tight nod, unsure what to say. Noah needed me too. I couldn't help him by staying here, or by going farther away.

Damerion echoed the nod thoughtfully, but he didn't leave until I swam toward the medic like he'd suggested.

I kept myself from looking back again while I continued toward the flattened tents. I felt like the rope in a complicated game of tug of war. The dehaians needed me. My family needed me. But so did Noah. Maybe he was unconscious. Maybe that's why I couldn't feel his presence, and why the distance didn't hurt. I didn't know if the Beast *could* fall unconscious, but that wasn't the point. He was still out there.

He had to be.

And meanwhile, Logan could be anywhere. He could be circling back here right now, for that matter.

I hugged my arms around my middle. Logan wouldn't, though. Somehow, I just knew he wouldn't. He'd head for the shore, for the wizards, and for the judges too. But first, he'd have fun.

My gaze slipped over the wreckage of the city. Fun like this.

And there wasn't anyone in his path with the power to stop him.

❧ 2 ❧

BAYLIE

"What the hell *are* you?" Declan muttered, his gaze locked on the vial of my blood in his hand.

I ignored him. It wasn't like I had an answer anyway. Ahead of me, Olivia's beautiful, two-story cabin was a ruin with a gaping hole blown straight through from the cellar to the roof. A good chunk of the living room and bedroom furniture lay on the grass around us, the majority of it little more than splinters and shredded fabric. Most of the windows were broken too, while in the cellar, pipes were still leaking water and who knew what else onto the shattered concrete floor.

My fault, all of it, even if I didn't have a clue what I'd done.

But I was pretty sure I knew why.

I shifted on the deck chair that Jace had salvaged for me from the back porch. Noah was gone. Dead.

For real this time.

The words weren't real, though. My mind couldn't accept them. I'd thought he was dead last summer, and then he wasn't. I'd thought maybe he wasn't fully *him* anymore, and then he was. So this…this was some kind of misunderstanding. This pain in my chest, this knowledge that was growing like a black hole inside me, waiting for me to believe it so I could fall and fall and fall into the dark. It wasn't real.

It couldn't be real.

Blinking fast to drive away the tears, I fastened my attention on the house again. The landwalker elders hurried in and out of the front door, carrying whatever they could salvage to the cars and trucks nearby. They were concerned the judges might be on their way here after detecting what I'd done. They were also concerned the house might collapse, which was fair. I was too. I'd seen the cracks I caused in the cellar walls. Their research equipment had come first—a motley collection of vials and sensors and machinery whose purpose I didn't know, all arrayed around the hardwood deck chair where I sat. Extension cords ran from the house, supplying the power for the machines, though even those had been cause for concern. Declan and I were almost seventy feet from the house now. The elders were fairly sure I hadn't caused a gas leak on top of everything else, but it paid to be careful.

"If you hadn't destroyed the microcellular regeneration analyzer…" Declan continued.

I gave him an annoyed look. I was tired of apologizing. I'd been doing it all afternoon. And it wasn't like it'd been his equipment anyway.

Or his house.

He hadn't even looked away from the vial. It was like autopilot for him, complaining and generally being an ass.

"Bite me," I retorted.

Declan's gaze flicked over to me, heated.

I glared at him.

His lip twitched. He went back to adjusting a setting on the metal box at his feet.

"Hey."

Instinctively, I tensed at the sound of Jace's voice. I'd barely managed three words to him since Angelica's not-quite-attack yesterday. The landwalker woman had an ability like Ellie, the unusual reversal of the "make you like themselves" power that all the elders seemed to have. Rather than project their own state onto someone else, rare elders could flip that around and get inside people's heads, make themselves like those people to get a read on what was going on with that person. Angelica had been trying to see if any of us was secretly changed by the judges and turned into a spy, and she'd started with Jace without a shred of his permission.

But it hadn't gone according to her plan. I tried to get between them, my arm bumped his, and my weird magic that I'd taken in from the Beast by accident a year ago had decided to intervene. The darkness inside me had rushed into him, *through* him, and driven Angelica's landwalker power back, nearly knocking the woman off her feet in the process.

And it had felt amazing. The first time he'd tried to share magic with me, I'd ended up hugging the porcelain king, my stomach doing flip-flops to get everything inside me *out*. But that had been an attempt to merge these forces inside us like they were the same thing. They weren't.

But when they worked together in balance like that…

"You thirsty?" Jace asked, seeming oblivious to the way I couldn't quite look at him. "They're getting the bottled water out of storage."

"Uh…" I glanced at Declan. Focusing on him was easier. "I can't leave just—"

"We're done for now," Declan interrupted, his attention back on the vial in his hand. Using a dropper, he drew out a small sample of my blood.

My attempted excuse summarily destroyed, I floundered for something else to say and came up with nothing. Pushing to my feet, I started toward the house again, leaving Declan muttering over what he was learning from his machines. "So how much longer are we going to be here?"

Jace shrugged, and I caught a glimpse of him from the corner of my eye. Dust from the wreckage coated the lean muscles of his arms in pale gray swaths. The thought that he looked like a model dressed as a construction worker flitted through my head.

I bashed it down fast. That helped *nothing* right now.

"We're going as fast as we can," he said, "but there's a lot of research to move. Twenty minutes, maybe less?"

I made a noise of understanding, but my attention still darted around the clearing. We were okay for now. The judges hadn't shown up, and maybe they wouldn't. Just because I'd blown up a house with magic a little while ago, and just because the landwalkers had figured out a way to spot my magic from a distance, that didn't mean the Judiciary would too. We could be panicking over nothing.

The anxiety thrumming through the back of my mind didn't quite believe that. We needed to get out of here.

"It'll be okay," Jace assured me.

I nodded.

"So… any change?"

I hesitated. "No."

He was quiet. His sister might have been part of this, I knew. No guarantees, obviously. Noah had been hunting for Ari, but there wasn't any way to know whether he'd found her, let alone know whatever else might have happened. But the judges wanted Noah dead, and if something had hurt him— yeah, hurt; I could say hurt, that wasn't as bad—there was a chance she could've been there.

"But," I tried, "no news is, you know…"

He didn't respond, and I couldn't blame him. I didn't buy that either.

We walked toward the elders in silence. Ellie was off to one side, finishing her phone call to her parents to reassure them of her safety—the call I'd interrupted by blowing up the house. Robin and several of the others were still hefting boxes into the cars and SUVs, but Olivia and a trio of elders stood by the vehicles, and when we walked closer, the reason for the annoyed look on Olivia's face became clear.

"—it only makes sense to go in that direction," Angelica argued. "Surely you can see that. We have three locations to choose from in Ohio."

Olivia scoffed. "With a known Judiciary base only a hundred

miles from all of them."

Angelica made an irritated noise.

"What about the Carolinas?" another elder offered. "There hasn't been any activity there in a few weeks."

Angelica shook her head. "The closer we stay to the center of any landmasses, the less likely we'll be to draw attention from the—"

"Sir!" A ruanir soldier raced around the corner of the house, a satellite phone clutched in his fist. He scanned the yard fast, spotting Declan and then hurrying to his side.

My anxiety kicked up a notch. This wasn't good. I had no idea what was going on, but the look on that guy's face...

And Declan's. The wizard stood up fast, and I could lipread enough to see him swearing at whatever the man told him.

"What is it?" Olivia called.

Declan barely spared her a glance, snapping orders to the soldier who was nodding so fast it looked like his head was going to fall off.

"Oh, hell," Jace murmured.

Warily, I walked back toward them. "Declan?"

The soldier nodded once more and then ran for the Jeep. Declan didn't move, his chest rising and falling in short breaths. His hand curled around the paper printout of the latest test results, crushing it.

My stomach became lead. "What happened?"

He didn't respond.

"Are Maia and Dhanya okay?" Jace asked.

I glanced at him. His cousin and her fiancée were helping

the resistance leader, Miguel, track the judges and the Judiciary's enforcers. But they should have been safe. Resistance hideouts were like fortresses. I'd never seen anywhere as well protected.

Jace didn't take his eyes off Declan.

"Their hideout was attacked," the man said. "Some goddamn infiltrating…"

My hand rose, covering my mouth. The judges had a way of changing people. Making them into spies against their will. Like the strakirin, only not as complete.

Like the woman who shot me a few weeks ago.

"Are they *okay*?" Jace's voice was hard. Tense.

Declan paused. "No."

A choked noise left me. Jace started shaking.

"Dhanya's hurt. Maia…" Declan shook his head. "There were judges. Davenport and a few others. They took prisoners. Maia." He paused. "Miguel."

"So they could still be alive," Jace interjected.

Declan looked over at him. "Do you really think your cousin is going to survive this?"

"You—" Jace lunged at Declan.

I didn't even think. I rushed between them, grabbing Jace's arm when it rose.

He stopped, staring down at me. His storm-cloud-gray eyes shone nearly silver with rage.

"What do they do?" I called over my shoulder to Declan, still holding onto Jace's arm. "To the people they take, what do they—"

"Ocean magic poisoning. Otherwise known as 'whatever

the hell they want,' and then that's what they claim."

"But Maia is Judge Davenport's daughter. Maybe she—"

"The judges don't care about family. They'll use her to make a point. About us, about not trusting the Judiciary. Her position as Davenport's daughter only means she'll make an even better statement for them."

My skin went cold. "And Miguel?"

"They'll sell him as the mastermind behind her condition."

"Which means what?"

Declan was silent for a moment. "Trial. Execution."

"They'd do that?"

He met my eyes. "They're already publicizing it."

Sweet God.

Declan turned away, packing up the machinery with swift, efficient motions. "I can get him out."

My grip fell away from Jace's arm. "What? No. Declan, you—"

"How?" Olivia asked.

I glanced back to see her walking toward us, clearly having heard him.

Declan kept packing.

"He knows how to use the weapon," I said. "He has since this morning."

Declan's hands paused for a moment, midway through setting several crystals into a crate, and then he continued putting the equipment away, never looking up.

"*What?*" Olivia demanded.

"It will kill him, though," I continued. "Him and any ruanir with ocean magic in them."

Jace made a choked sound. "And if they've already poisoned Maia? If Ari is still out there somewhere?"

Declan didn't stop.

"Dammit." Jace started toward him again. "If you do that, you'll kill them too, you—"

Declan jerked his arm out of Jace's reach. "Ari is *dead*, boy, whether or not her body is still breathing. And if they've gotten their hands on Maia, she's dead too."

Jace stared at him.

"You don't know that," I said softly.

Declan glanced at me. I wanted to wrap my arms around myself at the cold certainty in his eyes. "They'll strap Maia down and pour their version of ocean magic into her at the first secure location they reach—and they have many. They'll flood her system with their power and then twist her around any way they see fit. Maybe drive her mad. Maybe make her a vegetable. And they'll do this in minutes because that's how fast they work. By tomorrow evening, she'll be on every station and channel in the ruanir world, held up as 'proof' that the resistance needs to be stopped at any cost." He shut the equipment crate lid and latched it down. "It's been an hour since the attack. She's already been poisoned."

I didn't know whether to vomit or run for the hills.

"Maybe I can bring her back."

I looked over my shoulder. Ellie stood behind us.

"And maybe you could end up in their hands too." Declan hoisted the crate. "There's no way to get her out now. Miguel, I can help. At least then, the resistance won't die."

"But my cousin has to?" Jace protested.

"Do you think I *want* this?" Declan shouted. "Half the soldiers we had are dead. Today, yesterday, in the days before that. The Judiciary has connections everywhere, and they've been using them to swat us like flies. Veronique is in emergency care, Willa might not make it, and there's not much of anyone left. We have been building the resistance for *decades,* and they've obliterated us in the space of weeks. And now, if they kill Miguel, *everything* could fall apart. I'm sorry your cousin got caught up in this, I truly am. But if you think I'm going to let the resistance die because you can't see the bigger picture—"

Jace punched him.

Declan stumbled back and collapsed on the grass, the crate tumbling away. His hand pressed to his nose.

"Fuck your bigger picture!" Jace yelled. "You think I don't see that? You think I don't know how bad this is?" He stared at Declan for a moment, breathing hard. "We are going to find a way to save them all, do you understand?" Jace cast a quick look toward me and Ellie. "All of them."

Ellie nodded.

I didn't know what to say. How was he going to do that?

"The only chance we've got," Declan said, his voice muffled by his hand, "is this weapon. Do you get that, kid? The only shot."

"What about her?" Jace pointed to me.

I froze. Wait, what? No, he couldn't just volunteer me to…

Declan grunted, the sound irritated and dismissive. "Her

magic isn't compatible with the spell."

"Her magic blew up a house!"

"Guys," I sputtered, "I'm not—"

Jace looked at me, and I couldn't continue. Frantic desperation filled his eyes, and it was painful to see. This was his family. What was *left* of his family. His father was dead, he might have lost his sister, and now Maia had been taken too.

But I wasn't a weapon. I was a person hanging on by their fingernails to normal. Yes, I'd blown up a house. Yes, I'd taken out a group of enforcers somehow. And yes, I'd even volunteered to be in the same room with an enforcer while Miguel interrogated him, in the hope I could stop the guy if he tried to kill my friend. But that didn't mean I could go charging at the Judiciary like Rambo. Helping Declan not need to *kill* himself was one thing, but I couldn't go to *war*.

"Jace…" I shook my head, struggling for words to explain. "I… I'm sorry. I…"

Hurt crept into his eyes. Disbelief too.

I didn't know what to say. "I-I can't. I'm sorry."

His expression started to shut down on me. The sight was like a blade of ice to my chest.

I turned away, retreating toward the line of trees across the yard. I needed space. Air. Something. I couldn't think with him staring at me, with all of them staring—

Noah stood at the edge of the forest.

My gaze snapped toward the line of trees while my feet slammed to a halt.

"Baylie?" Ellie called from behind me.

He was gone.

A short gasp left me. I looked around, frantic. He'd been there. I'd seen him. From the corner of my eye, yeah, and not actually all that clearly, but I'd sworn…

I hadn't felt him, though.

Yeah, but so what? Maybe something had changed. Maybe I'd just not noticed it this time. Maybe…

"Baylie?" Ellie came up beside me.

Maybe…

My arms drew around myself, clenching down on my middle, while my gaze slid back to the swaying tree branches and the black-green shadows of the dense underbrush where I thought he'd stood. I'd been four when my mom died. Too young to remember much of her beyond a few details, all of which were like gold to me. The smell of her strawberry-vanilla shampoo in the soft waves of her blond hair. The sound of her laugh when I'd do something goofy or try to tell a joke. The way she'd hold me at night before I went to bed, and say that she loved me to the moon and back.

I'd stared at the moon a lot after she died, wondering if she was up there.

But for weeks, years even, I would think I'd see her. In a store. Down the street. Beyond a crowd. To this day, I'd catch a glimpse of someone in a car, their face blurry through the windshield, and sometimes for a moment, just for one *brief* moment…

And now I'd lost Noah too.

Shivering rocked me, radiating from my core.

This wasn't about the resistance. This wasn't about volunteering for war. They'd killed him. Those judges. That Judiciary. They'd gone after a guy who was as much a brother to me as any stupid title of "step"-whatever, who was kind and sweet and thoughtful and funny even after everything he'd been through, and they'd murdered him without a second goddamn *thought*.

He was dead because of them.

Black smoke drifted from my skin, so faint it was just a shadow on the breeze.

"B-Baylie?" Ellie backed away warily.

I glanced over my shoulder to the wizards. "How do we find them?"

Jace faltered. Relief spread over his face, along with something that really might have been gratitude.

I snapped my gaze over to Declan. I couldn't deal with that look on Jace's face right now. I needed to focus. I needed this rage.

Because that black hole was calling. The one that wanted to pull me down into the hell of having *one more person* I'd think I saw who would never, ever be coming back again.

"You're not enough," Declan said. "One person isn't going to be able to take on all the forces they'll have around Miguel. Now, if I use this weapon—"

"No." My voice was flat. Cold.

"Goddammit, Baylie!" Declan swore. "My life doesn't matter! Do you get that? Not if it stops them. Not if they're destroyed. I will *gladly* give up my life if it means they die, so stop stalling and—"

"I said *no*." The ground quivered beneath my feet. "No one else dies, understand? No one."

"Except them," Jace said quietly.

I trembled. I wasn't a killer.

They'd also never stop.

"We need more than just you," Declan stated with a tone of forced calm. "And unless you know any other superpowered magical monsters…?" He nodded at my silence. "Right. So you killing *yourself* isn't a goddamn option. We—"

"Chloe."

I glanced at Ellie.

"Chloe," she repeated. "And Zeke too. Plus he has an army."

I stared at her. If Chloe came here…

Declan pushed up from the ground. "Who the hell—"

"The king of Yvaria," Ellie interrupted. "And his girlfriend. She, um… she's not like a regular dehaian. Neither is he."

"A dehaian king," Jace repeated, a touch incredulous. "Will he and this Chloe person *help*?"

Ellie shrugged. "We can ask."

"You'd be asking the dehaians to start a war," I said.

Her brow rose and fell. "Isn't there one already?"

I stared at her. Yes. But it wasn't theirs.

"The judges are already targeting the dehaians, Baylie." Ellie gave me a look like she could see my thoughts on my face. "Those fake attacks meant to look like they were orchestrated by Yvaria, the fact they've made these strakirin creatures capable of going in the ocean…" She made a helpless gesture. "The judges are coming after them too."

"What can these two do?" Declan demanded.

Ellie watched me as if weighing what to say. "A lot."

Jace nodded, appearing sold on the idea. "How do we get in touch with them?"

"They have communications relays off the coast of Santa Lucina," Ellie replied. "Other ones elsewhere too."

"Devices that let you send a message to dehaian cities out in the ocean," I explained when Jace gave me a questioning look. "But you need magic to use them," I finished, directing the statement to Ellie. "And they're underwater."

"So we find a dehaian," Ellie replied.

I hesitated. Zeke had servants, ones who stayed on the coast to pass messages for us in case I needed to reach Chloe while she was underwater. But given everything that was going on, we had no way of being sure they were still around.

California was a long way to travel only to find out all the dehaians were gone.

"Assuming they're not all hiding after what the judges have done," Jace said, putting words to my concern. "The strakirin, the fake 'dehaian' attacks, and who knows what else… They could be gone. And they're not exactly easy to tell apart from humans, regardless."

"We could find one," Ellie insisted. "I've been working with them all year. I'll recognize them."

"Unless the ones you know are gone, like Jace said," I argued. "We could be going to California for nothing."

She gave me a betrayed look.

I turned away, unsure what to say. I wanted the judges to

pay for this. I did. But that didn't mean I was on board for risking Chloe's and Zeke's lives, on top of the lives of whatever soldiers they'd send. Enough people had died.

And anyway, I wasn't really sure I was ready to tell Chloe what happened to me, what I sort of *was* now.

Olivia cleared her throat. I glanced over my shoulder to see her watching us all, that sharp look back in her eyes. "Ellie's right. We need the dehaians. And as far as finding them goes…" Her gaze slid over all of us equally. "…if you'll trust me, I think I have a plan."

3

THE VOID

Memory, cold and distant, flickered like a dying star. Oblivion had a shape. A space. A form amid the emptiness. Walls. Pillars. Stone and dust, white, gray. Chipped figures carved in the rock.

Familiar shapes…

It knew this place. It had been to this place before the fire, before the satisfying death with the orange-black flames.

And after.

Fear arrived then, fluttering like the heart of a trapped liar, pinned down while they screamed. This was wrong. There should not have been an after. The why was gone, but the why didn't matter. It didn't want to be here. To see this place, to come to this place.

It had died in this place.

…would have died.

…could have died.

It had to go. Escape. Leave now because it remembered. Liars had been here. Were here. It had to get away before the liars came back. The poisoners, the corrupters. The ones who promised peace before they sent the merciless darkness to devour—

Calm.

Fear stuttered, overwhelmed by alarm. It wasn't alone. There were two of it here. Itself and a whisper. A whisper and itself. But neither was complete. Something was missing now.

But what was it? Who was it, and who was the whisper?

The whisper echoed softly through the silence. *Who are we?*

It didn't know. The memory was lost to this place, to the pain. So much had been lost here. Something important now; even that had been taken.

It had to leave. This time had been like before, but worse. Worse than when the soft warmth turned to cruel lies. It remembered that pain, remembered, and that was enough.

Again the whisper came, so quiet, so faint. *Show me…*

4

LOGAN

I sailed through the ocean, an invisible force unrivaled by anything on land or in the seas. In my grasp, I still held a half-dozen dehaians and over a hundred strakirin—my supposed allies and my tools. The water was like air to me, nearly frictionless, and I flew through it, untouchable, unstoppable. Sure, I'd lost a few strakirin back at the canyon. Ari too, not that she mattered. And while I could feel the pestering call of the judges, trying to summon me as though I was some sort of trained dog, the noise was easily ignored and inconsequential.

I'd get to them. Eventually.

But in the meantime, there was the ocean spread out before me like a kingdom all my own. Miles and miles of cities, towns, and villages full of creatures whom I could kill, control, or keep, all based on their usefulness to me. Miles of hills and valleys too, that no silly human could easily reach—and no judge either. Every strakirin with me served as my eyes and ears now. Every dehaian either lived in fear of my presence or provided me a thrill of excitement when they died. Everything was mine, created for me. And in it all, there was only one problem.

The seafloor was too damn empty.

I flicked a tiny bit of my consciousness down, finding a stra-kirin close to the dehaians I held. "Where is the next closest settlement?" I asked through the strakirin.

Osias hesitated.

My strakirin lashed out, the spikes on its arm drawing lines of blood that streamed away from Osias' chest like ribbons. The cuts weren't deep. Nothing more than slightly aggressive papercuts, really. A warning that I wouldn't tolerate obstinance, not when I'd put up with that dehaian spy's attitude for days on end just to get to the canyon.

Not when there was a new god in town, and it was me.

I did understand that he was angry. He wanted to destroy Yvaria. Getting revenge on the nation that wiped out his peo-ple was all that shortsighted fool cared about, and while his rage helped me—his contribution to the judges' plan had led to the creation of the strakirin, after all—it wasn't the most important thing in the world. I'd get to Nycicna. I would. By the time I was done, there wouldn't be a dehaian settlement left standing for a thousand miles.

But that first city had been too much fun to pass up any other settlement on my path. And the thrill I'd gotten from killing those dehaians…

The water shivered with me, a rush of memory and antic-ipation combined. Taking their magic in and watching them die from the draining force of my power had been incredible. Still, I couldn't help but wonder if the emptiness of the ocean around me owed something to the fact I'd left a few alive in that first city. I'd figured they'd warn their allies, but that was part of the point. The taint of fear permeating the ocean. The entire Pacific and beyond, dreading where I would go next.

I just hadn't figured they would all hide so *quickly*.

"Another village." Osias twitched his head; all the motion I would allow him. "That way."

The strakirin slashed him again.

"Sir," he ground out.

That was more like it. He'd barely hesitated that time.

Maybe I could afford to be magnanimous.

"And Nyciena?"

His eyes lit up from more than their normal magical glow. His focus flicked to the strakirin.

Amusement rippled through me. Mortals were so simple, really. I knew what he wanted.

"Straight ahead."

Well, then. What the hell was he upset about?

I sped up. Seconds slid by. Then minutes. Had he lied? He'd said straight ahead, but how far away was this place? I was moving so fast, I would have outdistanced a strakirin in a heartbeat and left any dehaian looking like a tired snail. Surely—

Magic tingled on the edge of my senses.

There they were.

I spread out wider, ready to take hold of the magic defense and tear into it like it was tissue paper. I loved these things. Veils, Osias said they were called. Protection, supposedly, from human detection and the elements and anything else. Except from me, anyway.

This one hurt.

I slowed down, my magic stinging and burning like a bad sunburn until I retreated from the veil. What the—

"What is this?" I asked Osias through another strakirin.

Osias looked irritated. It seemed to be his default expression, though it was tempered by an edge of caution now that his chest looked like a scribble of red crayon. "They must have installed defenses… sir. Most likely for the Beast."

I was the damn Beast.

Lashing out fast, I released a burst of power at the veil, the magic flying out from me like an explosion of lightning from an invisible thunderstorm.

Blinding heat shot through me as if I'd just skinny-dipped in the sun itself. Screams like tiny firecrackers went off around me, inconsequential in the grand scheme of my own agony. The water around me rumbled with my pain.

I withdrew, shaking. They had defenses. Defenses against *me*. Those sons of…

This was all that goddamn former Beast's fault. That waste of space, waste of time, waste of goddamn *power* that it had been, the stupid creature had never taken advantage of what it could do. Except to get in my way, anyhow. It had even stopped me from catching Ari in the canyon, though in the grand equation of things that part was irrelevant. But instead of destroying their cities, that useless monstrosity had bumbled around, giving them ample time to build defenses against it. Against *me*.

If the pathetic creature weren't already dead, I'd bring it

back just to kill it all over again.

Niggling pains still pulled at me. My attention flicked away from the veil.

My strakirin were hurt. Burns, scorch marks, a few were even unconscious—all of which explained the distracting little aches I'd been feeling. Meanwhile, from what I could tell, Osias and the other dehaians seemed dead. Their skin and scales were a mess of red burns and blackened welts.

Dammit.

I tossed all of the dehaians down to the sand and rocks outside the city. A few of them started to crumble in on themselves, disintegrating as they fell, while the others bounced off the boulders like ragdolls and then lay motionless on the ocean floor.

Goddamned Yvarians. Now I'd lost my tour guides as well.

I retreated farther from the veil, baleful irritation boiling in me. This was like that defense around their garrison. A thousand times the size, sure, and with a lot more juice behind it, but still, it was similar. And I'd torn through that—or my strakirin had, even if it'd taken who knew how many of them flinging themselves at the barrier and dying to do it. So I could break through this. I knew I could. I almost wanted to, just to show those uppity little dehaian bastards what happened when they messed with me.

But then, I hadn't even wanted to come here.

I drew back, pain still thrumming through me. This was *Osias'* destination. *Osias'* goal. I was simply being magnanimous, traveling here when there were countless places in the ocean that would be just as much fun to destroy.

Like hell I would hurt myself for a corpse.

I sailed on until the veil of Nyciena disappeared from my senses and the open water was all around me. The pain faded, though the throb of burned skin carried through from my strakirin. But they didn't matter either. I'd get more.

Wait. *How* would I get more?

I slowed down. I hadn't considered that. My strakirin were a finite resource—not necessary for my survival, mind you, and Ari wasn't either, not that one girl mattered—but they were useful as eyes, ears, and hands for when I wasn't in human form.

Could I even return to human form?

I drew to a total stop. What if I couldn't? The judges never anticipated that I'd retain my own will once the transformation in the canyon was complete. They'd planned for me to be their slave. So who knew what they intended for my ability to change form? As it was, I could still hear their pestering little signal, telling me to come back so I could give them my power. They'd never intended *me* to survive at all.

But I had. More than merely *survive*, I'd become a god. And every god needed servants.

Every god needed to punish the wicked who didn't fall in line.

My focus turned to the east and the distant shore I knew waited there. I could go back, see if I could change form like that waste-of-space former Beast had, and then…

Then I'd have the judges make me more strakirin. Thousands upon thousands of strakirin. I'd find Ari too, if I really wanted to bother. And if the Judiciary tried to stand in my way…

Amusement rippled through me. Maybe it was time to show the judges the new god in town.

5

BAYLIE

"This is insane." I stared up at the four-story, gothic edifice in shock. The place looked like it should have lightning flashing behind it, complete with a stormy sky. Maybe a vampire going *mwa-ha-ha* inside too. Instead, the sky was a clear, almost crystalline, late-afternoon blue, and floral landscaping lined the cobblestone circle drive with a profusion of cheerful color.

Holworth Psychiatric Hospital, read the sign outside. We'd traveled for hours to get to it, the elders and the wizards driving in shifts the whole time. Robin and the others were setting up shop in a motel now, several miles away. Meanwhile, Declan, Olivia, and Angelica had kept us with them as they rushed to get here before the place closed for the day—because, of course, showing up after closing would make our presence even more absurd than it already seemed.

Not that it really could get any more absurd. We were meeting Wyatt. *Wyatt*, the guy who'd murdered his own father, who'd hunted Chloe, who'd helped torture Zeke.

Who'd tried to kill me.

If we'd all shown up here in *clown* makeup, this couldn't have been any more insane.

"When you said you had a plan," I continued, "I didn't think—"

"He will work with us," Olivia interrupted. "The past several months have been quite good for him."

"*Good* for him?" I sputtered. "He's a homicidal *maniac*. How could they have been—Wait. How do you even—"

"Angelica has been working with him. We arranged his transfer some time ago, with the blessing of your stepfather."

"Peter knows about this?"

"It was his request. He approached me shortly after I moved to Santa Lucina. As greliarans, your stepfamily's ability to control their innate craving to kill dehaians is nothing short of a miracle. But Peter wanted to do more, to help others of his kind. Given our abilities, and the abilities of someone like Ellie or Angelica, we were his best option." She glanced to Declan. "Of course, we were not aware of the existence of the ruanir at that time."

"But..." I floundered, at a loss for what to say. Months. *Months*, they'd had this bastard locked up here, barely a few hundred miles from where I'd been living, rather than in prison where he belonged.

And where I'd reassured myself he was, each time I woke up from a nightmare of ever seeing his grinning face again.

"Why didn't we call Peter, then?" I tried. "Or Maddox? Or *anyone?*"

Olivia gave me a curious look. "And if something goes

wrong? If Peter or Maddox are injured, or worse, captured or killed by the Judiciary?"

My stomach turned. I couldn't handle that. Not on top of everything else.

"Thus far, very few greliarans have come forward for us to help. Almost none, in fact. He is our best choice."

"But why didn't you tell me?" Ellie asked her mentor, a touch of hurt in her tone. "About him. About this. I could've helped or…"

Olivia's annoyed expression faded. "Peter requested that we didn't."

I blinked. "Why?"

"He was concerned the topic would bring up painful memories, on several fronts."

I didn't know what to say. He'd been right. But at least when Noah was alive…

"We should go," Olivia said. "Angelica?"

The woman reached into her purse and drew out a black wallet. "We shouldn't need it." She extended it to Declan. "But in case we're wrong and your judges have infiltrated this place too, this is your cover. Your name is Jeremiah Barnes. You're a graduate of Harvard Medical School, and you took a second PhD in psychiatry after your mother's diagnosis of schizophrenia. You live in Salt Lake, where you are single, childless, and own a pug named Sigmund. Lately, you've been working with the Future Mental Health Leaders of America pilot program on a volunteer basis because you enjoy giving back to the community."

Declan's eyebrow crept up. "And when exactly did you—"

"We put the IDs together on the way here," Olivia said. "An amalgamation of several false identities we already had prepared." A faint grimace crossed her face. "The past several weeks have not been kind to my people. We have numerous fallback identities in place for all of us now."

She tossed a look to Angelica, who retrieved several other ID cards from her bag. "You're Joe Hargrove," Angelica said to Jace, handing him a driver's license. "College student at UCLA and intern with the Future Mental Health Leaders of America program. You're Samantha Alicort." She handed an ID to Ellie. "Another intern from UCLA. And you're Juliette Graves." She hesitated, not extending the ID my way.

"She doesn't bite," Declan said, a note of amusement in his voice.

Angelica's face tightened. She shoved the ID at me. "You're an intern as well." She clipped her purse shut. "And they are expecting us."

She strode toward the building.

Olivia gave us a small smile. "It'll be fine." She walked after Angelica.

Declan scoffed and followed them, muttering something too low for me to hear.

"So this guy tried to kill you?" Jace asked.

I couldn't come up with any way to explain. Nothing would make this sound less demented than it already was.

Giving him a helpless shrug, I followed the others.

Cool air surrounded us the moment we stepped inside,

making my skin pebble. The waiting area was large, with a ceiling almost two stories above our heads. Like the outside, with its profusion of flowers, more bouquets filled the room here. The multitude of colors continued in enormous paintings that looked taller than I was. The only hint this place was something other than a colorful art exhibit was the security guard in the corner and the heavy steel door blocking access to the rest of the facility, with the words "Permission Required to Enter Beyond This Point" printed in red, blocky letters on its surface.

"May I help you?" said a young woman behind the front desk, her skepticism about us clear in her eyes.

"Hello." Olivia smiled. "I'm Doctor Priscilla Ellison. We're here to speak with Doctor Neuhaus. He should be expecting us."

The woman blinked, appearing alarmed. "You're..." Her gaze darted over us again. "Where are your orderlies? The restraints? When they said you'd—"

Olivia cleared her throat delicately. "Please tell Doctor Neuhaus we've arrived."

The woman stared for a second and then picked up the phone.

I glanced around warily while she spoke in a low voice to someone on the other end. The waiting room was mostly empty, barring the security guard in the corner. He didn't seem to be watching us, not that I believed the middle-distance, not-focused-on-anything-in-particular gaze he'd adopted. The guards at the resistance hideout had done the same thing.

The receptionist set the phone back in its cradle. "He'll be with you shortly."

"Thank you," Olivia replied.

Seconds crawled by. A buzz from the metal door made me jump.

A short man with gray hair emerged. He was wearing a white lab coat and carrying a clipboard like some stereotypical doctor in a commercial. He gave Olivia and Angelica an anxious smile that looked more like the rictus of a Halloween skeleton. "Doctors," he called. "So, uh… so nice of you to come see us today." He flinched, seeming to spot the rest of us for the first time. "And these must be your, um…"

"The interns we discussed, Doctor Neuhaus," Olivia interjected smoothly. "And another psychiatric professional to observe."

"Of course." He smiled the same Halloween-skeleton smile. "Well, then. Uh. Yes. This way?" He gestured to the metal door.

"Indeed," Olivia said.

The others started after him. I hesitated, glancing to the security guard again. Why was this Neuhaus guy so nervous? And the receptionist seemed like Olivia and Angelica freaked her out too.

"Are you coming?" Angelica demanded.

I flinched. "Uh, yeah."

Anxiety still thrumming through me, I followed. The doctor paused at the metal door and pressed a large red button on the wall nearby. He waited for a buzzing sound before pulling the door open and continuing through. A vaguely greenish hallway lay on the other side, with an elevator door at its end.

A security station was visible through a window in the wall, though the steely-eyed guard inside didn't comment on our presence, but instead simply flicked a switch without a word. Another buzz followed, and then the elevator opened.

The doctor rocked nervously the entire ride up to the fourth floor. A white hallway greeted us when the elevator door opened again. Metal doors lined the corridor, each with a small window at eye level in their surface. Cries carried from behind some of them—and those were the most recognizable noises. At the end of the hallway, a security station surrounded by safety glass held several medical personnel and what looked like a miniature pharmacy under heavy lock and key.

Doctor Neuhaus stopped at a door halfway down the hall. "He's been very agitated recently, though up till now he'd been doing well. We haven't seen any sign of combative behavior, at least until yesterday morning."

I fought to keep from shifting my weight nervously. No reason to think that was connected to us. To me.

To Noah.

"Fine," Declan replied.

The man hesitated, glancing to Olivia and Angelica.

"Thank you," Olivia supplied, and then she turned to Ellie. "Stay out here, please. He still has nightmares."

Ellie nodded and backed up beyond the view of the door. The doctor stared after her.

Olivia smiled at him. "We'll be fine."

The man watched Ellie as if she was a wild animal who may not be on his side. "She's the doll, isn't she?"

Huh?

No one explained. "The door, Doctor?" Olivia prompted again, her smile unchanged.

The man nodded, but he still tossed a nervous look to the security station. When he spoke, his voice was just above a whisper. "If you don't get him back here in a few days like you promised, I'm out of a job, you understand?"

"Elders keep their word, Johan. You know that."

I looked the doctor over again. He was a landwalker?

Of course he was. The elders had connections all over the place. Even the chief of police in my hometown had turned out to be one of them.

Doctor Neuhaus seemed barely mollified by Olivia's response, but he opened the door all the same. The room beyond was white from the floor to the ceiling, with a white mattress on the floor and white bars on the single window. The walls were padded, as was the ground.

And in the corner, curled into a ball with his head tucked against the padded surface, huddled a guy I'd hoped never to see again as long as I lived.

"Hello, Wyatt," Olivia said.

The guy flinched at the sound of her voice, but he didn't move from his near-fetal position in the corner. He wore a straitjacket, both his arms pinned inside it, and his brown hair was tousled like it'd been ages since it saw a comb. I knew if he stood up, he'd tower over all of us, a muscled mountain of a twenty-something-year-old with enough strength to crush the life out of us with his bare hands—and that was without bringing his greliaran powers of rock-like skin and unbeliev-able strength into the mix.

Who was I kidding? Even curled in a ball on the floor, he still looked enormous.

"That'll be all," Angelica said to the doctor.

Doctor Neuhaus hesitated. "The orderlies are nearby if you need any…" He seemed to search for a word that probably wasn't synonymous with "protection."

I trembled, not taking my eyes from the homicidal monster who I *knew* could rip out of that straitjacket in a heartbeat if he wanted to.

The doctor gave up. "A few days," he repeated, and then hurried away. Angelica started into the room.

I bit back a nervous protest. This wasn't like last year, I reminded myself. I wasn't trapped in a forest, this guy's deranged brother holding me so tight I thought my ribs would crack. I was in a secure psychiatric hospital. I had wizards around me, and Ellie only a few feet away.

Not to mention whatever the hell *I* was. If Wyatt tried anything, he probably wouldn't live long enough to regret the attempt.

"Good afternoon, Wyatt," Angelica said, her voice cool and calm.

He shifted position a little at this, but he didn't respond.

Angelica sank into a crouch by his side. "How are you feeling?"

A long pause followed. "The… the air is wrong."

My skin crawled. I'd never forgotten his voice, muffled

though it was now. It made my heart race.

A shoulder brushed my own, and I flinched, glancing over fast.

Jace was next to me, his eyes locked on Wyatt. He may not have even known he'd come this close to me.

Maybe.

"How is the air wrong, Wyatt?" Angelica prompted.

For a moment, the massive guy didn't respond, and then scratching sounds of fabric on plastic padding followed when he shifted around. His eyes were locked on the floor, but when he stopped moving, he dragged his gaze up to mine.

I couldn't breathe.

"Please don't hurt me," he whimpered.

Huh?

"She won't, Wyatt." Angelica glanced at me, wary as hell. "Right?"

Wait, she wanted *me* to promise *him* that he was safe?

The woman's eyebrow rose. She was waiting for my answer.

"Uh, yeah," I stammered. "No. I mean… sure."

"See?" Angelica urged him.

Wyatt ducked his face away again. "She…" He was trembling so hard, I could see his tangled hair shaking. "She's different… now. More. Couldn't tell… last year."

Oh, hell.

He swallowed hard, dragging his gaze up to me again. "Can you tell?"

Something in the room changed. The air. The light. The whisper of the air conditioning on my skin. The hairs on my arms rose, goosebumps racing over me.

I could feel his presence like I'd felt Noah's. I cried out, backpedaling, and in my head, I shoved the feeling away as hard as I could.

Wyatt shrieked, cramming himself as far into the corner as possible. "Don't hurt me! Don't hurt me! You said she wouldn't hurt me!"

He was wailing like a frightened child. "What…" I tried to regroup, looking quickly to Olivia and then back at the crying monster in the corner. "What the…"

"What just happened, Wyatt?" Angelica's calm tone seemed forced. When he didn't stop crying, she looked to me. "What did you do?"

"Nothing."

Angelica stared at me.

My mouth moved. "I-I could feel him. Like Noah. Inside my head." I hesitated. "I pushed it back."

"You felt his presence?" Olivia asked. "But only just then?" That sharp look was back in her eyes. The one that measured and evaluated everything she saw.

"You said he's a greliaran, correct?" Declan asked.

Olivia barely spared him a glance.

"Yeah," I answered. "And yeah."

"What happened, Wyatt?" Angelica tried again.

"It *hurt*! She hurt me! She said she wouldn't, but she—" He looked up at me. I tensed, waiting for him to rip out of the straitjacket and charge at me. "*Why?*" he pleaded pitifully.

I gaped at him.

"He was hiding his presence, wasn't he?" Declan turned to Wyatt. "Weren't you?"

Wyatt nodded miserably.

Declan's dark eyes pinned me. "And you could feel it when he stopped."

It wasn't a question. There was no point to it being a question. The answer was obvious.

Except for the part about how.

"But," I tried, "I'm not a—"

"Wyatt," Declan interrupted. The guy flinched. "Did you ever encounter the Beast?"

I knew he had. He'd been there, with us, when the Beast attacked Joseph's place on the coast. When the Beast slammed into all the magic that old wizard had stored, and Chloe, Noah, and I had all ended up…

A ragged breath slipped from me. Oh, God. "Wyatt… were you… could you feel the Beast's presence too?"

He nodded again, whimpering.

My mouth moved, searching for words. I knew what had happened. Sort of. Maybe. That blast changed Noah, changed Chloe, changed *me*.

And it must have changed Wyatt too, which meant he was like us. *Connected* like us. Except not like us, because I'd never picked up on Chloe. She'd never felt anything about me.

Neither of us was greliaran.

My heart was pounding so hard, I could feel it choking my throat. This was horrible. A nightmare. The monster could find me anywhere, because he was inside my head.

"Baylie..." Jace murmured.

I jumped. His storm-cloud-gray eyes flicked down toward my arms. I followed his gaze, pausing at how the amber prayer beads on his wrist were glowing brighter than could possibly be natural. But he wasn't looking at those.

Dark lines flickered through my skin like the ghosts of black lightning bolts.

What the *hell?*

I staggered backward a step, staring at my arms, but with every passing heartbeat, my alarm drained. My eyes lingered on the black lines, mesmerized by their twisting and flashing. This should scare me. I should be freaking out right now because this was new. Something I'd never seen, even after I blew up the house.

Instead, the sight of them felt... right, somehow. Peaceful, and beautiful too, and not scary at all. They soothed the panic inside me, leaving only clarity and calm.

"When the air went wrong," I continued to Wyatt more firmly, "that was yesterday morning, wasn't it?"

"Mm-hmm." He didn't lift his head.

I took a step closer. He whimpered again. "Wyatt... the Beast died yesterday morning." I wet my lips, making myself say the next words. "*Noah* died yesterday morning. And if you make one crack about that, I swear to God I'll kill you, do you hear me?"

The threat came out in a rush. He drew in on himself with a whining noise.

I took a deep breath. "We need to find some dehaians,

Wyatt, and Olivia thinks you can help us. But you don't get to kill them, understand?"

He shook his head hard, his hair making rustling sounds against the plastic padding of the wall. "No. No, no. Please. No."

"No, what?" I asked, my voice hard.

"Don't want to… please. Please, they…"

I glanced at Angelica. "They what?"

"They frighten him," Angelica explained. "Or, rather, wanting to hurt people frightens him, and thus them most of all."

My gaze slid back to him. Was that so?

I walked closer. "Wyatt."

He whimpered.

"Why does Olivia think you can find dehaians?"

"They… they move funny. They feel weird."

Right. Okay. "You're scared of me… aren't you?"

It barely needed asking, but he nodded all the same.

"And…" I tossed a quick look to Olivia. "And the doll?"

He shrieked. Twisting in his straitjacket, he tried to scramble his way into the wall.

"Wyatt," I tried. "*Wyatt!*"

His frantic motions slowed.

"The doll and I are looking for the dehaians," I said. "And if you help us… we'll keep you safe from them. Understand?"

His motions stopped. Hesitantly, he lifted his head.

The face from my nightmares stared up at me, desperate with hope. "Y-you'll protect me?"

I made myself speak. "Yeah."

His lower lip quivered. His eyes turned watery. With a whining cry, he suddenly switched directions, flinging himself toward me rather than at the wall.

The black power inside me flared out as if on instinct, smoke and force alike, racing at the sobbing greliaran worming his way toward me in a straitjacket. The magic hit him, stopping him in his tracks but not blasting him away.

The smoke absorbed into his body.

I stared. Greliarans had been designed to absorb magic, I suddenly remembered. I'd learned that last year. But they did it by killing. They took it in when they killed something—like dehaians or that wizard, Joseph.

Oh, hell.

Wyatt lifted his eyes back toward me. He didn't rip out of the straitjacket, and he didn't look crazed. Not exactly, anyway. Chewing on his lower lip, he stared up at me like I was the kindest, most wonderful and generous person he'd ever seen in all his days.

I couldn't tell if that was a good thing.

"Will you help us find dehaians, Wyatt?" I made myself say. "And not hurt them?"

He nodded fervently, tears scattering from his eyes.

"Good." I backed away from him. I still looked calm on the outside, I was fairly certain—or, at least, calm to anyone who didn't know me that well. But somewhere inside, incredulity was catching up to me. Maybe hysteria too. The lightning bolts were fading, reality was reasserting itself, and oh-my-God-what-did-I-just-do was starting to ricochet around inside my head, making my heart pound. I'd given a murderer some of my magic. I'd given a psychotic killer more power.

I'd made a deal with *Wyatt*.

Taking a breath, I pushed past the anxiety as best I could. "How do we get him out of here?" I asked Olivia, my voice hard.

She studied me for a moment. She had to have seen what just happened with Wyatt, how he'd absorbed whatever this was inside me. They all must have. But she didn't say anything about it, instead simply replying, "Doctor Neuhaus has that handled. Angelica, if you will help him prepare to move?"

The other woman watched me warily, but she nodded. Turning, she spoke to Wyatt in a low voice.

I trailed Olivia out the door, glancing over my shoulder to keep an eye on Wyatt. He didn't *seem* like he was putting on an act.

But I wasn't ready to turn my back on him. I never would be.

"So this is how you're helping the greliarans?" Declan asked Olivia when we reached the hallway. "Turning them into sniveling children?"

Olivia blinked, regarding him with arch offense. "Excuse me?"

Declan gestured at the open doorway. "This creature is—"

"And your people have done *what* in the thousand years since you created them? Left them to rot, helpless in their madness?" Olivia scoffed. "For your information, *no*, we are not trying to break them, nor reduce them to this state. Quite the contrary. With most greliarans, we are trying to uncover the root of the craving woven into their genetic and magical makeup, and see if we can counteract that in some way. Our goal is for them to live as close to a normal life as possible for a magical being."

She glanced over her shoulder at Wyatt and Angelica. The woman was nodding to him, urging him to stand up. It didn't look like it was working, at least not quickly.

"Wyatt is a special case," Olivia continued. "He is a killer, and prior to actually committing murder, he was, like many of his kind, a homicide-obsessed psychopath. To stop him from killing Baylie… for lack of a better phrase, Ellie took him apart. Peter was concerned that, sooner or later, Wyatt's fear might drive him to hurt Baylie or Ellie anyway, and so we have been attempting to put those pieces back together without returning him to a psychotic state of homicidal rage. What you see here? This is a young man who has recurrent nightmares about a doll because that's how he saw Ellie—small, fragile, breakable—until she defended herself and Baylie with powers she had only begun to understand. This is a young man who couldn't be in a room with *anyone* six months ago without screaming and trying to claw his way through the walls to escape."

Declan was quiet.

"If we can help him," Olivia finished, "there is a very good chance we can help them all."

I watched as Wyatt finally clambered to his feet. I wasn't sure how I felt about their help. About this. He'd tried to kill us. I'd never forget that look in his eyes, that day in the forest.

He *enjoyed* killing, and to believe it was just the magical craving inside greliarans that caused it…

Noah wasn't like that. He had never been, before or after what had happened with the Beast. Neither were Maddox or Peter. If you took that out of Wyatt, would it make any difference?

Without that urge to kill, what was he?

Angelica led him to the door. Wyatt's eyes were locked on the ground, and his feet shuffled like he wasn't sure the ground was safe beneath him.

I backed away again while they set to leading him down the hall. Even if he was trying to help us, even if the elders were working to heal that craving that had been put inside the greliarans when the ruanir made them a millennium ago, that didn't mean I'd ever trust him. He wasn't like Maddox or Peter. He'd never be like Noah, no matter what the elders did.

Magic had nothing to do with being a monster.

6

LOGAN

The judges could have picked a more desolate spot to hide, but it would have taken doing. This place was a dump.

I swept up to the isolated, gray swath of coast, leaving my strakirin to shift back into their human-like forms and follow me out of the waves. They weren't in good shape, those strakirin, thanks to that goddamn dehaian city and its defenses. Burned, exhausted, with blackened scorch marks on their skin and tails—or legs now—the strakirin looked like they'd been through a war.

Not that their damage was important, considering I was here to get replacements for them anyway. And besides, no one was around to see them.

I hovered, concentrating on reshaping my massive, invisible self into human form. The wind churned, spinning up sand devils and whipping around the bleached grass clinging to the edges of the colorless beach. Electricity crackled in the air, and black wisps of cloud threaded through the overcast sky.

Human form was *tiny*. Pathetic, even. My God, how had

that stupid Beast ever made itself human-sized, let alone human-*looking*.

The answer presented itself immediately. I was the more powerful one. The former Beast had been weaker. I'd killed it, after all. Drawing *this* much energy and power down into human form obviously took more work than the old Beast had ever had to do.

My torso appeared, hazy like a mirage and mostly transparent. My arms and legs followed, and my three-hundred-sixty-degree, from-everywhere vision let me know my head was in place too.

I was also nearly twenty feet tall.

For a moment, I considered remaining that way—the better to look like a god and whatnot—but it would probably cause trouble too. If some idiot happened to be flying a drone nearby, I didn't want to risk the chance of ending up on the human news. At least not until I was ready to let the human world know about their new leader.

Though really, humans overall were annoying. Bombs, guns, squabbling like children all the time. I could understand why the Judiciary worked from the shadows rather than rule them. Trying to rein in the humans would be like riding herd on rabid mice. To add insult to irritation, they were damn near useless to me.

My body shrank, and my view through the strakirins' eyes confirmed that I was roughly the same size as I'd been before my metamorphosis in the canyon. On my way here, I'd tried killing a few humans—just a couple of fishermen on a boat far enough away from shore that no one would notice them dying. I'd wanted to know how it felt, if killing them was as good as killing dehaians—or as I imagined it'd feel to kill ruanir.

The former Beast had that, after all: the magical rush that served as payoff for killing dehaians and ruanir. Why else would it hunt them for so long? Story was, the thing practically got high from it, and I'd wanted to know if that trait had carried over. And humans had some sensitivity to ocean magic. Not enough that they could use it or channel it worth a damn, but enough that they liked being near the water. I wanted to see what killing them did.

The answer was nothing. Sure, it was fun, swooping down on them like an avenging angel, and striking them dead like one too. Their screams had been hilarious, considering they couldn't even figure out what was attacking them or where I was coming from. But as for power or a magical thrill from killing them…

Nothing.

I concentrated on clothes. Maybe a long black coat. Black pants as well. I'd look like a judge—a better, more stylish judge—but wasn't that part of the point? There were some custom-made, black leather shoes I'd been eyeing a few months back too. I could create some of those for myself.

My human form shattered. I rushed outward before I could stop myself, bowling over the strakirin and blasting the waves back from the shore.

Dammit. I struggled back into human form and tried again.

One of my strakirin shrieked when my next explosion sent

him tumbling and snapped his arm the wrong direction.

This was absurd. That old Beast had appeared to be a regular guy, clothes and all. Nothing interesting, sure, which showed the creature's utter lack of imagination—or, really, how boring its mistress had been. But then, she was dehaian. What did she know about good-looking humans or decent clothes?

I tried again. My strakirin toppled over as my body flew apart, blasting the sands a third time.

Screw it. That damned creature had been weak. I wasn't. That was why I couldn't confine myself with something as pathetically mundane as skin and clothes and whatnot.

I drew down into human shape, letting my body become black as night, swirling with storm clouds and flaring with lightning. Really, there was something to be said for looking like a thunder god. Assuming I stayed away from—or killed— any humans who might see me, anyway.

I made my human shape walk toward my strakirin. My senses didn't want to cooperate with my form, though. I could still see all around me with that amazing, three-hundred-six-ty-degree vision my Beast form had.

Which, really, was fine. I was the same size as I'd been before the canyon—a hair over six feet tall, with perfect muscles that made ruanir girls drool. Magic tangled through me, making the storm clouds inside me churn. With all that, why bother limiting myself to human-like sight? This way, I could see the judges no matter what they tried.

The thought made me smile.

I continued across the beach, half-floating, half-walking

with my legs making fewer strides than should have been necessary for the distance I crossed. The strakirin followed. The judges were just beyond the line of wind-beaten trees at the edge of the sand, in a building I'd seen from the air. The place looked like a collection of massive concrete blocks. Their magical signal for me to come back to them wouldn't be audible to humans, but to me, it bleated out of the gray structure like the world's most annoying alarm clock.

I knew what the judges probably planned. Most likely, they intended to trap me like they'd trapped the old Beast in that town, Santa Lucina. Then they'd try to drain me, use me, feed off me like the funereal leeches they were.

It'd almost be funny to watch them try.

I strode past the weathered tangle of trees and into a clearing. In the middle of a swath of sand and grass, the building squatted. A collection of rectangles and cubes, it scarcely had a window or architectural feature to its name. But for the human-sized entryways on the north and east side, and the massive garage-style door to the east as well, the place looked as if a giant had simply arranged some cinder blocks on the grass and then abandoned them.

In other words, it was boring, like the former Beast. Like the judges too.

I chuckled to myself, the sound coming out as a windy rasp. I might want to work on my voice, I noted. Get it back to what it had been. But for now, this might have a good effect.

The rolling garage door creaked, clanked, and then began to open.

I almost chuckled again. Here, Beastie, Beastie. Come right in.

Morons. How stupid did they think I was?

I waited, watching it roll higher till, with a final clank, it stopped. Nothing moved in the clearing. With the sound of the door gone, silence reigned.

Seconds ticked by.

Seriously? They meant to wait this out? I debated walking in, just to show them how idiotic this all was. It might be entertaining, after all.

Black forms moved in the shadows of the massive entryway. Judge Engle stepped out into the clearing, looking like a goddamn undertaker with his black clothes, white shirt, and dead-pale skin. But the white bandage on his forehead and the sling holding his arm disrupted the look. Someone had managed to bang him up pretty decisively—an accomplishment, considering the enforcers would throw themselves in the path of any judge in danger of so much as a papercut.

I couldn't decide if I was more amused at his wounds or irritated that someone had gotten to the bastard first.

Another judge followed him, called Quinlan or Quinford or something like that. Shorter than Judge Engle, the man had the stocky build of a weightlifter, though his pasty complexion and sallow hair made him appear anything but healthy. Several enforcers trailed him.

As if they'd do any good.

The judges barely spared me a glance, skimming their attention over me and then dismissing me like I was some kitchen utensil they weren't bothering to use. I seethed at the implicit disrespect, but I didn't move. Not yet. Not when I wanted to see what they were going to try first.

"They're not dead," the second judge commented.

Wait, what? Who?

"Perhaps some among the strakirin were far enough away to avoid the effects," Judge Engle replied.

"An alarming number, if that is the case. We anticipated they would be consumed by the transformation. Perhaps there was not as much power available at the target as we thought."

Excuse me?

"That is possible." Judge Engle regarded my strakirin like they were broken toys. "But clearly the overall transformation took place, even if a few survived. We can examine them in more detail once the transference is complete."

What "transference"? And what was this about being consumed? They thought my strakirin would be dead? What about me?

Did they even know who I *was*?

I could show them.

The temptation passed as quickly as it had come. It was better to wait. After all, who knew? Maybe this would have some benefit for me, what with the surprise and all.

The thought made me want to smile.

"Our dehaian allies are conspicuously missing," the other judge commented.

"A pleasant convenience. There is little doubt they'd lived out the majority of their usefulness."

"Agreed."

Judge Engle returned his attention to me. "Come."

Wow. Come. Like a dog.

But sure, why not? I sauntered forward, not saying anything. Let them think it was working. Let them think I was obeying their absurd command. I wanted to get a better look in that place, anyway. See what other judges were inside, along with whatever else they had going in there.

Because whether or not they'd been meant to survive, these strakirin sure as hell weren't enough. A hundred, at best, left from what I'd had, and maybe fewer. I'd lost too many crossing the ocean originally, and in the canyon as well. I wanted more. I wanted thousands. Eyes and ears everywhere, hearing everything.

Finding Ari.

My feet faltered. Where the hell had *that* thought come from? I needed more strakirin, not to find some broken, useless girl who was most likely dead. Ari was irrelevant. Everyone was. I'd keep a few judges around to make my strakirin, but as for the rest of them…

"Inside," Judge Engle ordered.

I looked past him into the building. It was pretty much what I'd expected. Steel girders by the door and farther in as well, forming the box that would become a cage. Monitors and machines in the distance, with techs in white lab coats watching them. Some enforcers too and, oh yeah, there were the judges.

So this must be that "transference" thing they were talking

about, the eager bastards. They planned to drain me like a god-damn battery.

Heh.

I weighed my options. I wasn't sure what they anticipated with the strakirin, whether the judges would expect them to move with me or not. They'd thought the things would be dead, after all. But then, the strakirin had been part of the hive mind—what was now just my mind.

Minus Ari.

I bit back a snarl. What the hell? Screw Ari! I didn't care about *Ari*!

Judge Engle shifted his weight, a flicker of question crossing his face. Dammit. I had no idea which option to pick, and the judges were waiting. The strakirin hadn't moved. I could make them stay, but… better to look like a hive mind.

I walked toward the cage and made the strakirin follow me. Thirty feet. Now twenty. With my three-hundred-sixty-degree vision, I watched Judge Engle turn his attention from me to the tree line, scanning it idly.

Moron.

Ten feet. The shadows inside thinned the closer I got to the entrance. They'd reinforced the metal beams since the last Beast tore through their pathetic cage in Santa Lucina, killing my mother in the process, not that I really cared about that any-more. Her position would have given me power, sure. But that power wouldn't have been a speck of dust compared to this.

Besides, I'd gotten my payback for that.

I concentrated on maintaining my human-like form. The

strakirin had lightning. The former Beast had too. I could see the magical carvings on the beams and the wiring, out in the open and just waiting to be fried. The judges hadn't thought to hide that, because clearly they believed they were dealing with a thunderstorm lap dog, obediently walking into the cage to let itself be drained like its "masters" wanted.

A smile flickered across my face. Five feet. Four. Three.

Good enough.

Lightning surged from my body, climbing the beams, the wires, and making the monitors on the far end of the room flare brilliantly in the dark. The magic surrounding the would-be cage tried to fight me, tugging at my power, pushing back on my assault.

It felt like a headbutt from a chihuahua. Like a kamikaze attack from a gnat.

Like nothing.

My grin widened. I wasn't even breaking a sweat, figuratively speaking, and yet the machines behind the cage exploded. The wires around the steel beams snapped, the charred ends smoking. My power ripped across the sigils carved into them, cutting into the girders themselves, scratching out the symbols and leaving molten metal dripping. Inside the building, the techs ran screaming and the judges did too.

A chuckle escaped me, like a rumble of thunder. So those bastards did feel fear.

Good.

I let the lightning die. My strakirin raced forward, grabbing the enforcers, the techs, and the judges too when they tried to flee. Spikes sliced through the enforcers' throats. The strakirin let the bleeding corpses topple to the ground. I withheld the poison; I knew it would only make the judges stronger, and I might need the techs for information. But the fear on the techs' faces was wonderful.

At my silent command, the strakirin hauled the judges and the techs out into the dismal, gray daylight.

"Now." I turned to Judge Engle. Like the others, my strakirin held him fast. "About our new arrangement."

Judge Engle's eyes filled with fury. "What is this? What—"

I scoffed. God, he was stupid. They all were. "You screwed up. You thought you'd become a god by making a slave. And you thought you'd make that slave be me." I shook my head, making a tsking sound. "Big mistake. So now you have a choice: work for me or, well…" I smiled. "What's it going to be, *Judge*?"

He didn't respond. His chin rose, his bearing proud, and behind him, the other judges were the same.

Fine, then. A demonstration.

Blades slid from the forearm of one of my strakirin, impaling the throat of Judge Quinlan or Quinford or whatever his irrelevant name had been. The techs shrieked, struggling pointlessly in their pathetic terror. With a swift twist, my strakirin tore his blades from the judge's throat.

The man crumpled to the ground. Blood pumped out onto the sand and grass.

I regarded Judge Engle.

"What do you want?" he growled.

That was more like it. "Your connections. Your hideouts. Your plans. Your bases of operation. It's simple, really." I smiled. "I want everything."

⟳ 7 ⟲

THE BEGINNING

Cycles of the earth, back and back, spiraling the ball of fire across the sky. The waters rose. Fell. Raged and tossed amid the creature's dreaming, quieting at last when the emerald land rose from the depths and the towers climbed. White towers. Glistening. It remembered them from the time that came after, remembered when they were splattered with red.

White walls then, curved and tiered like steps, spreading outward and upward for hundreds of feet like the cupped hands of a liar beneath the sky. One side was open, facing out on the deep blue bay. Ocean water covered the stairs halfway to their utmost height. White pillars rose in the middle of the space, supporting a glistening platform of pale glass above the shining water and then climbing higher still to tower taller than the stairs and walls. Beneath the surface of the clear blue liquid, more steps extended down to a base where swirling sigils were carved into the smooth ground. Above the pillars, shining statues of the liars glistened in solid gold.

Gold… gold hair like flowing strands of molten metal, like

glistening threads of sunlight, shining in the depths of the sea…

The memory slipped away, an incongruous fragment of another time, another place that came before and after and amid the pain. Now, there were only the white pillars and the glistening water, the warm light and the gentle waves. Now, vision came only as a blur; shapes and colors resolving slowly, slowly. Perception was new. Awareness as well. The creature had known neither before this.

This was the start.

Newborn, came the whisper.

The old ones stood on the glass platform. The liars, but that came later. The torturers. That was later too. Now, the creature rested beneath the pillars at the center of the space, aware of itself as something different from the water for the first time. But it wasn't afraid. The water was still a part of it. The earth and the sky and the drifting breeze too. Everything was warm and soft like a gentle current on the surface of the sea when the ball of fire was high in the sky. The old ones chanted around the creature, hands raised, hoods fallen back, scales curling across the faces of some, others showing only plain skin.

Two kinds, the whisper noted.

It hadn't noticed.

Time drifted. The old ones were no longer on the platform above it. They stood on the steps now, near an archway with tall, thin trees beyond. They shook hands, smiling, and shared drinks from gold cups while they motioned to where the creature hovered. Their words were ancient and warped by time, but their faces, their movements…

Peace, said the whisper. *They were making us in peace, not war. But for what?*

It didn't know. Flickers of feeling came from them, like small tongues of fire, licking at the edges of the creature's awareness. Warm feelings. Bubbly feelings like vents of heated water deep beneath the cold sea.

Happiness, said the whisper.

The creature liked happiness. But then, the old ones turned toward it, their eyes widening and their words coming to a halt.

They're surprised.

Their words became fast, their drinks forgotten, but the bubbling sensation returned, along with a feeling like a wind that didn't know which way to blow.

Confused. Excited. They didn't know that we could feel them. Know their feelings.

Warmth came then. Warmth from the old ones like the sun on the waves, like rain pouring down on the dry ground. *Love,* explained the whisper. The creature rose toward them, eager for more.

But then the feeling stuttered, shot through with cold. All the old ones tensed then, looking around in short, fast movements.

Alarm. Something confused them. Surprised them.

Others stormed in, rushing through the archway, racing down the steps. They held blades of metal in their hands and bore translucent spikes on their arms, and where they cut, red splashes followed. Some of the faster old ones—*dehaians*, said the whisper—defended the retreat of the slower old ones, slashing with their own spikes, falling when the blades came too fast. The slower old ones ran toward where the creature hovered, and their mouths moved, their words blurred and confusing and yet drawing the creature forward, summoning it into a space, a dark space, a space of nothingness where awareness ceased for a time.

Flickers of firelight against dark walls. Dank air, cold air, and water that dripped and dropped from teeth of stone on the rough ceiling. Awareness returned with no sign of the sun or the sea, no sign of the white pillars or shining stairs. The old ones, the slower ones, crouched beneath the creature with smudges of grime on their faces and water glistening in their eyes.

Ruanir, said the whisper, *and they're scared. So scared.*

Explosions then. Dust and rock clattered down from the ceiling above. Growls followed. Snarls too, outside the rough-hewn room, and screams cut short by gurgles. The faces of the ruanir were wet—*tears,* the whisper explained, *crying. They're being hunted. They're hiding.*

The noises were coming closer. The ruanir raised their hands and began chanting, and their magic flowed into the creature. More feelings came, unknown feelings it had never experienced.

Sorrow, said the whisper. *Grief. Loss.*

Awareness flickered. Began to blur. The stones and the ground became part of the creature again, and the water beyond them too. The feelings of the old ones started to fade, and sight did as well. But it didn't understand. What were they doing?

Unmaking us, came the whisper. *Releasing us to the earth.*

The far wall disappeared in a shower of rocks and grit, and the chanting stopped. New people poured into the room, people who were bigger than the old ones, with their rock-like skin cracked by fissures of light like lava boiling up through the earth. Their eyes glowed red, and they charged at the old ones, teeth bared.

Those creatures... breathed the whisper. *They're familiar. Why...?*

Spikes of metal lunged through the chests of the attackers. Relief poured through the old ones as their would-be assailants fell, only to turn to horror again when different people strode into the room. Scales twisted across their skin, visible only around the black hoods and robes they wore.

That man...

The creature recognized him. The dehaian had been there, at the place of stairs and pillars, and had joined with the other old ones in their feelings of happiness.

His feelings were cold and hard like ice now.

A traitor, came the whisper.

They all were.

With several other new ones, the man raised his hands while, behind him, the ruanir fell to blades and spikes and splashes of deep red.

And then a new sensation came, twisting and sharp.

Pain.

The creature didn't understand. It had never felt such a tormenting sensation before. And why would they do this? Why? This wasn't right! The creature could feel itself changing inside, the pain molding it around like burning clay, corrupting it into something else, something inexorably and eternally separate from the dreaming peace of its home in the water, never to return. And that wasn't right either. It wasn't supposed to be a weapon!

...wasn't supposed to be a weapon. The whisper seemed stunned.

Awareness shifted and warped then, like there were two of the creature inside itself. Then one grew larger, grew stronger, grew to encompass the world. One that was the dehaian at the center of the newcomers, and his will hurt. His will crushed down like the weight of a mountain, and there was no hope of disobeying him. The creature was tied to him now, as surely as vines wrapped a tree trunk. More feelings reached the creature, stronger than any of the rest. *His* feelings, ones of anger and satisfaction, bloodlust and anticipation. And everywhere, there was only pain.

The air changed. The warm, gentle peace was gone, burned to ash by the dehaian's will. Now everything became sharper, became cold. A sensation permeated its form, like invisible colors the creature could feel. Taste, that was the word. A taste like the coldest saltwater from the icy depths, or like blistering sand scorched by the ball of fire in the sky. Taste coming from the old ones and new ones around it, and that taste would stop the pain.

The dehaian said so. Said so without words amid his chanting. One taste, the dehaian taste, meant obey. Meant an end to pain through obedience, and that taste was to be left unharmed.

And the other…

A new feeling snarled through the creature.

Hunger, the whisper explained with quiet loathing.

The creature didn't want to be in this memory anymore. It didn't want to see these horrible times. It wanted them dead. All of them. *Any* of them. The torturers, the corruptors, the ones who twisted the creature against itself. They all needed to be gone so they could never hurt it again, because only then would the creature be safe. Only ever then.

I'm here, came the whisper. *You're safe. I'm with you.*

8

ARI

"Nyciena command, this is Commander Damerion, come in. We are outside the city and request entrance. Nyciena command, come in."

Silence radiated from the pool of teal magic in the hollow of a rock. Around me, soldiers tightened their grips on their weapons, eyeing our surroundings between quick glances toward the shimmer of power I could feel more than see in the distance ahead.

The shimmer that flickered and then fell.

Damerion glanced at Ezio. "That's not procedure."

Ezio didn't look away from the city. "They might be injured."

Damerion's expression made his opinion clear. "Four teams," he ordered. "Tidal, scout ahead. Get into the city. Find out what happened to those security stations. Hammerhead, you're point. Maelstrom, you follow us. Dogfish, your job is Lady Chloe and Ari. Anything happens, you get them out of the city and to the nearest encampment, understood?" At the affirmative responses from his troops, Damerion nodded. "Go!"

The soldiers took off.

"Stay close," Ezio murmured to me.

I nodded, not that I had any intention of doing otherwise. I wasn't quite sure why, but Ezio, Damerion, everyone I knew—who knew Noah—had started to feel like a lifeline. Like I needed them for something, even if I didn't know what, even if it didn't make any sense. They couldn't feel Noah, not like I could. They weren't able to tell he was alive like I could… like I *would*, the moment he was able to reach me again.

Because he *would* reach me, and then everything would be better.

Shivers crept over me, cold and weird like an envelope of melting ice on my skin, but no one else seemed to notice anything. My chest ached as if a strange lump inside me was turning to mush, and I didn't want that. Didn't like it. Couldn't even explain it, but…

I wrapped my arms around myself, hating the way it felt like everything inside me was shaking. But I'd be okay. Noah was out there. And the fact I felt like I needed these people around me who weren't even really my friends… well, it was irrelevant.

Because he'd come back again.

I swam onward, sticking close to Ezio. On the other side of him, Chloe hadn't taken her attention from the direction of the city. Tension seemed to thrum through her body like a live current, practically making the water quiver.

But then, she had powers like Noah, I suddenly remembered. Like me, too, in a way. Maybe the sensation of electricity around me wasn't my imagination.

Maybe she'd pick up on Noah too when he came back.

The city came into view ahead, a collection of towering stone and glistening light surrounding a mountain that would dwarf anything back home.

And everything was still standing.

Relief spread through the Yvarians like a palpable force.

"Easy…" Damerion cautioned in a low voice. "That thing could still be here."

The relieved atmosphere chilled at his words.

"Anything?" Ezio asked me.

"No. I—"

A shout went up from ahead of us. Spikes shot from my arms and the arms of those around me. The dehaians swept the water with their guns, seeking anything at which to aim.

Several soldiers swam toward us, hauling people between them.

Dehaian people, not strakirin, but that wasn't much of a relief. Logan could still be close by, and I wasn't sure a single person around me breathed while we waited to see who the newcomers were.

The guards racing toward us slowed. My mouth fell open before I could stop it.

"They were on the seafloor." The soldier hefted Osias higher. The Driecaran had started to sag. Clearly unconscious, with burns and welts covering him, the man looked like he'd been thrown straight onto a stovetop burner.

A cold, dark feeling churned in me at the sight, not quite nausea, not quite rage.

"Any sign of that thing?" Damerion asked me.

I shook my head, my attention still locked on Osias. Poison rushed up in my veins, pressing on my skin and ready to be released. Because he'd unleashed the spell that hurt Noah. He'd smiled as the judges changed me. He'd made all of this nightmare possible.

And I'd promised myself I'd kill the ones responsible for this. I'd promised *Noah*.

"We need him," Ezio murmured to me.

My eyes twitched over to find the mercenary watching me intently, like he could see the thoughts racing through my mind.

"Ari…" A hint of pleading touched his voice.

I trembled, but I let the poison fade.

"How many Driecarans?" Damerion continued to the soldier.

"Five, sir. That we've seen, anyway."

"Okay. Use the nets to hold them. We'll lock them up when we get to the city."

The guards obeyed, moving quickly to haul the Driecarans away.

"Perhaps the creature left them for dead?" Ezio offered.

Damerion scanned the empty ocean. "Perhaps." He turned back, regarding me briefly. "There will be justice on the Driecarans for the Beast's death. I promise you that."

He swam after his soldiers.

I bit my lip. He hadn't missed what happened. What *almost* happened. But he was wrong too, about Noah. He was wrong, and everyone was wrong, and goddammit, they just couldn't see that.

But they would.

We passed over the outskirts of Nyciena. Small hills rolled up against stone slabs larger than skyscrapers. Leaves and lights peppered everything while more lights and plants separated yards. Streets. Parks. A complex that looked like a children's playground.

There wasn't a single dehaian anywhere.

"Down," Damerion commanded in a low voice. "It'll be harder to catch us all in the streets than open water."

That wasn't comforting. The soldiers didn't react, though, merely diving for the city streets as commanded. Sticking close to Ezio, I followed.

The stone slabs and hills—small mountains, really—seemed to grow in size as we swept down among them, though I knew it was only an optical illusion. A trick of distance and perspective.

And the size of the ocean itself. How high had we been?

I pushed the thought aside, making myself keep breathing. I'd never really liked heights, honestly. Being able to basically fly through them thanks to the water didn't change the vertigo that started swirling in me at the realization of how far away from the ground we'd been.

Damerion ordered a stop in the middle of what appeared to be a marketplace. Openings were carved into the stone around us, all at street level, and all of them reminding me of the open-air stalls at farmer's markets back in Arizona. Lights dangled from the tops of the openings. Signs too, with markings that looked similar to ones I'd seen at the Yvarian garrison a million years before. But these seemed to be advertisements, not warnings.

Dehaian "For Sale" signs.

Home felt a million miles away.

"Commander," one of the soldiers up ahead called. "Scout approaching."

On the rollercoaster of reactions in the guards around me, the tension eased incrementally.

"Report," Damerion ordered when the woman came closer.

"Security station overloaded, sir, but the shield held. Communications devices were damaged, though. And they have injured."

Even Damerion looked relieved this time. "Okay. Take the medic. Tend the wounded and get me a status on where the hell that thing went."

"Yes, sir."

The woman darted off again.

My gaze landed briefly on Chloe. Near a street vendor's stall, she hovered with her arms wrapped around her middle like she was trapping all her fear inside. Pity pulled at me. Zeke could be dead, for all we knew, and so could everyone who'd lived here. All these people she knew, all these people she loved, could be—

Discomfort fought for space with my pity like an unwelcome guest forcing its way into a house, and I turned away, my hands chafing my arms. Logan hadn't killed us, though. Maybe he hadn't killed Zeke or the people of Nyciena either. Maybe any minute now, the others would find that out, and then we'd all know they'd been wrong.

Or I was.

My gut flinched like I'd suddenly dropped a hundred feet in the water. That… No. I was… I meant, I wasn't… Everything would be—

"Sir!"

The tension coming off the dehaians shot through the roof again. Another soldier raced toward us, coming from the south this time. Around me, the Vetorians and the Yvarians drew in, spikes emerging from their arms.

"Dehaians, sir." The man gasped to catch his breath. "A large number of them. Coming from the south."

"Survivors?"

"Unknown, sir. A contingent from Hammerhead is approaching them."

Damerion nodded. "Defensive positions. Lady Chloe, if you would please take shelter?" The commander gestured to the doorway of a store nearby.

Chloe hesitated, her gaze darting to the south with clear reluctance, but she nodded. Ezio swam after her toward the store.

"Ari?" he called.

I faltered. Hiding. Right. We were hiding now.

I twisted past the store counter and toward the doorway beyond, my movements made awkward by the ache in my side. The leaves of the door whisked over my skin and scales when I slipped by them, brushing the bruises above my healing rib.

Past the doorway was a room that seemed to be the stock area. In truth, it was a cave like so many other dehaian structures I'd seen. Shelves had been carved from the walls and stone boxes were stacked atop them. A multicolored rug covered the floor too, incongruous to the clearly utilitarian purpose of the room. Toys lay scattered on the ground—a collection of blocks, a woven doll—all abandoned as if on a moment's notice.

"If you would please stay at the back of the room, valya Praelex?" Ezio prompted Chloe, his voice quiet like he didn't want to risk being heard outside.

Water moved to my left while she swam to where he directed. I reached down, my gaze lingering on the doll while I picked it up. It looked like a little girl. Dyed strings of yellow hair, twisted into pigtails. A stubby blue tail.

Thrashing, flailing, bawling for her mommy while I swept down on her, the hive around me and the blades on my arms ready to strike. Cold poison surging through my body. Lightning coursing over my hands, my arms, my tail. The stra-kirin drone rising louder, buffeting my defenses, drowning the cries of terror from the village around me with the excitement of the swarm.

No. No, I wouldn't remember this. I wouldn't—

Blood in the water. Children shrieking in fear. Parents dying. Me, screaming in the darkness, trapped behind my walls, fighting not to be crushed beneath the weight of the hive mind—

I squeezed my eyes shut. Spikes crept from my arms, and my skin tingled with electricity. My heart raced, my breaths coming in short and silent gasps. But this wasn't now. Wasn't here. I was safe—as safe as I could be, anyway. And Noah…

I grabbed for our connection, desperate to feel something, *anything*. He had to be there. Had to be on the other side of it.

What would it feel like if he was dead?

I set the doll down swiftly and turned away, crushing my lips together to hold a whimper inside. The walls were too close. Too tight, really. I… they weren't helping. If I could get outside of them—

"Ari?"

My gaze snapped over to Chloe. "Yeah?"

She hesitated. "You okay?"

"Fine."

Her brow twitched downward. She didn't respond.

I turned away again. It wasn't really safe here. The walls were probably okay, though. But perhaps we should look for ways to barricade the entrance, in case the dehaians coming weren't on our side. Maybe those boxes. They could work. They were—

The leaves of the door loosened. "My lady?" someone called.

Chloe hesitated. Ezio too. They both were still watching me.

"All clear, my lady," the person continued.

Chloe glanced between me and Ezio and then swam for the door, ignoring Ezio's sound of protest. He darted after her.

I hesitated, suddenly reluctant to swim after them. But then, I couldn't feel the strakirin. Couldn't feel anything, actually. Inside, the room was totally silent, a lack of noise that just seemed to get louder and louder and—

I bolted for the door.

"Who was it?" Chloe was asking the others when I got

outside.

"Make way for the king!" came a shout from down the street.

A relieved gasp escaped Chloe.

Dehaians swam along the street, heading toward us. The ones in the lead moved aside, and I caught sight of Zeke behind them.

Chloe sped toward him. He caught her as she came near and pulled her into an embrace, being visibly careful not to crush her wounded arm. Holding her close, he ran his hand over her red hair as if to reassure himself she was there. She nodded to something he said.

Pain took up residence in my chest, like my lungs were suddenly full of glass. I dropped my gaze away, only to have it land on the other dehaians. Families. Kids.

They were staring at me. Some of the kids seemed scared. Most of them, actually, and a number of the adults too.

Self-conscious discomfort prickled through me, making me hyper-aware of my appearance for the first time in a while. The soldiers, the Vetorians, Chloe, and the others… they didn't seem to react to my utterly *non*-dehaian glowing hair, eel tail, or snake-like, yellow-green eyes anymore.

But those kids looked like they were in the presence of a monster.

I crushed my lips together, shaking all over as I turned away. The dehaians were alive. That's all that mattered. Several little ones were even swimming with their parents toward the store we'd just left, which was great.

Damerion came up beside me. "I could have some of my soldiers accompany you to one of the parks nearby, if you'd like?"

I glanced at him, but his attention was on the Yvarians around us. So he'd noticed the stares too. Gratitude nudged at the pain inside me. He and Ezio had both been so kind, ever since the canyon. Cautious of me too, but not like they were scared, exactly.

Just… careful. Careful and kind.

"Mommy, what's that?" A little girl pointed at me.

Her mother shushed her quickly.

"But what *is* it?"

The mother hurried her child around the corner, holding onto her tightly while watching me as if I might attack.

I nodded to Damerion. "The park, sure. Yeah, I guess, that'd be—"

"Hey."

I looked up at the sound of Chloe's voice. She was coming toward me, Zeke at her side.

I fought the sudden urge to swim away.

"Zeke," Chloe said, "this is—"

"Ari. I know. We met." He was silent for a moment. "I'm so sorry."

I opened my mouth, the words "he's not dead" on the tip of my tongue. But they hurt. They hadn't hurt before.

I closed my mouth again.

"What happened?" Chloe asked Zeke. "Did everyone get out?"

Yeah. I drew a breath. I could focus on that, maybe. Or on the lights of the storefront near us, shining blue-white in the twilight, meaning nothing and yet so much better to concentrate on than what was happening around me now.

"I believe so." From the corner of my eye, I saw Zeke toss a look to Damerion. "Your brother, Tiberion, led the forces to the north. Have you had contact with him yet?"

"I will send a squadron to check, Highness," Damerion replied.

"Good. And the defensive shield?"

"It held, but the station overloaded. They have injured. Our surviving medic is tending to them now."

Zeke glanced to the soldiers at his side. "Get another team up there. Help them."

"Yes, Highness." The man turned, calling orders to other soldiers.

"I want a defensive perimeter around Nyciena," Zeke ordered. "Raise the veil again and get me a status on the shield. I want it back at full strength as fast as possible. Do you have any information on where the… whatever-the-hell-it-was went after this?" He directed the last to Damerion.

"I have soldiers trying to ascertain that right now, sire."

Zeke nodded and then turned to me. "You could feel the presence of the other strakirin. Can you detect this thing?"

My mouth moved for a moment. "Yeah."

His brow rose, waiting.

My gaze flicked around. "He's not here."

"He?" Zeke asked immediately.

I hesitated.

"One of the strakirin, highness," Ezio filled in. Relief took the edge off my tension. Back in Periantrea, Ezio had saved me explaining to Kreyus the details of what happened. It'd helped then. It still helped now. "Damerion and I can give you a full report at your convenience."

Zeke nodded. "Very well," he said, but his attention had mostly turned back to Chloe now. He said something to her in a low voice, and she smiled, but the expression was pained.

"I'm fine," she insisted.

His lip twitched, something so loving in the expression. It looked like an argument they'd had before, though God knew when.

The shattered-glass feeling in my lungs expanded through my heart and veins, making my whole body hurt.

I wanted to be anywhere but here.

Zeke glanced back up at us. "Okay, then. Welcome to Nyciena."

Dehaians never had a nighttime, I learned. Not really. In a city where everyone could go for what humans would consider days without sleep, somebody was always awake.

But they were nothing like me.

I closed my eyes, pressing my forehead against the woven seaweed blanket covering my knees. The others were asleep in their own rooms somewhere—Damerion, Ezio, all of them—finally getting the rest they'd gone without for all the days it took us to get to the canyon and back. They'd be up again in a few hours, and then they'd make their plans, maybe to help me, maybe to stay and guard the city.

The minutes felt like knives, slowly cutting deeper as they inched across my skin. The city beyond the window of this palace suite was beautiful—a wonderland of glistening lights and merpeople—but I needed to get out of here. Go back to the canyon, go search for Logan, or head for land to help my family.

Something.

I made myself keep breathing. Guards hovered beyond the window and the door, out of sight but present whenever I leaned my head outside. Zeke put them there, to ensure my privacy and as a protection against any would-be gawkers.

Unfortunately, the soldiers also meant I couldn't leave unnoticed—not that I was certain I could find my way out of the ocean on my own, regardless. That hadn't gone well last time.

Jace and the others would be okay, though. Miguel would make sure they hid. Veronique and Willa—even Declan, for that matter—had magic to rival the judges, and their instruments had been able to pick up on Noah in his invisible form. They'd see Logan coming, and they'd stay safe. Everyone would be safe.

Except for the one who possibly wasn't.

My fingers curled into the blanket, crushing the woven fibers while my entire body shook. Noah had to be alive. I wasn't wrong.

I couldn't be wrong.

But why couldn't I feel him?

Rough, ragged breaths lurched in my chest. My body felt tight and hot, like I was trapped in cellophane. I couldn't feel Noah because I couldn't. Who cared about the rest? He was fine. He'd find me again, or I'd find him, and everything would be—

A laugh echoed up from the palace grounds, making me flinch away from the blanket. A cluster of young dehaians shot along the barrier wall surrounding the castle, teasing one another as they played chase.

I stared at them, lost and uncomprehending, as if I watched a scene from another planet. Life was getting back to normal around here, like nothing had even happened. Damerion's brother, Tiberion, had returned from the north with the other half of the evacuees, all of whom were fine. The overloaded security stations had already been repaired. Nyciena was a city that had bounced back from worse than this, Damerion told me, though he hadn't gone into details and I hadn't asked.

I didn't really want to know.

A knock came on the hardened leaves of the door. "Ari?" Chloe called in a quiet voice.

I straightened, alarmed and shaking. "Um, yeah?"

"Can I come in?"

My mouth moved as I searched for an answer. I couldn't exactly say no. It was her boyfriend's palace.

But I wanted to. I didn't want to see anyone right now,

especially her.

"Uh…"

"Please?" she asked.

Dammit. "Yeah. Sure."

The leaves made soft sounds as they loosened. Chloe slipped past them and caught sight of me on the window seat. "Hey."

I didn't know what to say. "Is something wrong?"

She hesitated and then swam farther into the room. Bandages wrapped her arm while a sling held it tight against her side. Her black eye was almost gone, though, thanks to the medicines they had down here. Even my rib felt worlds better. The doctors had seemed surprised that their healing gel worked on me—apparently non-dehaians ordinarily went into shock and sometimes died from exposure to the stuff—and they hadn't wanted to use it until I told them the judges already had. But when it came to bones, the sieranchine would still take a while to work its magic fully.

Chloe sank down on the edge of the window seat, several feet away from me. "I just wanted to see how you're doing."

I searched for an answer.

I had nothing. I loved him. How was I supposed to tell her that? I loved the guy she'd sort of dated or loved too the year before. And, if I *was* wrong…

Then I'd killed him. With a promise, with the fact he loved me back. He might be dead right now, simply because he didn't get out of that canyon when he should have.

All to protect me.

My insides knotted with pain. I looked away. "I'm fine."

She didn't move.

"Listen," I lied, "I'm really tired, so…"

"It's not your fault."

I glanced back at her sharply. How the hell had she—

"That's what everyone told me," she said. "Over and over again when I thought I'd killed him. I barely even remember the first few hours after—"

I shoved away from the window seat, the blanket falling from my tail while I swam farther into the room just to get away from her. "I don't need to talk about this, okay? You're a very nice person, and I appreciate your concern, but I'm fine. I just need to—"

"It's not your fault."

I looked back, her quiet words somehow shutting down mine.

The knowledge in her eyes was terrible. Old. Certain. Sharp like it had been honed by a thousand attempts to see things another way, only to be refined down to this. She was maybe a year older than me, but suddenly, that age difference might as well have been centuries.

"I thought I'd killed him," Chloe said quietly, "last summer when the Beast dragged him away right in front of me. And Noah himself swore to me that I hadn't." She paused. "He'd say the same to you."

Her green eyes didn't waver from me, and it hurt. The surety bore through my ice, my anger, every defense I had.

Leaving only pain.

"But he shouldn't have been there," I whispered.

Chloe nodded.

She didn't get it, though. She couldn't. "He should have *left*," I insisted. "He *could* have. But I made him promise to help me, and I called out for him in the dark, and if he'd just *gone* instead of staying, he—"

Chloe rose up and crossed the distance between us. All of a sudden, I realized I'd started crying again, and then the sobs took hold. Great gulping sobs, wrenching from me like they were determined to wring my body dry. I couldn't stop them. I couldn't even hope to slow them down.

"I know." She hugged me while I cried. "He came beneath the sea a year ago because of me. Trust me, I know."

My tears slowed. I wasn't sure how long it had been. A minute. An hour. Feeling splotchy-faced and disheveled, I looked over at her. She gave me a sad smile.

"Are you…" I glanced at the sling. "Is your arm okay? Did I hurt—"

She shook her head. "It's fine. Dehaian medicine, right? Crazy."

I managed a smile, nodding.

She twitched her head toward the window seat. Following her back over, I sank down onto the cool stone and, after a moment's hesitation, pulled the blanket around me.

"Did you…" I searched for a way to ask, "feel it? When the attack happened?"

She smoothed her hands over her cream-colored tail. "Yeah." She glanced up at me. "So you knew about the, uh, the connection we had?"

I hesitated. Noah hadn't told her about us? Why?

A twist of pain stabbed at me. Maybe I'd never know.

"We have one too," I said, rushing my words.

She paused. It took me a heartbeat to understand why.

Present tense. I'd still spoken in…

"He was miles from us," Chloe said. "Hours and hours away, and it felt like I was being flayed alive." She stared at me. "You were right there."

I didn't know what to do. I nodded.

"I'm so sorry."

I floundered, at a loss for how to respond. She was so kind, this girl Noah had been in love with a year ago. Compassionate like Baylie. He drew good people around himself, Noah did.

And left a great gaping hole in the middle of them when he wasn't there.

My chest ached, more tears threatening to spill out. I managed another nod.

Silence hung between us, quiet with shared pain.

"It's weird," Chloe said, her gaze turning to the city beyond the window. "The farther he was from me, the less I could feel of him, but even for all those months when there was nothing, it wasn't like this. Silent like this. *Empty* like this."

I wrapped the blanket tighter around myself, shying from the words and how horribly they rang true. How the link between me and Noah ached with the simple, terrible reality that there *was* no ache, no sensation, no emotion or connection or anything. Every attempt to reach for him only felt as if I was fumbling around in the vacant dark, not finding what I *knew* should be there. His presence, warm and real and true amid the shadows and the lost, ancient dreams of flames, of white stone, of cities torn down before he knew of a thing called time. Before the darkness came, bearing the eternal silence of a long-delayed grave, swallowing down any scrap of self into an endless moment among the ruins of history, utterly alone and yet—

"It's so cold."

I drew a sharp breath, Chloe's words snapping me back to reality. "What?"

She gave a lopsided shrug. "Now, I mean. Knowing he's not out there. It's just… cold." She shook her head, seeming to give up on her attempted explanation. "I don't know."

I blinked at her, my weird daydream dissipating like a droplet of ink in clear water. Shivering, I pulled the blanket tighter around myself. "What if he is?" I managed. "Still out there, I mean. And we just can't, you know, feel—"

Leaves rustled behind us. "Lady Chloe?"

A soldier appeared at the door.

"Yes?"

The man hesitated, his gaze flicking to me. "We've received a message from the American coast. It's your friend, my lady. Baylie."

My heart climbed my throat.

"Is she okay?" Chloe asked.

"We're not sure, my lady. She is with landwalkers." The soldier glanced toward me again. "And wizards."

Chloe turned to me, questioning.

I didn't know what to say. How much she knew. For that matter, last I'd heard, Baylie had been shot and was lying in a coma no one could explain.

But that wasn't exactly something I wanted to tell Chloe.

"Our messenger states she is calling for your aid," the soldier said. "The wizards have come under attack. The king has requested your presence right away."

Chloe pushed up from the window seat, already nodding. "Okay." She glanced back at me. "You coming?"

Absolutely, I was. I swam after her out the door.

9

BAYLIE

"Are they here yet? Do you see them?" Wyatt chewed his lip, shifting back and forth like a child in front of the enormous windows while his gaze zigzagged across the landscape as if it contained monsters.

Though, I guess, to him, it did.

"Not yet, Wyatt," Angelica said patiently for what had to be the millionth time. We were hiding out in an isolated house several miles from the coast, a property apparently owned by the landwalker elder Robin, not that she'd accompanied us to confirm that. The elders had split up after I destroyed their latest hideout—the better to protect their research, they said, though I suspected in more than a few cases they were just relieved to get away from me. Empty land surrounded us now, brown and sandy but dotted by scrub brush and the occasional tree. A single gravel track was the only path through the terrain, while a gatehouse guarded the fence that surrounded the property. The main house itself was beautiful enough from the front, but the back put it to shame, featuring floor-to-ceiling windows and two levels of decks, both overlooking a sheer cliff and the ocean in the distance. It was breathtaking.

It was also on the outskirts of Santa Lucina.

"They're really fast," he whined. "You have to watch constantly."

"I'm watching, Wyatt."

Of all the places we could have gone, coming back to the town where the judges had been—whether or not it's where my family had lived too—seemed like a crazy risk. But Olivia assured us that, beautiful or not, Robin had purchased the house for a reason. It had been the former mansion of a paranoid Hollywood celebrity, and thus the defenses on this place were formidable. Video cameras surrounded the area. Armed guards monitored the perimeter, hired through shell accounts from security agencies around the country. Panic rooms down in the subbasement led to tunnel exits somewhere beyond the property's edge. A hippie to the core, Robin had taken the trust fund she inherited from her parents and planned to turn the entire property into an artists' retreat for landwalkers, albeit one with plenty of security in case their new peace with the dehaians ever went wrong.

I doubted she ever envisioned this.

I shifted uncomfortably on the couch. Declan and the elders believed that if there was anywhere the Yvarian dehaians might have remained despite the attacks on their people, Santa Lucina would be it. And they'd been right. A few hours ago, we'd spotted a dehaian on a beach on the outskirts of town. Ellie hadn't recognized him, and I hadn't either, but Wyatt had freaked at the mere sight of the man. The dehaian had known the coded phrases and responses Zeke and Chloe had set up for us, and in short order, he'd hurried off to send a message just as we'd hoped. So far, everything was going according to plan.

In a world where basically nothing had done that for the better part of a year, that didn't reassure me in the slightest.

"You'll tell me if you see them, though, right?" Wyatt begged.

"I've promised I will," Angelica reminded him.

He nodded jerkily, still rocking back and forth by the window.

I returned my attention to the magazine in my hands. A mix of fashion, makeup, and celebrity gossip. I'd enjoyed this stuff, once. The latest makeup releases. New colors for the season and different skincare techniques. It'd been my guilty pleasure and favorite hobby, all rolled into one.

Now I couldn't remember a thing I'd just read, because I was too busy hoping I didn't get killed by magical monsters. The only reason I was up here was the fact the second-floor windows let in a stronger breeze from the ocean and, God help me, that felt better. The touch of salt on the air. The stronger touch of magic.

But that didn't stop me from wishing I was actually deep in a resistance bunker, with armed soldiers and foot-thick walls of concrete surrounding me, preferably also with Wyatt a thousand miles away. I mean, Declan had set up magical defenses outside the house on top of all the human-like ones, but that didn't guarantee the Judiciary might not be closing in on us at this very moment.

"What if somebody tries to sneak up on us?" Wyatt continued.

Ice shot through me at the echo of my own thoughts.

"They won't," Angelica said.

I set the magazine down on the end table and pushed away from the sofa, making Wyatt yelp in alarm. He couldn't hear what I was thinking, I reminded myself. He was edgy as hell, and he could tell where I was all the time—which was a nightmare in and of itself—but he couldn't actually read my mind. "I'm going downstairs," I said to no one in particular.

"You won't hide, though, right?" Wyatt asked.

He meant the greliaran ability to know where each other was. So far, between the two of us, it only seemed to be a one-way street.

And I couldn't stop it.

"No," I told him, though if I'd had a clue how, I would have done it in a heartbeat.

Wyatt nodded, looking reassured. He trusted me.

The world had gone insane.

I jogged down the stairway from the second floor, my footsteps muffled by the thick, beige carpet. I wanted out of this house. Away from this part of the country. New Zealand had beaches. Maybe I could go there.

Except that did nothing about stopping the judges.

I let out a breath, struggling to calm down.

Seated on the couch in the living room, Jace glanced up from a book that I wondered if he remembered a word of reading.

I avoided his curious gaze. He'd offered to come upstairs with me—Wyatt being near any of us made him uncomfortable, shocking as *that* was—but I'd convinced him we needed more people watching the first floor. It was bullshit; I doubted he bought it.

But I felt awkward enough this close to the ocean without him watching me too.

I made a beeline for the kitchen on the slim hope there was some coffee still left in a carafe. Declan, Ellie, and all the other elders were still outside, working on those defenses they'd found in another one of the elders' old records, along with some magic Declan used at one of the bunkers I wished I could be in right now.

Sofa springs squeaked in the living room.

Dammit.

"Hey." Jace's voice was so neutral it could have vanished into the beige carpet. "You doing okay?"

I hefted the carafe, silently thanking the coffee gods that a bit remained. "Yeah."

"I wanted to say I was sorry about earlier, at the house."

My brow twitched down, but I didn't look at him while I twisted open the lid on the carafe.

"I should never have volunteered you to take on the judges like that. It was wrong of me. I'm sorry."

I hesitated. "Thanks."

A moment crept past, filled only by the sound of coffee pouring into my mug.

"Listen," he began. "About the other day…"

My hand didn't shake. It really didn't, which I considered a minor victory. And there wasn't enough coffee left to overflow the mug either. Nothing to give away how I trembled inside at the memory of how whatever was within me had reacted to the magic inside him when Angelica had tried to take him over with her power. How *good* it had felt, this thing inside me sweeping under him, his magic sweeping over me...

I bashed the memory down hard. "What about it?" My voice was cold.

He hesitated, seeming alarmed like some new thought was occurring to him. "Did it hurt you?"

God, no.

I bashed that down too. "And if it had?" I tossed out, picking up the coffee mug. Anger was good. Anger helped keep the fact I wanted to reach for his hand and try it again right now at bay.

And that scared me.

He blanched. "I-I'm so sorry. I would never have—" He struggled to regroup. "From the way you looked after, it didn't seem like—"

I set the mug down before even taking a sip.

He waited, his storm-cloud gray eyes watching me warily.

A scowl fought its way onto my face. "No, it didn't hurt me." Far from it. "I'm just..."

I struggled for a way to describe why I'd been avoiding this topic for the better part of two days, without *actually* getting into why I'd been avoiding it.

Jace didn't say a word.

"I don't even know you, okay?" I glared at him. "Your favorite food, your favorite color, your middle name. I don't know *anything* except the insanity of these past few d—" I grimaced. "—*weeks,* and I was in a coma for most of them. And what happened back there…"

My words ran out. Chest heaving and heart pounding, I snatched after some way to explain that didn't involve the *least* hint that I was attracted to him, that I wanted to share magic like that again, or that I couldn't get the lure of it out of my head.

Because the idea this dark power inside me could be something *besides* a force of utter destruction was oh-so-tempting. And the possibility of freeing that power with *him*—

"Gideon."

"What?"

"My middle name. Jace Gideon Moreau." He paused, seeming to take in my expression. "Mom was obsessed with being an aristocrat. I got out of it better than Ari—or Ariabella Celestina." His lip twitched.

I wasn't quite sure what to say. Yeah, his name was aristocratic, or, you know, strong like he should be running a bank or maybe be a movie star, but…

I liked it.

"Chicago deep-dish pizza, preferably with pineapple."

My nose wrinkled. Seriously?

His grin spread, just for a moment. "And blue." His gaze searched my cornflower-blue eyes. "My favorite color is blue."

Shivers went through me, way too warm for my own good.

"You?" he asked.

I blinked fast. This wasn't going the way I'd planned, not that I'd really planned anything beyond getting out of the conversation and staying away from the topic—and quite possibly him—for the better part of forever.

"Um…" I reclaimed my coffee mug from the counter. "Annabeth."

His brow crept up, not cruel, just surprised. His smile returned.

I didn't like what that smile was doing to me, purely because I liked it way too much.

"Blueberry waffles," I continued, focusing hard on taking a sip of my coffee and then grimacing at the bitter taste. Black. Not the way I'd normally drink it. Cream and about a candy store's worth of sugar was my typical go-to.

"And color?" he prompted.

I avoided his eyes. "I like all kinds of colors."

Including gray.

He was quiet for a moment. "I'm sorry about what happened with Angelica. I didn't mean to—"

"I know."

"And I'm not trying to push you. I'm only…" A frown twisted his face.

"What?"

"Ruanir have to work to keep ocean magic out. Whenever we're near the ocean, it's there, testing the edges of our control, tempting us, weakening us. We've always been like that. It's why ocean magic poisoning—even if the judges' version is bullshit—has always been a threat. But now…"

Alarm prickled through me. What did he mean, now?

His attention was on the windows beyond the pass-through in the kitchen. "When I was in Santa Lucina before, I could feel the ocean tugging at me the entire time. But ever since we got here today, it's like I can feel it, but it doesn't bother me. It's not a tugging or tempting, not doing anything to weaken my magic at all. It's just… there. Outside me, but not trying to come in, like somebody built a floodwall." He met my eyes.

It was impossible to miss his meaning. Me. I'd done that. *We'd* done that.

"Do you feel any different?" he asked.

I pulled my gaze from his, focusing on setting the coffee mug down again. "Um…"

No. But then, was I certain? I'd seen black lightning crackle through my skin, for God's sake. Maybe that was simply part of whatever the hell I *was* now, but who was to say that wasn't related to this instead?

"I'm not sure," I admitted.

He hesitated and then stepped closer. I tensed.

"Look," he said, "I know I don't know you that well. I know you don't know me either. And if things were different…" He gave a rueful chuckle. "Let's just say I would've loved to ask you out for coffee sometime."

My stomach fluttered, and I tried to cram the sensation down into a box. It wasn't helping.

"But they're not." His mouth tightened. "I don't know what sharing magic with you like that last time *was,* or what it *did* to me, but it… it felt…"

"Amazing," I whispered.

He stared at me. "Yeah."

I swallowed hard.

"And it helped," he continued. "So if you'd ever be willing to try again—"

I couldn't stop myself. I reached out, placing my hand on his where he rested it on the counter.

He watched me, wordless. Nervousness trembled through my insides because I didn't know what I was doing. What this was *going* to do.

Anything.

The front door opened.

My hand jerked back from his, a sharp breath entering my lungs.

"Baylie?" Ellie called.

I picked up my coffee mug again, clasping it tightly. "In here."

Jace stepped away from me, his hands reaching behind him to grip the edge of the countertop like he was hanging onto something steadying.

Ellie rounded the corner. "Hey, the—" She glanced between us. "Everything alright?"

"Yeah, fine." My response was too quick. I knew she caught it.

"Um, okay." She fidgeted with one of her curls. "Well, uh, the dehaian guy called Olivia."

I tensed, my heart climbing my throat.

"He was able to reach Chloe and Zeke," Ellie said. "They're coming… and they've got Ari with them."

～ 10 ～

THE BEAST

Show me, urged the whisper. *Show me what happened then. Show me who we are.*

Splashes of red, faster, faster. Red on white marble, red on green grass, wet and glistening in the bright summer sun. Screams, always screams, as the ruanir who tasted of hot sand and green grass died. Time had no meaning. Days and nights blurred, if they were noticed at all. Through its link to the dehaian man whose will had replaced its own, it learned of new abilities. The ability to send fear, send dread, send dark and terrible feelings to the little ones who ran and hid and cried. The ability to lash down with lightning and shake the earth, to sweep up waves of the sea and wipe out buildings, trees, people. And in those days, it learned its name, a name screamed by those who feared it and howled by those who died.

The Beast.

At the dehaian man's command, it opened fissures in the earth to swallow the little scurrying ones whole. It sent spears of lightning to burn them alive and swept them up and threw them on the white, cool stones. Bursts of pure, sweet peace followed. It craved the peace, that rush of satiation from a hunger that only ever seemed to briefly end with their deaths.

It craved a respite from the pain.

The one who commanded it waited beyond the place of buildings and roads, inside a quiet forest that the dehaian planned to burn once the killing was done. None would escape. None would hide amid the tall, green trees. It wouldn't let them. They needed to die.

The one who commanded it said so, and to disobey was agony.

But that day, a new taste suddenly filled the air. A taste of cool water and hot grass combined with the churning fires deep within the earth. The taste dulled the pain, muffled the pound-pound-pound of the dehaian man's will with warmth like the ocean on a gentle wave, softness like the earth after rain. It knew that taste. Remembered it now.

Home.

Confusion and elation filled the Beast. It could return to a time of peace. If it followed that feeling through the air, if it found the source, it could be free of the dehaian man and the pain.

It chased the taste of home, tracing the flavor that flowed upward like a river into the sky, to a space of white steps, glistening pillars, and clear blue water. And it knew that space. This place had been there in the beginning, in the time before the pain. A small collection of people stood atop the glass platform now, with black, oily markings slashed and swirled on the translucent floor beneath them.

And they were familiar. They were some of the old ones, the original ones, the first it'd seen. They came from the gentle dreaming time in the cool water, back before the pain.

They lifted their hands into the air, chanting words it didn't understand. But the feeling of home intensified. Home was pouring in around it like water, drawn from all over the island, from the ocean beyond, and from the sky and the earth to this one place, this one moment. Home was here. The Beast only had to come to them, and then, at long last, everything would be all right.

But the old ones were liars.

Black light flared from the dark oil on the translucent platform. The air became charged, crackling and burning, dragging the Beast down like a whirlpool. The blue water frothed, churning in the black light, and the feeling of home turned sickly and sticky, smothering the Beast like quicksand.

And it couldn't escape.

Fear filled it, like the terror it would send upon the little scurrying ones. Down, down, down pulled the sticky black energy. Down toward the old ones who chanted without ceasing. Down toward the inky markings that swirled beneath their feet like a whirlpool to make the world drown. Darkness surrounded the Beast, black like the core of the earth and the depths of the sea, but with nothing of their security or peace. Just emptiness. Nothingness.

An end, when it had barely had a beginning.

Everything had been a lie. Home was a lie, bait in a cruel trap that waited like a hungry maw. The liars and betrayers had only sought to trap the Beast, end it. The darkness warped reality, warped awareness, drawing the creature down into itself, into the markings that had not grown any larger and yet seemed to encompass the Beast's world. The trap dragged the creature into oblivion while the liars stood fast, now above the Beast, above the magical symbols of the trap, untouched and unharmed by the black, sticky magic roiling beneath their feet. And all around, the feeling of home rushed in, drained from across the island to pour into this place, this prison, like dirt onto a grave.

The black power tugged at the Beast, whipping away the creature's energy like wisps of fog in the wind. More and more of its strength vanished into the void, devoured by home, by all that should have been safe but had only proved a lie. The darkness began to seal over the light, to close the Beast inside this trap and consume it fully, and, in a panic, the Beast reached for something, anything to save it, and felt the dehaian man racing toward it. His power built of pain stabbed into the abyss over and over, seeking to reclaim mastery of the Beast and fracture the trap built by the liars.

And their trap shuddered.

The flicker of lost control was enough. In desperation, the Beast surged for the last fragment of light beyond the abyss.

The darkness around it rumbled and roiled, the nightmare built of home seeking to reclaim its hold. Pain burned through the Beast's amorphous form as the darkness fought to hold it in this place, but at the moment the Beast thought it could take no more, the darkness failed.

Lightning erupted from the Beast as it surged up from the trap and back out into the light. Beneath it, the darkness churned out of control, destabilized by the loss of its prey. The black oil frothed and boiled as the trap clawed after the Beast, its quarry. The translucent platform began to crack. The liars fled in terror, but they couldn't escape the battle they'd started. Lightning tore into them, scorching their flesh, while the darkness wrapped around them, devouring the ground beneath their feet and dragging them into nothingness.

But more scurrying ones were coming. The dehaian man, his people, countless others who would hurt it. Liars, all of them! None could be trusted. No one would help it be free. In a burst of agony, it shared with the dehaian man, it tore him down and crushed him to the churning earth before he could secure his hold on it again.

A flare of peace followed, like the rush from the death of a hot-sand one, but different. Like a reduction of pain, rather than satiation of hunger. But the dehaian man had made the Beast believe his death would be agony. Liars, again! Always lying!

And the darkness was coming.

With lightning and winds and shaking of the earth, the Beast hurled the liars at the dark, hurled buildings and trees and chunks of hillsides too. Fires spread wherever its lightning struck. Blazing orange flames billowed black smoke into the air. Still, the darkness did not slow. Buildings and roads fell into oblivion. Mountainsides sloughed down toward the abyss, and trees tumbled into the widening void. At the edge of the roiling shoreline, boats fought the churning tide in a desperate attempt to get away. Ocean water poured into nothingness. Boats and screaming little ones were lost. Still, the darkness reached for the Beast, scarcely held at bay by its blasts of lightning or surges of power that tore up entire swaths of land and hurled them at the steadily encroaching oblivion.

But finally, the darkness began to tire. The feeling of home diminished, draining into the darkness while the last of the island disappeared beneath the waves. The green hills and the white towers were gone, swallowed by the waters that frothed, white-crested, beneath the blue sky. Nothing remained of the island, of home, of the place where all the gentle warmth had turned to cold cruelty. Even the liars were gone, drowned in the depths of the tumultuous sea. But if any remained in hiding, the Beast would find them. It would be safe. Alone, and forever safe.

We destroyed the island, came the whisper. *But they did too.*

The ball of fire arced and vanished so many times through the sky. Hundreds, thousands of times while it hunted the liars.

But with each cycle of the earth, they were fewer. Both kinds. Either kind. Fewer and fewer, until another feeling shared space with the fury to make the world safe. A gnawing feeling, one that it remembered from the first days with the liars.

Hunger.

They changed their magic to escape us, said the whisper. *We were starving.*

It sank into the ocean then, tired, slipping into dreams while the earth cycled and the waters rose and fell. It drifted along the current at the edge of the quiet, eternal darkness, but in all of time, it never came close to the *place*. It didn't like the place, had to hide and stay safe from the place. It didn't remember why, not back then, because remembering was frightening and something it didn't want to do. There were simply… reasons. And then even those faded away.

Until one day…

Power like lightning through the deep, dark water. The feeling, the hunger, lessened for the first time in all of time. There was an old one in the water. An old one had returned. Red hair. Cream scales.

A girl… came the whisper.

It hated the girl. Wanted to kill the girl. Reach into her mind, send her fear. Hate. Little old one, all alone, but there could be others. Had to kill her, even if she stopped the gnawing feeling, because she would hurt it if she could. Bring others to hurt. She was a liar. They were all liars. See! See how they chanted already, summoning it into a cave with the girl on a table. They didn't feel the same, it couldn't even see them now, but still, they were there in secret. Hidden liars! It would never be safe unless it killed them all and—

The boy.

Memory stopped. Tall. Blond hair. Between it and the girl, struck by accident as the Beast reached for her to kill her.

It knew that boy. He wasn't like the others. He—

I, said the boy.

The boy had been created to kill, but he didn't want to kill. He lived without hunger, without fear of anything except himself. He didn't want to be what the lying ones had made, and so he wasn't. He simply… chose differently.

Didn't want to be a weapon, the boy murmured.

Together with the boy, it could be different too. It could be *safe*, protected from the darkness and the dragging deep. It could live and be more than what the traitors and the liars made. And so we were. Together, we did something right, something good. The thing we needed, and because of that, the little scurrying ones were changed. The *world* was changed, our hunger faded, and the ones who hurt us didn't hurt us anymore.

Because I became Noah.

I was Noah.

I am Noah.

But something was still missing.

11

ARI

"They trust these *humans* for their protection?" The dehaian soldier's tone was heavy with skepticism.

His companions didn't respond while our SUV rolled closer to the gate blocking the gravel road. Five other vehicles were behind us, all of them as heavily fortified and bulletproof as this one seemed to be. Inside, soldiers waited for one word of warning from me about Logan or any strakirin in the area—though many of the dehaians didn't seem too keen on trusting me, either. Unlike Damerion's troops, this group had come from Nyciena with their king, and though Zeke made it clear that I was on their side, they still eyed me like they were daring me to prove him wrong.

I'd barely moved a muscle as a result.

Chloe and Zeke, along with Damerion and Ezio, were in the middle vehicle, however. I doubted anyone would hurt me without an order from one of those four. Meanwhile, a half-dozen people stood on either side of the gate in front of us, all of them dressed in black with guns, Tasers, and who knew what else on their belts. They were security, obviously, but guarding what seemed to be an empty swath of California landscape.

I swallowed nervously, resisting the urge to shift on the plush back seat. The dehaians had retrieved the vehicles from storage near the coast, along with tactical gear and enough guns to invade a small country. It was a novel thing for them, according to Chloe—the cars, the storage, even the weapons— all of it owing to their recent ability to go more than a few miles beyond the coastline without pain. Now dehaians were learning how to drive, were looking into human currency and bank accounts, even jobs. It was a whole new world, according to her.

I hadn't known about any of it.

But it meant we were sitting here in a new-looking SUV, dressed in clothes the soldiers had stored along with the weapons, following directions on a GPS to a location a landwalker elder had given us. We looked practically human.

And like an armed caravan that would put the Secret Service to shame.

"Name?" one of the security guards asked when the dehaian soldier rolled down the window.

"Why do you need my name? We're expected. Let us through."

I stifled a groan. This was going well.

All the security guards put their hands to their weapons. "*Name*," the first one spat.

I cast a nervous glance to the dehaians and then shifted forward a bit on the back seat. "Ari," I called. "We're here to see

Olivia?"

The security guard leaned over to see me in the rear of the SUV. His cool gaze skimmed me, the soldiers, and then me again.

He leaned back. "Let them through."

The other security guards pushed the gate aside. The dehaian soldier made a rude noise and then drove onward.

I closed my eyes. Though Tiberion and a large number of soldiers had stayed behind in Nyciena to guard it, hundreds of others waited off the coast in case of an attack. The ones around me were the advance force of an army, basically, and if things went wrong…

But things wouldn't. This was a… I wasn't sure what this was. A peace summit? A war treaty? I couldn't settle on a metaphor, because I wasn't sure which it would turn out to be. The message had asked us to come at once because the resistance was under attack. They'd suffered losses. They needed help, the kind only the dehaians could give.

They'd been vague on the details.

But the messenger had described Baylie perfectly. Ellie too, plus another woman I didn't recognize but whom Chloe seemed to know. Somebody named Olivia. From Chloe's and Zeke's reactions, the woman possibly, most likely, almost *certainly* seemed to be on our side, which meant this was all going to be fine.

I glanced through the rear windshield to see one security guard closing the gate while another spoke into a walkie-talkie attached to his shoulder.

Totally fine.

The SUVs rumbled along a rise in the gravel road, and a house came into view. Two stories, standing alone amid the rough trees and dry-scrub landscape, it backed up on what seemed to be a sharp drop. Blue-gray rolls of hills waited beyond it, while beyond them…

The ocean. That way.

Right.

I swallowed hard and pulled my focus back to the house. To the landscape around us. To the security guards I could see patrolling the property beyond the trees, their attention pinned on the perimeter and not us.

They wouldn't stand a chance against the judges.

I drew a slow breath. Their guns would. Tasers too. Ruanir magic was slow. For my entire life, that had been something that scared me, that meant we couldn't reveal ourselves to humans, because they'd most likely shoot us. Now, when we were the ones with guns, it just meant we'd be safe.

Except against Logan.

The SUV pulled to a stop a hundred feet from the front door. The soldiers climbed out, their gazes scanning the house and surroundings intently. Damerion and Ezio emerged as well, clearly checking the area before they'd allow their king and valya Praelex to leave the vehicle.

I couldn't make myself move. The message said the ruanir resistance would be waiting, and that meant my family. Probably my family. Maybe, anyway.

Or maybe they weren't here.

My stomach churned. That wasn't the better option. If they weren't, then anything could have happened. And sure, it'd been months. Sure, last I'd seen them, I'd been a monster. But Noah had said they were okay.

That thought just hurt.

"Ari?" Chloe peered into the vehicle while the others walked past, heading for the house.

I made myself get out.

"You okay?" she asked.

I nodded, the motion a total lie.

She nodded back, not looking convinced, and then continued on till she reached Zeke again and took his hand.

I started after them. The landwalker hideout was a far cry from the rundown houses and abandoned buildings that the resistance used for bunkers. Two stories of architecture that looked like a mix of mission and colonial, the house had unblemished white walls, dark tiles on the roof, and a broad porch flanked by white columns. Windows with beautiful crisscross patterns over their panes looked out on the expansive yard. Double doors of dark, polished wood led into the house itself, while on the second story, smaller doors led out onto a terrace with white railing above the front porch.

It was beautiful.

It couldn't possibly be safe.

"Area secured?" Damerion murmured, like he was having the same thoughts I was.

I glanced at the commander.

He nodded at whatever he heard over the communication

device in his ear. "Good, then move on the—"

The front door opened. "Ari!" Jace ran down the steps.

I froze, a thousand reactions crashing in on me at once. I wanted to cry. Laugh. Throw myself into my brother's arms and hug him till the end of time, even if I knew I couldn't, because of ocean magic and poison and just being strakirin. And I wanted to run and hide because I wasn't ready for this. I'd *never* be ready for this. I'd possibly killed the guy I loved. I was a murderer with countless resistance dead at my feet, slaughtered by my own hand when the judges had me in their research lab. And now here was my brother, who didn't know any of that, who thought I didn't have blood all over my hands, who—

I couldn't breathe.

He skidded to a stop ahead of me. "You're… are you…"

"Hi." The word blurted from me, and it was stupid. *Hi?* After everything that'd happened and months of being away, all I could come up with to say was—

Jace grabbed me into a hug. I choked on a protest, paralyzed for a moment in a wash of relief and guilt and fear and ever-increasing aches from my healing rib.

"You're alive," he said. "You're actually… oh my God…"

"Yeah." I nodded. My rib was starting to hurt worse. From the house, I saw Baylie and Ellie emerge along with a bunch of people I didn't recognize. "Yeah, I—"

He let me go abruptly, pushing me away at arm's length like he wanted to look at me. "Are you okay?" His gray eyes were intense, searching mine.

My mouth moved. What was the answer to that?

Noah might be dead.

That was the answer.

Jace blinked suddenly, registering the others around us. His grip on my shoulders tightened while he scanned the dehaians behind me.

"This is, um…" I wasn't sure what to say. "Well, that's Ezio, and that's Damerion, and that's, uh, the king—"

"You're here!" Ellie hurried down the steps, grinning. "We were getting concerned you were…" She slowed, catching sight of all the soldiers around us with spikes on their arms.

"Stand down," Zeke ordered. A smile softened his expression. "Good to see you again, Ellie."

Her grin returned, albeit nervously. "You too. Both of you. I was worried… you know." She gave a lopsided shrug. "I'm just so glad you made it."

"Where's Baylie?" Chloe asked.

Ellie glanced over her shoulder. "She was here. But maybe Declan had more tests or—"

"Tests?" Chloe interrupted.

Ellie hesitated. "Um, right. Uh…"

Declan appeared at the door, and Ellie cast him a look that was practically relieved. An African-American woman followed him out of the house, and I could feel the tension in the air ratchet higher as she approached.

But I didn't see Maia. Or Dhanya. Or anyone else from the resistance at all.

"Welcome," the woman said, smiling.

Declan's expression looked anything but that word.

"Olivia," Zeke replied evenly. His gaze rested on Declan, waiting.

Olivia's smile didn't waver at the neutral greeting, though I noticed she marked it. She had a sharp edge to her, I could tell. An intelligence that reminded me of Ellie, but without the shyness.

"May I present Declan, head scientist of the ruanir resistance, Highness," Olivia continued, unperturbed. "And currently our ally in this undertaking."

I noted the use of "currently." It wasn't hard to guess the others around me did too.

Silence greeted the introduction.

"Well," Olivia said. "It would probably be best to continue this conversation inside. You've all had a long trip, and there is much to discuss."

Another lengthy pause followed her words. The soldiers made no move to go, but simply watched Chloe and the king, waiting.

Chloe and Zeke glanced at each other, a different question seeming to pass between them. Wariness rose in me at the look in their eyes. They'd seemed to recognize Olivia when the messenger described her, back in Nyciena. Were we not safe around her? Had something happened in the past to make them wary of landwalkers?

I made myself keep breathing. The resistance was here, though. Somewhere. At least…

I glanced around. They should have been.

"Agreed," Zeke allowed. He twitched his chin to the Yvarians.

The dehaian soldiers melted back beyond the trees surrounding the property, with the exception of Damerion and a handful of others. Falling in around Zeke like an entourage, they started inside.

I looked at Jace. "Where is everyone else?"

Chloe stopped, overhearing me. Ellie did the same, nervousness flashing over her face.

My brother was silent.

"Jace…" My heart started galloping. "Where are Maia and Dhanya?"

Noah had said they were okay.

The thought was a quiet plea inside me, desperate in its fear. It had to still be true. It just *had* to.

"Jace?" I whispered.

"There was an attack."

Oh, God.

"Maia was taken by the judges. Miguel too. Dhanya's hurt, but…"

"They're on their way here," Ellie said when he faltered. "Whoever's left. Whoever could be moved."

I couldn't breathe. My legs wobbled beneath me.

Jace reached out, catching my arm. I yanked it away fast. He shouldn't be touching me right now. I couldn't guarantee I wouldn't lose control.

Hurt flashed over his face.

"Is she *alive*?" My voice was hoarse.

Again, that horrible pause came. My mouth worked soundlessly, searching for the words to make this not be real.

"Declan says they'll poison her. Use their magic and…" Jace couldn't finish.

I wanted to throw up. She wasn't like me, pre-adjustment and able to be turned into a strakirin.

Like this was better?

Of course it was. This was… She could *survive* this.

Except now there was Logan to consider too.

I clutched my arms to my middle, fighting to keep the nausea down.

"Is this something to do with the tests you mentioned?" Chloe prompted warily. "Was Baylie poisoned?"

Ellie floundered. "Um, no. You, uh, you really should just talk to her. But this is why we hoped the dehaians would come," she continued to me. "Chloe and Zeke most of all. The resistance doesn't have the forces left to deal with this, but with the dehaians…"

I hesitated. Chloe had powers like the Beast, sure. But that didn't mean she could take on Logan.

Ellie glanced to the house with a helpless expression. "We should really get inside."

I nodded distantly. I'd find a way to help Maia. I would.

Even if I had no idea what to do.

∾ 12 ∾

BAYLIE

I could hear the others downstairs, moving around the house. I'd seen the dehaians outside, fanning out to survey the rough landscape like they'd been born to it. The rest were standing guard around the house. It had never occurred to me that they could move as stealthily on land as they likely could through water, but then, if they were with Zeke, they were probably soldiers who trained everywhere, land and sea alike. The better to protect their king.

And the people close to him.

Anxiety gnawed at me. I should have gone out there, pretended to be normal, and said hi to Chloe and all that. I mean, honestly, if I wasn't there, then who knew how long it'd be till someone made a comment, slipped up, and let my best friend in on my little secret-that-wasn't-a-secret? And it was more ordinary than hiding out up here, with only Angelica and a psychotic killer as company.

I couldn't make myself walk down the stairs.

"Too many." Wyatt rocked back and forth in the corner.

"Too many…"

"It's okay, Wyatt," Angelica murmured. "It's okay."

I glanced at her. She appeared worried, and there was an edge to her voice that I hadn't heard before. There were probably *hundreds* of dehaians down there.

But then, what had we expected? We'd asked for the Yvarian king.

"Too many…"

I froze when Wyatt looked up at me, tensing for him to change like greliarans could. But the expression on his face paralyzed me for a whole new reason.

He looked *terrified*.

"Don't want to hurt," he whimpered. "Please. *Please*, don't want to hurt…"

Every rational bone in my body screamed to run, but I found myself moving closer anyway, a weird surety inside me that had nothing to do with history and everything to do with the childlike terror in his eyes. I rested my hands on his. "It's okay. I… I won't let them hurt you."

He bit his lip, his grip shifting to clutch my hands hard. I hissed with pain, and he whimpered again, loosening his hold immediately. But the desperate hope and the unwavering faith in me didn't fade from his eyes.

What the hell had Ellie *done* to this guy?

He tensed, his gaze snapping beyond me and a choked cry escaping him.

I turned, my hands still clasped inside his massive grip.

Chloe stared at us. On the landing ahead of her, a dark-haired guy I remembered as her bodyguard did the same.

Wyatt's breaths came short and fast. I could feel him shaking.

"What the…" Chloe started.

I glanced back at Wyatt. He hadn't taken his eyes from her. I wasn't sure he could.

And his hands were getting unnaturally warm.

"Wyatt…" I cast a quick look at Angelica, but her attention was fixed on Chloe too.

Great.

Short, growling huffs came from Wyatt. Hair-thin cracks of light flashed and vanished in his skin while his face twitched between terror and hunger.

Oh, hell. "Wyatt!"

His gaze snapped to me. There was nothing sane in those eyes. "*Fish… my fish…*" His voice was the growl I remembered from my nightmares.

Panic drummed an ever-accelerating beat through my veins. This was going bad and could go so, so much worse in no time at all. And I didn't know what to do about it. Tell Chloe to go downstairs? What if he tried to follow her? It wasn't like I could stop him. I couldn't even—

An idea occurred to me. A terrible one.

The heat from his hands was starting to burn. I could see red flares popping like embers in his eyes.

Barely breathing, I didn't move, my entire body tingling with the effort of control, control, control. Don't let her see…

Shielded by my body and engulfed in his grip, my hands shivered with a twist of black smoke and even darker lightning.

Wyatt's breath caught. His eyes focused, like I'd snapped him out of a daze.

"Don't. Do. *Anything.*" I bit off the words.

The cracks faded from his skin. His grip on my hands relaxed. He jerked his head in a short, tight nod while his eyes twitched away from mine, flicking across the carpet as if he was searching for something. I couldn't guess what. But a strange confusion was on his face now, different than what I'd seen before. Like he was lost, maybe, or waking up from a bad dream.

This wasn't the time to wonder about it. I extracted my hands from his, glancing down quickly to check for smoke. It had already vanished. Maybe it'd never even been there.

Wyatt's reaction would seem to belie that.

God, don't let her have seen anything…

Cautiously, I looked over my shoulder to Chloe. She was staring at us. I couldn't tell if her expression was for me or the psychotic killer currently huddled in a ball on the ground.

"Downstairs?" I suggested tightly.

Wyatt gave an inarticulate grunt behind me. "No… don't… don't go."

I glanced back at him. His eyes were still scanning the beige carpet. He looked like he didn't even know where he was.

Anxiety prickled through me. "It's okay, Wyatt."

I hoped.

The protesting expression on his face strengthened, but he didn't say anything more.

"Um, yeah," Chloe answered me. "Downstairs. Sure." She

gave a slow, wary nod, still watching us. With a brief glance at Angelica and the dark-haired man nearby, she retreated toward the first floor.

A breath left me. So much for pretending things were ordinary.

She was waiting when I reached the first floor. Her dark-haired bodyguard stood by the base of the stairs, watching the second floor as if daring Wyatt to follow. From the living room, Declan's voice carried, his tone vaguely annoyed as always. He was explaining something about the ruanir, presumably to the dehaians.

Chloe didn't take her eyes from me.

"Um, hey," I tried.

"You have *Wyatt* here?" she blurted.

My mouth moved. Okay, good. She was shocked about that, not me.

Hopefully not me.

"And what the hell was that?" she continued.

Dammit.

"You're… you're…"

"Look, I'm sorry I didn't tell—"

"How the hell are you *controlling* him?"

Oh.

I blinked fast, rewriting my answer to something not

magical. Not about me. Not—

"Are you okay?"

I looked over at her again, confused. "Huh?"

Chloe's worried eyes searched my face. "Ellie said something about tests? That Declan guy needing to do tests?"

Damn, damn, *damn…*

"Are you okay, Baylie?"

"Yeah." No. "I'm fine." I'm a wizard.

Or something.

Chloe didn't seem convinced.

I grabbed for the first distraction I could find, glancing to the dark-haired bodyguard who was now watching me as much as the stairs.

Awesome.

But I remembered him now. He'd come with her father on a visit to see Chloe. Ezio. That was his name. "Is your dad here?" I cast a quick look around.

"No. He stayed in Periantrea."

"Oh. Is he—"

"Why was Declan doing tests on you, Baylie?"

Dammit. "It's just…" The truth pressed at me. This was my best friend. Surely I could tell her.

I *knew* I could tell her. That wasn't the problem. The problem was I wasn't human anymore. Or, really, that I couldn't *be* human, not with her, not after I told her the truth.

Chloe being different wasn't an issue. Noah or anyone else in my family, either. Chloe had always wanted out of Kansas, and Noah had talked of traveling the world long before he'd become a flying storm monster who could go anywhere. And me?

I'd wanted a family. Friends. A house not far from my dad. My family had been blown apart when I was four years old and my mom died, and I'd grown up being that girl whom people worried and whispered about. The girl whom the other kids avoided for fear that somehow I was to blame, contagious, or a curse, and if they hung out with me, then their moms would die too. All I wanted in life was to stay close to the people I loved, to have friends and fun and cookouts on Fridays, and be *normal*. And if I told Chloe…

"What?" she prompted, worried.

A response popped into my head. "Um, it's just that Ellie stopped Wyatt last year, and it had, you know, side effects."

"On you?"

"No!" I regrouped. "No, just Wyatt. It made him scared of everything. But we needed someone to help find dehaians and…" I was botching this. "It's fine. I'm fine. Everything's… you know… fine."

Chloe hesitated, a new sort of worry coming into her eyes, along with something that looked a hell of a lot like doubt.

She suspected I was hiding something from her.

My chest ached. Over the past year, Chloe had become comfortable with not being ordinary. It hadn't been a hard jump for her, regardless. She'd embraced not being human and all that it entailed.

All the things magic had destroyed.

The ache deepened. Telling the ruanir had been one thing.

Declan, and Maia and Dhanya… even Jace… I could compartmentalize that. And sure, the walls were cracking. Ellie and the elders knew now too. But I could swear the landwalkers to secrecy and hope that wouldn't affect anything else. I could swear the ruanir to silence as well and leave them behind when this was all over to just go on with my life. But if I told Chloe…

There had to be a way through this where I could carry on as human after all this ended. Where I could still be *me,* still have my normal life without being a wizard or whatever the hell magic had turned me into. But Chloe… what if she didn't get that? There'd be no going back once she knew. What if, instead, she wanted me to be comfortable with magic, comfortable like her, and she tried to fix the fact I knew I could never be? It could tear our friendship apart. It could mean magic ruined even more than it had already.

It could hurt her.

"Okay," she allowed. She was trying to trust me anyway.

And that hurt too.

"Well, um…" She cast a quick look over her shoulder to the living room. Olivia was talking now, saying something about landwalker resources. "I should probably get, you know, back in there."

I could hear the invitation to join her in her voice, and the worried expression on her face didn't fade.

I hesitated. I could go back upstairs. Sit this out.

Funny how hanging out with the psychotic killer was the less terrifying option right now.

But then, Declan or the others might say something. Might

let her in on my not-secret.

Being in the room with them wouldn't help anything.

It might stop them.

"Yeah," I agreed. "Sure."

I hurried for the living room, trying to ignore the way my best friend watched me.

13

NOAH

I hadn't been a weapon, not at first. I didn't know what I'd been.

But I knew I was in trouble.

The silent darkness dragged at my amorphous form, trying to pull my consciousness back toward black oblivion where nothing would exist and nothing would matter. And it was tempting, so tempting. I'd existed as no more than non-sentient magic since the beginning of time, unconscious, not alive. What memories I had of my life were fragments, shredded snapshots of an ancient history that I—no, the Beast—had tried to forget for a thousand years. Snapshots the Beast had never understood because why would it?

I had only been a child. And more than that... less than that... I...

Never alive.

Thought that together we could be.

That was me. The other me. Noah. A... a year ago, when I became me and I tried to explain why to the red-haired girl...

to Chloe, why I…

My thoughts scattered, and the memory slipped away again. It wasn't the memory I needed, though. Something else was gone, and it would help me survive this draining darkness, help me remember. I needed to remember…

Gold and glitter, twisting like threads of pale fire in the night. Eyes like yellow-green jewels or gray like the summer sky in a storm. A smile like the warm sun, filling me with a feeling the Beast had never had in a thousand years. A feeling the other me had never expected to have again.

Love.

For Ari.

More memories tumbled back, bringing the image of her beautiful face, the softness of her incredible skin and scales, the sound of her laughter, and the warmth of her in my arms. The rush of protectiveness I felt when she was in danger. The respect I felt for how strong she was, no matter what stood in her way. The quiet, blessed quiet, she brought to all the rage and pain of a thousand years of hunting the ones who hurt me, or to the past year of fearing I'd lost all that the greliaran side of me had ever known.

Everything came back. Logan, the fight, the Driecarans, and the judges and the ruanir and—

Instinctively, lightning flared inside my formless shape to beat back the darkness, but the impulse was a mistake. The draining power of the darkness intensified even as my three-hundred-sixty-degree vision instantly took in every detail around me. Numbness spread through me, carrying the lull of an endless oblivion where I wouldn't exactly be dead, but I'd never again be alive. I groaned with pain as I struggled to fight it, my growl barely a whisper in this silent tomb. They'd wanted to kill me here.

They'd almost succeeded.

Darkness beneath them, spreading across the glass platform and dragging me into oblivion, while they stood above it, untouched, unharmed.

I'd become Noah for a reason.

Desperately, I concentrated on drawing down into the infinitesimally small form of a person. Of me. My other form that I'd taken for a reason, because the liars had been safe. The liars hadn't feared the darkness.

Till I ripped the ground from beneath them.

But my body wasn't real. Wasn't human or greliaran, just a shape made out of a storm, that wouldn't stop the darkness from devouring me.

Warmth in my skin. The ghost of a heartbeat. I could feel alive again.

I remembered.

With everything I had, I focused on what I'd learned from sharing magic with Ari. Heat rushed through me, bringing with it the distant ghost of a heartbeat and an awareness of the bitter cold around me. I didn't need to breathe—couldn't down here anyway—but the change was enough. The pulling of the magic around me slowed, becoming a faint tug like a current in the otherwise still water.

For a moment, I hovered, trembling. I was okay. I was still

alive. A soft chuckle escaped me, barely more than a quiet rasp in the heavy silence. Ari had saved me. From this, from the poison of the strakirin, from losing myself to rage and pain. Over and over and *over*, she'd saved me.

But where was she?

I reached for the place in my mind that had been our empathic link. It wasn't dead, not like it had been when that Shannon woman broke our connection and nearly killed Ari. The bond I'd restored between us was there, stronger than it'd ever been, but weirdly muffled too, like a massive tree trunk wrapped in cotton batting. I knew it existed, knew it was strong, but couldn't feel much definition or shape to it. A whisper of anxiety came to me as I followed the link toward her, and the unexpected impression of… of gravel? Maybe trees too? And was that a house ahead of her? That was odd. How in the world would I know if she was near a—

A sludge feeling engulfed me like I'd driven straight into a patch of dense mud. No, more than mud now. A wall.

One that hurt.

I recoiled from the connection, my body aching like I'd been burned. The pain faded.

What the hell? Cautiously, I felt for my link to Baylie and Chloe, needing to try even if I knew Chloe was probably too far away for me to feel much, let alone let anyone know I was alive, and Baylie was in a coma no one could explain. But maybe…

The faintest shadow of impressions came from Chloe. Maybe a whisper of discomfort. Of worry. And Baylie…

A distant, pale blue glow, but cool like the breeze before

a storm. Somehow dark and strange as well, as if I'd caught a glimpse of a mirrored reflection in a nearly pitch-black room. And yet, a hum in my skin like a low-level electric current too? I'd barely felt anything from her when I visited her in the various makeshift medical centers that the resistance used. Was this some effect of the prison around me? Or had something happened to her? What the hell?

The ache returned, as if I was covered in burns and coming too close to a fire. I retreated cautiously, and the impression of Baylie faded like a dying circuit drowned by mud.

I hovered in the darkness, baffled and alarmed and unable to see or hear anything at all. Even my weird echolocation ability seemed stifled down here, and the changes to my vision that let me see in the depths of the ocean were meaningless. I might as well have been in outer space.

I reached out my hand and encountered nothing. The brief flash of lightning I'd tried earlier had revealed rocks around me, with more overhead, but nothing else. Certainly no sign of whatever the hell was stopping me from reaching the others.

"Ari?" My voice bounced from the rocks, and a dull groan carried through the water as if the stones around me were unstable. Sand and gravel sifted down to brush my face, and I tensed. The boulders wouldn't kill me if they fell, even if I was in this human-like form. Probably not, anyway.

Except that I'd need to lose that form to escape the collapse, and then the darkness would start draining me into oblivion again.

My hands chafed my arms. The stones wouldn't collapse.

I'd be fine.

Something moved at the corner of my eye. My attention snapped over, and then I froze.

People were coming out of the walls.

My mouth moved, no sound emerging. The darkness thinned, taking on a translucent quality as the glowing white figures drifted from the crumbled pillars and stones. Their bodies were like smoke, and their clothes like the liars… the *ruanir*… I'd seen in my memories. Dehaians too, scales on their faces, and that wasn't all. Burn marks. Gashes and ragged wounds. Limbs missing, and the sides of some of their faces too.

They were dead. All of them. I was surrounded by the dead.

A strangled noise escaped me, nothing articulate in the sound. I'd lost my mind. There was no other explanation. I'd officially, unequivocally, *lost* my mind somewhere in this darkness between life and death and…

A chill shot through me. Oh my God, was I *dead?*

Frantically, I grabbed for the connection to Ari again, only to slam into the painful wall between us. I shoved at the wall in my mind, shaking from the burning pain it caused even as fragmented images came to me of a table and chairs and people whose faces I couldn't see. But surely this wasn't what death was like. Surely there wouldn't still be this connection between us.

Unless I was imagining it. Unless this was all some last-ditch attempt of my mind to make me believe I was still—

The dead turned toward me.

Like a reflex that bypassed any rational thought, I spun,

frantically seeking a way out, but they were everywhere. Drifting down from the rocks overhead, coming from the pillars and the walls. Even the ground beneath me released them, sending them up from the sand and gravel like… like…

Ghosts.

"Get back!" Lightning burst from my body, crackling all around me.

Instantly, the darkness dragged at me again, as if even the slightest display of my powers was enough to trigger the pull. I cringed with pain, the lightning vanishing. My abilities retreated into my human-like form as if to hide.

The ghosts came closer.

Fear gripped me. The existence of the dehaians, strakirin, the judges… Hell, becoming the damn Beast. Those were nothing compared to watching the *dead* float toward me. Reach toward me. They were all around me now, crowding in, and I couldn't escape. Their smoke-like hands stretched for me, their fingers like cold claws as they touched my skin, and with the contact came images. Sounds. Noises and impressions and pictures too fast to perceive, distilling down from a cacophony into words that repeated over and over.

…triedtostoptriedtostoptriedtostop…

Stop!

All of the ghosts became motionless.

My eyes darted across them. I barely dared to twitch a muscle. Like photographs, they were utterly still. All around me, and utterly still.

One of the ghosts began to move again. She looked like a

dark-haired woman dressed in robes that could have been any color in life, though now they were as white as the rest of her. The right side of her face and arm was marred by wounds like deep shadows on her too-pale skin. Wisps of smoke drifted up from the injuries, almost like she was still burning, but no pain showed in her eyes.

Just grief.

Precious one.

The words poured into my mind like a collection of strange sounds and impressions that found their way down into speech, but only inside my head. Around me, the other ghosts shifted into motion again, drifting away almost absently, like they'd forgotten why they'd appeared in the first place. They made languid gestures that stalled a few heartbeats after they started, only to skip back to where they'd begun and restart again, as if they were caught in an endless loop of their own.

I shuddered. This was beyond too weird. This was insanity. Coming here at all had been bad enough, and watching Osias wake this place with that spell had been terrible.

No one ever should have woken this place.

But this was madness. I couldn't be *dead.* I didn't want to be dead. Not after everything I'd—

Changed.

My gaze darted back to the woman. What the hell did that mean?

You.

Wait, could she *hear* me? I'd heard Ari, back in the brief moments before the darkness took me, back when I restored our connection. I hadn't been sure that was real, though.

Maybe it hadn't been. Maybe I'd just imagined it, right before I died.

The thought hurt, and almost as if in response, the grief on the woman's face deepened.

Not dead. Trapped. Trapped in this place. Wasn't supposed to be this way.

Confusion hit me, and then a slew of images and impressions did too, like pure information pouring into my mind. They'd created this place. They were the liars. The ruanir and dehaians—those ones who made me—but so many other dehaians and ruanir besides. The woman and her followers tried to destroy me, back in the days when I'd been turned into the Beast by the ones who betrayed them. They thought they had no choice. They thought it was the only way to stop the weapon I'd become.

But their plan had gone wrong. The dehaian man's attempt to regain control of me destabilized their spell, and my attack—my self-defense—had disrupted it entirely. And then the island had been devoured by the backlash of my magic and the destabilized spell alike, and for those whom the spell hit...

My eyes slid across the pale figures around me. When I was in high school, my class studied the Second World War and my teacher showed us pictures of the aftermath of the nuclear bombs dropped on Hiroshima and Nagasaki. Among the images of horrific devastation, one of those that stuck with me was the photograph of a man's silhouette burned onto the ground by the heat of the blast. He'd held a walking stick in his hand. He'd been standing beside some stone steps. His body, I supposed, had been vaporized. But his shadow, his afterimage, remained as testament to the horror that killed him.

Like a ghost.

"I'm sorry," I whispered.

You changed. The woman's pale hand rose to brush my cheek, the sensation like a cold breath of winter drifting along my face. *Became this.*

I hesitated. "I wanted to live."

A sweet, sad smile lifted the edges of her mouth. *And did you?*

Not enough. And she made it sound like my life was over.

I shoved the thought aside. "How do I get out of here?"

Her smile faded. *You don't.*

"No, I can't stay. There are people out there I need to—"

Her hand withdrew, and her expression became firm, like someone sharing horrible news that wouldn't change, no matter how anyone else argued against it. *The trap is shut. It was made to destroy you. To seal your power away for all eternity.*

She shook her head. *There is no way out.*

$$\sim 14 \sim$$

LOGAN

"Damn." The word blurted from me, a momentary loss of composure. But it was justified.

I'd walked out of a doctor's office and straight into a caco-phonic hell.

The thick, metal door swung shut behind me, sealing off the silence of the previous hallway. From my vantage point atop a walkway, the warehouse floor beneath me looked like an exercise in barely controlled chaos. Chain-link cages cubed the space like a collection of dog kennels with roofs, leaving only narrow pathways between them. Each one held a chair inside like a reclining version of an electric chair, all leather-bound with metal restraints for the arms, legs, and neck. People were strapped into them, and judges stood to the side. They seemed to be running some kind of experiment.

A loud one.

The test subjects screamed against the gags in their mouths and thrashed in their restraints. Bruises and scabbed-over wounds covered many of them. Others had blood on their clothes. The walls rang with their shouts, their howls, their muffled shrieks to stop, to spare them, to go to hell.

It was a far cry from the place I'd just left. Beyond the metal door behind me lay neutral-toned halls with thick, abstractly patterned carpet and equally abstract art. Potted plants dotted the corners, and elevator music played in the foyer. Candy dishes waited at every nurses' station, while children's books and magazines lay elegantly on the end tables in each waiting area. Even the judges had endeavored to look welcoming.

All the better to con the masses and so forth.

The hive hummed in my mind. I'd gained four new strakirin this afternoon, thanks to the charade on the other side of that door, and ten more ruanir teenagers were waiting their turn. Not that those kids knew what they were signing on for, of course. The idiots had flocked to answer the Judiciary's call to "fight the dehaians and save our people." Whole *families* had volunteered to be changed by the judges after a few well-placed "attacks" on ruanir neighborhoods. The adults thought they were becoming like the enforcers, and sure, most did.

But the teenagers…

The hive grew louder as another one was changed. The Judiciary had been carting in volunteers by the busload for months. Smiling and oblivious, the hapless morons walked into neutral-toned, pleasant little exam rooms like eager sheep, and came out as my eyes, ears, and hands, without a single thought of their own.

But none of that explained what was going on here.

"What is this?" I glanced at Judge Engle. Straight-backed

and proud as a medieval priest, he stood with his hands clasped behind his back and his chin held high in the air. You'd never know there were two strakirin behind him, holding him hostage. You'd never think I'd nearly killed him three times over on the way here.

The man was a nuisance. I was sure he was planning something to take the reins back, not that I'd ever let him. If I could have, I would've killed him before we ever left the coast. Too bad he was one of the most powerful judges this side of the Mississippi, and therefore, valuable.

"You wanted to see the headquarters of our efforts to create strakirin, as proof of our loyalty to you." An undercurrent of anger roiled beneath the words. "So be it. That was the public face of our effort." He nodded sharply to the door behind me. "In the western wing, we have the laboratories. In the east wing are the defectives, for further analysis and, if necessary, dissection." He gestured sharply to the two walkways leading off to my left and right.

"And? Answer the question."

"And these are the new… experiments."

"They're—" I searched for a word. "—*old.*"

Judge Engle's gaze slid to me. "Indeed. Most are soldiers of the so-called 'resistance,' recently retrieved following a successful attack on one of their hideouts. Others are landwalkers, mostly commoners, though we did obtain an elder recently."

I regarded the people screaming in the restraints. The landwalkers didn't matter. Elder or not, they were just weird humans, and therefore pointless. But the resistance was interesting. I'd wondered about them. Ari had been found with them, months ago.

Like. That. Mattered.

I forced myself to focus. I'd worry about why I kept worrying about her later.

Or never.

"So how many have you managed to make into strakirin?"

And why didn't I feel them in the hive?

His imperious gaze turned back to the test subjects. "None. The experiment continues."

I scoffed. Seriously? God, the Judiciary was incompetent.

Judge Engle drew himself up further. "Some have been made into spies, of course." He sounded like he was giving a lecture. "But their effectiveness is limited by their persistent and unfortunate ability to resist their conditioning—and, of course, that is not the same as a full strakirin, nor is it the goal of these experiments." Was that defensiveness I heard in his voice? "We wish full conversion of an adult subject. As you know, however, the process has thus far been unsuccessful upon any ruanir who has already gone through the adjustment to extend their lifespan. We have been endeavoring to correct this issue, but have lost nearly twenty prisoners without any detectable change."

As if I cared about the numbers.

"We are hopeful you can assist us with changing that situation."

Huh? I turned to the judge, incredulous. He wanted my help?

That was as good as an admission they couldn't do anything

without me. That they *needed* me.

About time the Judiciary recognized that. All it'd taken was me becoming a god.

The idiots.

"How?" I asked.

"By forcing the conversion."

Well, now that was interesting. I hadn't tried that. Could I make my own strakirin?

Excitement spread through me, enough that my strakirin began to smile. I wouldn't need the judges. Hell, I wouldn't need anyone. And if I could change the ruanir who'd already been through the adjustment into my strakirin too… well, that was just too good an opportunity to pass up.

Because I needed more. Hundreds more. Thousands.

Ari was out there.

I snarled with irritation and saw the judge tense. "Fine," I said calmly, trying to cover for the momentary lapse in control. "Let's get started."

Judge Engle hesitated. "Perhaps not yet."

I turned to him. "Excuse me?"

"There is another prisoner we would like you to examine first."

"Why?"

"Because their conversion would be valuable, and if there is a limit to your power—"

The judge cut off, wincing, as the strakirin suddenly grabbed his shoulders, their grip crushing down. Limit? Me? Oh, I'd show that self-righteous geezer *power*.

"Where are they?" I demanded.

Judge Engle's face twitched, his only admission to pain. "Through that door."

I glanced to the door. It could be a trap. A cage like they'd tried before.

Then I would kill him for it. Simple.

"Fine." I made my strakirin release him.

We continued across the walkway and through a door leading deeper into the building. Stairs led down to another corridor that almost certainly had to be underground. The walls were concrete with metal reinforcements. Enforcers were on hand at every entryway, standing ready to defend the Judiciary against… something. The resistance, I supposed, though from the sound of it, that group wasn't doing too great.

And it wasn't like the enforcers would stand a chance against me.

"What's with all the enforcers?" I asked when we passed another cluster of them blocking a doorway.

"A precautionary measure only."

"For what?"

He was silent while he unlocked a door halfway down the hall. "We anticipate whatever remains of the resistance will attempt an assault."

I glanced to the hall behind me. Enforcers here, not where most of the prisoners were being held.

Who the hell were they guarding in this place?

Judge Engle pushed the door open.

It looked like an office if you ignored the location and the people inside. Beige carpet, slightly lighter beige walls. A desk, a chair, even a few filing cabinets and a ficus tree in the corner. Panel lights in the ceiling lit every inch of the space with an unrelenting glare.

Including the heavily restrained occupants.

Alarm flashed over the man's face at the sight of me, before turning to something closer to rage. His arms and legs were bound to a chair by metal chains, each limb padlocked down with no hope of breaking free. Enforcers stood on either side of him, hands clasped behind their backs in a military stance. Behind the desk, a dark-haired judge sat, idly perusing the screen of the tablet in his hand.

And across the room was a girl.

I regarded her curiously. Strapped down from head to toe on a contraption that looked like a bed frame propped upright, she slumped in the restraints like a rag doll. Sweat dampened her tank top. Her head hung with exhaustion, and her brown hair draped forward in wet strands, obscuring much of her face. Bruises showed past the bonds on her wrists and ankles.

She wasn't dead, though. Ragged breaths made her chest rise and fall. Behind the tangles of her hair, her dark blue gaze slid to me and anger flared in her eyes.

"You son of a bitch!" the man snarled. "You swore you were on our side."

Huh? I glanced over to find him glaring daggers at me, though what the hell he was so upset about, I had no…

Understanding clicked. My pitch-black form, laced with lightning and storm clouds, only barely bothering to hold the shape of a human… this dimwit thought I was the old Beast.

Now that was funny.

I sauntered over to him, studying the man more closely. Darker skin, a few strands of gray in his black hair. Obviously a ruanir, given where we were, so that made him probably around two hundred or so. He hadn't let the age get to him, though. The guy clearly worked out, though the calluses on his hands meant the muscles weren't just the result of gym rat bullshit.

Interesting.

"Excuse us, Judge Davenport," said Judge Engle from behind me. "I wished the… Beast to see the prisoners."

I noted the pause, and the lack of a name, as well as the odd look that passed between them and lasted a heartbeat too long. *Did* they know who I was? Surely they'd planned for me to be the one who survived. After all, they'd made me into the leader of all the strakirin.

They also hadn't intended any of the strakirin to survive with a trace of will or identity intact. I had Ari to thank for that.

To hell with Ari!

But maybe the Judiciary hadn't cared who took control. Maybe they thought we'd all just be one big hive, subservient to them and mindless otherwise.

The temptation to show how unfathomably *wrong* they'd been was overwhelming.

But I could be patient. Now would be satisfying, sure, but later might be even more beneficial.

"Indeed." The judge at the desk stood. Like all the judges,

Davenport wore a black suit with his hair trimmed back and firmly under control. His face had softer lines than Judge Engle, though, who could double for a scarecrow if he really wanted. But this guy… oh, he was unremarkable to an extreme. Bland, even. Face like the beige walls around him. Body like any suburban dad. He looked like the kind everyone would describe as "such a nice man, never any trouble."

When they saw him on the six o'clock news after his arrest as a serial killer.

A smile tugged at my mouth. His eyes, though. His eyes gave it away. They always did.

Except for my own, of course.

"Well," Judge Davenport continued. "Here we have Miguel Salazar, lately the leader of the so-called resistance, and—" He perused the tablet in his hand. "—ah, yes. Maia Davenport, one of his followers."

Davenport? I glanced between them, catching the resemblance now.

Father and daughter. Judge and victim.

Amusement pulled my grin wider. I walked toward the girl.

A grunt escaped the man behind me. With the three-hundred-sixty-degree vision I still had, I could see Miguel struggling against the bonds holding him, rage on his face. He didn't want me near the girl. Probably why they had her in here to begin with.

She wasn't the only one being tortured.

"As you can see," Judge Davenport said to Judge Engle, "the girl seems to be exhibiting a stronger effect on Mister Salazar than the soldiers. We believe this is because he considers her an innocent in this situation, based on some of his more colorful comments over the past several hours. He persists in denying us the requested information, however."

"Ah." Judge Engle studied Miguel like a bug pinned beneath glass. "I assure you, Mister Salazar, this is not the extent of our power, nor have we even *begun* to exhaust all the measures we can take to gather the information we need." He smiled. "The ruanir populace eagerly await your execution. No one is calling for your release or your salvation. On the contrary, they want you to die. Your stubbornness will only delay the inevitable and subject this young girl to further suffering. Are you truly so heartless that you would force her to endure such torment for nothing more than your pride?"

"Rot in hell, pendejo," Miguel growled.

Judge Engle's smile did not fade. He glanced back to the other judge, unperturbed by the insult. "And the process?"

"Well, the girl is a curious case," Judge Davenport said. "The treatments seem, for lack of a better phrase, to be unable to find a grip on her. Even with our biological connection, my magic does not seem to produce any lasting effect on her. The magic settles in, only to…" Consternation showed as he searched for a description. "…slide off, as if something has inoculated her against the exposure."

I studied her while they talked. I remembered her now. Ari's cousin. Older cousin, but not by much. She was pretty, though I'd never much been interested in her. Girls who pretended to be lesbians for the sake of catching a guy's attention were one thing. The real ones were just boring.

Maybe she would know where Ari was.

Irritation made my face twitch. I didn't *care* where Ari was, goddammit! She could be on the moon, for all I—

I should check the moon.

My hands curled into fists. Lightning crackled in my skin.

Maia's blue eyes rose to meet the black shapes where my own would be, glaring, then hesitating with a flicker of some kind of understanding.

"It's not the Beast," she said, looking beyond me to Miguel. "He wouldn't do this. It's a trick. A Judiciary—"

Judge Engle reached out, placing a hand to her bare shoulder. She choked, her mouth gaping and gasping for air like a beached fish. Her head fell back, the agony and fear in her eyes melting into dazed oblivion.

An enraged snarl left Miguel. He yanked at the bonds holding him to the chair.

Judge Engle took his hand away. Maia sagged in the restraints, her breathing hoarse and stilted, her body lurching spastically.

"It won't last," Judge Davenport warned.

"Perhaps," Judge Engle replied.

I bent down, studying Maia's face beyond her curtain of sweaty hair. Her eyes held that woozy, nobody-home look I recalled from the faces of the few victims of ocean magic poisoning I'd seen over the years.

So that's what they were doing—and what wasn't working.

Yet, failure shouldn't have been possible. No one came back

from ocean magic poisoning. Or any kind of poisoning, for that matter.

Ari had escaped me.

I scowled. Not. The. *Point.* What the hell was *wrong* with me, that I kept thinking about—

Screw that girl. I didn't need her.

A shudder left Maia. Even as I watched, the light seemed to come back on in her blue eyes. Her breathing steadied. Pain showed on her face along with fear like she was realizing what they'd done, what she'd escaped.

Again.

The fear didn't last long, though. With every second, the anger and defiance in her expression grew stronger. I knew that look. I'd seen it on Ari's face too.

Goddammit, stop thinking about Ari!

I straightened, turning toward Miguel, though I'd already spotted his brief flash of relief at the way she was recovering.

"Why is that happening?" I demanded.

Miguel's eyes narrowed. "She's right. You're not him."

Displeasure thinned Judge Engle's lips. He'd really wanted me to pretend I was, hadn't he? But then, of course he had. I would've needed to be silent for that to work. Play along. Let him lead. Be the obedient Judiciary lapdog again.

Not likely.

I grinned. "I'm the one who killed that thing."

Miguel's eyes narrowed.

"He's lying," Maia countered. "No way some Judiciary monster could kill the Beast."

I turned back to her.

She shook her head, her attention locked on me. "No way."

I chuckled. She was scared, sure, but she really believed in that waste-of-magic monster. "I shredded him alive," I told her softly.

Maia trembled. "Bullshit." Her gaze raked over me, and over the judges too. "What is this? Some enforcer you experimented on just to scare us? You think storm clouds shaped like a person will make us talk? I've seen the Beast in action, you bastards, and he's coming for us. You don't know who you're messing—"

I grabbed her by the throat, pushing her head back against the metal frame holding her.

"Logan Marseilles," I said. "Not an enforcer. Me. That's who *you're* messing with."

I could read the alarm in her eyes. She recognized my name. She knew who I was.

Good.

But then the defiance came back. "Bite me, you wannabe-rapist *pig*," she hissed.

I kept my fingers from snapping her neck, but only barely. She thought she could survive whatever my magic could do to her. That I wasn't a threat, just like the judges behind me with their stupid poison that didn't work and their idiotic questions that she and Miguel never intended to answer.

"Release her, Mister Marseilles," Judge Engle said. "This was a mistake. If our power has not even phased her defenses in this long, there is little chance your abilities will do any more good."

Excuse me? He was *comparing* us? Who was the god here?

Judge Engle glanced to Judge Davenport, practically dismissing me from attention while he commented, "If the former Beast was behind this, possibly nothing is strong enough to overcome her protections."

I barely restrained a scoff. They thought nothing was strong enough to overcome that waste-of-magic's little trick? Oh, to hell with that.

The storm inside me lashed out, pouring into her. I'd never tried to make a strakirin before, and making one from someone who'd already been through the adjustment was supposedly impossible too. But I was the Beast, dammit. I was a *god*.

I could do anything.

And she could help me find Ari.

Maia's body went rigid, her eyes wide and locked on the ceiling, unseeing. Behind me, two enforcers kept Miguel from lunging across the room, chair and all. To my right, the judges watched me with idle curiosity, as if they were observing a particularly interesting experiment.

One that wasn't cooperating. The magic inside her twisted and slipped from my grasp like an eel. No matter how I grabbed after her power, it was gone by the time my own might reached it.

"Fascinating," Judge Engle commented. "Perhaps I was mistaken."

Damn right he was.

But he was also distracting, and this defense inside her hadn't ceded any ground. With my other hand, I reached up, grabbing Maia's shoulder where the judge had touched her. More of my power poured in. All of my attention focused on her. I *would* defeat this, goddamn it. That waste-of-magic monster wasn't stronger than me.

The room faded. The judges, Miguel, even Maia… they didn't matter. Distantly, I could hear Maia screaming, but this power… this defense she had…

Someone had taken magical poison from her before, impossible as that seemed, and her system had *learned* from that, like a vaccine against a virus. She'd been safe because of it, though I wondered if she was even aware of the protection till now.

But who… *how*…

A shred of my magic gained a foothold, like a pick in a rockface, and I felt the girl's defenses start to give. It'd work. I could do this. Just a few more seconds, a little more pressure, and I wouldn't need the judges to make me a single straki—

Fragmented images flashed through my mind. A dark-skinned girl, a late-night movie, a quick and anxious kiss. God, will she think I'm weird? Too shy? Too awkward? I like her so—

Sadness overwhelmed me, clogging my throat. And fear followed. I wanted to see the girl again. I loved her with my whole heart and soul, and I was so scared I'd never—

Blech! I shoved the images and the emotions away, but on their heels came more. And more. I was drowning in the onslaught. Between the stubbornly tenacious magic around me, still sliding from my grasp, and the images that just wouldn't quit… What the hell was this?

Memories.

The answer spread through me, sure knowledge amid the chaos that kept fighting me, kept slipping away like it was covered in oil. I could… I could *see* fragments of her *memories*.

Had Ari been able to do this?

Goddammit! I didn't care about *Ari!* Just because I needed to find her, and I had no clue where she'd gone, and I didn't know what I'd do if I didn't—

The hum of the strakirin hive died.

I staggered back from Maia, the room swimming into focus. Miguel was still strapped to his chair, a gag shoved into his mouth. Maia hung in the restraints, appearing nauseated yet nothing like a strakirin. Meanwhile, the judges were beside me and my strakirin were on the ground, their throats slashed. Enforcers stood behind them with bloody knives in their hands.

The *bastards*.

I surged forward to kill them all.

Except I didn't. Nothing happened. My body stayed in human form, and my abilities…

Nothing. No lightning. No magic at all. My attention flickered, three-hundred-sixty degrees of bullshit, but it showed me something new.

My hand went to my neck. A metal collar encircled it, but my hands couldn't touch it. Every time I tried to grasp it, my fingers passed straight through.

What the *hell?*

"So, Mister Marseilles." Judge Engle clasped his hands behind his back calmly. "Shall we discuss a new arrangement?"

Judge Davenport chuckled.

I stared at them. They'd planned this. Her magic, the way they couldn't get a grip on it. They'd planned it all.

And they'd bargained I wouldn't be able to get a hold on it either, or at least that I'd get distracted. They'd had her here for who knew how long; of course they'd tested the hell out of what she could do.

The bastards *played* me!

"Judge Davenport, if you would be so kind as to send the all-clear and notify the others that they can meet us here?"

The judge glanced at the enforcers and me before nodding. "Of course." He walked back to his desk and picked up the receiver of an old rotary dial phone.

Judge Engle shifted his weight, bringing himself slightly closer to me. "Give me your hand," he murmured.

Screw him.

A condescending look passed across the judge's face. His thumb moved over something tucked into his palm. A shock went through the collar, making me tense.

"Now, Mister Marseilles."

Oh, I was going to kill him. I should have hours ago.

Another shock, stronger. Pain sizzled through me like every nerve ending I no longer possessed had somehow been set aflame.

Judge Davenport paused mid-phone call. "Judge Engle?" he asked, curiosity tingeing his voice.

"The creature attempted to attack," Judge Engle said without turning around. "I am illustrating its new situation in terms it will understand."

The other judge regarded him, his eyes narrowing briefly, but then his gaze flicked to the enforcers. Seeming mollified by whatever he saw, he returned to his phone call.

A hint of a smile pulled at the edge of Judge Engle's mouth. "I assure you, Mister Marseilles," he continued in a calm voice that the rest of the room could easily hear, "the Judiciary prepared for your more… aggressive tendencies. The dehaians made a version of this little device, and we have adapted it especially for you. You may note the runes carved on its sides. They keep the device… shall we say, located properly for maximum efficacy? Upon command, you will be able to shift to your more… natural form, though the device will remain inside you. When shifting back to this form, the device will resume its current location. Attempts to remove it, or to disobey, will have consequences, as you have just felt. Right now, we're at a level that would give a regular ruanir seizures. Next up are levels that would kill, followed by enough power to overload the electrical grid of a city block. So tell me, will you do as you are told, or would you wish to test further degrees of these shocks?"

He was dead. He was so dead. I'd snap his neck. I'd make him bleed from his eyes. I'd—

Pain screeched through my body. Judge Engle's eyebrow rose.

I'd bide my time.

"Judge Engle." Judge Davenport set down the phone. "Step away from the creature."

I extended my hand.

"Judge Engle! Enforcers, stop him!"

The enforcers didn't move. Judge Davenport rushed to get around his desk as Judge Engle rested his fingertips on the back of my hand, like he had a single right on earth to touch me.

His eyes glinted with dark anticipation. "Release."

"No!" Judge Davenport shouted.

Huh? What the hell was that supposed to—

Magic rushed from my hand to the judge as if on command. Judge Engle gasped, but not with alarm.

With enjoyment.

That… no. This wasn't happening. I wasn't under their control. I never had been.

Black lines of magic climbed through Judge Engle's veins, racing up his neck, across his face. Behind him, Judge Davenport lunged for us both only to be stopped by two enforcers who grabbed and restrained him, ignoring his shouts.

A yellow-green stain spread around Judge Engle's black veins, mottling his skin in a pattern like ghostly scales before seeming to sink into his body. All color leeched away with them, draining his skin to the too-bright color of bleached paper. His eyes rolled back, the irises vanishing while the whites swirled with marbled gray then black, and then a darkness that spread, seeping into the skin around his eye sockets, swallowing them in shadows that glittered like a starry sky and crackled with lightning. A rapturous smile spread across his face, and in the black gash of his mouth, his white teeth glowed. Thick smoke billowed around him, so dark it seemed to drag in all light, while black lightning snapped and snarled inside his too-pale skin.

He lifted his other hand. His arm seemed to skip through space as if I was blinking quickly and interrupting my eyes' ability to see his movement, or as if he wasn't quite a part of the world around us. Tangles of impossibly black electricity played across his palm. He closed his fingers into a fist, the dark energy vanishing as if at a silent command.

More of my magic poured into him. More and more, and dammit, this was mine! What the hell was *happening*?

"Now…" He grinned and placed his free hand to my chest.

Something lurched inside me, like he'd grabbed hold of the lungs I no longer possessed and was pulling them out through my ribcage. But then the feeling went deeper, stretching into me, *through* me, like I was a tunnel and he could reach all the way along it to whatever lay on the other end. I couldn't stop him. Couldn't even move.

And then the sensation stopped, jerking hard as if it had caught on something, as if it was a wire that had found its connection. From somewhere inside me, and yet behind and beyond me, a new feeling surged toward me.

The ocean. Lightning. The earth, rolling in a wave, and a tsunami rising like a harbinger of annihilation. And another power, like clay, like water, molding and moving and changing.

Always changing.

It crashed through me and into the judge, and he didn't stumble. Didn't fall before it like surely, *surely* he should have. The power was too much.

What the hell *was* this?

"Finally," he breathed. Black smoke wafted from his lips

with the word.

"You bastard!" Judge Davenport struggled against the enforcers' grips.

"Oh, as if you weren't planning the same, John," Judge Engle chided. "As if every single one of us wasn't intending to steal the power for themselves. I merely got there first."

Judge Davenport seethed, and I could read the look in his eyes. Of course he had. But from the way he glanced to the enforcers, I guessed he hadn't believed someone could turn them against any judge, let alone him.

"I supervised their processing myself," Judge Engle commented. "Leaving a few extra instructions during their conversion wasn't exactly difficult."

"The power was meant to be *shared*," Judge Davenport growled.

Judge Engle scoffed, his hand dropping from my chest. The connection inside me seemed to go with him, like a rope I hadn't known was inside me, now fully in his possession. "And what sort of sense does that make, John? Truly? Mister Marseilles carried a connection to the power of the island back for us, and then we were meant to… what? Share little samples around? Content ourselves with only a tiny portion, to be *fair*, rather than embrace the full extent of what we could become?"

"The Judiciary—"

"Answers to me now."

Judge Davenport stared at him, aghast. I wasn't far behind. I'd had a connection to that power? To *this?*

And I hadn't known it. Couldn't touch it, even now.

My body shook with the desire to reach out and strangle that glowing white bastard where he stood. Maybe I couldn't grasp this power while he controlled it, but I bet if I *killed* him…

Judge Engle ignored me entirely. "You have a choice, John. Resist and die, or adjust. Which will it be?" Flickers of lightning danced in Judge Engle's dark eye sockets as he waited for the other judge's response.

"What would you have me do?" Judge Davenport ground out.

Judge Engle smiled. "Continue testing the young woman and Mister Salazar. I want as much information as you can get from him prior to the time of his execution. And in the interim…" He glanced to the door as a commotion arose in the hallway. "Ah, yes."

Several enforcers hauled a woman into the room. Her long, brown hair was in tangles, her long skirt was torn, and she had a nasty bruise over one eye. Thrashing in the restraints and shouting blistering insults at the enforcers, she was like a pissed-off hippie with the vocabulary of a sailor.

I glared at her. Like she had anything to be upset about. I was the god in chains here.

"Conversions." Judge Davenport's voice was flat.

"You would have me wait?" Judge Engle sounded amused.

"She's a landwalker elder. If you kill her—"

"Then I will find others." He gave Judge Davenport a condescending look. "Yes, the landwalkers were once similar to dehaians, but they've also had so many centuries of genetic differentiation from their source that there is every chance she'll survive the conversion where the dehaians would not." He paused, turning his pitch-black gaze on the woman. "Or she'll provide an interesting autopsy."

Judge Engle motioned toward the enforcers. "Let's bring an end to this little resistance, shall we?"

The enforcers dragged the woman forward. I watched her squirm as Judge Engle reached for her, the woman shouting obscenities while Miguel struggled to break free and Maia hung in her restraints, crying. No one noticed me. No one even glanced my way.

But that wouldn't last. I wouldn't let it. That bastard had taken power from me, but somehow, I'd get it back. I'd make a thousand strakirin. Ten thousand, from every ruanir on this planet. And I'd crush Engle and all the judges. Crush the bastards who thought they could control me, till they begged and pleaded for my mercy. I *was* still a god, after all.

And one way or another, I wouldn't be in chains forever.

15

ARI

Political debates were a nightmare.

Ones where my family was at stake were straight from hell.

I rubbed my eyes, relishing the calm of the house around me and the way my head had finally stopped throbbing. I'd had a killer headache for most of the afternoon, though I supposed that was understandable. The negotiations had taken hours, finally called off at sunset when the human-like among us needed to eat. Declan had been like an angry cat in a cage the entire day, and by the end of the evening, even Zeke and Chloe had started to show signs of temper in dealing with him. Baylie was the only one Declan seemed to listen to, though God knew why, and Olivia had barely kept the landwalker elder Angelica from lunging across the table to strangle him on more than one occasion.

And we'd gotten nowhere. Well, almost nowhere. We hadn't started a war between us, which was a minor victory, I supposed. But no one knew what to do about the judges, and this mysterious weapon that the elders and Declan had been exploring would kill the good guys as well as the bad.

So we had nothing. My cousin was locked up in a Judiciary prison somewhere, with the judges or—God forbid—Logan doing who knew what to her, and we had nothing.

I wasn't relishing the calm. I was clinging to it to keep myself from racing out the door to find Maia right now. I didn't want this to be my reality, or hers. I wanted us all to be back in Maine, missing the judges' party that night due to a headache or a cold or just playing hooky, and watching movies all night in our hotel room instead.

Of course, then I never would have met Noah.

Maybe that would have been better. Maybe then he never would have gotten hurt.

And he wouldn't have possibly died.

Something twisted in my chest, and I shoved the thoughts away, hugging my knees beneath the crocheted blanket I'd stolen from the living room couch downstairs. The second floor held so many nook-like spaces at the ends or turns of the hallways, each one perfect for bookcases and chairs. Most of them also had windows for admiring the view.

I'd taken the most secluded one I could find and hid till everyone else had laid down for the night.

I hadn't told Olivia I didn't sleep anymore, and I'd pleaded insomnia when Jace asked if I was headed to bed. The elder would have just given me that same analytical look she'd had all day, the one that made me feel like she wanted to put me under a microscope, and Jace…

He didn't know how much I'd changed. Somehow, I wanted

to delay the moment when he'd learn the truth.

Murderer. Monster.

Least of all that was how I didn't sleep or eat anymore.

Shivers crawled over my skin, and I hugged my knees tighter. The dehaians had given me more of their magical gel, sieranchine, and now the ache of my rib was pretty much non-existent. Meanwhile, dawn was only another hour away, maybe less. The moon was long gone, not that there'd been more than a sliver of it to begin with, and the night was an abyss of black, broken only by the dim glow of Santa Lucina beyond the hills and the horizon. The ocean's magic felt stronger, though, carried on the breeze through the open window at my side. Maybe it was the direction of the wind. Maybe it was just my imagination. But soon the others would be back up, and I could resume pretending to be normal—or however close I came to that these days.

Something moved in the darkness outside.

My breath caught, my fist clenching on the blanket, and then embarrassment filled me. The dehaians were out there. Most of them, in fact, armed to the teeth and in tents they'd brought with them in their SUVs. I could have joined them, except that would have resulted in a weird look from Jace and more questions again. But there wasn't anything out there to be—

Baylie's blond hair caught in the glow of a porch light. She turned and looked up at the house with an anxious expression.

Confusion overtook my embarrassment. Why did she look scared?

She crept out of view, heading around the house and away from any of the dehaian camps. I pushed away from the chair, letting the blanket fall. I liked Baylie. Trusted her, even. Why was she sneaking outside but avoiding the dehaians? This wasn't normal.

Maybe she knew something about all this that I didn't.

My skin tingled, and the tips of my spikes slipped from my forearms. My eyes changed, just a bit, just enough to dispel the shadows and hopefully not terrify anyone who happened to be in the dark corridor too. All the debates from today aside, I hadn't heard anything that would make me believe the dehaians or landwalkers were going to betray us. But then, Baylie was Chloe's best friend. Maybe she'd read something between the lines, something that made her scared.

Barefoot, I crept down the hall. The house was incredibly silent. Even that weird guy, Wyatt, had finally gone to bed. The thick carpet absorbed my footsteps while I snuck downstairs and over to the entryway. My flip-flops, borrowed from Chloe, waited by the door, and for a moment, I considered slipping them on. Not the most silent thing in the world, though, flip-flops. If something was going on here, I'd need to be as quiet as I could.

And besides, Chloe had explained how the dehaians' feet could change to handle different terrain anyway. A few seconds on the beach had proven I'd gotten that trait too, as disturbing as *that* was.

But then, all the traits were disturbing. Even the helpful ones.

The well-oiled hinges made no sound when I slipped past the front door. The night was warm, still hanging onto summer, but the hint of salt on the air made the fine hairs on my arms rise and shivers creep across my skin. Something in me wanted to go back to the water even now.

I focused on following where I'd seen Baylie heading instead.

The enormous house sat on a cliff, surrounded by scrub brush and scraggly trees that were nothing but darker spots on the black sky. But amid the trees and brush, brief glimmers of green and blue and brown like glowing gemstones let me know the dehaians were there.

That or wolves.

Something rustled to my left, and I froze, adrenaline shooting through me and making my vision flare brighter when my eyes changed fully.

But I didn't see anything.

I stood paralyzed for a heartbeat. Okay, that... that had been dehaians. Just dehaians. Not wolves.

Definitely not wolves.

My feet rushed into motion, carrying me faster while shivers wracked me. I was safe out here. I had my defenses against the strakirin up so high that there was no way they could find me. I couldn't feel Logan, couldn't hear anything beyond the night, and that completely harmless rustling beneath the trees was gone now anyway, so everything was fine. Totally fine.

The tips of my spikes stayed on my forearms.

Baylie was sitting at the cliff's edge.

I crept toward her, my eyes darting around warily, but of

course there was nothing here. Not that there would have been. Besides dehaians.

God, I couldn't stop shivering.

"Baylie?" I whispered.

She flinched, gasping.

A shadow moved over her skin.

I stopped. That'd looked like… like smoke. Like threads of black too, but…

But I couldn't see anything now. I wasn't even sure I'd seen anything in the first place.

Baylie stared at me. "Ari?"

It hit me that, between my glowing, snake-like eyes and my spikes, I probably looked like a monster. It was a miracle she hadn't screamed. "Uh, yeah." I changed my eyes back to human quickly and then walked closer, trying not to be obvious about the way I kept glancing to her skin. "What're you doing out here?"

She gave an awkward shrug, turning back to the view from the cliff. I sank down nearby, wishing I had the blanket still with me. My shivers were getting worse, warm night or not.

"I could ask you the same," she said.

I hesitated. "I saw you."

She didn't respond.

"Everything okay?" I tried.

A long moment passed. "Couldn't sleep."

That didn't seem like all of it. I glanced around, nervous. There wasn't anyone here, though. Besides the dehaians in the woods, anyway.

"It's just… nice out here," she said. "Nice night."

I made an agreeing noise, watching her. It *was* nice, my incessant shivers aside. But that hadn't been the look on her face when I saw her from the window.

She drew a breath. "I'm sorry about your cousin. If there's any, um… any way to help her, I know the dehaians will."

I shifted a bit on the grass. I didn't want to talk about that. "Sorry."

I nodded.

"I guess all the topics suck right now," she said. "Anything I'd say, just…"

I knew what she meant. "Same here."

Crickets chirped in the silence. Between the trees, glowing eyes of green or blue or yellow flashed into view and then moved off again.

I trembled. "I'm going to stop them," I said softly, not even sure why I was admitting it. Maybe because she was Noah's sister. Maybe because she'd want to know someone cared that he wasn't here, for more than just the strategic loss.

She turned to me.

"The ones who did this," I continued. "Who hurt Noah." Magic tangled beneath my skin. "I'm going to find a way to make them pay."

Baylie was silent for a long moment. "Me too."

I met her eyes, finding only solemn agreement. I wasn't sure how she'd be able to help, but… however she could, I knew she would.

I gave a small nod.

A minute crept past, filled with crickets and silence but for the occasional rustle of undergrowth between the trees.

"Why'd you come out here, Baylie?" I asked.

She was quiet for so long, I started to think she wasn't going to answer. "Getting some distance. It's… crowded in there."

"I saw you from the window. You looked scared."

"Just concerned somebody might know I was outside." She chuckled, a helpless sort of irony in the sound. "Guess they did anyway."

I didn't know how to respond to that. The dehaians would have seen her leaving too.

Who was she hiding from?

"I'm sorry I worried you," she continued. "Nothing's going on. I just… I'm going to sit out here for a while, so if you want to get back to bed…"

She trailed off, waiting for me to take the invitation.

My hands chafed my arms. Telling her I didn't sleep wouldn't help anything. She wanted to be alone. I could read between those obvious lines.

"Yeah." I climbed to my feet, my body still shivering from the salt on the air and the magic twisting through it. Much more of this and my teeth would start chattering. "Well, um, goodni—"

The strakirin drone brought me to my knees.

I gasped, my fingers curling into the grass and dirt. What was this? How had they—

Two strakirin emerged from between the trees. Baylie shrieked, scrambling up from the ground and backpedaling.

Glowing yellow eyes tracked her and then returned to me with laser-like intensity.

The drone lessened.

I pushed away from the ground, my heart pounding in my throat. Spikes stood out fully from my arms, and every trace of strakirin power I had inside me boiled just beneath my skin. I had no idea if the poison would work, but by God, the lightning probably would.

But where were the dehaians? And for that matter, where the hell was Logan?

My gaze flicked to the sky and back. Just stars. Just the dark.

But Noah had been able to go invisible…

"W-what…" Baylie stammered.

I cast a quick glance to her, not daring to take my eyes from the strakirin for long, and then I froze. Wisps of black smoke rose from her arms, like fragile ghosts. Threads like dark lightning flashed beneath her skin.

What the *hell?*

Baylie caught sight of my stare and fear darted across her face.

Later, I ordered myself. Focus on that later.

Stop the monsters now.

I tugged my attention back to the two strakirin in front of me. Both of them had eyes like a snake, yellow-gold and slit with black. A suggestion of emerald scales stained their cheeks and temples, as well as their arms and legs. Faux swimsuits covered their bodies. The one closest to me was female, her skin beyond the scales an amber-toned brown, and the dark waves of her hair tangled with twigs. The other behind her was male, and amber-skinned like the girl. Dirt and sand smudged their legs and hands, and neither of them looked over eighteen years old. Maybe younger.

But they weren't moving, and the drone…

The drone wasn't a drone. Not exactly. It was an erratic, humming, staccato mess, like a swarm of discombobulated bees.

"Logan?" I demanded. "Is that you?"

The strakirin hissed like poked cats, recoiling as if my words offended them.

Huh?

Dehaians hurried from between the trees, spikes on their arms and guns in their hands. "Don't move!" one of them shouted, a tall, brown-haired man with a scar across his chest. In the house, the lights came on. Someone had probably snuck around to warn them, I realized. Others were almost certainly heading back to the tents to get the king and Chloe out of here.

But the strakirin didn't even twitch. They were just staring at me, like no matter how many soldiers were around them, I was the only thing that concerned them in the world. I watched them, barely breathing as I waited for the attack, the trick, something. "What do you want?" I asked, attempting to give no sign of how I was shaking.

The girl made a hissing, trilling noise to the boy behind her. My pulse ratcheted up another few notches from anxiety. I didn't understand that.

Something inside me understood that.

Instinctively, I backed away, shaking my head to clear it. What the… It was a question. That trill. That'd been a—

"Ari," Baylie said. "What the hell…"

The strakirin girl had been checking with the boy about something.

I didn't want to find out what. "I don't know," I said to Baylie.

Not taking my eyes from the strakirin, I shifted my weight to put myself between Baylie and them. I had no clue what those black wisps coming from her arms had been, but smoke sure as hell wasn't going to stop these things.

Maybe I could.

"When I say run," I started.

"P-pleassse…" hissed the strakirin girl.

I froze.

"Please…" The girl grated out the words like speech was difficult. Like she was fighting to make the words emerge. "Please… help… us…"

I could feel the drone in my head, pulsing and fractured and unsteady, and yet it echoed her words.

"Ar… ee…" the girl pleaded.

I stopped breathing.

The drone resonated with my name.

"Logan," I warned, trembling. "If that's—"

The girl hissed like a cat again, flinching as if the words burned her. "Don't… say his… name."

I stared at her. There was desperation in those snake-like eyes. Fear too.

You're in them, temper and all.

Shivers coursed through me. I'd hated my eyes down there, under the water. Hated how inhuman I looked, how inhuman all the strakirin looked. Their eyes were dead. Alien. But Noah hadn't seen that.

Not once I'd broken free.

"Please…" the boy gasped. "Make… it… stop."

What?

"You're… the key…"

Chills rushed through me. The strakirin prisoner Damerion had taken from the garrison said that. Noah had even told me that Shannon said that. People kept calling me the key, and I had no clue on earth what they meant.

But the girl was staring at me, pleading. Beyond my defenses, the drone ricocheted against itself. The kids were fighting to escape it, I realized. They were trying to battle their way out of the hive mind.

Memory came back to me. The kids in the hive, in the canyon. The strakirin, swimming for their lives after I'd showed them how to defend against the drone, after Logan had swept down on us all, killing so many. Killing Noah. But some of them had survived…

I stepped toward them.

"Ari!" Baylie protested, while around me, the dehaians tightened their grips on their guns.

I kept myself from looking at the soldiers. "Breathe," I told the strakirin. "Feel for the ocean."

Gratitude showed on the strakirins' faces. The girl nodded,

closing her alien eyes.

In my head, I could feel the erratic drone shift, reaching for the water and the magic there. But it wasn't enough. They were still struggling. And there was something else, something different about the kids in front of me.

Except that didn't make sense. The judges used what they'd done to me to make the strakirin. I was their template, their mold. Their original from which they'd made a thousand copies.

Copies…

An idea flashed through my mind, too quick to grasp. There was something to that, though. Copies had smudges. Copies weren't identical, not down to every pixel and molecule. So maybe the judges hadn't gotten everything. Maybe it wasn't something different about these kids. Maybe it was me…

Ragged breaths escaped the girl. The strakirin kids were shaking, terrified.

They weren't going to make it.

Cautiously, ready to retreat behind my own defenses at any moment, I reached out for the desperate sound of their minds.

Their presences swelled around me, and I gasped. Luna Rosario. That was the girl's name. She was sixteen and from Las Cruces. The guy behind her was her brother, Leo, one year younger than her and a sophomore at Las Cruces High. Their dad had been in the human military; he'd died in Afghanistan three days before Luna's ninth birthday. They'd lost their mom in a supposed dehaian attack a few weeks ago, so they chose to answer the Judiciary's call for volunteers.

Information poured into my mind like an avalanche of

snapshots. I was losing myself in their memories, their pain, their fear that they'd be taken again and drowned in the mindless swarm. It was there, waiting, ready to consume them, and they clung to me, drawing on me, *needing* me like—

"No!" I stumbled backward, shoving the drone away. A shudder raced through me, hard enough to make my world spin. Deep in my core, something cold and dark stirred.

Frantic, I slammed my defenses back into place. The sensation vanished.

The strakirin stared at me, and I could see their fear, their worry. Leo made a stuttering, hissing sound.

I could tell it was an apology.

"No," I gritted out. "Don't… speak like them."

A heartbeat passed. I knew Baylie was behind me. I could only imagine her expression. And the dehaians too, with their guns.

"S-sorry," Luna said.

I dragged my gaze up to theirs.

Two pairs of snake-like eyes watched me. "Human eyes," I snarled. "Change them."

Luna and Leo flinched like they were scared of me, but then Luna hesitated. For a heartbeat, she didn't even seem to breathe.

And then the scales faded from her skin and her eyes turned a brown so deep it was almost black.

Human.

She glanced at Leo. His skin and eyes changed too.

"Why are you here?" I demanded.

"For help," Leo said.

"For you," Luna added.

I tensed.

"You…" A smile flitted over Luna's face, and I could feel it. Her joy at speaking more easily again. Her relief at her freedom from the droning hive mind.

My jaw clenching, I threw more energy into the wall separating us, trying to keep her out.

Luna winced. Hurt flickered in her eyes. "You saved us. From it. From him. You saved…" Her gaze didn't quite make the trip to her brother this time. "They told us we'd be like the enforcers. That it wouldn't hurt, but it did. We were trapped there, inside our minds, and the things they made us do…"

"You signed on for this." I tossed the words back.

"We signed on to defend our people from annihilation by dehaians, not—" Luna cut off, struggling for words, but it wasn't about the language this time, I could tell. It was memory. "Not to kill *children*. Families."

I saw the dehaians behind them shift position, their hands flexing and then crushing down on their weapons.

"We couldn't stop them," Luna continued. "Not from the inside. The… the *thing* they made would have killed us. But you…" Her brow twitched down, her expression confused yet knowing. "We needed you. *Need* you. We can feel that, inside our heads."

"Why?" I demanded.

She shook her head, giving a small shrug. "We don't know. It's just like a space inside, and it's… you."

I stared at her. I knew what she was talking about. Maybe,

anyway, because I'd said something similar to Noah. That there'd been a space inside me, a place where our connection had been, and that had allowed me to hide from the monster they'd put inside my mind. But...

My body went cold, chills pouring through me.

But that space had been *him*, not *me*.

Luna bit her lip. "We got away after the dark place. Others didn't. We hid from him, but it was so hard to stay out of his..." Again, that glance to her brother. They were communicating, I realized. Still talking to each other with the drone.

I felt sick.

"He dominates the hive, but he doesn't listen to it. He doesn't hear it like we do, and he doesn't care. The judges made him different. Not fully, but... different. He wasn't erased like we were supposed to be. And he's powerful. More than us. More than *any* of us. He... he's just..."

"Evil," Leo finished.

I shivered. The word fit.

"He claimed the rest," Luna continued, "but we got away."

"How did you find us?" Baylie asked.

Luna wrung her hands together and then froze when the dehaians made cautioning noises, tightening their grips on their guns. "The judges sent out warnings about dehaians. They said to avoid Santa Lucina because it wasn't safe. We knew you were traveling with dehaians at the canyon, so, you know, we decided to risk it." Her shoulders twitched in a tiny, helpless shrug. "We got lucky. We saw you come out of the water."

I stared at her. They got lucky. The dehaians had SUVs.

We'd driven on highways, on country roads, all the way up into these mountains. And they'd gotten lucky.

But the strakirin were fast.

"The judges lied to us," Luna said, her voice choked. "They claimed we'd be defending our people from attacks, not murdering children. Not *babies*."

Behind her, the dehaians looked ready to kill the two of them where they stood.

She cleared her throat. "But we heard the rumors, the resistance broadcasts, where they said it wasn't dehaians at all—"

"It wasn't." Baylie's voice was cold.

Luna nodded quickly. "I know. We didn't believe the stories, not before. But when the judges sent us down there..." She looked ashamed. "We didn't mean to start a war. To erase ourselves so that they could start a war." She turned to the dehaians. "We know our apologies will never be enough, no matter how... how *horribly* sorry we are. But we are so, *so* sorry, and that's why we want to help you."

"How can you help?" I couldn't stop shaking. This was insane. Wrong. These monsters—

Except they weren't monsters. No more than I'd been when I let the judges connect me to the Beast. When I'd doubted what little I'd witnessed of Noah, and believed instead that the Judiciary were right and honorable and honest, because they had to be. Because I was a ruanir, and they'd been our trusted leaders for centuries, and everything I knew proclaimed they were a force for good.

Rather than a bunch of megalomaniacal lunatics hellbent

on crushing anyone and anything in their path.

"You're like us, but different too," Luna said. "You haven't… you don't hear it like us, either, do you?"

Her question was nonsensical. And it sounded rhetorical too. "What?"

"The song." She tapped her temple, watching me.

Song? Oh. "The drone?"

She blinked, like she couldn't believe I described it that way. "Y-yes. I guess. It doesn't sound the same to you as it does to us."

Clearly not.

"It's changing," Luna said. "He's changing it, and we can hear that, which means we can help you find him." She looked uncomfortable. "He's hurting people. We can hear them screaming. He has to be stopped. But we can guide you. Help you find the others, and the judges, and even *him*." She stepped forward, trying to take my hands even as her eyes darted warily to the soldiers. I flinched away, and dismay flashed over her face. "You're not like us, but the strakirin need you, now more than ever. You're the key, and if you don't—"

"What does that mean, the key?"

Luna hesitated. "We think it means you can save the world."

16

NOAH

I didn't care what some ghost woman said. There had to be a way out of here.

Swimming through the darkness, I scanned the crumbling canyon around me. Boulders the size of houses shifted and groaned above me, sending waves of dust and gravel drifting down. How this place hadn't collapsed on top of me was a mystery, though I supposed the magical prison that held me might have had something to do with that.

And if I broke out—*when* I broke out—maybe the place would finally cave in completely.

I pushed the thought away, filing it under "stuff I'd worry about once I could get the hell out of here."

The ghosts drifted around me. Most of them didn't seem to notice my presence, though every so often, a few would pause like I'd distracted them from whatever moment they were caught in. But most simply repeated the same motions over and over in an endless loop, as if they were frozen in time. The pale white glow they emitted lit the darkness with a light that defined creepy. It didn't cast shadows from the boulders around us, and it made my eyes ache, as if it somehow wasn't *quite* touching the stones and sand. Instead, it seemed like an optical illusion, ending just a hair's breadth away from whatever surface was nearby.

On second thought, creepy didn't even come *close* to describing this.

The canyon turned ahead of me, and warily, I swam around the corner, my hands and feet kicking to keep me moving. I'd figured out early on that there were certain parts of this place that, if I came close, hurt like hell. The walls of the prison, I supposed, and even in my human form, drawing near them set the draining force of this place on me like a pit bull. The ceiling was one of them, meaning I couldn't just shove my way up through the rocks and debris suspended above me. Random walls in the canyon were the same, forming an invisible net whose boundaries I only found by accidentally swimming too close to them.

I'd never moved more cautiously in my life.

The space beyond the turn looked the same as the rest of the canyon behind me. More fallen pillars, more boulders big enough for a dehaian to carve into a home. Gingerly, I let my powers extend out from my human form, bracing myself for the draining effect of this place. It was relentless, ready to start dragging me toward nothingness if I let my control slip for even a moment. Even passing through the water like I was accustomed to—moving like I was flying, like the water itself propelled me—was enough to set it off.

So I swam like a human, and I was starting to feel as tired as one too.

No way out.

I bit back a snarl at the comment. The ghost woman drifted up from behind me, pity on her half-burned face. It was getting easier and easier to hear her even without touching her, though God knew I didn't want to examine the implications of why. I wasn't dead. She'd even said so. And I wasn't going to die. I was going to get the hell out of here, no matter what it took.

Prison of the magic that made you. Of what you were. Holds us all.

"Then why can't I use it?" I snapped, still swimming forward. "If it's my magic, why is it trying to drain me into nothing instead?"

Because that is its purpose. To close around you, to drain and destroy what you became. It is what you were. Not alive. Force alone, nothing more.

"But I'm not just that anymore. I wasn't even that when you first made me."

Exactly.

I sputtered, at a loss. "I… what? So why can't I—"

*This prison is made from what you were. Formless magic, pure force without any awareness or sense of self. We crafted you from that energy and separated you from it. We did not know you would obtain true consciousness, true identity and self, beyond what you had in our time. We did not know you would become this—*she gestured to me—*or the good that you would choose to do. We made this trap when our enemies turned you into a monster, into* *a weapon, and into a creature of struggle and war. We could not save you, so we tried to unmake you.* She paused. *We did not know what you would become.*

I could see the sorrow in her expression. The guilt.

You were born of this magic, so we shaped a snare for you from it. But when you escaped, the trap closed around us all… and yet its purpose was not complete. You are the spell's reason for being, and without your destruction, that spell will never find its end. It waited for you. It exists only to drain you back into itself. But now that you are here, now that it has captured you, it will do this. Every trace of your power it absorbs draws the noose in tighter, draws the spell closer to its end. Ultimately, the spell is destined to return to the magic from which it was made, and we will join it.

As will you.

Chills crept through me at the calm certainty in her voice.

Magic cannot be destroyed. It is energy, and energy cannot be destroyed. It can only be changed. Used. You were once what this magic still is, and fighting it is to fight yourself. A cycle, never ending. If you hold onto yourself, if you hide in this form, your uniqueness also holds you separate from this prison, imprisoned in its grasp like your palm is imprisoned by your own fist. But if you were to surrender and become the power from which you were born, to allow yourself to change back into the unconscious energy that you once were, this place could not hold you. The trap would cease to be.

"But becoming like that again… it'll kill me."

Her pitying expression was infuriating. *Yes.*

I stared at her. If I let go of who I was, if I released my human form and let this place drain me into nothing more than the unaware magic I'd been before these people ever created me, I'd be free… and dead. Dead in every way that mattered. I'd be nothing, not even a memory of myself, just non-sentient energy. And if I wanted to stay alive, stay myself… I'd be a prisoner forever.

Fear, panic, and sheer, desperate denial boiled through me. "So let me out. You made this. Reverse it."

She regarded me sadly. *We cannot.*

"*Why?*" I shouted.

We are fragments. Afterimages. Scraps of memories that once were. An image holds power, but it cannot unmake what has been done. It cannot change the past.

I floundered, searching for words and finding nothing, and then I started swimming again, faster than before. Futility and rage tangled into a seething mess inside me because this couldn't be it. This couldn't just be *it*. I'd die in a trap set a millennium before, all because a dehaian bastard forced me to become a weapon and my creators' only solution had been my *death*.

Screw that. "Dammit, why did you even make me in the first place? I wasn't a weapon. What the hell was I supposed to be?"

She drifted beside me, silent for a moment. *Salvation.*

I blinked, slowing down. "What?"

The water ahead of me quivered.

I came to a stop, scanning the shadows, but no one was there. The boulders remained motionless above me, suspended like hundred-ton guillotines. The walls were unchanged. Nothing was different. There were only the ghosts. Only me, and I hadn't done that… that *whatever* it was.

Had I?

An eerie blue-green glow arose in the water, seeming to come from everywhere with no source I could see.

Okay, that *definitely* wasn't me.

I inched forward cautiously. The quivering in the water intensified, becoming a pulling sensation. A twisting, churning feeling like I was a fish caught in a swirling drain. Around me, the ghosts stopped their repetitive motions, and impressions of panic and terror suddenly filled my mind.

My throat closed. I couldn't breathe. Oh, God, I couldn't breathe.

But I didn't *need* to breathe. What was this? My heart was racing so fast, it felt like it would explode, and I didn't even *have* a heart. I wasn't really human, and this—

My powers retreated deep inside my human form, like they were slamming a barred gate on a fortress. My back collided with the rough canyon wall, and my hands crushed into the stones as if to secure me there. The churning feeling was still there, still beyond my skin, but it wasn't gripping me the same. I'd found an anchor, I realized. I *was* the anchor.

Whatever the hell that meant.

I turned, looking for the ghost woman. She hovered beside the wall too, and the edges of her form shivered and wisped away like tendrils of smoke in the wind.

Danger.

No kidding. "What is this?"

Danger.

"*What* danger? What's happening?"

Puncture.

"Huh?"

She didn't respond, and the absurdity of my situation hit me. I was arguing with a thousand-year-old ghost. Demanding answers from a thousand-year-old ghost.

One who was just as trapped as I was.

The enormous stones overhead groaned. Showers of sand and gravel cascaded down, bringing a few of the smaller boulders with them.

Oh, that couldn't be good.

I looked back in the direction of the pull. This wasn't some new feature of the prison. It couldn't be, because the ghosts probably wouldn't be freaking out like this. But there was a world beyond this place, a world with Ari and the dehaians and the strakirin and…

Oh, hell.

My fingers crunched further into the stone wall behind me as my grip tightened. Logan was out there. The judges too, and either of them could be behind this. They'd sent Osias and the strakirin to draw power from this place, and if they still had a hold on it from out there…

I glanced around. Magic was keeping this space from collapsing, and it was holding me prisoner at the same time. I'd like to think that if whoever was out there drained that, I could get free, but I doubted it'd be that simple.

Nothing was ever that simple.

The pulling sensation grew stronger, trying to drag me from the wall. No, whatever this was, it affected me too, which meant I probably wouldn't escape that easily. But more to the point, the judges had wanted my magic and wanted me dead. They'd taken my power just to make the strakirin in the first place, and they'd sent those strakirin here to get even *more* power.

If they had a hold on the magic here, there was no telling what they could be doing out there.

I had to stop this.

I focused all I had on holding every last trace of my abilities inside me, away from the dragging hold of whatever the hell was going on, and I made myself let go of the wall. The strange suctioning sensation in the water had less effect on me, no longer trying to pull me toward itself when I buried my abilities so deeply hidden inside. Staying close to the seafloor, I swam forward slowly, ready to retreat at the first sign that this force had gotten a hold of me.

Nothing happened. I kept moving, my eyes scanning the chasm amid the eerily glowing water, every instinct I had screaming to lash out, to retreat, to opt for fight or flight or anything at all if it got this *thing* away from me.

I edged around the canyon wall. Dread sank over me.

The amphitheater. I was outside the amphitheater again. The fight must have knocked me away from it, or maybe I'd retreated from it in the dark without realizing.

It was spooky, seeing it now, so soon after finally remembering what it had looked like once upon a time. My memories and current reality overlaid one another like a double exposure photograph, bringing up a jumble of guilt and rage and pain.

It hurt, remembering what I'd destroyed. I hated the feeling.

My fingers curling into fists, I ordered myself to focus. There had to be something I could do to stop this, even if I couldn't even see what was happen—

The ground at the center began to change.

I retreated instinctively, my attention locked on the gravel. To my eyes, nothing was different. There were simply crumbled white rocks resting at the base of an amphitheater a thousand years old. But my mind said the ground at the center of the floor glowed brighter than all the water around me, as if a visual signal was reaching my brain and bypassing my sight entirely, making my head throb.

The invisible glow-feeling shifted, pushing through the gravel and twisting up like a sprout bursting from the earth. Shoving through the sand and debris at the base of the amphitheater, the strange sensation grew like a weed, thin as a rope and stretching higher and higher toward the boulders overhead. A pulse went through it when it reached the rocks, a throb of invisible light that I felt in the water.

Our van bounced over the rough road, the expensive shocks struggling to offset the dilapidated nature of the gravel track. Enforcers in tactical gear filled the vehicle, their snake-like eyes turned yellow and black from their anticipation of what lay ahead. Later, I would chastise them for allowing their control to slip. Now, I preferred they remained focused on the target at hand. The road climbed, and sunlight pierced the van's interior, lighting my folded hands and absorbing into the muted lines of my black suit. A house came into view beyond the next rise, its brown siding and pointed roof showing past the trees.

I flinched away. What the hell?

The vine of power twisted over the rocks, finding small spaces, continuing its climb upward.

Like a link. A connection to whoever was on the other end, feeding them the power of this place.

Oh, crap.

Panic drummed through me. I had no idea what was going on, but those were enforcers. Somehow, I'd seen enforcers. And that terrain… I'd only caught glimpses from Ari, but the similarities were enough.

She had enforcers after her. Maybe a judge too.

Oh my God, had I connected with a judge?

I shoved the thought aside. I'd worry about it later. Right now, this rope thing was clearly linking itself to someone out there, and that someone was after Ari. I couldn't let my own abilities out, or this place would kill me, and I couldn't get close to the walls of this prison without it trying to do the same, meaning…

Meaning I was screwed.

A growl of frustration escaped me. I had to do *something*. I couldn't come near the magic of this prison, and yet—

Wait.

I looked around, but the ghosts were gone. The odds were split on whether they'd answer my question anyway.

I swam closer to the invisible vine of magic twisting up from the center of the amphitheater. This couldn't be a product of the prison around me. The ghosts wouldn't be freaking out and hiding if it was. But the ghost woman had said "puncture," and clearly this was magic. In unleashing the spell he'd gotten from the judges, Osias had woken this prison and woken the power that fed the creature Logan had become, but maybe... maybe those weren't the same thing, and maybe the one was leaking through the other, and since—unlike when Ari and the others had been here—this time, I wasn't fighting to stay out of the trap that already held me...

Maybe I could use that power too.

And if I was careful, the prison wouldn't try to kill me at the same time.

My hands flexed as I battled back the trepidation railing at me to not be an idiot and to stay clear of that throbbing, invisible rope. The prison lurked around me like a monster breathing down my neck, waiting to strike. Memories flashed through me of what it'd felt like when Osias woke this place. I was gambling on a veritable *truckload* of unknowns, and if this went wrong...

Then I was dead. But if I did nothing, I'd be leaving Ari to the judges.

I reached for the vine of magic.

17

ARI

"What?" I stared at Luna and her brother, Leo, torn between trying to keep my jaw off the ground and wanting to run for the hills.

Save the world? They thought I could save the *world*.

No pressure.

Hysteria bubbled up in me. Luna had to be joking.

Luna didn't look like a girl who knew how to joke anymore.

Nausea followed on the heels of the hysterical urge to laugh. Save the world. Hadn't the judges said something like that too, back before their procedures? That I could save us. Help my people. I just had to let them connect me to the Beast and everything would be fine.

Yeah, I was looking at how well that had turned out.

"The Judiciary wants the hive to be their weapon," Luna said. "But… there's more to it than that. The hive is a life force. A living thing, and it needs you. You… you *matter* to it. Maybe it's because you were the first strakirin, or maybe it's something else, but the hive is drawn to you, and if you abandon it…"

I needed to sit down.

"You have to embrace this," Luna begged. "Please. Let the song in. Join the hive and—"

My head was already shaking no. No, no, no. Forget sitting. Forget hysteria, because I was way past that. I didn't need to stop this.

I needed to run.

"*Please*," Luna begged. "It's only a matter of time till he finds us, and when he does, we..." The fear was plain on her face.

I had no idea what was on mine.

I shook my head again, harder. This was... this wasn't...

"And we're supposed to believe this isn't just some kind of trick?"

I jumped. Jace was behind me. All around us, the dehaians watched, visibly tense as hell with their guns aimed and their bodies radiating readiness to shoot.

My brother glared at the strakirin. "You show up and tell her to, what? Join some 'hive' thing and trust that it's a good idea simply because you say so?" He scoffed.

Luna stared at Jace, something almost alien coming into her eyes. Beyond my defenses, I could hear the drone get louder for a moment.

And then it faded, and the look in her eyes did too. "We know you. Jace. Her brother. Leo saw your picture on the news—"

I couldn't take this anymore. I retreated, vaguely aware there was a cliff nearby and, on some level, not even caring.

It'd get me away from them.

That hysterical laugh tried to bubble up again.

I turned and ran, tearing across the yard and out into the rough terrain beyond. The trees were a blur. Branches swiped at my face, my legs, my arms. Tents flashed past, and startled dehaians too. The darkness was thinning to deep indigo. Dawn was finally starting to arrive.

"Ari!" Jace cried, far in the distance behind me.

I kept running. Save the world. I was supposed to do something that saved the…

This was madness. Total insanity. They wanted me to let the hive in, when my defenses were the only thing keeping me *safe* from the oblivion that had nearly killed me?

A hungry oblivion—thick, and dark, and filled with ghosts. It surrounded me now, finally coming for me after a thousand years. Something dragged at it, feeding like a leech on a wound. It would devour me if I didn't—

I tripped on a log and crashed headlong into the dirt. Pain shot through my outstretched arms when they caught me against the ground. I gasped, the shock blinding me for a moment before my hands and forearms started to sting.

It wasn't the spikes. I pulled one hand away from the dirt, wincing at the scrapes up and down my flesh, all of them starting to well up with blood.

Dammit. Shifting around on my elbow to keep from pressing my bleeding hands onto anything else that might hurt, I climbed to my knees awkwardly, hissing with pain when the air stung my cuts too.

Tears welled in my eyes. It wasn't the cuts. Not only the cuts.

It was everything. The pain. My life. The hive and the strakirin and the "song" that would probably kill me. For all I knew, Jace was right. This could be a trick. Two strakirin showed up out of nowhere and told me to do the *one thing* I've been avoiding this entire time—and with good reason?

Yeah, right.

I wished Noah was here.

My eyes squeezed shut, trying to trap the burning tears while I sank onto my heels. I was so sick of crying. So sick of pain. It didn't fix anything. For a moment there, I could have almost *sworn* I felt him, but that was just…

Just…

Hope flickered up inside me—a desperate, you-know-you're-wrong-but-you-want-to-believe-it-anyway kind of hope. Everyone thought Noah was dead. I'd worried I was wrong. But what if…

"Ari?" Luna called. She was close now. Leo probably was too, considering they both could move with all the considerable speed of a strakirin. Hell, they'd chased down SUVs.

But they didn't matter right now.

I remained kneeling on the ground, my thoughts racing. White towers. When I'd been in Nyciena, I'd imagined something about white towers and tall trees on a summery island. One I'd never seen.

But I'd bet Noah had.

Was it possible? Was he still out there, finally reaching for me?

Tears choked me. I crushed a fist to my mouth to keep the

sob inside. Oh, please, please let him be out there.

From the corner of my eye, I saw Luna and Leo dash from the trees, only to stop when they saw me. I didn't even glance toward them. I couldn't breathe as I stretched out in my mind, feeling for the space inside that had been connected to him, the place that had become so much the two of us that we'd been sharing memories without even realizing it. And maybe…

I pushed farther, concentrating with everything I had. Just *maybe…*

Cold darkness flared up ahead, small and bright as a distant star, empty as a black hole. It brushed the edges of my mind like a chilled wind ahead of an oncoming storm. And it wasn't alone. Something equally dark, equally deadly followed it. I couldn't see it, could only feel it, but I knew one thing. None of it was Noah.

Oh my God.

Luna shrieked. I retreated fast behind my walls while Leo grabbed my arms, shouting for Luna to run. With his help, I scrambled to my feet, ignoring the pain in my hands because a few scratches didn't matter. Nothing mattered except getting the hell out of here.

Strakirin lunged from the scrub brush and charged at us. Over the rise, a dark monster strode, a ghostly pale man at his side and more strakirin and enforcers behind.

It was Logan.

Logan and God knew what else.

Lightning leapt from me, instinctive and desperate, striking the strakirin charging at us. I spun, tearing across the dirt and rocks with Luna and Leo at my side, my muscles screaming for more speed, more speed. We had to warn—

Something bit my neck. My hand rose to slap it away, and then the world tilted.

The hard earth vanished before I reached the ground.

18

BAYLIE

Ari bolted into the forest, and the strakirin kids raced after her so quickly, all the dehaians could do was shout with alarm—though that didn't stop them from raising their guns all over again and aiming like they didn't know who to shoot.

"Get to the king!" yelled the one who seemed to be in command, motioning to some of the others. "You three, watch them!"

The soldiers ran for the forest.

"Dammit." Jace started after his sister. "Ari!"

Guns in his face brought him up short. "Stay there!" shouted another dehaian.

Jace shook his head. "You can't—"

"*Stay put!*" the soldier bellowed.

"Jace!" Ellie ran from the house, only to skid to a stop at the sight of the dehaians aiming their weapons at us. "What are you doing?"

"The girl led those things toward our king," the dehaian snapped.

I gaped at him.

"You—" Jace sputtered. "That's not what happened!"

"She ran and they did too. Until we know the king is secure—"

"Enforcers are coming!" Ellie interrupted.

My stomach dropped. Chills raced over me, bringing with them smoke and black lightning in my skin. The soldier spat something in a foreign language and then ran after the other dehaians.

Jace swore and took off too.

"Baylie, please," Ellie begged. "They've broken past the perimeter. You have to get inside, down to the subbasement—"

A brilliant light flared beyond the trees, like a lightning bolt at ground level.

Oh, hell. "Jace!" I yelled.

I ran, tearing through the brambles and branches and over the rough terrain. I'd briefly been a runner in middle school; one semester of cross-country followed by one semester of nursing a torn hamstring and the decision that running was something our ancestors probably would have quit too, given half the chance.

For the first time, I wished I'd kept it up because damn that guy was fast.

"Jace!" I caught a glimpse of him ahead of me and tried to put on an extra burst of speed. The undergrowth swiped at my legs. Shorts really weren't appropriate attire for this either. Another note for "next time I'm chasing a guy in the middle of the forest."

The sarcasm was only distracting for so long. I was running *toward* the bad guys. This was stupid on any day of the week.

Jace shouted ahead of me. Adrenaline did what willpower couldn't. I ran faster, finally catching sight of him again.

Strakirin surrounded him, and enforcers weren't far behind. There was no sign of Ari or those kids who'd gone after her anywhere. And that wasn't the only thing.

I slammed to a stop, my feet nearly skidding out from under me at the sight of the monster, the creature, the black-abyss, impossible *thing* that stood at the edge of the ring of strakirin around Jace. Human in shape alone, lightning tangled inside its too-tall form. Storm clouds too, churning and twisting inside its body like that first day on the beach when Noah had come back after becoming the Beast.

But it wasn't Noah. No way in *hell* that thing was Noah.

"Ah, the brother and… a landwalker, perhaps?"

For a heartbeat, my attention couldn't quite pull itself from the creature enough to register the man who'd spoken. And then my mouth fell open, a garbled shriek strangling itself inside my throat. Pale skinned, tall, and dressed in a black suit, the guy looked as if the world could end right in front of him and he would only comment on the inconvenience. But that wasn't what froze me.

Black lightning snapped and flared inside his too-white skin. Eerie smoke that seemed to absorb all light rose from his body, and strange shapes twisted in the haze, like half-formed monsters from my childhood nightmares. His eyes were bottomless pits of darkness, and his body moved like it wasn't quite in sync with his muscles, or maybe with reality itself. He twitched and shifted in unnatural ways, like he was a film strip pieced together with some of the frames missing. Sauntering up beside the monster like they'd both simply been out for a pleasant stroll, the man folded his hands in front of him and regarded us both with a black slash of a grin, as if we were mildly amusing insects.

A judge, I realized. Oh, God, this had to be a judge. But no one had ever mentioned them looking like *this.*

But he didn't know who—or really, *what*—I was?

Maybe the enforcers Miguel captured a few days ago hadn't made it back to tell him.

I couldn't be grateful. I was too busy trying not to panic.

"Take the boy." The judge made a dismissive gesture to the strakirin, his hand skipping through space in a staccato motion that made my eyes hurt. "He'll make a good test subject, given his genetic proximity to Zero-Zero-One. The rest of you, to the house."

The enforcers took off running while two of the strakirin started toward us. Jace retreated, staring at them with this strange expression on his face, and it took me a moment to place why.

Robin. Oh my God, that was *Robin.* Her face was stained green, and her eyes were yellow-black, and only the shock about the black-storm creature had kept me from recognizing her in the first place.

My gaze darted over the others, panic gripping me. I knew them too. Not well. Not hardly at all, but… I'd seen them.

They'd been part of the resistance.

I couldn't breathe.

The judge's attention flicked to me, and he smiled, the expression like ice and a knife had a baby. "And now—"

He staggered, his words cutting short. Alarm flashed over his face, and indignation too, as if he couldn't imagine what had possessed the audacity to interrupt him.

But I couldn't see anything. Couldn't feel—

Oblivion dragging at me, black and terrible. Hungry like a thousand starving mouths unfed since the dawn of time, all of them eager to gnaw at me, tear at me, and once they got a grip, I knew they would never stop. I had to stay free of them. I—

Reality came back in a rush of sunrise and snake-eyed nightmares. Only a moment had passed. The strakirin were still surrounding Jace, and they hadn't reached him yet. The storm monster that I would never call the Beast hadn't moved, though I would have sworn something in its body language screamed confusion.

But the judge looked furious. His head snapped to the west, rage in his eyes. "How…?"

He reached up, grasping something on the storm creature's collar. "Destroy them all," he snarled.

The creature exploded into smoke, into clouds, an eruption of black thunderheads that grew and grew over our heads, rising higher with a growl that reverberated through my chest and body. For a moment, the creature hung in the sky, the clouds of its form churning in on itself. Purple lightning flared in its core, lashing in on itself from the right and left, like it was trying to strike something inside its enormous form.

"Now, Mister Marseilles!" the judge ordered.

The storm monster snarled and took off over the trees, heading for the house.

And then the judge vanished too. One moment he was there, and the next he had disappeared, leaving only an impression of wispy black smoke.

I stared. I'd lost it. I hadn't woken up this morning. This was a crazy dream.

"Baylie, run!" Jace shouted.

I tore my gaze from the space where the judge had been.

The strakirin had Jace.

Instinct took over. Air vanished around me, sucked inward for the split second it took the magic to build, and then the power burst outward again, erupting at the strakirin. The magic slammed into them, ripping them away from Jace and driving them back over the underbrush and up against the scraggly trees beyond.

Black smoke twisted up from my body. Threads of dark lightning flared and vanished beneath my skin. A shudder went through me for the magic that looked so similar to the judge, but surely I wasn't like him. Wouldn't become like him.

Oh, God, please don't let me end up like him.

Jace stumbled upright. He threw one quick look to the fallen strakirin and then raced toward me, grabbing my arm. "Come on!"

We ran for the house.

Shouts came from beyond the rise. Lightning flared, rising

from the ground and blazing against the dawn sky.

Chloe. That would be Chloe. And she…

I couldn't finish the thought, because the only option was for her to be fine. But the monster was already there.

Where the hell had the judge gone?

Scrambling up the incline, I caught a glimpse of the storm creature beyond the trees. Black tentacles of thunderclouds whipped down on people I couldn't see. Screams followed every time, and lightning too, while a rumble came from the monster.

Horror choked me. It sounded like *laughter*.

Jace swore, desperation in his voice. My gaze flicked to him and then caught on the nightmare I would have already seen if not for the creature up ahead.

Tents. Dozens of them, crushed.

And the people nearby…

Bile rose in my throat. Dead didn't begin to describe it. Their skin was slashed by burn marks and marred by a sickly green stain. Their eyes were fractured with yellow, with black, like a mosaic from hell. Their hands wrapped their throats as if they'd choked to death, or else gripped the ground like they'd been trying to drag themselves away.

The image of the strakirin behind me filled my mind. Resistance members, now strakirin.

The creature had been trying to change the dehaians too.

But they'd died instead.

My feet were moving before my brain caught up. I tore past the tents, the bodies, racing for the trees. The screams were fewer now.

I hadn't seen lightning again.

No. No, Chloe would be okay. She'd be—

"Baylie!" Jace yelled behind me.

I darted past the trees. Storm clouds billowed through the yard like thick smoke, engulfing parts, leaving others hazy enough to see the bodies on the ground. Lightning flared inside areas of the smoke, and if there was any mercy in the universe, it'd be coming from Chloe and Zeke. I couldn't tell, though. I could hardly see anything. The creature hung over the house. Tentacles of black smoke twisted through the gaping door, through the shattered windows and back out again like a snake.

I let the magic inside me go.

Power rushed into me, like a deep breath before the plunge, and then exploded outward, upward, straight at the monster. The blast struck the creature at its core above the house, the magic driving deep into the black clouds. The tentacles tightened on the house; wood and stone crunched in its grasp. The black clouds in the yard retreated enough for me to catch sight of Chloe with Zeke beside her, both of them alive and surrounded by a handful of soldiers, all beneath a glowing dome that sparked and flared like it was on the verge of giving out.

Relief hit me, and then a hand took mine. Jace, his eyes on the creature, his magic just beyond my skin and waiting. "Don't stop!" he shouted.

A growl rose from the monster. Black smoke rushed toward us.

Jace's magic poured into me. The darkness within me

responded, water and land, like the force of the earth itself surging through my bones. I threw out my hand, barely able to hear myself screaming over the rush in my ears, and released the magic at a creature who would never be the Beast.

The monster shuddered, slowing down, but still coming. My hand clenched on Jace's while I poured everything I had into stopping the clouds swooping down to attack us.

Light burst inside the creature, like a grenade had gone off inside the storm. The monster jerked back, tumbling in on itself, thrashing as if in horrible pain. The tentacles whipped away from the house. The clouds retreated from the yard, collapsing in as the creature fled upward with a roar so loud, I could only crush my hands to my ears while my entire body shook from the sound.

The creature surged over the trees, vanishing to the west.

I lowered my hands. My breaths came short and fast, and I couldn't hear them. My ears rang, and my body felt as shaken as a baby rattle. I turned, finding Jace, who stared at me in shock. Beyond him, Chloe, Zeke, and the others climbed to their feet, the glowing barrier around them gone.

But we hadn't won. I knew we hadn't won, even if the creature was gone. Something had exploded inside that thing, something that wasn't my power. Something else had driven it away, saving us, at least for now.

I just had no idea what.

❧ 19 ❧

LOGAN

If I'd had a body, I would have been screaming.

I fled through the sky, racing away from the stupid house in the California mountains. I could barely think from the pain. Barely even see where I was going. I caught glimpses of trees shredding in the wind, of a plane tumbling in the sky. It didn't matter. Nothing mattered.

Holy god-that-I-was, that had *hurt!*

But then, the collar was also gone.

I slowed down over a snowy mountaintop somewhere a few hundred miles north of the house. For a long while, I hovered, shaking as the pain gradually began to fade. My focus started to return, my attention shifting to the important questions, rather than the radiating, burning agony of Judge Engle's idiotic collar shattering inside me like a miniature magical bomb.

God… I'd make him pay for that. All of it. And then some.

But first, the Judiciary had Ari.

My irritation grumbled out of me, a low growl of thunder. No, no, no. That wasn't *important.* Getting revenge on that son-of-a-bitch Judge Engle was important. The blond girl was important. That bitch had power. As for what kind, or what the hell she even *was*, I had no clue, but that wasn't the point either. I'd figure it out. I'd take it for myself. And if I turned her into one of my strakirin at the same time…

Wait.

Curses raced through my mind while I took stock of the complete lack of strakirin in my grasp. In my haste to get out of there, I'd left them. And sure, the individual bodies weren't important, given that they were only mindless husks filled by my will. But they were still an asset. My eyes and ears elsewhere, and—I checked quickly—yeah, dammit. Most of them were dead.

Most, though. Not all. I could probably use that.

To find Ari.

My snarl of irritation was louder this time and sent a wave of snow cascading down a mountain slope. What was wrong with me? That useless strakirin girl had all the importance of naval lint! Why the hell did I keep thinking about her?

This was ridiculous.

I stayed motionless in the sky, calming myself while the spruce trees beneath me drowned in the deluge of snow. This *was* ridiculous. It was beyond ridiculous—as was the fact that this obsession obviously wasn't going away no matter my efforts, which meant it was someone's fault.

And thus someone deserved to pay.

My attention swept over the mountains. I needed answers for this bizarre obsession with some irrelevant strakirin girl, whether it was a trick the judges had pulled—screwing with my mind somehow—or something else entirely. And I wasn't going to get those answers hovering here.

I needed a judge.

Now wasn't that ironic? *I* needed a *judge*. Admittedly, it was only for information—well, information and an epic ton of payback. But still, it was amusing.

And, oh, so tempting... I knew just who to pick.

I drew my attention inward, hunting for that weird twist of magic that Judge Engle had used. He'd drawn on something, drawn on it *through* me, but I couldn't feel whatever the hell he'd done anymore. He'd taken something from inside me into himself, like I was an ingredient to a recipe where he held all the other components. But taking something still left a space where it had been, and if I searched...

A faint awareness of... of *something* flickered in my mind, like a blush of color on a radar screen. It wasn't that I was connected to him. No, more like I could just tell that something was out there, something disturbing the magical currents in the world around me.

And it had to be him. The other Beast was dead, and Ari wasn't anything but a damned annoying strakirin, so that left Judge Engle...

Judge Engle, who was racing west like his proverbial feet were on fire.

Where the hell was he going so quickly?

I started after him. He was already miles beyond the California coast. What was he after?

Ari couldn't be out there.

I snarled, the thought pulling me up short more by reflex than any act of will. And I couldn't make myself move forward again. She wasn't… she wasn't *there,* and so I couldn't go that way. Not until I knew where she was. The need became like ants crawling all over my skin—and I didn't even *have* skin. The sensation was mindboggling. Overwhelming. *Intolerable.*

Growling like thunder, I turned my attention inward again. Dammit, fine! If I could locate Judge Engle, then why couldn't I just locate—

The ant-crawling sensation increased. She wasn't here. She wasn't *here,* goddammit, and I needed her! I needed her like I used to need air, and if I didn't find her soon, I would—

I slammed into a mountainside blindly, but the impact jarred me back to reality. The overwhelming panic receded enough that I could pick up on the world around me again. For a long moment, I hung motionless in the air while the slope beside me collapsed into crumbling rock, pouring down in a tumbling landslide of boulders the size of minivans to crush the trees and who cared what else.

Judge Engle disappeared over the horizon, a distant blot of irritating magic vanishing from my mind.

I growled, vibrating with enough rage and thwarted craving to make the clouds fragment and dissipate. To hell with that bastard. I'd get to him in good time. I'd shred that pathetic copycat and make him rue the day he ever dreamed of stealing power and abilities from me. But first… oh, first, I'd locate one of those "lesser" judges and make them tell me exactly why the *hell* they put this impulse to find Ari inside me and yet hadn't given me a goddamn clue how to do it. After all, this was someone's fault, and I was pretty sure that someone was *them.*

I knew she wasn't going to be out in the ocean, though. Not when I'd just seen her taken by enforcers who couldn't change themselves into amorphous rip-offs of my form like Judge Engle. They'd loaded her in one of the vans, along with some other broken strakirin, and raced off for the highway before any of her allies could be the wiser. So she had to still be on land, or near it.

But then, if I did get near a judge, there was still that little "release" command to consider. If all they had to say was one word and suddenly my power would drain into the bastards…

It was unconscionable. But that had probably been part of the control from that collar. It could be gone. And if by some chance it wasn't, well, I was prepared now.

If I'd had a body, I would have grinned. I'd act fast. Grab them. Silence them. See about that little trick with reading someone's memories. It'd be easy. The idiots were still calling for me too, out there with their silly signal beckoning their supposed slave home. I could feel it, inside my mind. The damned thing was as good as a homing beacon.

Or a target.

I started off toward the closest source of their idiotic call— most likely another research station, if I had to wager a guess, even if it was hundreds of miles from the Judiciary's main one that I had already seen.

I'd get my answers. I'd get more strakirin as well.

After all, I could change anyone I wanted now, those useless dehaians notwithstanding. There were sure to be at least a *few* ruanir neighborhoods along the way.

～ 20 ～

ARI

—do you think she—

—but what if we—

Wake up!

I lurched awake with a gasp, the whispers from my dream vanishing. My gaze flashed around the room at high speed before my mind caught up to my eyes. Gray walls. Bars. No windows. A lightbulb inside a cage overhead. A screened square like a speaker behind another small cage high up on the wall and a camera at its side.

A prison cell.

I scrambled up, my hand slipping on the edge of the camp bed and nearly sending me tumbling to the floor. I staggered upright, my head spinning and my vision too. I'd been… somewhere. At the house, that big house, and then…

Shivers crept over my skin, and spikes inched from my arms. Then…

The judges. The enforcers.

Logan.

I blinked, reaching out to steady myself on the concrete wall. Scabs covered the scrapes on my hands and arms that I'd gotten from falling, hinting at the fact I'd been unconscious for a while. The cell around me was barely five feet wide, and three of those feet were taken up by a camp bed that had clearly seen a better day. Brown stains that I hoped to God weren't something more disgusting than blood dotted the gray blanket while rust spots had eaten away at the army green finish of the bed frame. The only other feature of the entire room was a toilet and a door, each of them on their respective ends of the cell, and on the door itself…

I swallowed hard, my gaze dropping to the tips of the spikes on my arms. I didn't need to cross the tiny room to confirm. The scratch marks were too far apart to be made by anything else.

But *I* hadn't made them I was fairly certain. Hopefully, anyway, unless I'd done something while unconscious—

A crackle of static made me jump.

"Hello, Miss Moreau. How nice of you to join us."

My heart pounding, I turned toward the speaker on the wall.

"As you can see, we've well prepared this room for your kind. It is in your best interest not to struggle; you'll only hurt yourself. Now, enforcers will be along to collect you soon. We have many questions."

Oh, God.

"Where am I?" I shouted at the camera, my heart pounding.

The voice on the other end chuckled. "Safe. That is all that need concern you. We have had a share of defective strakirin before, Miss Moreau, though admittedly none who had successfully joined the hive mind prior to malfunctioning. You are quite secure."

My heart raced. I couldn't be back in their hands. I couldn't. Before I even finished registering the thought, I was already at the door, scrambling for a lock, a crack, something to give me purchase so I could get out of—

Electricity jolted me. I toppled backward into the camp bed and then crashed to the floor.

"As I said, Miss Moreau. Quite secure."

A click came from the speaker.

I stared at the door, breathless, my entire body vibrating from the shock. My mind was blank. I couldn't get out through the door, and the rest of the room was a box. A concrete box.

Panic choked me. I couldn't breathe. I scrambled backward on the rough ground till the wall met my back. This wasn't happening. This wasn't...

Alone in the dark, hiding from the sounds, the pain, the cuts they made over and over again, testing, testing. The glittering gel, repairing the damage fast so they could try again. Bodies collapsing to the floor. The rush of joy as the strakirin killed and killed and—

A frantic whimper escaped me. My legs crushed up against my chest. This couldn't be happening. I couldn't be here again.

Noah! I screamed in my head. Noah, please...

Seconds crawled by. I trembled, calling out again. Please...

My breath hitched, the only sound in the echoing silence.

He wasn't there. Maybe he never had been. Maybe Noah was dead, this time for real.

And I was alone.

I buried my head in my arms and cried.

❧ 21 ❧

NOAH

Explosive power ripped me away from the vine of magic, throwing me back across the amphitheater and slamming me into the white stone steps so hard that, if I'd still possessed a truly human body, the collision would have broken every bone of it.

No.

Reeling from the impact, I blinked hard, trying to make the amphitheater resolve into anything but a blur of rocks amid the water's eerie blue-green glow. My body shook like I'd just been electrocuted, or how I remembered it felt when I'd lifted so much weight that my muscles didn't want to work anymore. My chest ached like I'd run a marathon, like the lungs I no longer possessed had been scorched dry. Memories flickered back as if they were a broken film, a series of disconnected images that made little sense. The judge. Ari falling. And… and Baylie?

Baylie was awake?

I pushed up from the steps and braced myself on the

crumbled stone, feeling relieved in spite of everything. Last time I'd seen my stepsister, she was lying in a coma no one could explain, and what I'd felt when I tried to reach her through our connection earlier had been bizarre to the extreme. I had no idea what was going on with her, and I hoped to God she was okay. But she was awake. She was up and alive and awake. That was the best piece of news I'd had in… in however long I'd been here.

Trepidation tugged at the edge of my relief. It couldn't have been long. Maybe a few days, trapped here. And only a few moments connected to that flood of power too. The energy pouring into me from that vine of magic had been overwhelming. Time had distorted along with my vision, and swiftly, I'd lost my awareness of anything around me. I thought it'd only been seconds, though, until the ghost woman blasted me away from that power source.

Raking a hand over my face and through my hair, I struggled to push my worry aside. My mind felt full of whispers and fleeting images that evaporated before I could grasp them, like my memories were in a blender and my brain was too. Meanwhile, the ghost woman hovered nearby, as close to the amphitheater wall as she could get without becoming part of it. She was staring at me.

"What the hell…" I managed to move to a sitting position, still so shaken that I didn't trust my body to fully support me. "Was that you?"

Her head jerked in a small nod.

"You stopped me. Why?"

Danger.

I groaned, the statement like déjà vu, and pressed a hand to my head to stop the weird susurrus of whispering noises still battering around in my brain. "*What* danger?"

Draining.

"Draining what? Me?"

Everything.

I stared at her, and the incongruity of all this suddenly hit me. "You made a prison to kill me. Why do you care if I die?"

A look crossed her face like I was the most obtuse, most unbelievable thing she'd ever seen.

And I'd swear my words had hurt her.

"Sorry," I muttered, even if I wasn't sure quite why.

A slightly mollified expression flickered over her face.

"This prison drains me," I tried. "And now you're saying that thing does too? So what's the difference?"

To everyone besides me, anyway.

She still didn't say a word. I waited, but as the seconds crawled by, nothing changed. She hovered by the wall, as motionless as any of the other ghosts had been.

I couldn't see any of the others around me now.

Muttering curses, I struggled up to my feet. My body hurt, but the shaken feeling was fading. I could still feel the draining power of the prison around me.

Even if it wasn't quite the same.

I hesitated, scanning the suspended boulders above me, before cautiously swimming away from the steps. The draining feeling was... uneven. Intermittent, in a way. Always there, but it felt stronger, then weaker, then stronger again as I moved.

As if I'd cracked it like glass, like ice, till it was on the verge of shattering.

Cautiously, I swam closer to the barricade. The whispering in my mind grew louder and softer in direct inverse to the cracked feeling—louder where the prison was weaker, softer where it was stronger—and wary hope nudged at me, like a kid who wasn't sure if today was Christmas. Whispers, that's what I called them. But what if…

Elation bubbled through me. I kicked hard in the water, rising closer to the boulders above the ruined amphitheater. Like before, it hurt to get near the edges of this prison, but the pain was definitely less in some areas now.

"Ari?" I waited, but no response came. "Ari, can you hear me?"

Seconds crawled by. The whispers didn't sound like her, if such a thing were possible. They sounded… well, weird. Like a bunch of unknown voices on the edge of hearing, like soft sounds coming from another room, but I couldn't make the words out.

What the hell?

Danger.

I jumped as the ghost woman appeared beside me. "Danger to you or danger to your prison?"

No answer.

That was helpful. "Danger to me?"

No response again, but something… something tightened in her expression.

I hesitated. Danger to me. "How?"

She reached out, placing a hand to my arm. I tensed, but the flood of information wasn't forthcoming. Instead, only one word reached me. *Changing.*

"Huh?"

You.

"Me what?"

Change.

"Change shape…? Change me?" I paused. "Why aren't you explaining yourself? You did before. What do you want me to—"

Her hand fell away, something like consternation on her burned, too-pale face. She reached up again and poked my chest.

"What the—"

She poked me again. Other ghosts appeared from the walls, coming to surround me. They reached out, jabbing at me too.

"Hey!" Their motions became insistent. "Stop that!" I tried to retreat, but they were everywhere, and the damn things had gone insane. Over and over, the word came to me, "change, change, change," drowning out the whispers in my mind and railing at me like an order. I twisted away, trying to shift shape just enough to escape the ghosts but keep the prison from killing me at the same time. "What the hell are you—"

I couldn't change form.

Shock froze me for a moment. The reflex to shift into the Beast's amorphous, storm shape was just… it didn't work. Like a muscle I suddenly couldn't move, like a limb that wouldn't even twitch. The ability I'd had more trouble *stopping* from happening than using in the first place was suddenly just *gone*.

This wasn't possible. It'd taken me a year to even manage to look human, let alone have warmth in my skin or the imitation of a pulse, and now I couldn't… I couldn't even change back to…

The ghosts stopped moving. I sank in the water, sank like a human who'd stopped trying to swim. The weirdest feeling of claustrophobia overtook me, clogging my throat with panic and sudden terror. A year ago, I would have been elated at being human-like again, but this wasn't that. Now my skin felt too tight, too close, like a plastic-wrap cage of flesh that I couldn't escape. The canyon seemed to grow around me, suddenly overwhelming in its size, and I floated at the base of it, small and alone at the bottom of the sea. Frantic, I tried to summon up the Beast side of myself, but it felt far away, as if it was buried and hiding so deeply inside me, I couldn't reach it anymore.

Oh my God, what if this didn't stop at simply being unable to shift form? What if the need to breathe followed, and the need for normalized pressure outside of millions of gallons of water too?

What if I drowned?

My eyes squeezed shut, and my fists clenched as I fought the terror. I wasn't breathing. Wouldn't start. I didn't actually have a heart that needed to beat, for all that it felt like the memory of my heartbeat was racing a thousand miles an hour, and the horrible things that happened to human bodies at this depth definitely weren't happening to me. I was okay. I'd *be* okay. I'd make it out of this.

Shaking, I looked toward the ghost woman again. "You could've just said!" Even to my own ears, my voice sounded bitter.

Choice.

"What choice? My choice? Yours?"

She didn't respond.

"What choice?" I shouted.

You.

I opened my mouth, closed it, and then opened and closed it again while frustration sent me floundering for a response. She wasn't making sense. Wasn't even trying to, it seemed. And what was with these one-word answers? She'd been a flood of information before…

Before…

Oh, hell.

The timing played back through my mind. She'd been all kinds of talkative, if rapid-fire impressions of language inside my head could be called that, until this magic in the center of the amphitheater had started up. Then her conversation started to consist of single words.

And warnings.

Was this magic creating some kind of interference? Was it doing something to the ghosts? Now that I thought about it, they looked… weaker, somehow, than when I first saw them. Like bit by bit, they were fading, though the difference was slight. A bit more rock showing through their bodies. Deeper shadows where their burns used to be. Maybe this was draining them.

Or maybe it was draining my ability to connect empathically too.

I looked up, as if I could see through the boulders and the miles of ocean I didn't want to think about, all the way to Ari. The whispers were different now. Fading in and out as I moved, like I was a radio antenna struggling to pick up a signal. The sounds were louder in some places too, or maybe just more distinct, but those same spaces kept shifting, fainter then louder, and then fainter again. But were any of them her? Panic thrummed through me, and it seemed to color the whispers in my mind too, but maybe that fear was just me. Maybe all of this was. A desperate hope, taking the form of a delusion that maybe I hadn't lost everything I—

Noah!

Ari's voice whipped through my mind like a scream on the wind, there and then gone, yet filled with so much pain and fear that I cringed. She was terrified. Beyond terrified. She…

The emotion faded like the scream, trailing off like a whimpering cry that was moving farther and farther away, swallowed down by the whispers that covered it like the ocean covered me.

But that'd been Ari. Not my imagination, not a delusion. She was still there, connected to me, and like those moments before I'd driven her away from the canyon to protect her, more than emotions had reached me.

We could communicate. Maybe, anyway. Or perhaps this was only her power reaching me, rather than anything of mine. It might not work in reverse, meaning it was possible she couldn't hear me at all.

The fear coming from her was like a stain permeating the water.

I closed my eyes, struggling to ignore the ocean and my fear alike. If I could still pick up on her, then maybe…

"Hear me, Ari. Hear me… oh, God, please hear me."

❧ 22 ❧

ARI

Hear me…

I gasped, my forehead snapping away from where it rested on my knees. I knew that voice. That impossible, wonderful voice.

Noah.

My gaze darted around the room, taking in the speaker, the camera. It could be a trick. It could, but…

Desperation made my hands clench tighter on my arms. Oh, sweet *God*, please don't let it be a trick.

I reached out in my mind, searching, straining. I didn't dare speak his name out loud, not when the judges might hear. But inside my head, I stretched out from behind the safety of my defenses, and…

A whisper. Words I couldn't make out, far away. Emotions, too, like distant strains of an instrument, just on the edge of hearing.

My breath caught in my throat. It was him. Oh my God.

In my mind, I chased him, but the feeling of him kept

moving, as if something was between us, blocking me. But still, I could feel him. He was… scared. Drained. Trapped and struggling and afraid of… of drowning?

Wait, what?

Doubt flickered in me. Was I making this up? Why would Noah be scared of—

Ari?

Tears choked my startled cry of joy, and I clamped my hand over my mouth to keep the sound inside. I couldn't let on, couldn't let the judges know. But I wanted to scream. To laugh. To burst into sobs because he was alive. Here. With me, in my mind, and he—

—how much longer—

—need to be patient—

—can't keep waiting—

She's here.

I shrieked, fleeing back deep behind the wall in my mind. I knew that sound, and it wasn't Noah, and it wasn't a dream.

That was the hive.

Shh…

I froze like a rabbit, eyes wide. It could hear me. Inside my head, past my barricades, it could—

Calm filtered through to me, like a soothing murmur to not be afraid. I was safe. Always safe.

I flailed, swatting the air and cringing back against the concrete wall like I could bat the hive away. I wasn't about to be calm, and there was no way in hell I was safe. Not with them. *That.*

With everything I had, I concentrated on my defenses, building them as high as I could, taller and broader than the Great Wall of China. But it hurt too. Noah had been out there. Beyond my defenses, so distant I could barely hear him.

But he was *there*.

Rage filled me, and tears burned my eyes. He was alive. He was alive, and I couldn't reach him because the hive, the damned, *damned* hive, was between us. Was out there too, waiting for me.

—lost—

—in the dark—

Not gone.

I stopped breathing entirely. They could still hear me.

Fractured.

Broken.

Yes.

I reached out a shaking hand, grabbing the concrete wall like it was the only stable thing in the world. On trembling legs, I climbed to my feet, my eyes darting over the empty room. I'd never heard this many voices from the hive before. The noise sounded… discordant, but only at first, like it was a concert of voices speaking, thinking, and feeling before continually drawing down to one thought, one statement. That had never happened. It'd always been a drone, uniform and terrifying, like a single mindless creature made up of multiple bodies, all obediently awaiting its masters' commands.

But then, Luna and Leo had broken out and still had the ability to communicate without speaking out loud.

I hesitated, not trusting the argument of my own mind. It was true that they'd been able to do that, but I'd still picked up on the hive from them. I'd still felt the way they were fighting that zombie drone that wanted to take their identity, their lives.

This could be a trick. A drug. Something.

The calming feeling filtered through to me again, spreading like a balm across my nerves.

I screamed.

The feeling retreated. One of apology followed.

My skin crawled. I wanted this out of me. Off of me.

But why had it said "not gone"?

I didn't move. Didn't even breathe. Not. Gone.

Could they hear Noah too? Those words could mean anything, they didn't necessarily have to be about him. Or the hive could be lying. It was in my head. It could do anything.

No.

I stopped. No? What the hell did it mean, *no?*

I couldn't believe I was doing this. Talking to that thing, even a bit. Even accidentally.

My fingers flexed against the scratchy surface of the concrete wall, bracing me, reminding me what was real. Maybe I was making this up. Or tripping on some gas the judges had filtered into the room without my knowledge. Or maybe it was a trick to get me to lower my defenses. But if this was a trick of the judges, then what was the plan? To make me insane? To tempt me back into the hive again?

Surety spread over me. Yeah, that was it. To tempt me back into the hive so that Logan could—

The drone of the hive lessened sharply, recoiling from me like it'd been burned by Logan's name.

I gave a cold scoff. Nice try. It had probably picked that up from my memories of those strakirin kids.

But then, where *was* Logan in this? None of the voices in the hive sounded like him. The few coherent, cohesive thoughts that came from this hive didn't carry the arrogance that dripped from his every word either. In fact, this felt… softer, but not like it was speaking quietly. Like there weren't as many voices behind it. Not as many minds forming the drone. And discordant too, like they were… what was the word it'd used?

Fractured.

This drone could argue with itself. I'd heard it, earlier, calming its own impatience. But that didn't make any sense. The drone was mindless. An entity unto itself, whose only thought, only purpose, was to serve the judges.

This one felt like a wolf pack.

For all I knew, it'd tear me apart.

Nothing answered the thought. I could feel the hive, though, beyond the walls in my mind, waiting. Distrust radiated from it like a kicked dog.

I'd hurt it. Or Logan had.

And as for how that made *no* sense whatsoever…

Called you. Wanted you. Needed you.

The thoughts bombarded me in rapid succession, lobbed at me as if from a distance by someone uncertain it was safe to approach.

But they made no sense either.

Needed you!

I recoiled against the wall, my vision whiting for a second. My hand went to my throbbing head. What the hell?

The drone lessened again, but… my God, why did I know it was angry? Hurt and offended too, like it thought I should have understood something that I didn't.

This was madness. Stupid too. I was thinking about that thing, thinking *at* that thing, when I should have been focusing everything I had on my defenses to keep it *out*.

Not that my defenses seemed sufficient.

No response came to the thought. No angry shouts, no weird whispers. Which was good. Great. I didn't trust it for a second, but—

Bad ones coming.

Panic colored the message, and on its heels came the drone, louder, more insistent. Begging. Pleading. Shouting.

Terrified.

I collapsed against the wall, sinking to the ground with my hands crushed to my head in a desperate attempt to keep the noise out. My eyes felt like they were bleeding. Maybe my ears too. I couldn't take much more of this, or I—

Please.

The thought filtered through the rest, like water streaming in from all sides, draining the shouts into itself, as if the drone was calming and overruling its own panic.

Again.

That didn't make sense.

Bad ones will hurt you. Coming for tests. For pain. The hive can help. Please.

What? I didn't understand. Didn't even want to.

Except for the fact I had a sinking feeling who the "bad ones" might be.

On the other side of the cell door, something made a beeping sound. Voices carried past the metal, muffled.

My heart climbed my throat. My gaze darted over the cell. Questions, the voice from the speaker had said. They had questions, and the enforcers would be along to collect me soon.

Panic drummed through me. My legs wanted to run. My arms wanted to tear down the walls, if only to get me out of wherever the hell I was. The judges were going to torture me again. Make me kill innocent people again. They were going to hurt me, and I was all alone and—

No.

In my mind, the drone rose, a wave of sound sweeping toward me, determined now. It spread around me, on the brink of crashing down.

You are strakirin. You are us. You are not alone. We will help you.

The door swung open. Two enforcers walked into the room, while three more waited in the hall. Thick metal restraints dangled from one man's fist, the forearm-length shackles looking eerily similar to the ones dehaians used. At the sight of me in the corner, the nearest enforcer's lip twitched in amusement.

Need you safe.

Not alone.

I retreated farther against the wall, spikes extending from

my arms, poison roiling beneath my skin. I'd kill the enforcers if they touched me. Any of them. I wasn't going to be tortured again.

The enforcers just smiled.

Safe. The drone was pleading with me now. *Safe to be with us. Not alone.*

It had to be lying.

Noah? I cried in my mind. I didn't have a clue how he could help me, no idea of what he could possibly do, but surely, *surely* there was something…

The nearest enforcer started toward me, the metal restraints clinking in his hands. He was wearing gloves, I realized. Big black ones that looked like they were designed to handle hot metal.

Or strakirin.

Noah? I tried again.

He was beyond the hive, beyond the drone. I couldn't hear him past the monsters in my mind.

Bad ones find out, they will kill you.

Find out what? I thought desperately.

What you are.

Huh?

The enforcer reached for me.

Let us in!

I shrieked, trying to escape, but there was nowhere to go. His hands wrapped around my arms, hauling me upright. Poison rushed from me, striking those thick black gloves, but the man didn't fall. Thin green wires began to glow in the black material instead, and the enforcer chuckled. "Nice try, bitch."

The enforcer slammed his fist down on my elbows hard, sending a shock through my arms like he'd punched a nerve, and my spikes withdrew as if by reflex. Swiftly, he twisted me around while I screamed. The metal shackles clamped down on my arms. "You try to electrocute me, and these'll electrocute you, get it?"

Let us in!

Never.

Grabbing the chains between the manacles, the enforcer dragged me away from the wall. I yelled, thrashing, fighting to reach anything past the shackles and the damned gloves protecting him. My knees slammed into the camp bed, my elbows and shoulder hit the wall. Concrete grated beneath my back, scraping any exposed skin while he hauled me toward the door.

"Sedative," the man snapped at the other enforcers. "The masters have a live one here."

No. Oh, God, please no.

A second enforcer chuckled. "Another one for the dissection table, then."

Let. Us. IN!

The second enforcer took out a syringe and came into the cell while the first man wrenched me around and yanked my head to the side, exposing my neck. "Thank the masters," the first guy said, "I hate the screaming ones."

Kill you. Bleed you. Please. PLEASE!

The other guy chuckled. From the corner of my eye, I could see the needle coming.

I dropped my defenses against the hive.

The drone swelled around me like a tidal wave, rising higher and higher on all sides. Fear gripped me for a heartbeat as I felt it hover around me, waiting, climbing above me, around me, surrounding me completely. Oh my God, I'd made a mistake. I shouldn't have—

It swept in.

The sound of the drone engulfed me. The room disappeared. The needles and the shackles and the enforcers too. There was only the hive. Dozens of minds and thoughts and wills and imaginations and dreams, and they were real. All of them were real, joined together in this one space for one purpose.

To make sure I survived.

Lightning flared across my body, and for a heartbeat, I felt the manacles try to shock me like the enforcer said they would. But the electricity coursing through me overpowered them. The enforcers shouted, backpedaling.

I scrambled to my feet. Three of them were still blocking the door. One was on the ground, electrocuted.

One was still in the cell with me.

Fear.

Confusion hit me for a heartbeat, and then I understood. I'd felt the strakirin do this under the ocean when they attacked a village. I'd seen the results too.

Innocents wouldn't be hurt this time.

My skin shivered, a cool sensation passing from me like invisible mist coming through my skin. The effect around me was immediate. Enforcers in the hall recoiled, their eyes going wide. The one in the cell choked on a cry and froze, motionless as a statue.

"S-stand your ground!" the man inside the cell stammered. "They've tried this before. The masters' process will hold against the—"

My gaze snapped over to him. Knowledge filtered through to me from the hive. It was true. The strakirin—the broken ones, the abandoned ones, the shadow that hadn't been broken by the judges' process—they had tried this. They'd done so much to try to defend themselves against the enforcers, and it hadn't worked.

They hadn't been me.

Chills swept through my body, dark like the depths of the ocean. I wasn't like the other strakirin. I was stronger. More powerful.

I'd been changed by more than just the judges, and that power didn't share without consent.

The words passed through my mind, but there wasn't time to examine them. The enforcers outside the cell shrieked with utter terror, abandoning their post and running for their lives. The one in the cell stumbled back, horror in his eyes.

The judges could change people any way that they wanted, but millions of years of human-like evolution would still win out in the end.

Fear was universal.

"Unlock me," I ordered.

He whimpered. His pants were wet, and a stink was starting to cloud up the room.

My stomach churned. I lessened the energy coming from me, just enough to where he could move. "Now!"

His hands shaking, he drew out the keys and fumbled one of them into the locks on the shackles. The metal restraints clanked to the ground.

Go.

An image flashed in my head, complete with sound like someone had just turned on the TV behind my eyes. Footsteps pounding on the concrete beyond a locked cell door.

The image vanished as swiftly as it had appeared.

Bad ones coming.

I raced for the exit. The cell was at the end of an empty hallway. Other metal doors lined either side of the corridor ahead of me. Square panels dotted the walls, one to the left of every doorway. A security camera perched near the ceiling at the end of the hall.

Oh, hell.

Enforcers raced around the turn ahead of me. I was trapped. The only way out was through them.

Confidence settled into me. It was the hive. I could feel it around me. In me.

I wasn't alone.

The enforcers charged.

Shivers ran over my skin, the magic radiating out of me, projecting fear. The enforcers stumbled. Some of them ran. Others collapsed.

One of them raised a gun.

I was moving before I finished registering the sight. Fast

as thought, my body ducked and raced at him from the side, snagging his arm before he'd even finished lifting it to aim. Yanking his arm hard, I twisted it around, pinning it behind his back like I'd seen people do on TV.

It worked. It also torqued his shoulder enough that he screamed.

Nausea clawed at my throat. I swallowed hard, my gaze darting to the panels on the wall. Strakirin were back there. I could feel them.

I pulled his hand back up, slapping his palm to the panel beside the door. The screen turned green, and the box beeped. Something clunked inside the door, and then it swung open.

A strakirin girl was waiting on the other side. Half her face and body was stained with watercolor green scales, and the other half was skin. Her eyes were the same, one of them yellow split by black, the other human-looking. She couldn't change all the way, nor change back again.

And her name was Jennifer. She was nineteen. She was from Ann Arbor. Her mother was dead, and her father…

Oh my God.

Declan.

She gave a small gasp, her mouth falling open in a tiny O. She could see him in my memory, and tears filled her eyes for the fact he was still alive. The judges had decided to fake her death and keep her as insurance because they'd heard whispers her father was out there working against them, despite how he'd vanished, despite how he'd been reported as dead. They were never one to waste a "resource," not even a child.

Though that hadn't spared her from being a test subject. A mindless slave was even better than a prisoner because they had no chance of betraying you.

The information flowed between us like water. A breath left me, but there wasn't any time for more. The camera was watching. The judges would be coming.

I took off, dragging the enforcer with me. Jennifer followed, I knew. I didn't even have to see her to know she was there.

Other doors. More and more. Luna was there, barely conscious, and Leo too. The other strakirin were like Jennifer, half changed, half human, some more so than others. One of them had part of their legs fused together, halfway through a change to a tail, while another couldn't bring his spikes back in. Some had their memories while others were fragmented like confetti, their pasts a tattered mess inside their minds.

The judges had left them here, the broken ones and the rejects, the ones on whom they didn't get the process right. The ones who couldn't join the hive the way they wanted. They'd left them because there'd always be time for further experiments and analysis later.

A thought flashed through my mind, unexpected. I could help them.

The key, whispered the hive.

Footsteps pounded on the concrete. The enforcers were coming.

Panic reached me, coming from the others. *Run,* urged the hive.

We did.

23

LOGAN

The first family I found didn't even have time to scream when I swept down on them, flooding into their home through windows left open for the warm autumn breeze. They gasped, sure. They choked on attempted cries for help.

And then my magic ripped into them, changing them, eradicating every stupid thing they thought they'd ever been and leaving something better.

Me.

My will.

My power.

And then the next houses were waiting.

It was child's play to spot them, really. Unlike the former Beast, who'd honed in on whatever the hell our ancestors had, I had been a modern ruanir. The most skilled, sure, and the most talented, obviously. But my affinity for modern ruanir magic had carried with me, which meant that unlike the former Beast, now I could pick the flavor of ruanir magic off the wind like the world's most incredible tracker.

Which I was.

I'd already taken five neighborhoods. I had dozens of ruanir who had been hiding in their homes, dutifully waiting for word that the dehaian "threat" had been eliminated by the judges. Now they all belonged to me. Most were currently making their way south, heading for the California coast and the places where it was most common to see dehaians. I'd left some in place, though. Whole neighborhoods vanishing would have undoubtedly raised human suspicion eventually. Plus, they were keeping an eye on their areas for me. Regular little sleeper cells of strakirin, scattered throughout the northwest United States, though of course they didn't look any different. No, they looked as human as they had when they'd been ruanir. No one would know I'd changed them. Not till it was too late.

I couldn't wait to go after the ruanir in London, in Mumbai, in all the major cities and tiny territories all around the planet. I supposed this had probably been the judges' plan too—converting everyone they could into strakirin. All the better to rule the world.

The world that was mine now.

I left a single-story bungalow—all the people inside now belonging to me—and I swept across the empty road to the ramshackle, two-story Colonial that looked just like any other on the street—or on *any* neighborhood street, for that matter. Clearly not as set financially as some other ruanir, the families on this road were probably dependent on the judges for their very survival. Problems like that had been getting more and more common, after all. The stock market had tanked during the Great Depression, or the Great Recession, or at some other point along the line, and lots of ruanir who hadn't planned as well as my mother or me lost everything. The Judiciary had been only too happy to step in and provide "help" in the time of need.

Of course, that help came with strings. Lots of them, considering it was really just another tactic to put the common ruanir under the Judiciary's control.

I could do better than that.

The thirty-something-year-old man by the window cut off sharply in the middle of his phone call when I took him, and every little memory, every flash of identity vanished before he could even take a breath to scream. Up on the next level, a brunette woman stumbled when I grabbed her, and panic filled her eyes before she was gone. Two teenagers were in the next room, clearly home from school or homeschooled, though it didn't matter either way when their identities disappeared. The bedroom beyond theirs was aglow with pale yellow wallpaper, light blue bows and a mural of the ocean that—for an ocean-magic-terrified ruanir—was practically treasonous.

And a baby.

A fricking *baby*.

Well, damn.

I slowed down, studying the squirming kid inside a wooden crib lined with blue blankets and teddy-bear sheets. A few tousled strands of blond hair were plastered to its head, and its face was turned toward the open door like it could see me, though maybe it was just searching for its former mother.

Irritation flickered through me. I could kill it, but the body would probably start to smell and attract attention. I could change it into a strakirin, but what was the point of that? It's not like an infant was *useful*. The dictionary definition of the opposite, actually.

Whatever. The brat would make it a few days before dying, and I'd have my strakirin seal up the windows before they left.

I headed for the open window and the next house. The source of the Judiciary's signal was less than a mile away. I'd seen it from the air, a plain brick building masquerading as an industrial repair shop. All the ruanir in the area probably worked there, or at least they *had*, prior to my arrival. But I wasn't ready to head that way just yet. There were at least three more houses on this block that radiated ruanir magic, and I wasn't one to waste a perfectly good resource like that.

The baby started to bawl.

I slowed down. God, that was an annoying sound. More to the point, it'd attract attention, something I didn't want. Not yet.

Fine, I'd take care of it myself.

I reversed direction, heading for the crib again. The little brat screwed up its fists and face, howling like a banshee for all the world to hear.

It was amazing anyone had kids, given how irritating these things were. Its parents should thank me for getting rid of this crying, fleshy—

Magic sizzled through the air, burning any part of me still outside the house. I flinched back instinctively, my focus going from the baby to the street and the yard.

No one was there. What the hell?

The feeling got stronger, transitioning from a crackle like a static shock to the thrum of an overloaded socket. But I couldn't see the source. There wasn't a single person outside, though I couldn't get far from the house before the burning sensation became painful. It was almost like the cages the judges had tried to—

There.

Little metal stakes were planted in the yard by the corners of the property, some of them askew, others with upturned dirt around them, as if whoever shoved them into place had not only done it quickly, but recently too.

But they couldn't have known I was coming…

Wait. The man on the phone. He'd been by a window, one which faced the house I'd just come from. And if he'd seen anything…

There wasn't any point in asking him. Judge Engle may have waited to comb through the memories of his newly made strakirin before wiping their minds completely, but I'd never been one to dawdle. Like all of my strakirin, I'd obliterated the man's memory the moment I changed him.

That had never been a source of trouble until right now.

But then, there weren't many options for whom the guy had been calling, given that there weren't *any* other options for who would have done *this*.

Irritation growled through me. There was a judge here, somewhere. The bastard couldn't have gotten far.

A ragged sob tore the air. The baby again. And now there was a neighbor stepping outside, heading for her car only to pause at the sound.

Goddammit.

The burning sensation of static electricity on steroids was getting worse. *Much* worse.

I tossed a command to my strakirin to make the baby stop crying and then withdrew from the house, condensing myself into a tight, invisible force in the middle of the yard. The last cage the Judiciary had tried to use on me hadn't held. No way in hell this hastily concocted one would.

Magic crackled against me, burning like fire ants. I growled, making the nosy neighbor stop in her tracks and look around with alarm. Damn, damn, damn.

The magic failed.

With a triumphant snarl, I burst past the cage. The neighbor was on her cell phone now and running toward the house I'd just left. Probably calling the cops. The woman was too damn curious for her own good—though most idiots just called it *being* good. Regardless, she clearly didn't have an ounce of sense at all. But killing her would attract even more attention, and a dead baby might too.

I ordered my strakirin to leave the kid alive. Help it, feed it, whatever. Just play human to get the neighbor and the cops to stay away. I had a bigger problem.

I had a judge to find.

It took less than a minute to cross the distance to the supposed industrial repair building. I could feel the Judiciary's signal beating the air like a drum from hell. A field of magical energy surrounded the place, like that defense I'd felt around the resistance hideout months ago, the one that red-headed bitch, Willa, had blown up just to try to stop me.

And it hurt.

I snarled, the air rumbling like thunder in the clear blue sky while I seethed at the small metal spikes stabbed into the soil around the property. The dehaians had defenses, the resistance had defenses, now the goddamn judges thought they could stop me.

The bastards. I was the Beast reborn, and if *anyone* thought they could protect themselves against all the power I—

Wait.

Amusement flickered through me, silencing my rage. I reached down, sinking my magic into the ground below me. Storms and strakirin weren't my only powers. At least, I doubted they were. After all, the old Beast could shake the earth if it wanted, and I was *damn* well more powerful than that paltry excuse for a wannabe god.

The ground began to quiver. To shake and rumble and send the parked cars around the building bouncing. I focused the quake, directing it around the building even as I made the shaking grow stronger.

Fissures opened in the grass and dirt. Down into the openings tumbled the metal stakes carved with runes that held up the building's defenses. The shield around the place flickered and fell.

Perfect.

I swept downward. The doors caved under my assault, and the ruanir secretary at the front desk didn't last a heartbeat before she was mine as well. The halls were as boring as the outside of the building, the better to hold the illusion of being normal, but the judge was still easy to locate, back in a tiny office at the far end of the building. Blond-haired with a hooked nose and blotchy, pale skin, he reminded me of a skinny nerd who used to hide from me in middle school, all because I found him entertaining. This guy was young too, and appeared like he'd just been elevated from journeyman status yesterday.

He screamed when I grabbed him away from his desk.

Moron.

I drew down into human form, albeit a human made of storm clouds, and watched his beady eyes go wide. "Rel—"

My hand clamped over his mouth and then continued on, stretching beyond human proportions and wrapping around his head in a vice-like grip. Horror filled his beady eyes, and his fingers clawed at my hand, and the sight was hilarious. I let his fingers slip through mine, and in his desperation, he unintentionally ripped his nails across his own skin.

God, I could get used to this. And I would.

As soon as I found Ari.

My face twitched as I shoved the thought away. I was *getting* to that, the goddamn persistent…

Whatever.

"I have a question," I snapped at the judge. "You're going to answer it. And if you say that goddamn R-word, I'll turn you inside out and leave your corpse on the front of this building for the humans to find. But if you help me, I'll let you have some of this power. More than all the other judges combined. Deal?"

His struggles slowed, and I buried a smile. I'd suspected that would work. Young judge like him, bottom of the pecking order and stuck at a desk in some random research facility… oh, yeah, he'd want all the power he could get.

The fact he believed me made him truly an idiot, though.

Behind me, several enforcers rushed toward me only to fall when twin blasts of my lightning tore them down.

"What's it going to be, Judge?"

The guy's face was turning purple in my grip. He mumbled something that sounded like frantic agreement.

I cautiously took my hand from his mouth. "What is Ari?"

The judge stared at me. "What…?"

"Why does she matter to me?"

"I-I don't know who you're—"

"Zero-Zero-One, for God's sake! Why the hell is she important to me?"

"I don't—She was the first strakirin we made. Just the first one. The template. But that doesn't mean anything. She's the exact same as all the—"

"The hell she is!"

The judge's confusion was clear. The idiot had no clue about what I was going through.

Or none that he would tell me at least.

Fury snarled through me. Fine. The other way, then.

I sent my magic pouring into him, same as I did when I made a strakirin, but careful too. The last thing I wanted was this idiot to absorb even a *trace* of my power.

Not that it would make him able to fight me. He just didn't deserve a shred of *me*.

Shudders wracked him. I could feel the power inside him, changed to be distinct from other ruanir, and it was trying to slip away, trying to resist me. They'd been thorough, the judges. They'd tried to make themselves invincible against being changed into a strakirin. They'd obviously planned for contingencies, just in case I wasn't fully under their control.

They hadn't planned well enough.

The guy in my grasp was choking. Garbled noises escaped him, like he was gagging on his own tongue. But that wasn't what was important. The power inside him was starting to give. As my own magic twisted around it, pulled and plucked and picked at it, the defenses were beginning to cave.

Images flashed in my mind. Memories. Thoughts. He was slightly older than I'd suspected. More like a middle-manager than a bottom-rung judge, though every bit as power-hungry. But there was his history, and there was his identity, and yes, there was the moment they planned to make the strakirin. There were the books, the records, and all the hours spent learning a dead language just to understand them. There were the discussions, the debates, and the moment again... a new moment... another, when they figured out what they had to do if they wanted the creature they were going to create to... to...

His defenses gave entirely, collapsing in a wash of magic

that burned through the memories, through his identity and his entire mind.

Leaving only ash.

I withdrew from the wreckage, my attention returning to the man hanging limp in my grasp.

Or, now, the corpse.

My lip curled. Blood dripped from his blindly staring eyes, and drool hung from his slackened mouth. I couldn't feel a pulse beneath my fingers. I couldn't see him breathing.

And I knew what had happened. I'd seen it, right before the end. Their final solution, in case their defenses against me didn't work.

Suicide.

I dropped his body, ignoring it as it toppled like a marionette with cut strings. Fine. Even if the judges would rather die than be made into strakirin, that didn't mean they weren't still useful. This one had been, after all, because their nuclear option of killing themselves hadn't been the only thing I'd seen.

I knew what had gone wrong in their grand little plan, what they'd never suspected, because they hadn't been asking the right questions or checking the right things, and what they still didn't suspect, even now. I knew why I'd been so focused on her. I didn't *need* Ari. Quite the opposite.

I needed her dead.

24

ARI

I lost the enforcers after the first turn, and couldn't hear them anymore after the third. The strakirin chased me, the ones who could run helping the ones who couldn't, and all the while, the drone carried on.

The song, Luna had called it. Even now, I couldn't hear it that way.

I wasn't sure I wanted to.

But I could feel the others. Even Luna and Leo now. They'd woken up fully a few minutes ago, though several of the others were still helping them run. It'd taken a bit to convince them to join this hive, that it wasn't some trick from the Judiciary—a fear I understood all too well.

I'd never seen a bigger grin than Luna's when they finally did, though.

It wasn't what they'd feared. What I'd feared. It was unlike anything I'd ever imagined, and *nothing* like what I'd been trapped inside before. The adrenaline of the hive pounded through me now, along with the strakirins' exhilaration at escaping the cells that had held some of them for weeks or longer. Jennifer hadn't seen daylight since she was a child, and a few of the others…

Memories flashed behind my eyes. Children of resistance members or other dissidents, held for leverage or experiments or both. Others were orphans, brought in when the Judiciary wanted more strakirin or more examples of "ocean magic poisoning" to keep the populace in line. Still more had been volunteers like Luna and Leo, leaving behind families who'd been hurt or killed by supposed dehaian attacks.

The ruin and refuse of the Judiciary's attempts to control the ruanir world.

I yanked open another door, only to stumble to a stop at the sight of the cages arrayed on the warehouse floor below us. We stood on a catwalk that extended around the massive space and crisscrossed it as well, and chain-link fencing squared off areas like cells nearly twenty feet below. Leather-strapped chairs that looked like they belonged in a dentist's office from hell stood inside each cube.

Shivers crawled over my skin. Strakirin. This had to be where they made strakirin, because I remembered those chairs. Remembered being strapped into one when the judges did this to me, months ago when the world still felt somewhat sane and I trusted that the Judiciary was only interested in the good of all ruanir.

It felt like a lifetime ago.

The cages were empty, though. Almost all of them, anyway, and the one that wasn't…

My stomach turned at the sight of the dead man sprawled on one of the chairs, his body prevented from collapsing fully to the ground by the straps still holding him down. He was blond, with a scar on his left cheek and dark brown eyes that stared sightlessly upward.

And he was familiar.

The memory took a moment to click into place, and adrenaline rushed through me when it did.

I'd seen him with the resistance.

I spun toward the strakirin behind me, eyes wide, and it only took a thought for my questions to be heard. Maia. Was she here? Had they seen her?

The drone grew louder, just for a moment, the hive thinking, remembering, seeing her image in my memory.

Yes.

A scene flashed through my mind like a movie. A dark-haired girl being dragged past the cages below, hauled up some stairs toward a heavily guarded door on the other end of the room from us. One of the newest recruits, newest failures in the strakirin conversion, had seen her when the enforcers brought them to their cell only a day ago.

New shouts broke out below me, yanking me from the memory. Enforcers. Lots of them. And they had guns.

The debate ran through the hive in a heartbeat, and then we decided.

Half the strakirin leapt the guardrail of the walkway while the rest of us took off running. The enforcers shouted, their guns rising, aiming. Bullets tore the air, too slow.

Almost too slow.

A snarl of pain ripped through the hive as a bullet drove through the shoulder of one of the strakirin who'd jumped. The boy crashed to the warehouse floor and curled in on himself, whimpering with pain and clutching his wounded shoulder.

I staggered, gripped by the pain radiating up from him. I couldn't tell if my rage was my own or that of the hive.

But it didn't really matter. Not right now.

Not when the enforcers were firing at us again.

On the walkway, we ducked and ran while the strakirin below us raced between the cages, faster than the enforcers could aim. Fear pulsed out of the strakirin in a wave. The enforcers struggled to hold their ground, terror obvious on their faces. Darting around the cages, the strakirin didn't hesitate, slicing their spikes at the enforcers and then speeding on to the next, tearing them down. Racing across the metal walkway, I didn't even need to look to know we were winning.

But where were the judges?

As if summoned by my thought, another door swung open at the far end of the warehouse. I glimpsed a carpeted hallway and something green like a potted plant beyond, and then the judges were there. Three of them, standing on the walkway on the opposite side of the warehouse, glaring at us like imperious, offended deities.

"Stop!" one of the judges declared. "Your masters command you!"

The hive growled, resisting the order. The strakirin with me hadn't joined the primary hive, hadn't been converted properly.

Even though they could feel the compulsion to obey, their wills were still intact.

Like hell they'd listen to the judges now.

The judges each raised a hand. A wave of dead-swamp magic rolled out from them, chilling the air, making it clammy against my skin.

Oh, God.

"Run!" I screamed.

The noxious magic hit the strakirin closest to the judges. Their hands flew to their throats, and I could feel their pain and their desperate attempts to breathe past the toxic, amorphous power flowing around them.

The judges smiled.

On the warehouse floor, one of the strakirin lashed out with lightning, trying to strike the judges.

An enforcer shoved their master aside, taking the blast.

Without even a pause for the death of his bodyguard, the judge turned, aiming his magic at the strakirin who'd tried to attack him, grinning as the kid began to choke and die.

Help.

Can't breathe.

Do something!

I didn't know how to answer the hive. The door was behind me, with Maia hopefully somewhere on the other side. The judges were on the other end of the warehouse and too far for me to hit with lightning, at least not without hitting anyone else. I couldn't reach them in time.

But I could feel the strakirins' pain, their struggle. The toxic wave of magic rolled across the warehouse floor, toward us like an invisible cloud of poison and death.

Do something! screamed the hive.

Pain radiated through me. My hands gripped the walkway guardrail as the strakirin, *my* strakirin, the broken and the abandoned… they all started to die.

Key.

I didn't know what that meant.

Save us.

I didn't know how.

Please…

"Please," whispered Jennifer next to me. "You're more of what he is than any of us."

I turned sharply. "What?"

The magic hit us. Jennifer started to choke. A sickly sensation of mud and decay rolled over me, coating my skin with invisible slime, pouring down my throat like sludge. I saw Jennifer fall next to me; the strakirin on the other side of me did as well. I gripped the guardrail, my gaze rising to the three judges, who grinned as their creations died.

Rage burned inside me. They killed and killed. They'd killed so many, claiming ocean magic poisoning, and it had always been a lie. They'd tried to kill Noah.

Now they wanted to kill us all too.

My thoughts slowed, the world drawing down toward a long, dark tunnel while lights flared at the edges of my vision.

Noah…

Here.

My grip spasmed on the guardrail. I could hear him again.

Memory flared behind my eyes. Declan on the ground gasping. My hand on the man's arm.

Noah holding me, taking in the poison too.

The poison I'd already drawn in.

My gaze rose again, finding the judges.

More like him than any of us…

"Find Maia," I gasped to the hive.

I grabbed Jennifer's arm and drew the judges' magic into myself.

Liars…

Torturers…

Let go!

My body was burning.

Magic poured into me, linked through Jennifer to the strakirin next to her, and the one next to that, on and on. I wasn't even touching them, and yet… I was touching them. My hands were holding Luna's, holding Leo's. I was down there, with the strakirin on the warehouse floor. And over there too, with the boy on his own, choking to death in a corner while his shoulder bled from a bullet wound.

My body was exploding.

The magic roiled inside me, building higher and higher. I couldn't contain it. The power was tearing me apart. I wasn't

Noah, the Beast, a magnificent creature miles wide. I was a person. One small, sort-of-strakirin girl standing on a walkway, screaming.

I was everywhere.

Ari…

Tears slipped from my eyes, turning to steam. I could hear him so clearly now, as if he was standing by my side. I could feel his hands on mine, his arms around me and his chest at my back, steadying me amid the onslaught. God, I missed him. Needed him. My body craved him, and my heart did as well.

Did he miss me too?

Love poured through me, surrounding me, engulfing me like the sea. *Yes.*

"Where are you?" I couldn't tell if I thought the words or said them out loud, but an image came to me. The amphitheater. Huge rocks suspended above me, an eerie blue glow to the water, and faces… burned faces surrounding me, and oh my God, they…

The image disappeared like someone had pulled it away. *I'm trapped here,* he said.

"What was that?" I asked.

He paused. *Old memories. It doesn't matter.* And then another pause followed, a pained one like he was torn. *Ari, this power is too much. You need to let go of it.*

"No. No, I need to find you. I need to—"

Heartache filled the voice in my mind. *Let go, Ari.*

I shook my head. I didn't want to lose him. And I didn't know how to do what he asked. People would die if I let go of this.

You have to.

No, I—

There…

The judges were moving. With sight that came from all the eyes around me, I could see them. They were running toward us. Their enforcers were aiming guns at us.

Now.

A shudder went through me, so hard it felt like my bones were going to snap. My hands crushed down on the guardrail, and my eyes locked on the judges. The bastards who'd made us.

The liars.

Magic erupted from me, waves of it pouring from my skin, from every inch of my body. Lightning crackled from the dark torrent. I was screaming, I knew, but I couldn't hear my own voice. I couldn't hear anything over the howl of the magic flooding out from me, coursing over the warehouse, evading everyone I didn't want it to touch.

Slamming hard into the ones I did.

The enforcers collapsed, and the judges stumbled back, their faces stricken with horror. They started choking, started falling, their hands clutching their throats for all of a moment before the end. Like rag dolls, they sagged limp to the ground, their mouths and unseeing eyes wide.

Rough breaths left my lungs. Sound returned, and sensation too. I was me, in my own body, one person standing on a metal walkway.

Without Noah.

I crushed my lips together, tears prickling in my eyes, and I tried to give no sign. I couldn't feel him anymore, not like I had. He was just… gone.

Beside me, Jennifer groaned.

"Y-you okay?" I rasped, my voice hoarse from screaming.

She nodded, appearing as unsteady as I felt. I looked around to the other strakirin, and confirmation came from them as well. They were okay. More than okay. A flood of elation built around me, surging up from the hive; a clamor of relief and joy and gratitude that made me gasp all over again.

They were alive. The judges weren't.

We'd won. We'd beaten judges.

I'd beaten judges.

I fought for a breath, trying to focus and stay standing against waves of joy that felt so strong, they could take me off my feet. We weren't out of the woods yet. We were in the middle of the judges' facility, for pity's sake, and we had to make it out of here no matter what the Judiciary tried.

The hive's elation cooled. They understood.

I nodded to their silent agreement and glanced around, still hanging onto the guardrail to keep myself standing. The enforcers were dead. The judges too. And that left the door to where Maia was being held on the far end of the walkway, along with whatever else was waiting behind it.

But first…

Tentatively, I reached out in my mind again, afraid of what I already knew. *Noah?* I waited. *Noah?*

I couldn't find him.

Not gone, the hive whispered.

I looked at the others in alarm. They'd said that before. They'd said it, and I heard him and…

"Can you feel him too?"

The hive was quiet for a moment. "He's far away," Jennifer said.

Trapped, the hive echoed.

He'd said that. "Did you hear that through—"

She was already shaking her head. "We can feel it. Something between him and… you."

I knew what she'd almost said. "Us."

She nodded, appearing uncomfortable.

I felt the same. "Is he part of… of the hive?"

She hesitated, but the answer came from the others around me.

Part of you.

"But," I looked around at the others, at a loss. The judges used me as the template, but they'd gotten the magic to change me from Noah. So why…

I reached for him again, more forcefully, grasping at the connection between us like it was a rope through which, by God, I would pull him home.

And then I staggered like I'd physically run into a wall. A murky, amorphous *nothing* wall that separated us like a barricade of solid fog. Only my hold on the guardrail kept me from collapsing to the ground entirely.

Shivers coursed through me. *Noah?* I called inside my head.

A whisper of… of something reached me. His voice, maybe.

Or a distant echo of my own cry.

Jennifer's hand rested on mine. Sympathy was clear on her face.

I closed my eyes tightly. Right. Escape now. Evaluate later. And save Maia.

I started to turn, but my legs felt as wobbly as a newborn foal's. My entire body was quivering like I'd just been electrocuted.

I drew another breath. I could do this. I was just me again. Me, same as always. Not… whatever that had been a moment ago when I'd thought I was everywhere.

Just me, on two legs, walking.

Repeating the crazy pep talk to myself, I made myself release the guardrail.

Imprints of my fingers were crushed into the metal.

I looked up at Jennifer in alarm.

"More like him than any of us," she said. The hive echoed her words.

My hand hung motionless in the air for a moment before I drew it back to me. Shivers ran through my skin, and hesitantly, I chafed my arms.

Once upon a time, Noah had said I *wasn't* like him. That I wasn't becoming like him. He'd held me on Baylie's porch while the dark waves rushed toward the shore and told me I was something else.

Later, I'd concluded that just meant I was strakirin.

The key, whispered the hive.

But what *is* that? I pleaded silently.

No answer, and then knowledge that didn't make anything better at all.

They knew what I was, insofar as the fact I was different than them. Unique and needed and vital for their survival, and the only word they had for that was "key." They could feel the truth of it, inside every one of them. But even the hive didn't know what it meant.

Or why.

25

NOAH

"Ari?" I stared at the boulders overhead, shouting like a crazy person in the middle of a park. "Ari!"

Or in a stadium of ghosts.

"Ari!"

The boulders overhead groaned as my voice bounced from the ruins of the amphitheater walls. A furious snarl escaped me, and I turned away, raking my hands into my hair like I was about to pull it out. Goddammit, I'd heard her. Felt her presence.

Maybe helped her.

I squeezed my eyes shut. There was that. Possibly, anyway. Though how the hell she'd managed…

Judges. That'd been their magic, floods and floods of it, and she'd taken it all in. But it hadn't killed her—thankfully. Oh, God, thankfully. And for one moment, one blessed moment, I'd heard her so clearly, it was like the magical prison around me was nothing. I'd been there, almost as if I was with her, and my whole body ached with the memory of it and the fact that it hadn't been real. Not like I wanted it, anyway.

If I got back to her—no, *when*—I was never going to leave her side again.

I dropped my hands from my hair and looked around. The judges' magic had helped us reach each other, as insane as that seemed, and that wasn't the only thing.

Liars…

That'd been me, not her. The Beast side of me, buried so deep down that I could barely even pick up on it anymore. But I knew who the liars were, and they hadn't been with her.

Had they?

I turned, searching for the ghosts. Back where I'd entered the amphitheater, in the ruins of an archway that led to the canyon, the woman hovered.

I'd swear she was watching me with fear.

"What the hell are they? The judges?"

She didn't respond.

Of course she didn't.

An infuriated noise left me. The ruanir had been part of creating me, and I remembered hearing how the judges possessed the closest thing to the kind of magic the ancient ruanir had. So maybe the Beast side of me had just recognized it. And it wasn't like the judges hadn't done their fair share of lying, regardless. What happened to Ari was proof enough of that.

But their magic had passed through the prison around me.

Their ancestors' magic had helped *make* the prison around me.

A prison that killed their ancestors, and everyone else, a

thousand years before.

I studied the rocks overhead while pale sheets of dust and gravel sifted down onto the amphitheater around me. That wasn't exactly true. Their trap hadn't killed them, my magic and the destabilized spell to create the trap had. Before I broke out, the spell had been passing around them, leaving them untouched even as it drained me down into nothingness.

Their magic hadn't been affected at all.

But how did that connect to the power currently pouring up through the center of the amphitheater, power that had cracked the prison around me but that was also somehow trapping me in human form?

Though the ghost woman called the latter part of that a *choice*.

I turned back to her. "Why can't I change shape? That wasn't anything I chose."

She didn't say a word, yet despite the burns and the damage to her face, I could still read her expression.

Yes, I had.

"I chose to be in human form. I didn't—"

She pointed to the invisible vine of magic pouring up from the center of the amphitheater. *Power.* She gestured to the area around us. *Change.* Her finger leveled at me. *Choice.*

I blinked. "What?"

She looked away like, if she were still capable of making sound, she'd groan with exasperation, and it was everything I could do not to laugh with incredulity. I was annoying a ghost. Awesome.

But then her irritation seemed to fade. Something like sorrow crossed her burned face while her eyes scanned the ruins of the amphitheater and the canyon beyond. *Choice,* she said again, something strange in the word, in the sound it made inside my mind.

Almost like sadness. Like resolution.

Like a sigh.

But she didn't say anything else.

I worked my jaw around, searching for a response that didn't involve shouting at a dead woman. I wasn't *choosing* to become like a human at the bottom of the ocean. Why would I ever choose…

My thoughts slowed.

…choose something like that.

I looked back at the invisible rope of magic climbing up through the amphitheater, chills creeping through me. I already knew the Beast side of me had chosen to become like this for protection, for a chance at life. But what would the greliaran part of me have given this past year to be human-like again? To be *normal* again, even if only by a fairly unusual standard?

Anything. That was the truth. Just about *anything*.

My gaze dropped to the gravel beneath me. Was that it? Was this power starting to turn me back to a real, flesh-and-blood person again because of some weird combination of protection and subconscious desire?

Could it?

The implications rolled through me, a wave of all the plans I'd thought I had to leave behind, back when I became this.

College. Family. A career and a house and a *life*.

Oh my God, a normal life.

What if it didn't stop there? What if this magic could help Ari too? Change her back, give her the chance to go through the adjustment like all her people did, and give her the centuries' worth of life she would've had if this summer hadn't happened.

And everything I'd become—everything *we'd* become—would be gone.

At the thought, a weird feeling twisted in my middle, warring with the elation holding me in its grip. The sensation wasn't worry. Not quite like fear, either. More like the sense that the ground beneath me was unsteady. That I was overlooking some important, integral flaw.

My eyes rose to the barricade of stones overhead. *Ari?* I called in my mind. *Ari?*

Whispers reached me, nothing else.

I looked away. If I did this, if I changed us both back, we wouldn't have our connection anymore. On top of that, Ari could become basically immortal—or close enough compared to me. I'd live a normal, human life span, dying an old man by the time she barely looked… what? Thirty-five? Maybe forty? God help me, I didn't want that.

But I also couldn't make the decision for her. If there was a chance for both of us to have our lives back…

Deep inside me, the Beast side rumbled.

My discomfort grew. It couldn't stop me. And if I wanted to, I could ignore it. Obliterate it.

Forever.

If I wanted to...

I looked up at the ghost woman. She'd drifted closer now, watching me like she could see the thoughts rolling through my mind.

For all I knew, she could.

"What was the Beast? Before the war, what was it supposed to be?"

She regarded me with the sad patience of someone who'd answered the question several times before, but knew their answer hadn't been sufficient. And I didn't know what I'd expected, anyway. The power pouring through the amphitheater was disrupting the way she spoke. Only single words reached me now, and "salvation" didn't make any sense at all.

Her expression unchanged, she reached out and interlaced her fingers with my own. *Take.*

"What?"

A cold sensation crept across my hand where she held it. Her magic. Her power, cold and clammy like thick fog. *Take.*

She wanted me to absorb what she had?

My eyes darted toward the center of the amphitheater. Using even a trace of the abilities I'd gotten from the Beast—the ability to survive underwater notwithstanding—set the prison to draining me. And that power there, it wanted to drain me too. To use those abilities now...

Take.

"Why?"

Understand.

That wasn't much of an answer.

Like I'd get more of one? We were down to single words here.

I closed my eyes. My greliaran side had been made to absorb magic too, albeit not like this. But I'd taken in magic once, under the ocean when those cultish bastards who wanted Chloe dead had attacked us. And no, this wasn't the same. I wasn't killing a dehaian with my bare hands—a memory that some-how still managed to make my skin crawl, even after spending a year as the Beast.

But maybe I could do this too.

I concentrated hard on only where she held my hand, on letting in her magic and nothing more, on keeping the entire world and everything around me outside myself except for this one tiny trace of magic that—

Light and color and sensation poured into me in a wave of impressions and sound, distilling into information like my mind was downloading an entire library in one moment. Centuries of life on the island, of dehaians and ruanir and even humans from time to time. History that turned to myth, that turned to nothing, after I destroyed their civilization. But before… oh, before…

Her hand withdrew from mine. Reeling, I opened my eyes again.

She was nothing but a faint shape in the water.

I stared, frozen with horror and guilt. Her body was almost gone, only a few wisps of gray-white fog in the water denoting her form. Her face consisted of only a hint of pale features amid the eerie blue-green light.

I'd almost destroyed her.

She smiled like she'd known what would happen all along. *Understand?*

I nodded. I'd been their answer. Centuries of dehaians and ruanir living side by side, of two civilizations intertwined, but never fully made one, forever kept apart because they were not the same, could not be the same. Even their biology was different. Ruanir lived for centuries, sustained by their power but unable to leave the human shape in which they'd been born. Dehaians changed form and lived beneath the waves, but only marginally exceeded a human life span. Their magic likewise seemed incompatible, for all that it came from the ocean, and every attempt to blend the two had resulted only in failure and death.

Until me.

Until millennia of magic use on the island had produced what even the long-lived ruanir could not. A form of magic that was made of both, that had merged naturally and gradually in the rocks and the sands, in the waves and the depths, until it was something new. And the ones who made me, the most advanced and skilled magic-users of their time, they'd drawn on that power together, crafting it and taking from it with only one goal.

To join their people.

To give the ruanir the gift of going beneath the waves. To give the dehaians longer lives. To bring peace to the tensions between the ruanir and the dehaians, and to give them both the ability to be one people, once and for all.

Salvation, the ghost woman whispered.

"But the others… the ones who tried to stop you…"

Purists.

I remembered. Remembered Osias describing his ancestors that way, back before he unleashed the magic here. Remembered watching the attackers race into the amphitheater on the day I'd been born. Remembered the fear the woman in front of me had felt that they might destroy what she and the others had made, the unexpected form of life they'd discovered, on the very day they'd finally achieved what generations of dehaians and ruanir could not.

Because the purists were afraid. Because they wanted power and believed that joining their people wouldn't make their civilizations richer; it would destroy them. Dehaian or ruanir, the purists never saw the irony that they were actually the same. They both wanted to lock the world into one moment, just as it was, because this was the moment they felt strong, and they were scared, so scared, that someone would take that from them.

And so they killed instead. The ruanir purists assassinated the peaceful king of the ruanir for his support of the merging, and then they blamed the dehaians. The dehaian purists retaliated and wiped out innocent villages and towns. And then they came for me.

Then they turned me from the force that could have joined their people, that could have changed all their lives, and made me into a weapon of death and annihilation instead.

The woman reached up, the wisps of her hand brushing my cheek like a cool breath. *Choice.*

I knew what she meant. The Beast had chosen this, chosen to be more than a weapon, chosen not to kill but, instead, to become the guy whose life it'd almost taken.

My discomfort returned, as if I stood at the fork in the road.

Because I could choose as well. That power pouring up through the center of the amphitheater had cracked the prison around me. Maybe it could destroy it entirely. But more than that, it could give me my life back. Everything I'd been. Everything I'd dreamed of being. Everything... at only one cost.

The death of a creature who was now at my mercy, who couldn't stop me if it tried.

"Is there another option?" I tried. "Some way to separate us or..."

I trailed off, discomfort stirring in me at the conflicted look in her eyes. I could hardly even feel the Beast, but I still remembered the truth. The Beast had wanted to live. To have a life, so it'd taken mine.

And not taken it. I was still here, after all. Still mostly, sort of, almost entirely me, minus the lack of warmth in my skin or any kind of real body. And even that had been changing over the past few weeks. Not back to normal, no, but—

The feeling of the water changed.

I froze. Nothing around me seemed different. Nothing in the invisible vine of magic even felt different. And yet something... something was...

Coming.

Goosebumps crawled over my skin, a more human reaction than I'd had in a year. Through the fractures in the prison, I could feel a whisper of something out there, small but growing larger with every second, descending toward me like an aster-oid falling to the earth. A roar built in the water like an aircraft carrier coming in to land, and cascades of rock tumbled from the canyon walls.

Oh, God.

The barricade above me exploded downward, chunks of boulders shredding through the water like missiles while magic surged in a technicolor display of blinding light in their wake. The vine of magic surged and warped, pulsing so hard that it made my chest feel like all the air had been crushed out. I had only a moment to try to swim away, only a moment to see the amphitheater coming down around me.

And then the blast wave hit.

I groaned. I hurt. Everything hurt. And something was tugging on my arm.

I opened my eyes and then froze. A slab of stone rested only inches from my face, so close that I could see minuscule flecks of silver and white in its brown surface. Sand and gravel pressed hard against my back, while my right foot was twisted awk-wardly, centimeters from being smashed by the rock above me.

Only the canyon wall behind me had stopped the massive rock from falling onto me fully.

My gaze skirted to the side. The ghost woman was there, the faint outlines of her fingers frantically plucking at my arm. Worry creased the pale lines of her face as she looked from me to whatever waited beyond the rock on top of me.

A hissing-scraping sound came from the slab of stone as it slipped a few millimeters farther down, its weight beginning to press hard on my foot.

Oh, *shit*.

I wriggled sideways as fast as I could move, twisting to crawl and swim and get myself the hell out of there the moment my upper torso was out from under the rock. The scraping sound grew louder, the slab sliding against the seafloor and then crashing down behind me, sending up a cloud of sand.

I treaded water, shaking all over and staring at where the block of stone lay. I was okay. I was alive. I hadn't been crushed.

Oh my God, I could have been crushed.

Frantically, I checked over my body for wounds, finding none, and then rubbed a hand to my face in a desperate attempt to calm down. The water was strange—or at least stranger than it had been. A gloomy blur of debris and grit illuminated by a harsh, coming-from-everywhere kind of light. It made me want to squint, as if it came from a lightbulb flickering so quickly that it was giving me a headache. Meanwhile, gray clouds of sand hovered in the water, casting a haze over the canyon.

What was left of it.

The ghost woman tugged at my arm. *Danger.*

No kidding. The canyon walls had collapsed around me, sloughing into the chasm and carrying the crumbled pillars and ruins of the island with them. Scarcely any of the seafloor remained uncovered by rocks and boulders now. And as for the barricade above me…

Shivers rushed over my skin. The rocks were still there—sort of, anyway. They were closer than they had been, much closer, but large gaps showed between them now.

Gaps with inky black darkness in them… and for reasons I couldn't even begin to name, that darkness felt really, *really* hungry.

"What is that?" In spite of myself, the question came out as a whisper.

Collapse. She tugged on my arm again.

I didn't look away from the darkness between the impossibly suspended rocks. "Of what?"

Trap.

Right. That's what I'd been afraid of.

She tugged at me a third time. *Danger.*

I knew that. I was staring right at it. The damned thing was only about twenty feet from my head.

But what caused the trap around me to collapse?

The thought pulled my attention from the barricade like a tether. Boulders lurked like hulking shadows amid the clouds of sand, hiding God knew what behind them, and all around me, the water seemed to vibrate with that strange light and the tingle of electricity that preceded a lightning strike. I was far outside the amphitheater, blown back into the canyon by whatever had just happened, and I couldn't see past the clouds of sand and grit to tell if the place still stood. Maybe it was buried under tons upon tons of rock.

Maybe that magic was too.

My eyes lingered on the direction of the amphitheater while my hands chafed my arms. That wasn't a good thing, obviously. I needed that magic to get the hell out of here. But as for what else it could do—

"Are you there, Beast?"

I froze all over again. The booming voice carried through the water like it came from a giant.

And I was Jack, standing out in the open like an idiot after I'd stupidly climbed the beanstalk.

Beside a boulder the size of an upturned semi-truck, the ghost woman appeared, waving her hands urgently. I kicked as hard as I could, struggling through the water to reach her side. A sliver of a gap revealed a tiny cave in the canyon wall, almost completely obscured by the enormous stone in front of it.

The ghost woman motioned for me to swim inside, and trepidation gripped me. I'd just survived almost being crushed. Being buried alive didn't sound like much of an improvement.

"Is that some tiny scrap of you," the voice called, "hiding as you try to steal my strength?"

The magic in the water warped like it had when that invisible vine had first appeared at the center of the amphitheater, drawing everything toward it and hauling on me like it wanted to drag me into oblivion.

Or hell.

I grabbed at the rock, my debate ending abruptly. Possible death by invisible, magical whirlpool, or potential imprisonment in a cave.

At least I might be able to get out of the cave.

Stones tumbled down from the top of the canyon, crushing smaller rocks around me. With a snarl of effort, I hauled myself around the edge of the enormous boulder shielding the small hollow. My fingers dug into the canyon wall, and then into the cave wall when I climbed inside the small space. Even here, the water glowed faintly, a dim blue-white illumination that I suddenly wished would go away, if only to give me shadows in which to conceal myself.

The tugging power in the water grew stronger.

From within the hiding place, the ghost woman snagged me, the cold wisps of her fingers gripping my shoulders as if to hold me there. More hands appeared, more arms too, coming from the walls in a way that would be nightmarish if it wasn't for the fact they were helping me. Ghosts upon ghosts crowded the tiny space, holding onto me.

Saving me.

Abomination.

That was the ghost woman. And it didn't matter if I couldn't see what was trying to hurt me, what was chuckling like a ravenous monster, somewhere beyond this tiny grotto.

I agreed.

"It was a neat trick," came the voice, "making a clone of your power out there."

What? I looked toward the narrow gap between the cave and

the boulder blocking it. What the hell was that thing talking about?

"As if that could save you." Derision dripped from the voice. "Or her."

A shape moved past the stone shielding the cave.

My fingers dug into the rock involuntarily, though thankfully the sound of the wall crunching in my grip blended with the rumble of the chasm collapsing around us. The thing out there wasn't human. Not anymore, though there wasn't really a chance it would be, down here at the bottom of the ocean. It wasn't dehaian or strakirin, either, but instead looked like a nightmare version of a man.

And I knew him. I'd seen him in the Judiciary lab that day when enforcers kidnapped Ari off the street outside Baylie's apartment.

Judge Engle.

His skin glowed like white fabric under a blacklight. The long folds of his suit were made from a darkness so deep, so hungry, that they seemed to draw all life into them. Lightning crackled from his black hair, and dark smoke drifted up around him. He floated through the water, hovering a few feet above the seafloor, his hands folded behind him and his radiant-white, contemptuous expression surveying the canyon like a preacher certain of his right to condemn the world to Hell.

Shivers crept through me. This was it, then. What they'd done to themselves. What I'd connected to, if only for a moment. This was what they'd used the strakirin and that magic pouring up from the center of the amphitheater to make themselves become.

But where were the other judges? And what did he mean, *her*? Ari?

Oh, God, what did he know about Ari?

I reached for her instinctively, desperate to make sure she was okay, but I couldn't get past the walls of the trap. Whatever this thing had done, it was making the walls shift and waver so much that any cracks I'd managed to form in them were moving too fast for me to hear anything.

"She's not going to stop me, Beast. The Judiciary worked for years to create the strakirin. You think one little former land-walker is going to change anything?"

Wait, *what*?

"Or was she human? Maybe a dehaian? How many little pseudo-wizards did you make out there, trying to protect your-self against what you had no hope of stopping?"

The ghost woman turned, and from the corner of my eye, I could see her staring at me. *Wizard?* she asked. In my head, she sounded shocked. Incredulous even, and maybe a bit excited. *Like… you?*

The creature was moving away now, his voice more distant than before. I couldn't ask what the hell that thing meant, though. Couldn't risk even a chance of being overheard. I didn't know what that creature was out there, but I wasn't an idiot. In human form, unable to change shape…

Fighting that wouldn't end well.

"Was it some old programming, Beast? Some vestige of your purpose?"

My attention snapped back toward the opening of the cave.

"Some memory of why those fools made you?"

I didn't move. I wouldn't be that idiotic. But it was difficult. This thing knew why I'd been made?

Of course he did. The dehaians might have forgotten, but Osias had also said the judges kept records. That they'd worked for a thousand years to recreate the spell and use it for their own ends.

To make the strakirin. To make themselves into this.

And, for some reason, to destroy me at the same time.

I watched the opening of the cave, motionless. The judges had wanted me dead. Maybe to keep others from using my magic to create other things, maybe to stop me from interfering. But whatever it was, my death was still their goal. He'd kill me the moment I left the cave. I understood that like it was written on the walls around me. This was bait.

"Are you connected to that little blond girl, Beast?"

Ice shot through me. Blond girl? Blond. Girl.

Oh my *God*.

It wasn't possible. He couldn't be talking about Baylie, but who the hell else was there for me to be connected to?

But… a wizard? Baylie wasn't a *wizard*.

Was she?

The memory returned to me of how it'd felt when I tried to reach through our connection to her. Dark and strange and like a reflection in a nearly pitch-black room. Like a low-level current of electricity too.

What'd happened? *How* had it happened? Shannon shooting

her shouldn't have done that, and a coma—weird and end-less as it'd been—shouldn't have either. And as for the magic around her, there was that bizarre experiment the resistance was trying, but surely no one had exposed her to enough of that energy to…

To…

The pieces fell into place in my mind like I was watching a puzzle assemble itself. A year ago, when the Beast side of me attacked Joseph's house and…

This *was* me. But why hadn't I felt it? Why hadn't I known?

Because I'd never checked.

My eyes twitched over the cave walls and the faintly glowing water all around me. Because maybe something had changed.

"Will it hurt you when my people cut her apart?"

My teeth clenched. He was trying to scare me, and I knew it was working. But more than that, he was trying to infuriate me.

And that was working too.

I glanced at the ghost woman and then to the others around her. To a person, their attention was locked on the opening to the cave, though at my movement, the woman's burned face turned back toward me again.

I couldn't speak. Even if it was moving away, that thing might still hear me. But then, early on in this nightmare prison, I hadn't needed to speak out loud, anyway. So maybe I could ask without—

I didn't even finish the thought before the answer came.

Take.

Wait, she wanted me to…

I shook my head. I'd kill her. Or something, anyway. But she'd be gone. There was barely any of her left, even now. And what good would it do? I'd still be trapped here.

A faint smile crossed the outlines of her face, and then she looked to the others. They were all watching me now. *Take.*

More words reached me from the ghosts around me.

Find.

Anchor.

Pull.

Way… out.

And I thought I understood. Some of it, anyway. The judges' magic had helped Ari reach me. Maybe this could do the reverse.

Except it would kill the ones who were helping me.

"I know you think you care about others, Beast. Would you like to know how we dissect our enemies? The traits we take from them, and how they scream as they die?"

I closed my eyes. My hands clenched into fists, my entire body shaking with the effort to keep from going out there and bringing whatever remained of this prison down on that bastard's head.

Cool fingers brushed my cheek. *Precious… one.*

I opened my eyes. She was watching me.

Take.

But…

Please.

I didn't want to kill whatever was left of this person who'd helped me.

Her hand cupped my face gently. *Already… gone.*

My chest hurt, the weight of what I could do crushing down on me. I never even learned her name, I realized. Never asked, and she'd never said.

A hint of a smile lifted the unburned edge of her mouth, almost amused. *Alessandra.*

Her fingers fell from my cheek to rest on my forearm. Around me, the others moved too, their hands touching my shoulders, my arms.

Take.

I did.

26

BAYLIE

After the first dozen bodies, I retreated to the edge of the yard, a gray wool blanket around my shoulders. I wasn't cold, but I couldn't stop shaking. Angelica was dead. Most of the dehaians and all of the human security guards too. Their bodies were laid out near the house, sheets and curtains and whatever else could be salvaged covering them.

But Chloe and Zeke were okay, as were their bodyguards, Damerion and Ezio. About two dozen other dehaians had survived as well, though that felt like nothing compared to the army they'd had yesterday. Meanwhile, Ellie, Olivia, and Declan were okay too. They'd hidden in the secure subbasement where, by some miracle, the monster hadn't found them.

No one could locate Ari or the strakirin kids.

"I couldn't… I couldn't…" On the ground next to the large, sand-colored rock on which I perched, Wyatt sat, his arms wrapped around his knees. He hadn't left my side since Olivia found him inside a closet upstairs, buried under a pile of coats, blankets, and crumbled drywall. Angelica's body lay a few feet away, crushed beneath a beam from the ceiling and sprawled toward the closet as if she'd been trying to join Wyatt in hiding.

There just hadn't been time.

"I couldn't save her," Wyatt whispered. "The… the clouds… I couldn't…" He fell silent, though I could see him trembling.

I glanced down at him, distantly curious at why it would have even occurred to him to save anyone, but I didn't say anything. Broaching the topic felt like too much right now, like it might shatter the quivering numbness protecting me from the death and destruction behind me. It was good he hadn't attacked the dehaians in the middle of all this, though. God knew why. Maybe he was just too shaken up from narrowly surviving a run-in with a storm monster.

He wasn't the only one.

I chafed my hands over my arms in a useless attempt to stop my shivering. The surviving dehaians were out searching the property now, rounding up the strakirin who'd come with the judge, though most of the creatures seemed to have fled when the monster took off. The judge likewise hadn't reappeared, something for which I was grateful, even if my ideal preference would've been for someone to have caught that thing and made sure it could never come near me again. But it was anyone's guess whether the Judiciary would come back with reinforcements. The ruanir and dehaians were packing up to leave as quickly as possible, though it still seemed to be taking forever.

Robin and a few of the others hadn't escaped, though. They'd been knocked unconscious by what I'd done in the clearing, meaning they were now tied up by a half-dead tree on the opposite side of the yard, restrained by chains that some-one had found in a utility shed. Dehaians were guarding them, weapons at the ready. Declan sat nearby. He hadn't said a single word since the attack, not one. He just watched the prison-ers with a look on his face that I couldn't hope to read. Jace was questioning them, though, and Ellie was too, trying to get information regarding Ari or anyone else.

So far, the strakirin had only stared at us with those yel-low-black snake eyes and smiled.

It made my skin crawl.

But they hadn't gotten away, the monster was gone, and some of us, at least, were still alive. On the measure of things, everyone else seemed to believe that counted as a win, only if barely. We'd been lucky.

A muffled thud came from across the yard. Another body. Another dehaian whose name I didn't know, or the corpse of a human security guard, retrieved from wherever the judge and strakirin had left them on the property.

I pulled the blanket tighter around myself, shivering. Lucky. But it didn't feel that way.

"Baylie?"

I tensed at the sound of Chloe's voice. Casting a quick look to the side, I saw her coming toward me, a blanket around her shoulders too. Blue crochet. Pretty.

I looked back to the horizon, hoping she'd go away.

Dirt scratched beneath her flip-flops. She hoisted herself onto the boulder on the opposite side of me from Wyatt, eye-ing him nervously. He made a worried sound and shifted like he wanted to get away from her. I reached down without looking, and black smoke drifted out of my hand when I placed it on his shoulder. He shuddered and then was quiet.

A short breath left Chloe. "Y-you were going to tell me about this… right?"

I didn't respond.

"I would have understood." Her voice edged toward desperate. "It's not like I would have treated you any differently."

"I know."

"Then why didn't you say any—"

"Because you would've."

I could see her confused expression from the corner of my eye.

"You would've tried to treat me the same, but I'm not. And you would've wanted me to be okay, but I'm not. And if you *knew,* if I told you and you knew, then… then things wouldn't have ever been the same, no matter how much you might've wanted to make them seem that way. This always would be there, every second, every day. It would've been there no matter where we went, no matter what we did. It would've been real, and… and it would've meant I *couldn't* have normal, no matter how we tried to pretend." I shook my head, searching for words. "I never wanted to be different, Chloe. You're fine with it, but I'm not. I wanted my friends, my family, cookouts on the weekends, and a house near Dad's. Sure, I'd go see Noah and the others in California, but it would have been an ordinary vacation, and then I would have gone home." I turned to her, almost begging her to understand. "I never wanted my life to be *magical.* I never wanted to be on the outside of everything I've ever known to be real. I just wanted my family and for everything to be okay."

"It's okay." Wyatt reached up, taking my hand and patting it carefully.

I pulled away, feeling nauseated.

"I take it he's part of this, though," Chloe said, only half asking.

I hesitated. I'd hurt her. I knew I had, and I hated it, because sharing the truth hurt me, but lying to her did too. I couldn't win.

I could only stop fighting.

"Yeah. He, um…" I wet my lips. "He says he can feel where I am like a greliaran."

Chloe blinked.

"I can't shut it off or hide or whatever it is they do, though."

"You can't?" Wyatt looked up, alarmed.

Dammit, I hadn't told him that.

"So then… is this like them?" Chloe nodded to Wyatt. "Some kind of…" She searched for a description.

"It's the Beast… we think."

"We?" The hurt came back into her voice again.

I winced. "Declan. Jace. The ruanir. It…" God, this was going to hurt her too. "It happened last year, at Joseph's, after the Beast… you know."

She didn't respond.

"I had no idea, not at first. Just gradually things started to get… weird. I kept it secret, but then after I was shot about two months ago—" A tiny gasp escaped her. I pressed onward. "—it seemed to get stronger. Until, when Noah died, it just…" There wasn't a good term. "Exploded."

Chloe shifted uncomfortably.

I took a breath. "Wyatt was linked up to the Beast too, though, after it attacked Joseph's house, so I'm guessing that's how we ended up… connected or whatever. Something to do with the Beast's power and how it affected me. Declan and the others think I'm sort of like the ruanir too, but not entirely… like the older ones who, I guess, made the greliarans, so…" I shrugged. "I don't know."

She was quiet for a long time. The urge to fill up the silence with words, any words, pressed on me, but I couldn't think of what else to say. I'd lied. Hidden this. I'd had good reason.

I wasn't sure it was good enough.

"Did Noah know?"

My chest ached. "I don't think so. I tried to tell him, but… there was never time."

She looked away.

I shifted on the boulder, my eyes tracking across the trees, the rocks, and the gray-brown dust. I wished I could have told him—this and a thousand more things. Maybe he would have known some way to control it.

Maybe he could have made it disappear.

Discomfort raced on the heels of that desperate wish. Maybe he could've, but then I would have died today. Chloe and Zeke, Jace and the other dehaians too. They all would have died.

The idea of being the savior of the day was almost more

uncomfortable than anything.

"Are you doing okay?" I asked her, my voice tight. "After the, uh…" I didn't know how to address it. Almost all your people died… but, hey, how's it going?

I'd be a bad friend if I didn't ask. I felt like a jerk for bringing it up.

I could never win.

Chloe hesitated, her gaze twitching toward the yard behind us but not quite making it. "Yeah."

I waited. She didn't say anything else.

Pain twisted in my chest like a sharp-edged rock. So this was how things were now. She lied, I lied. We both just lied and lied to each other about the uncomfortable things, rather than trusting—

"No."

I looked to her, gripped by relief and uncertain whether to put any faith in it.

She was watching the horizon beyond the house, but didn't seem to be seeing any of it. "They died right in front of us." Her green eyes turned to me, filling with pain. "And I couldn't…" Her face tightened. "If we dropped the veil to help them, we would have…"

I didn't know what to do, so I did the only thing I could think of and reached out and hugged her. She turned quickly, hugging me back in that wonderfully warm, determined-not-to-let-go way she'd had since we were kids.

Tears stung my eyes, and when we pulled back, I could see a grateful smile lifting the edges of her mouth.

Another thud came from the yard behind us, and her smile faltered even as I flinched. Her hand found mine, and I squeezed it hard, neither of us turning around.

"So, um," Chloe tried, her voice strained, "you ever get a chance to try that new coffee place on Orchard Street?"

I glanced at her. Her eyes were locked on the horizon with an intense expression like, if she tried hard enough, we could find ourselves back in Santa Lucina, hanging out in my apartment.

Back in the ordinary world, before so many of her people had died.

"Yeah." I nodded tightly. "They, uh… they've got great caramel mochas."

"Extra caramel."

I managed a weak chuckle. "And extra choc—"

A hard shiver shot through me as if the air had suddenly plunged in temperature. I gasped, my gaze snapping toward a seemingly random spot on the western horizon where the ocean lay beyond the hills.

"Baylie?" Chloe asked.

"D-do you feel that?"

"Feel…?" Wary confusion filled her voice, and then she took a sharp breath, like she'd picked up on something too.

I couldn't take my eyes from the horizon. Nothing like this had happened to me before, not here, not in Kansas. Never. But I knew exactly what it was. What it had to be.

What it couldn't be.

"Noah?" Chloe whispered, as if afraid to say his name out loud in case this shattered like a dream.

The cold deepened. A small sound of alarm left Chloe. From the corner of my eye, I saw her recoil.

But something inside me responded.

Wisps of smoke drifted up from my arms. Black lightning ghosted beneath my skin.

Chloe gasped, staring at me.

Impressions started to reach me. A sense of being trapped. Of being hunted and infuriated and maybe even afraid because I couldn't get out, and there was danger… some kind of danger. Of reaching, but it was hard, so hard…

I choked as the icy sensation increased tenfold, like I'd been plunged into the heart of the Arctic, and with the cold came darkness. Living darkness that took shapes and forms like people, and oh my God, they were dead. Their faces were decaying. Their bodies were too.

Baylie?

I gasped. That was Noah. I could hear *Noah*.

You're… what is this? He sounded shocked. *Are you okay? What happened to you—*

Wizard. A new voice cut him off, a hundred voices, all of them coming from the dead who were turning, looking at me, watching me like they could see across the miles straight into my brain.

And their voices rang through my mind. Not with words, exactly. More like concepts. Impressions carried on my connection to Noah. Emotions that boiled down to ideas that found words inside my head.

Prison.

Help.

Save him.

Pull.

Anchor.

Salvation.

A vision flashed behind my eyes. Me, the ocean around my feet, the water carrying my magic through the waves. My hands extended over the surf, black lightning and smoke tangling in my skin. I could feel the spray hitting me. Feel the cool waves and the sand beneath my feet, and I wasn't really there. I was in a dark abyss with my stepbrother, surrounded by the dead, trapped by a hungry magic I couldn't touch but that could kill me. I was on a hillside with my best friend, next to a house that a monster had destroyed. I was… I wasn't… I…

My world spun, the vision swirling into a whirlpool of color and light that was too much, too overwhelming. I couldn't breathe.

The whirlpool tilted, tumbling toward a blur of gray and brown. Something warm and hard like muscle caught me. Wyatt's face emerged from the maelstrom only to be swallowed by darkness.

And then everything else was too.

I lunged away from the grass and dirt, gasping for air.

Wyatt was right beside me, his arm supporting my shoulders.

I shrieked and tried to scramble back from him, my palms shoving at the rough ground to propel me away. Wyatt retreated, his hands raised as if to show he wasn't a threat. The motion was so incongruous, so insane, it was almost laughable. But I also stopped moving.

My attention darted to the others in brief glances. The dehaian bodyguards, Damerion and Ezio, were here now along with a handful of other soldiers. They formed a semi-circle around Chloe, their hands on their weapons, and their body language screaming a readiness to use them. Zeke was right beside her, watching me and Wyatt alike. Chloe crouched next to me. Lightning flickered around her trembling hands, the tiny sparks crackling from her fingertips every time she glanced toward Wyatt.

"What is it? What happened?" Jace called, running toward us. Ellie hurried after him, and Olivia did too, while Declan watched us all from across the yard.

"You okay?" Chloe asked me warily.

I nodded, attempting to climb to my feet, but then memory started to rush back. "Noah." I froze, looking up at her. "Noah's alive. Did you feel that?"

She hesitated and then gave a small nod. "I felt something, yeah."

I echoed the motion more firmly. "He's... he's trapped somewhere. He..." I struggled for a way to explain. He needed me to go to the ocean? Was I sure of that? Because those *things* had sent that message, or whatever that rush of images had been, and they sure as hell weren't my stepbrother. I had no way of knowing if I should trust them.

But then, if it helped Noah…

My God, I was debating whether to trust *ghosts*.

"He what?" Jace asked me, ignoring the dehaians like they weren't even there.

I shook my head, pushing away from the ground. I teetered slightly with residual dizziness, but I managed to stand. "I don't know."

"He's in the dark," Wyatt said. "There's nothing but darkness where he is, and he can't get out. But he's not alone."

I stared at him. "You saw…"

"Just a feeling." He gave a small shrug, seeming uncomfortable and maybe a bit embarrassed.

But not scared.

Anxiety prickled through me at the sudden realization. He… he hadn't looked afraid for a while, now that I thought about it. Nervous, yeah, but calmer than I'd seen him since before the attack. Calmer than he'd been since the dehaians arrived.

And now there were dehaians all around us. Dehaians with weapons, and he wasn't even looking at them. He was just watching me.

"Wyatt…" I wet my lips. "You, um… you okay?"

Chloe glanced between us. The crackles of electricity on her fingertips grew stronger. The dehaians around us tightened their grips on their weapons.

Wyatt hesitated. My heart started to pound.

"Better," he admitted softly.

"Better how?"

"It's quiet."

I didn't know what to make of that. Greliarans could hear a pin drop at a thousand yards, I remembered. "Like, your hearing?"

He shook his head. "Just… the noise." His eyes twitched toward Chloe and then away. "The noise to hurt them is… quieter. It's never been quiet before."

I stared at him.

"The craving, you mean? For their magic?" Olivia asked. I flinched, startled for no reason I could name. She watched us all with that intense, analytical expression she had, like she was measuring us down to the millimeter.

Wyatt nodded hesitantly.

"When did this start?" she continued.

"After she came to the hospital." Wyatt pointed to me, almost apologetically. "Her magic makes it better." He seemed to search for a way to describe it and then gave up. "Quieter."

"No," I protested, shaking my head. "No, I'm not—"

Tires rumbled on the gravel path. I turned, alarmed. The dehaians drew their weapons immediately, some of them aiming at Wyatt and some aiming at the road. Two vehicles appeared over the rise, an old and beaten-up red sedan and an SUV with massive dents on the front and side.

"We expecting visitors, sire?" I heard the dehaian commander, Damerion, mutter to his king. Zeke shook his head.

Declan rose to his feet, his cold expression firmly in place. "They're ours."

I noticed he didn't tell the soldiers to put the guns down.

The two vehicles drove closer. In the morning glare, I couldn't tell who was behind the wheel. Wisps of smoke rose from my skin, barely visible. Moving cautiously, Wyatt rose to his feet and stepped in front of me, his eyes on the approaching vehicles.

The protective stance was disconcerting, but right now, I wasn't going to argue with it.

Both vehicles came to a stop. The doors opened. I held my breath, begging the universe that, for once, this wouldn't be another attack.

I couldn't take it if more people died.

Hands appeared above the open door of the SUV. "It's… it's us. It's just us."

Harvey's head popped up. The nervous little man gaped at us all owlishly. His hair was tousled and matted intermittently, and one cheek looked puffier than the other, as if he'd taken a hit to the face. The brown tweed jacket he always wore had a rip in the shoulder and stains darkened the fabric. I had the feeling they were blood.

"Jace?" Dhanya rose from the passenger side of the red sedan. Her long, dark hair was lashed up in a messy ponytail, and her right arm was wrapped in a discolored bandage with frayed edges and dirt smudges.

But she looked like herself, not strakirin, and not crazed like the spy, Shannon, who'd shot me two months ago. Both she and Harvey seemed normal, as did all the others climbing from the vehicles.

I wished I could trust that.

"Check them," Olivia called immediately, like she'd read my mind. "They could be spies."

Ellie nodded and walked toward them. Zeke twitched a hand at his soldiers, who immediately moved to accompany Ellie toward the vehicles.

"Just, uh…" Ellie prompted, coming to a stop and watching the newcomers warily. "Don't come any closer, okay?" She closed her eyes. Harvey gave a panicked shriek and froze. A heartbeat passed, and then Dhanya went still, alarm on her face. The other ruanir followed, each of them tensing and then relaxing a moment later.

Ellie let out a breath, seeming a bit unsteady on her feet. "They're good."

Jace strode past her, heading for Dhanya, who made a beeline for him as well. He drew her into a tight hug.

"Where's Ari?" I heard her ask.

Jace didn't respond.

"W-where is *everyone*?" Harvey looked around, clearly at a loss. "When you sent your location, you said an army was here."

"It was," Declan said shortly. "The Judiciary killed it."

"They have a… creature," Jace explained. "It's like Noah, only not on our side."

Harvey blanched. Dhanya stared at Jace and Declan, horror spreading over her face like they'd just cut the only lifeline she'd been hanging onto.

I couldn't stop myself from checking the sky.

"Do any of your people need medical assistance?" Olivia's dark eyes skimmed the ruanir as if she was running a total on them, our supplies, and the difference between the two.

"N-no." Harvey stepped away from the SUV, wringing his hands. "We got help at the outpost in Utah." He paused. "What was left of it."

My stomach twisted with nausea at the clear implication. Shaking his head, Declan muttered a curse.

"We have a lead on Maia and Miguel," Dhanya managed. "Everyone else too. If we—" She glanced across the few remaining dehaian soldiers like maybe, if she hoped hard enough, they could multiply. "If we hurry, we could—"

"What's the lead?" Declan demanded when she faltered a second time.

Dhanya gave a quick glance to Harvey, who scrambled toward the back seat and began rustling around.

I bit my lip. A lead was great. Saving Miguel, Maia, Ari… all that.

Anxiety tugged at me. Noah was out there too.

Harvey retreated from the vehicle, rolled and crumpled papers bunched in his arms. "Blueprints." He carried them to Declan, eyeing the dehaians warily as he went. "Before the attack, we'd received indications that the supposed hospital that was recently constructed on a Judiciary property on the outskirts of Arley, a small town in California, was actually a new research center. Based on an algorithm I created, and factoring in their recruitment efforts, their security, and the patterns of the volunteer transports, there was a sixty-nine-point-three percent probability that the location was meant to serve as their new headquarters for the next stage of their plan."

"Which is?" Olivia asked, her sharp gaze pinning the nervous little man.

Harvey blinked, seeming thrown. "W-we're not sure. But after they took Miguel and…" he cast a worried glance to Dhanya, "and Maia, I calculated an eighty-two percent probability they would bring them there, especially given the security features and the direction of their retreat—as far as we could track it, anyway." He hesitated. "Seven of our people went after them. The last made it as far as Carson City before they were detected and… stopped."

I shuddered, but Declan didn't react to the implication. "There's a lot of territory between Carson City and California," he replied.

"I-I know, but there's an eighty-two percent—"

"Probability," Declan interrupted. "You said that."

"And what?" Dhanya cried. "That's not good enough?"

"It's the best we've got," Harvey added, still seeming apologetic.

"What's this 'research' center supposed to be researching?" Jace interjected before Declan could speak.

"The, uh—" Harvey gave the strakirin prisoners a wary look and then froze like he was registering their appearance for the first time. "Wait." He blinked fast. "Wait, that's—"

"We know," Declan cut in. "Answer the question."

Dhanya made a rough sound, gaping at the strakirin too. "Screw the question! What—" She spun to Declan. "You all were sure the judges couldn't change people who were past the adjustment!"

"Apparently, now they can."

I winced at the cold anger in his tone.

Dhanya just stared at him. "*Apparently?* That's Roger from weapons' storage, for God's sake! He's a hundred and sixty-three! How…" She reeled away, pressing a hand to her mouth like she was trying to stop a scream. "Maia. We have to find Maia. We—" She looked to the dehaians. "Your army, is it *all* gone or…?" A pause followed her words. "Answer me!"

"You will *not* speak to King Zekerian like—" one of the soldiers snarled.

Zeke held up a hand. "We have soldiers in the bay, but the thing that attacked us here kills dehaians just by touching them. I can't order my people to go up against it again without a way to protect them."

He didn't look at me, and I was grateful. But a number of the other dehaians did.

I wanted to sink through the ground.

Dhanya floundered. "But—"

"What makes you think they're at the research center?" Declan directed the question at Harvey.

"The, um… the security, mostly." Harvey couldn't quite take his eyes off the strakirin prisoners. They were smiling at us. "Their other research stations have experienced a twenty-three percent increase in volunteer transports over the past few weeks while Arley experienced a commensurate drop. That indicates they're routing converts to alternate destinations from the Arley station, and yet security at Arley is forty-one point five percent higher than anywhere else." He paused. "They're creating a prison. A research prison. We're not sure for whom else, but statistically—"

"Maia and Miguel are there," Dhanya interjected firmly, as if she'd personally seen them delivered to the door.

She needed to believe that, I realized. Otherwise, the resistance had nothing. The woman she loved could be on the other side of the planet for all they knew.

"That's where they'll take Ari too," Jace added, nodding.

Harvey blinked. "Ari's—"

"She's back," Jace said. "They took her."

Dhanya nodded. "We need to go. Now. The dehaians don't have to come. We can—"

"How do we get in?" Declan interrupted.

"Utility access, northeast corner. There's a ventilation shaft on the west side that could serve as a way in too. They're both guarded, but there's a blind spot—"

Olivia cleared her throat. "We need more evidence before we assume that's where your people are, or before *any* of us risk our lives against a Judiciary installation and this new creature they've devised." She met Dhanya's stare, iron behind her pacifying expression. "You have no weapons to fight that thing." She paused. "We need the Beast."

Relief and terror hit me simultaneously. We were going to find Noah. Great. It was somehow on me to do that. Oh, hell.

I wanted to run. I just couldn't decide on a direction.

"Okay, fine." Dhanya looked around. "Where the hell is he,

then? Let's go."

"He's not here," Olivia said.

Dhanya choked on a scoff. "Okay, so contact him, and tell him to get—"

"We can't," Chloe said. "Baylie and, uh… and Wyatt think he's trapped, wherever he is. But if we can help him, then he could help us against this Judiciary you're talking about. And hopefully against that creature too."

Unless that's what nearly killed him, I added silently.

My stomach churning, I glanced at the strakirin on the far end of the yard. They all still wore creepy grins. A few of them even seemed to be chuckling.

"Help him how?" Dhanya demanded.

Chloe hesitated. "I'm not sure."

Dhanya shook her head. "We don't have time for that. They've had Maia and Miguel for days."

I couldn't make myself look away from the strakirin. Now all of them were chuckling.

"Without the Beast, we have no guarantee this creature won't slaughter us before we even reach the door," Olivia insisted. "We're no good to anyone if we're dead."

"Guys…" I started. Something was wrong. Something was *really* wrong. What were those things finding funny?

"Y-yes." Harvey nodded to Olivia. "That's true. But our most recent intel indicates the judges don't know we've secured these blueprints. A longer wait raises the statistical probability that, given the length of time that has passed, they'll—"

"There's no *guarantee* that this creature will even *be* at the facility," Dhanya interrupted, glaring at Olivia. "And even if it is, you drove it away from here somehow. What did you do?"

"That's not the point," Chloe interjected quickly.

"How could that not be the point?"

"It's just not."

I ignored them, my thoughts racing. I was able to feel Noah's presence. Ari had been able to do more than that. The two strakirin kids who'd disappeared when she was taken also seemed like they could communicate without a word. And these creatures…

Oh, God. "Shut up," I gasped.

Dhanya made a desperate sound, taking a step toward the dehaians. "You say you can't help, because it'll kill you, but you're not willing to share how you drove that thing out of—"

"I said shut up!"

Dhanya spun toward me, furious.

"Look at them." I pointed to the strakirin.

The strakirins' expressions instantly became stone.

Nauseated shivers raced through me, like I was in a horror movie and I'd suddenly realized that the monster in the shadows was just toying with me.

"It can hear us," I managed. "Through them. It knows what we're saying."

Silence followed.

"Oh, hell," Chloe whispered.

Wordlessly, Olivia motioned us all toward the trees on the opposite side of the yard.

"Keep an eye on them," Zeke ordered two of his soldiers,

not taking his eyes from the strakirin either.

The dehaians nodded. Still watching the strakirin, Zeke crossed to Chloe's side, the remainder of the guards staying with him. Wyatt trailed after me as I followed them, watching the strakirin as he went.

His body language felt protective, and I hated how that was almost a relief right now. One monster to protect me from another, assuming the magic inside me didn't stop the strakirin first.

I made myself turn away, rubbing my hands over my arms again even though nothing about this day was cold.

"We need to get away from this place," Chloe stated the moment we reached the far end of the yard. "Now. Are the wounded ready to go?"

Zeke glanced at Damerion, who nodded.

"We need Noah too," Zeke said. "We can head for the ocean and figure out our next steps from there."

Dhanya stared back at the strakirin, desperation clear on her face. "But… it might take this creature thing time to get to the Judiciary facility. If we go now…"

She was clutching at straws, and I could tell she knew it.

"This new creature can move like the Beast," Olivia said. "Even in a jet, we wouldn't be but a few minutes ahead of it. We have to find Noah first if we're going to stand a chance."

"I-I agree." Harvey sounded apologetic. "If those… *creatures* are in contact with what attacked this place, then that changes the equation significantly. The likelihood of an ambush is almost—"

"Um, everybody?" Ellie interjected from the edge of the group.

"What?" Olivia asked.

"Where's Declan?"

Cold dread sank over me as I scanned the yard, finding nothing. There was only one reason Declan would vanish like this, though, and it wasn't to go find Noah. "Oh my God."

"What?" Chloe asked.

"There's a weapon," I relayed breathlessly. "An old dehaian spell, and it's bad. It'll kill every ruanir with ocean magic in them. And he knows how to use it."

Dhanya made a choked sound. "But Maia might—"

"Go," Zeke ordered his guards. "Head for where our vehicles are hidden. He didn't take these cars, but he's going to want some kind of transportation."

Several of the soldiers raced off.

"W-we can go," Harvey said. "The rest of you can find the Beast. We'll watch the research center. Stop Declan if we see him."

I stared at the little, anxious man, trying to imagine how he could stop anyone.

Dhanya just nodded, though. She started toward the vehicle she'd arrived in, only to pause when Jace didn't follow her. "You coming?"

He hesitated, glancing from me to Wyatt and the dehaians.

"Go," I urged him.

He still didn't move, though I could see he was torn. "You might need..." He gestured vaguely. "You know."

I read between the lines. His magic. What we could do together.

I could feel Chloe and the others staring at us.

"We'll find Noah," Jace said, turning to Dhanya, "and we'll head for the research facility." He paused. "Don't go in. Just wait for us. Please."

She hesitated before giving a tight nod.

Jace nodded too and then glanced at me, a question in his eyes.

I took a deep breath. I didn't know what the hell I was supposed to do to help Noah break free, but I also didn't want to pass up any help I could get.

No matter how insane this all was.

"Yeah, okay," I agreed. "Let's go."

27

ARI

The door clanked shut behind us, and only a flick of my power to induce fear sent the enforcers running down the stairs on the other side. Trailing the sound of their footsteps, we chased them past reinforced concrete walls and utilitarian strip lights that made everything glow an eye-searing shade of blue-white.

Until the enforcers dashed around a corner up ahead, and suddenly the sound of their footsteps stopped.

We slowed, a feeling of warning radiating through the hive. Why would the enforcers stop?

In the lead, one of the strakirin kids crouched at the corner, a small boy with white-blond hair. Worry threaded through me for him, from myself and the hive alike. He peered around the corner with all the speed of a strakirin, just a flinch forward and back to see what lay beyond.

Bullets shattered the wall behind where his head had been only a heartbeat before.

A short gasp left me, but he was okay. Scurrying backward, he retreated from the corner.

I'd already seen what he saw. Enforcers. Lots of them, all blocking the next corridor.

Almost certainly protecting their masters behind those doors.

I inched forward. Wariness and worry came at me from the hive. I motioned behind me without looking, begging silently for calm. They were distracting.

And I needed to be fast.

I crouched at the corner like the boy had done and placed my hand on the floor. They would aim at chest height. Or the height where they'd last seen him. But the ground?

Biting my lip, I slipped my hand around the corner and let the lightning go.

Screams rang from the hallway, cut short fast. Bullets hit the wall beyond me, a wild spray. I ducked back again, my heart racing.

Muffled thuds came from beyond the turn. I started to lean around the corner.

No, came the hive.

I looked back at the strakirin. The boy crept toward me again, an intent look on his face while he gently pulled me away from the turn. The other strakirin took my arms, holding me back, urging me silently to stay, to let him go.

He sneaked forward and, swift as a thought, glanced around the corner again.

Nothing. A vision of fallen bodies and charred skin flashed behind my eyes.

I started breathing again. The strakirins' hands fell away as

I rose to my feet. I started toward the turn, the others moving with me.

A bullet tore through the air, striking the pale blond kid as he rounded the corner.

Pain exploded through my mind, shrieking from my chest, my lungs, my back as I hit the ground. As *he* hit the ground, because I didn't. Everything blurred around me, the boy, the hall, an enforcer on the pile of electrocuted bodies ahead. The man lay on the ground, his skin burned and his body shaking while he clutched the gun amid his fallen comrades.

He died with my spikes in his throat.

I gasped. I was down the hall, surrounded by dead enforcers. The kid was behind me, and oh, God, he was choking on blood. So much blood.

I ran back along the hallway, the walls blurring and the ground too. I crashed to my knees at the boy's side.

Ryan. Sixteen. His mom had been a part of the resistance three years ago, killed in the same fight where the judges kidnapped him.

My hand took his cheek, sorrow flowing out of me. He coughed, red bubbles frothing from his lips, and then rested his face against my palm.

His chest hitched and fell still.

The hive grew quieter as he left.

I couldn't breathe. Couldn't even cry. I hadn't known him more than a few moments.

I'd known his whole life.

Hands took my arms, my shoulders. The hive was there,

and I lost myself in their sorrow and their comfort. They were there, and they remembered him.

Ryan was never truly gone.

I turned, scanning the faces around me. What had the judges intended when they created us? Because it wasn't this. It couldn't have been this.

They didn't have enough of a soul to ever have created this.

Gently, I let my hand fall from Ryan's cheek and closed his eyes. We'd remember him. He wasn't gone. But there were judges ahead, behind that door. Judges that would kill us if they had the chance.

Anger filtered through to me from the others, matching my own. I climbed to my feet, stepping carefully around Ryan and starting toward the door. When I reached it, I paused, a thought occurring to me.

I glanced to a strakirin nearby, a tall boy with a broad chest and green scales forming an erratic Rorschach pattern on his face. He'd considered becoming an enforcer one day, though he'd decided to become strakirin first. The better to serve the Judiciary.

Back before he knew it was all a bargain from hell.

The thought passed from me to him. He nodded. "All clear," he called in as deep a voice as he could manage.

A moment passed.

The handle turned. The door started to open.

We burst past it, rushing into the room and taking the enforcers inside by surprise. Six of them, blocking the room beyond, though they fell fast to our spikes, never having fired their guns.

"Stop!"

I skidded to a halt at the shout from the judge across the room. Judge Davenport, my uncle, stood beside an upright bedframe that held his own daughter.

And he had a knife to Maia's throat.

"One step," he warned. "One flicker of that fear magic you do, and she's dead."

Shudders went through me. From the others, I could see the rest of the room. Miguel was there, chained to a chair with the lone surviving enforcer beside him. Like the judge, the man held a knife aimed at his captive's throat.

"So," Judge Davenport continued. "Zero-Zero-One."

Rage flickered through me at the numeric designation they'd given me.

"And…" He seemed to search for the memory. "Oh, yes. This one's cousin. My niece."

The rage turned to hate. He couldn't even say his own daughter's name. Chances were, he scarcely bothered to remember it.

Even as he was *torturing* her.

My gaze ran over Maia. Her brown hair, always so shiny because she took meticulous care of it, hung in dull and bedraggled tangles around her face. Sweat coated her sickly pale skin, and dried blood crusted the straps that held her wrists to the metal supports.

Trembling, my hands curled into fists. Ocean magic poisoning was bad enough, but what they'd done to her wasn't it. I knew what that looked like; I'd seen it when I was growing up, some girl who the Judiciary probably wanted to use for leverage, not that I'd understood it that way at the time. But it hadn't looked like this.

This was just torture.

Of his own daughter.

And he'd kill her too. I knew that. In a heartbeat and without a moment of hesitation. Even though she was his daughter, he'd never even care.

Judges never did.

"What do you want?" I asked, stepping farther into the room and urging the others to stay still.

A whisper of wariness swept through them, but they didn't move.

An imperious expression returned to Judge Davenport's face. "Obedience, obviously." His gaze skimmed us all and then returned to me. "And an explanation. You…" His eyes raked over me as if to encompass the mere fact I was standing in front of him. "You were tested. Proven to be part of the collective. And yet here you are. Are you another of Engle's tricks?"

"What?" I asked. All around me, confusion came from the hive. They hadn't heard of this either.

His eyes narrowed. "We know he's gone to the sunken island. The fool stayed above water almost the entire way there, making it only too easy to track him. He can't return in time to protect you, so there's no point in feigning ignorance. It won't save you."

I glanced across the enforcer, Miguel and Maia, and then back to the judge. I had no idea what he was talking about, but if Judge Engle had somehow gone back to the island…

Noah? I called silently.

No response. Fear prickled inside me. What if Judge Engle was hurting him? It didn't make any sense how he could even reach Noah, all the way underwater, but—

A whisper of anxiety suddenly came to me, flickering through my mind before washing back into silence.

I started breathing again. Noah was alive. Worried and hiding, but alive.

And he needed help. He needed us to—

"What is Engle planning?" Judge Davenport demanded, snapping my focus back to the present. "Why has he returned to the ocean? Where is Mister Marseilles?"

"Go to hell," one of the strakirin said.

He tightened his grip on the knife with a cautioning noise. "As your master, I command you answer me."

I motioned quickly, begging the others to be quiet. To stay still. Please.

He would kill her.

So stop him, said the hive.

Images raced through my mind. Me, in the moment after Ryan fell, crossing the space to the enforcers before the hive could see my body move.

A tiny breath left me. I'd seen Noah do that.

Yet, Noah didn't have a body. Not really. And I wasn't like him. He'd *said* I wasn't.

"You will obey me, strakirin," Judge Davenport ordered, pulling Maia's hair back and making her gasp against his grip.

I was something else.

The room shifted and flowed around me, and then I was on the other side, behind the judge, grabbing his hand and wrenching it away from my cousin's throat. Judge Davenport shrieked, the bones of his hand crushing beneath my grip, while across the room, the others raced at the enforcer, yanking him away from Miguel. I felt spikes tear through the enforcer's throat, a distant sensation.

The hive thrummed with the idea to kill the judge too.

My stomach churned. He was my uncle.

And he'd almost killed Maia.

Spikes grew from my arms. Lightning sizzled beneath my skin.

He might know how to stop Logan.

The thought made the lightning fade. I wanted to hurt him for what he'd done to Maia. The hive wanted him dead for a thousand injuries too horrible to name. But we needed him— at least for now.

I released my uncle. He crumpled to the ground, cradling his hand. "Stay down," I warned him.

He glared up at me.

The others watched him while I reached up, cutting Maia's bonds. She sagged against me, limp and breathing hard.

"Maia?" I tried. "Maia, can you hear me?"

I glanced to one of the other strakirin. The kid crossed the room, cutting the bonds around Maia's ankles and then helping me get her down. Her legs couldn't support her. I sank to the floor, my arms around her.

"Maia?" I brushed her hair from her face and then I looked

to Miguel. Unsteadily and with the help of the strakirin, he was climbing to his feet. "What did they do to her?"

Miguel eyed me for a moment. The other strakirin too. I suddenly became painfully aware of how long it'd been since I'd seen him.

And the last time, I'd become a monster. A murderer—or close enough. I'd been the cold, mindless, obedient *thing* the Judiciary had tried to make us all.

It felt like another life right now. Like a million years had passed since then, even if it had actually only been a few weeks.

"They've been poisoning her," Miguel told me. "Over and over again."

My brow furrowed. "What?"

"It wouldn't stick. Some kind of protection inside her, keeping their poison out. They thought it might be from the Beast."

A short breath left me, and I looked back at my cousin. An even longer lifetime ago, he'd saved her. Noah. From an enforcer's poison.

But he'd never mentioned any kind of protection.

Maybe he hadn't known.

Maia made a weak sound of protest, pushing at me, moaning like she thought I was trying to hurt her. "You're okay," I urged. "It's me. You're safe."

Her blue eyes opened, bleary and unfocused. "A-Ari?"

"Yeah. I'm here."

She looked around, her breath catching at the strakirin around us.

"It's okay," I said immediately. "They're with me."

Maia gave me an incredulous look, but it didn't last long. "Dhanya. Is Dhanya—"

"She's fine. She's on her way to meet Declan and the others."

Maia exhaled and then dragged in a breath like she suddenly remembered how to breathe. "Good. That's… yeah. Okay." She swallowed hard, nodding like she was reassuring herself with the words—or maybe just clinging to them. "Good."

Her gaze landed on her father. For a heartbeat, she barely moved, staring at him as her chest rose and fell faster and faster.

"You *bastard!*" Maia scrambled up and flung herself at him, fists swinging. I grabbed her, pulling her back. She screamed, fighting me, thrashing to reach him. "You sick, twisted *bastard!*"

I winced, hanging onto her while she screamed. God knew I had poison inside me, but I was controlling it with all my might. The judge wouldn't do the same. He'd hurt her if she touched him. He could hurt her even now with that swamp-like magic inside him.

An image of the dead judges in the warehouse flashed behind my eyes. The hive wanted him dead too.

Maia wasn't the only one he'd hurt over the years.

"We need him," I told the hive and Maia alike. "We—" Maia's screams were turning to sobs. "I'm sorry. I'm *so* sorry, but we need him."

"*Why?*" Maia demanded.

"Because he might know how to stop Logan."

Maia's struggles slowed. She turned, her eyes meeting mine. There was something in her gaze. Fear, but cold. Some knowledge I couldn't place and wasn't sure I wanted to.

My God, had Logan been here too?

For a moment, she didn't move, and then slowly, carefully, she drew herself up and looked at her father again. The silence hung heavy for a moment. I didn't let her go.

"He wouldn't stop." Her voice was quiet. "Even after they knew it wouldn't work, even after they'd tested the poison over and over, he wouldn't stop. Because he was my father. Because he was *curious*." The word scorched the air with its heat. "And because they wanted to break Miguel. They changed all his people, didn't they?"

She wasn't looking at me. I didn't know what to say.

But she didn't seem to need an answer. "They left Miguel for public execution, and me…" She trembled so hard her hair shook. "He didn't stop."

Her eyes found me this time, burning into mine. "You remember that, when you're done *needing* him. Because I damn well will."

Without another word, she walked away on legs that seemed to be held steady by rage alone.

Judge Davenport struggled to get to his feet, still cradling his hand. "You defective children! There is *nothing* you can—"

A flicker of lightning slashed out from me, striking the judge. Just enough to shock. Not enough to kill.

Barely.

Judge Davenport collapsed backward against the wall, his shattered hand clutched to his burned chest. Gasping, he stared at me.

"I'll remember," I promised quietly.

∽ 28 ᴄ

LOGAN

The way through California was almost devoid of ruanir to change into strakirin, a fact that was annoying but not unexpected. Short of the judges, no ruanir would choose to be close to the ocean—and certainly not as close as this excuse for a town. Lost somewhere between Santa Lucina and No Man's Land, but still within sight of the sea, this rinky-dink excuse for human habitation probably didn't even warrant a blip on a map.

I sailed toward the edge of town where I knew I'd find the research facility. The judges had long since stopped broadcasting their little signal to draw me to them, though it didn't matter.

Not when the resistance had been so incredibly helpful.

Amusement filled me, and if I'd had a body, I would have smiled. I knew where the facility was, I knew where the entrances were… hell, I knew everything, thanks to the idiots carrying on about all their plans within earshot of my strakirin. That they thought the Beast could still be alive was such a joke;

they hadn't seen what I did to that thing. What I'd do again, for that matter, if it *had* somehow survived. And sure, the blond girl had eventually figured out that I was listening in, but I'd still gained more than enough information to end this once and for all.

I swept over the town, scanning the little buildings and insignificant people going about their pointless lives. It'd been damned helpful of the judges too, bringing Ari back to the main facility where they'd put that damn collar on me like a dog.

I was looking forward to tearing the place down.

My target came into view by the edge of an abandoned lot. A tall fence surrounded the Judiciary property, enclosing the building, a large parking lot, and some half-hearted landscaping that looked as boring as the judges themselves. A few trees. A couple of bushes. Close-cropped grass. A lonely picnic table sat under a tree near the edge of the property like a lame excuse for a break area for the employees inside. The building itself was massive, spanning several city blocks, though it was constructed of bland, tan brick that somehow conspired to make it fade into the background, thoroughly unremarkable. In fact, short of a sign proclaiming it as Los Angeles Area Medical Research, there wasn't a single aspect to draw human curiosity about what lay inside.

For maybe a heartbeat, I debated being subtle, but why? Humans were irrelevant—they'd figure out their blasé little world had changed soon enough—and more time would only give the judges further opportunity to be annoying before I killed them.

I started down toward the building, when a sudden movement on the abandoned lot caught my attention. I paused, watching a solitary man sneak along the line of trees, his focus clearly on the enormous Judiciary building across the street.

I recognized him. He'd been at the resistance hideout. I scanned the area around him, but I couldn't see anyone else. Had that moron seriously come here alone?

The man slipped toward a break in the bushes, still watching the building. Understanding clicked. He was trying to sneak in.

Oh, like *hell* he'd ruin this for me by finding Ari or alerting the Judiciary to the fact something was wrong before I was ready.

I swooped down and snagged him. He shouted as I pulled him back and dragged him into a thicket of bushes because, let's face it, I'd like some privacy for questioning him before the judges tried to get involved and became annoying.

Though "questioning him" was a loose term, really. No need for words here.

My power poured at him, ready to take his mind, his memories, every little trace of "him" that had become irrelevant now. After all, having an extra strakirin here would be beneficial. My other strakirin were closing in; ten minutes, maybe less, and they'd be here. Because I willed it, they'd done everything short of break the sound barrier to get here to help.

But I could always use more. Like this guy. *Declan.* What a pathetic name. He didn't need it anymore. He would simply be another weapon in my—

The man gasped, and a strange twist of magic lashed out from him. I recoiled, not dropping him but shocked nonetheless. What the hell? That wasn't ruanir magic. Not entirely.

Wait. The resistance. They'd had some special magic. That Willa chick had blown up her grandmother's bed and breakfast with it, back a lifetime ago when I'd hunted Ari and the Beast with the enforcers.

Fine. I'd take that from him too.

My power rushed back at him. He choked on a scream. How dare this little—

New magic hit me, not remotely the same as what I'd felt before. It was heavier. Darker. *Weirder.*

And it hurt.

I dropped him to the ground and coalesced into human form. "What the hell was tha—"

Pain choked off my words. The man scrambled backward, gasping, choking while his mind and body rebelled against itself, half strakirin, half *whatever* he'd been, because he sure as hell wasn't purely ruanir. More like a judge, but without the oily, swamp magic they used. And as for the magic he'd turned on me...

The power inside me began to burn hotter, and then hotter still. It flared white-hot like magnesium.

I staggered away, my body exploding outward and then drawing back to human again while I tried to fight for control of this... this *poison*. Anger surged through me for the injustice, the indignity. I was a god, for pity's sake. How dare some jerk with a prissy little name like *Declan* try to poison *me*? I owned his stupid ass. I owned the *world*, and I was capable of changing anyone I touched into my goddamn *slave*.

I'd change this too.

My magic roiled inside me. My body was gone, and I barely recalled letting it go. The landscape became a blur around me. The sunlight was a kaleidoscopic flare giving me a migraine. But it didn't matter. Nothing mattered. Nothing except this poison burning and eating through my magic like it stood a chance against me. But now I could feel the edge of it. Just the barest edge out ahead of it, and I could feel the way it was working too.

The poison slowed. I was ahead of it now, pushing it back, and I knew this. I could change ruanir to strakirin. I could take in magic.

That's what that old Beast had done. Take things in, change them. And I was stronger than him. Better than him.

I was winning.

A growl rumbled through me while I twisted and changed the poison inside me. It wasn't gaining ground anymore. In fact, now that I had a handle on it…

I drew back to human form, grinning. "Now let's see how you like it, buddy."

The guy was gone.

I spat a curse. The bastard had used my suffering as an excuse to run, that coward. He was dead the next time I found him, strakirin or not.

But meanwhile…

I looked at the Judiciary building. There were secret entrances, I knew. The resistance had said that in front of my strakirin, and that Declan guy had been aiming for them too. But what kind of sense did it make for me to slither in through the back door, as if I needed to fear the judges detecting me?

I was a god.

I let my human form go and rose into the sky. On the streets around the building, I knew my strakirin had arrived, pulling up in their own cars or whatever vehicles they'd needed to steal to get here to serve me. They hurried out, moving to surround the building in preparation for my next order.

And somewhere inside, Ari waited. Did she know I was here? Could she feel my presence looming above her as I prepared to sweep down and wreak my vengeance?

Amusement moved through me. She would soon enough.

And after that, I'd show her the new spell I'd just found.

29

ARI

Alarms screamed through the halls only a heartbeat before all the lights around us died.

"What—" Maia gasped. "What's happening?"

My eyes flashed into strakirin form, bringing the hall back into view. The other strakirin did the same, twin yellow glows springing to life all around me. "What is that?" I demanded of Judge Davenport.

His jaw clenched. His eyes moved with that blind focus that told me he couldn't see a damn thing.

I grabbed him. "What the hell is—"

A gasp came from the strakirin, and through them, suddenly I could feel it. The black cloud. The droning hum that still thrummed with cruel laughter.

Oh, God, no.

My walls rose in my mind, burying me as far behind my inner defenses as I could go. "Run!" I shouted.

The hive was already moving. Two of the kids took Miguel's hands, pulling him after them while they raced away. Another two snagged the judge and hauled the man between them down the hall. Grabbing Maia's arm, I kept her beside me as I took off after them.

"What's happening?" Miguel called over the blare of the alarms. "What are you running from?"

"Logan," I called back.

I could see the horrified look he threw over his shoulder. Miguel had seen what Logan had become, I'd bet on it. Gripping the strakirin, he fought to run faster.

The floor shuddered hard, nearly taking my feet from under me. A roar came from deeper in the building, like several tons of concrete tumbling to the ground.

"Ari…" The call singsonged through the building, loud as a jet engine. "Oh, *Ariiii*…"

Panic clenched my throat shut. The monster was hunting me.

The hive, *my* hive, swelled inside my mind, protective, sheltering, as if they were a part of my own defenses in a way I couldn't understand. But they wouldn't let him have me. We wouldn't let him have any of us.

But if we didn't escape now, we'd all die.

Jennifer turned immediately, grabbing Judge Davenport by his shirt. "How do we get out of here?"

He glared up at her glowing eyes.

"*How?*"

"Unless you want to die at the hands of that thing you made," I managed, "you'll tell us."

His glare slid toward the sound of my voice. His face twitched with rage. "Whatever this ploy of Engle's is, it won't—"

A crash carried from farther in the building, and the walls groaned like they were shifting under the weight of the destruction.

"Does this seem like a *ploy* to you?" Miguel spat back.

"Logan *will* kill you," I said. "And as for Judge Engle, he's going to answer for every second of what he did to us… and so will you."

The judge scowled at me, but I could see the wheels turning behind his eyes. "Utility tunnel. That way." He jerked his head toward the hall ahead of us. "It leads beyond the outer wall." His lip curled. "We left the security measures around it off the building records as bait for Miguel's little resistance."

Rage quivered through me. "Show us."

"*Ariiii*… I've got a new toy to show you, Ari…"

Grabbing Judge Davenport again, the strakirin took off running. The halls twisted ahead of us. The floor shuddered beneath our feet, making dust and debris rain from the ceiling. Logan was bringing the building down around us.

The darkness thinned beyond the turn of the hallway. We slowed. No sound reached us, but after a moment, the light moved slightly, as if someone was holding it.

Silently, I urged the others to stay put before I inched toward the corner. One of the other strakirin caught my arm, a girl with scales slashed across her cheeks like dark green blush. She shook her head and then crept ahead of me.

They didn't want to risk me. I didn't want to risk them.

The girl peeked around the corner, the motion so swift it set her long hair swinging. Through her eyes, I saw a half-dozen enforcers, their arms crossed and their feet planted body-guard-style while they watched the hallway. One held a crow-bar while another had a flashlight. But nothing else was around them.

Except the hidden escape hatch.

A snarl of rage came from beyond the turn of the hall. They'd seen us.

Poison surged through the strakirin. The kids darted around the corner, slashing out with their spikes before the enforcers made it more than a few steps. The crowbar clattered to the ground, and the flashlight did too, spinning a beam of brilliant light across the suddenly wet walls.

My stomach churned when I followed them around the turn, but there was nothing for it. The enforcers would never have let us leave with the judge. They would have tried to poison the first one of us who touched them.

"You think you have a chance of winning here?" Judge Davenport snapped at me. "That, what? You'll aid the resistance? We know all about them. We're tracking them right now! The enforcers who captured you survived to tell us of that freak wizard your Beast made. Judges are circling in on them *as we speak*. She won't—"

A rumble overhead interrupted him. Dust rained down on us, then tiny chunks of cement. Cracks formed in the ceiling, and threads of smoke twisted through, moving like tentacles across the concrete.

Logan.

Two of the strakirin kids turned quickly, yanking at the gap between the panels on the wall with speed that seemed borne of adrenaline. A hatch ripped from the wall, revealing a tunnel. Narrow and dark, it was only high enough to crawl through, but that hadn't stopped Judge Davenport from already trying to beat a steady retreat.

"Go!" I cried to Maia.

We ran for the tunnel.

Tentacles lashed down, swiping the space between us and our escape. I spun out of the way, shoving Maia ahead of me while the ropes of black smoke flailed and other tentacles pulled at the ceiling. Larger chunks of concrete rained down. I caught a glimpse of darkness beyond the gaps.

It was pulsing. Snarling.

And it saw me.

A rumble came from the darkness above me, and it sounded like laughter. He could see me. Us. More tentacles twisted down into the space between us and the tunnel, whipping like wild ropes and growing denser with every second. I saw Maia reach the tunnel. Miguel too, and Luna and Leo scrambled in after him.

But they weren't fast enough.

A tentacle lashed, connecting with Leo's wrist and then twisting around sharply, wrapping him faster than even he could move. He screamed, and the hive screamed with him as poison flooded into him, trying to change him, trying to drag him back into the drone that was just made of Logan now.

An endless oblivion of serving Logan alone.

Luna slashed out with her spikes, tearing through the tentacle like it was flesh rather than magic. The tentacle wrapping her brother's wrist faded.

The rumble grew louder. "Now that's not nice…"

My chest shook at the reverberation of the words.

More tentacles rushed in. The shadows were thick with them, and the paltry glow of the flashlight just made them more terrifying, backlighting a monster of ropes and darkness that could see us with every molecule of its being. Wordlessly, I cried for the others to run for the tunnel, and through their eyes, I could see some of them made it.

But not all.

"Mmm… aren't you all a mess?" Logan purred as the hive screamed.

My heart hit my throat. I couldn't breathe. I could feel their pain, hear them screaming in my head. He was killing their minds and leaving their bodies alive, and for what? For nothing. For fun.

When it was me he wanted.

My eyes went to the path back into the facility, away from the tunnel, and from Maia, Miguel, and the hive.

My hive.

"Logan!" I shouted.

His amused chuckle rumbled through the air, but the tentacles slowed. He was looking toward me, at me. I knew it.

I ran.

"Ari!" Maia shouted.

I bolted around the corner and kept going, pouring every

ounce of speed I had into my legs, my pumping arms. The hallway blurred, and the debris did too. Broken chunks of concrete and shattered doorways shot past. I scrambled over a pile of cement so fast, it was behind me in only a heartbeat, and ahead, I could see a glimmer of what looked like thin sunlight through the shattered ceiling.

And he was leaving them. Their pain was less now.

He was coming after me.

"Ari…" he called.

I raced up a fallen slab of wall. There was a gap ahead. Open air beyond.

"You're not going to get away this time."

Maybe not. But I'd buy the hive time to escape. Maia too. And Miguel.

My hands gripped the rough edge of the concrete ceiling. Dirt and clumps of grass crushed beneath my fingers. I yanked myself up over the top.

The sunlight vanished above me, swallowed by a low and thick black cloud. Logan had been waiting, baiting me with sunshine.

Laughter rumbled through the air. "God, you're so pathetic."

The black storm swooped down and engulfed me.

∽ 30 ∾

BAYLIE

"I want Hammerhead to the east, and Tidal to the south, understand? Watch that damn road in case anyone—and I mean *anyone*—comes down it."

The dehaian commander, Damerion, glared at the isolated stretch of sand and the single gravel track leading to it. Rocky cliffs circumscribed a crescent shape around the beach, sheltering it from view of just about anybody, and large slabs of rock washed by centuries of ocean water stood up like jagged teeth in the sand. It was nothing like the nicer, smoother beaches near where I lived. This was nature that nobody had bothered trying to control. We were miles from the closest town, though that hadn't stopped the dehaians from being nervous. Me either, for that matter, considering I was one of the stars of the show now.

And I had no idea of my lines.

I glanced back at the ocean. We were going to try to reach Noah, to bring him back if possible or to get a better idea of what was keeping him from coming back on his own. I'd admitted to Chloe that I was still picking up on him on the way here, just faint flickers, even though she couldn't detect anything. She'd just stared at me for a moment and then nodded, absorbing the information and planning what to do next.

I wondered when she'd become such a strategist—and at the same time, I didn't care. I was grateful. It saved me from having to pretend to be the one who had this all under control.

Drawing a deep breath, I tried to calm down. True, I had no idea what I was doing. True, if you'd told me a year ago that I'd be standing on the beach outside Santa Lucina, preparing to use magic—my *own* magic—to bring my supernatural-thunderstorm stepbrother back from an underwater prison populated by ghosts, I probably would have laughed at you. Or, really, run like hell because that was insane.

Now all I could think of was how it'd be my fault if this didn't work.

"You okay?"

I jumped. Coming up beside me, Jace eyed me as if I'd just answered his question without saying a word.

"Yeah, just…" The truth fit. "You know, worried."

He watched the ocean for a moment. The surf tumbled over the shore like hungry hands never quite able to reach us, but desperately continuing to try.

"It's going to work." He sounded confident. I envied him. "We'll get him back."

I nodded, doing my best to believe the words. We would. Noah would be fine. As for what happened after that…

"You ready?" Chloe called. I glanced over my shoulder to see her walking toward us, her bodyguard Ezio not far behind.

"They're about as happy with the security around here as they're ever going to be."

"There aren't enough of us to cover everything," Ezio said, as if repeating something he'd already pointed out before. "It would be safer for you to return to the remaining reserve troops off the coast."

"I'm not leaving Baylie," Chloe replied.

And that sounded like an old argument.

I fought the urge to fidget uncomfortably. I wasn't sure whether to be glad she was here—she could electrocute anything that came near us, same as Zeke, and weirdly same as me—or whether I wished she'd listen to her bodyguard and go find somewhere safe to wait. We'd taken a complicated, circuitous route to get here, making sure we weren't followed, and there were easily two dozen dehaians on the beach, and another dozen atop the cliffs, all of them armed like they were expecting the apocalypse. But I agreed with Ezio. More would be better. An entire army would be better, though God only knew what regular people would think, if any of them wandered down the gravel track toward the beach and spotted us.

Who was I kidding? The dehaians were so edgy, they'd probably shoot anyone before they got within a hundred yards of us.

"So what do we need to do?" Jace asked.

Gratitude nudged at me, if for nothing else than the change of subject.

Chloe's eyebrow rose at me. I faltered. Right. My line.

What the hell was my line?

"Um…" I looked back out at the ocean, wishing I had more than a few snapshot images in my head to go on.

Images from ghosts, no less.

My stomach churned at the thought. I'd accepted mermaids. I'd accepted greliarans. Hell, I'd accepted wizards and that I was sort of, kind of, one of them. Nobody had told me there would be *ghosts* involved too.

But what had those ghosts said? What had they shown me? Pulling. Something about an anchor. Was I the anchor?

A whisper of anxiety threaded past me, coming from Noah. We were running out of time.

I nodded at no one in particular and slipped out of my sandals. No reason to get them soaked.

My God, what was I doing?

I pushed the incredulity aside and walked into the water, leaving the others on the sand. The surf swept around my ankles with a suddenness that always made me gasp, no matter how many times it happened. The water was always too fast, too sudden, like it would drag me with it down into the depths if I wasn't careful. If I didn't hang onto the land.

A shaky breath left me. The waves rolled around my knees before pulling on my legs as if to haul me out to sea. The fear inside me whimpered that I'd gone far enough. My worry for my stepbrother—for everyone—wasn't sure.

I closed my eyes, willing myself to release my death-grip on that shivery, dark power inside me. I might as well have been forcing myself to step off a cliff, all based on the promise that, somehow, I'd be able to fly.

Someone shouted on the shore.

A weight slammed into me, throwing me forward into the waves. Water flooded my mouth, choking off my instinctive gasp. Before I could lash out, hands grabbed me, yanking me from the tide almost as quickly as I'd been shoved into it and then pinning me behind something large and *way* too warm.

I shrieked, tugging one hand free and dashing the water from my eyes. Wyatt was in front of me, his skin changed to the rock-hard, lava-cracked form of a greliaran. A growl rumbled in his chest while his attention was locked on the shore.

More shouting reached my ears. Screams as well, and oh my God, that was gunfire. Frantic, I struggled to see around him because Chloe was back there. Jace too, and Ellie—

Shock froze me, and then Wyatt shoved me behind him again, but not before I'd caught a glimpse of the beach. It was chaos. A scene from a war movie, only I was no soldier. Several dehaians lay dead on the sand. The survivors were pinned down behind the slabs of stone on the beach, firing at enforcers who held the high ground atop the cliffs. Of the dehaians who'd been up there, there was no sign. But Ezio was wounded. Blood soaked his bare chest as he lay against another stone, and Chloe was on her knees beside him, pressing a bundle of fabric that might've been his shirt to his shoulder. Damerion crouched near his king, soldiers surrounding them both. Zeke was striking out with lightning, hitting whomever he could on the cliffs, while Jace had Ellie with him behind a stone several yards to their right.

Wyatt snarled, lurching hard like something was striking

him, but he didn't fall. I couldn't even scream. Those were bullets. Actual *bullets*, and they were hitting him.

They would have hit me.

Dark clouds stuttered up from me like frantic smoke signals. Black lightning flashed in my skin like a light switch was flicking on and off. I couldn't let the magic out here, I'd hit Wyatt.

But, God, it was hard to control. Power poured up around my feet from the ocean, coursing through my legs, my torso, so strong that it was all I could do to keep it from exploding out of me.

"Stay behind me," Wyatt growled over his shoulder.

I couldn't make a sound.

He started forward, still keeping me behind his back, and I stumbled after him. The waves tugged at me, sending rushes of magic coursing through my body. In brief glimpses, I saw the beach. The soldiers were gesturing for Zeke and Chloe to make a run for the ocean, but she wouldn't go. Jace was saying something to Ellie, who was nodding. Wyatt lurched as more bullets struck him, but he didn't stop moving. Greliarans were damn near bulletproof, I remembered. I'd never been more grateful for that fact than I was right now.

We neared the shore, and Wyatt moved faster, rushing for the closest large slab of stone. Twisting quickly, he pulled me around him and down behind the cover. I crashed onto my hands and knees in the sand and then huddled up against the rough, wet stone.

"Stay down," he ordered.

I nodded, glancing around frantically. To my left, Chloe struck out with lightning, tearing down an enforcer who had been making his way around the top of the crescent-shaped cliff to shoot at her. Nearby, Zeke was helping his soldiers hold back the enforcers trying to come down the gravel track. To my right, Jace had his palm plastered to the sand, his eyes closed, while Ellie kept watch beside him with a handgun clasped in her trembling grip. On Jace's wrist, the amber prayer beads he always wore glowed bright like tiny suns.

A rumbling noise came from the cliffside. Fear froze me for a heartbeat, and then I twisted to the side, risking a quick glance toward the sound.

A swath of the cliff was crumbling beneath some of the enforcers.

I looked back to Jace. Strain lined his face. The beads on his wrist were growing dull, like all the color was draining from them.

A rough breath escaped me. I had an idea. It was probably a bad one.

I lunged up from behind the stone.

"Baylie!" Chloe shouted.

Bullets struck the sand behind me as I scrambled across to the stone hiding Jace and Ellie. Tumbling down next to them, I snagged Jace's arm. His eyes flew open.

"Take it," I cried.

His other hand grabbed mine. Magic poured from me into him, sweeping beneath his power and then around it, through it, swirling with it like a dance. But only for a heartbeat. Only for the moment it took for him to slam his hand back down into the sand, driving our combined magic through it, across the beach, and up into the rocky cliffs all around.

I felt the ground fighting him. It hadn't moved in a million years, and it saw no reason to start now. But our magic wove through it, loosening it, convincing it to let go.

And then it did.

Enforcers screamed as the crescent-shaped cliffs roared down beneath them, swallowing them in cascading rock.

Jace opened his eyes as the rumbling stopped. Sweat dripped from his forehead, and he was breathing hard, but he smiled at me all the same. On his wrist, the prayer beads glowed again, their amber shade turned to a strange, faintly purple color.

Gently, his hand lifted from mine. Swallowing hard, I released him as well, my entire body quivering. I felt drained. Emptied into the ground like a watering can. But I still nodded at the silent question in his expression, reassuring him I was okay.

I glanced at the others. The soldiers were scanning whatever remained of the beach, guns at the ready, though from the way none of them fired, I guessed that the enforcers were gone. Still in greliaran form, Wyatt rose, scanning the beach as warily as any of the soldiers.

"All clear?" Damerion shouted from behind a stone, keeping one hand to Zeke as if to stop him from moving.

"Yes, sir! All—"

The soldier cut off with a strangled sound, but I didn't hear any gunfire. Any noise at all. Just the surf and—wait, were those more choking sou—

A wave like a mudslide swept over us, except nothing was there. No earth, nothing at all. But suddenly, the air was too thick and I couldn't breathe. Dense, invisible sludge rolled across my body, engulfing me in nothing, encasing me as if to bury me alive. On instinct, I tried to scramble away from it, out from behind the cover of the stone, and I threw a desperate look over my shoulder to see what nightmare was chasing me.

Half a dozen people in black suits and white shirts strode down the track toward us, a collection of armed guards behind them. The cliffs were gone around them, crumbled toward the sea, but the gravel road remained mostly clear. The men and women paid no attention to the destruction, didn't even glance toward the dead. They fanned out once they reached the beach, their enforcers around them, their hands extended toward us, and contemptuous smiles on their faces.

Judges. Those were judges. They must have been there the entire time, willing to let their first wave of enforcers lead the way in attacking us.

Because why risk themselves? Why use their magic when guns would do?

My eyes flashed over the others. Oh, God, they were in trouble. The soldiers were on their knees. Some had collapsed fully to the sand. Chloe struggled up, striking out with lightning and managing to hit one of the judges before she crashed back to the ground. But even as the judge fell, the attack didn't stop. Bullets from the enforcers with the judges peppered the stone that hid Jace and Ellie, and struck the slabs of rock protecting

Zeke and all the other dehaians too. Wyatt fought to get up, trying to reach me while his hand clutched his throat and he gasped for air.

The judges spotted me, and their grins broadened. They shouted a command to their enforcers, and the gunfire increased, pelting the rocks behind which the others hid, keeping anyone from trying to reach me, even if they could.

I grasped for the magic inside me, but I felt like I was shaking the last few drops from an empty bottle. Lightning faltered and flickered in my skin, pale as the smoke I could barely see coming from my body. The air was too thick to scream, too thick to even breathe, and only instinct kept me scuttling backward in a frantic attempt to get away, get away, get—

A wave struck me, carried in by the tide I'd crab-crawled into. The water swept around my body, startlingly cold and shocking the remaining oxygen from my lungs, but the dredges of power inside me didn't care. The darkness in me latched onto the magic in the ocean, drawing it in like the air I couldn't breathe, drinking it down like water on parched ground. I'd never felt it this strong, never let the ocean in like this. Like it was the only thing keeping me alive.

Inside my skin, lightning flared.

"Stop her!" one of the judges shouted.

The enforcers aimed their guns. Wyatt struggled to his feet, his legs stumbling on the verge of giving way as he fought to block them from shooting me.

Another wave struck my back, stronger. Magic flooded into me like a storm surge.

Several of the judges turned their hands toward me, abandoning their attack on the dehaians.

Air rushed into my chest. My hands sank into the rough sand. Another wave struck, tumbling past my shoulders, lashing me with its cold and soaking me with its power. Darkness spread around my fingers, twisting in the water like ink, sweeping back out to sea with the tide.

The judges' magic rolled toward me. I could feel it coming, a noxious surge of mud and sludge like a polluted lake, like a dead ocean.

But I was the ocean.

A wave hit my back and kept coming, holding me in its grip as it lifted me up from the sand. Black clouds filled the water, all of them crackling with lightning as they rushed around me toward the shore. The judges' power faltered before them, too slow, too corrupt.

Too dead to resist this much life.

The tide crashed in, sweeping around the dehaians and my friends like they were invisible islands in the sea. The judges shouted, their enforcers scrambling to get them out of the way, but there was no time. Like a tsunami, the black storm surge tore over them. The mudslide of their magic disintegrated beneath it, crumbling to nothing as the wave threw the judges and the enforcers back, driving them against the rocks of the destroyed cliffside.

A breath left me as the wave receded, the black tide running out toward the sea. My bare feet sank into the sand, and inside my skin, the lightning faded. The power wasn't gone. Wasn't even drained.

But the threat was over. The magic inside me knew that.

And somehow, the knowledge of that fact didn't scare me anymore, as if for the first time—and maybe finally—I and the power inside me had an understanding.

I swiped my soaked hair back from my face. All around me, black shadows melted from the water as the last of the magical tide slipped from the shore to rejoin the waves. On shaky legs, I walked from the surf, looking for the others as I went, confirming that they were all still alive.

Most of them were staring at me.

Jace shoved up from the ground and strode toward me, ignoring the tiny rivulets of ocean water running past his feet. "Are you okay?"

I kept myself from looking toward the judges, what was left of them. I knew I'd had no choice. They would have killed the others, and maybe even me.

Or worse.

It didn't make anything easier. "Yeah, I'm… I'm fine."

Relief spread over his face. He faltered like he wanted to reach out to me but wasn't sure it'd be welcome.

I met him halfway, taking his hand and hanging on tight, but he didn't stop there. Quickly, he pulled me closer, wrapping me in a hug.

"Thank you," he said. "For the… you know, magic and…"

Air slid from me as he trailed off, my heart rate slowing even though, honestly, this was intense enough that it should have sent my pulse through the roof. Hugging him. *Being* hugged by him. His arms were so strong, so warm, and the rich, earth-and-spice smell of him mingled with the salt in the air.

But who was I kidding? Compared to what we just went through, this was… well, this was nice.

Really nice.

"You too," I said against his chest.

He hesitated, and when he spoke, I could swear there was something deeper than simple courtesy in the words. "Any time."

Quivers ran through me, strangely warm, and maybe he felt them, because his arms tightened. Another few heartbeats passed before he released me.

Drawing a slow breath, I turned toward Wyatt, who stood several yards off. Threads of light still cracked his skin, though the effect was lessened from before. He watched the cliffs, and the water too, scanning everything as if searching for even a hint of a threat.

"Thanks," I said. "You saved my life back there."

He paused, but didn't turn around. "Protector."

I didn't understand.

He looked back over his shoulder. There was something different in his face, I realized, and it had nothing to do with the cracks of light in his skin.

It was calmness, despite the fact I could tell he was still on guard for any danger. A peace I could almost feel from him, as much as see.

"Greliaran," Ellie said, rising from the shelter of the boulder.

"What?" I asked.

She walked toward me, watching Wyatt. "That's what the word used to mean."

Wyatt nodded. He returned to watching the cliffs.

My mouth moved, no words following. Had I known that? Had I heard it a million years and one summer ago when I first learned greliarans existed? Whether or not I had, I certainly hadn't thought about it since, because why would I? Whatever the greliarans were meant to be in the past, they'd categorically become terrifying, psychotic killers. Of every single one of them, my stepdad, Noah, and Maddox were the only exceptions to that brutal, bloodthirsty rule.

Until now.

"Baylie?"

I blinked, looking away from Wyatt. Chloe hurried toward us. Behind her, Damerion crouched beside Ezio, holding the bundle of bloodied fabric to his shoulder. Zeke was speaking with the other soldiers, and at his order, several of them strode toward the fallen cliffside.

Chloe threw her arms around me, making me stumble. "Good job," she whispered to me.

I hugged her back, not sure what to say.

After a moment, she released me, a relieved smile on her face. "We okay?" she called over her shoulder to Zeke.

He glanced to the soldiers on the gravel track leading up from the beach. At their confirmation, he nodded.

Chloe echoed the motion. "So…" Her eyes twitched toward the ocean. "You, um… up for what we came here to do?"

I followed her gaze to the waves, crystalline and cool,

washing in toward the shore. Noah was out there, somewhere far beyond them. He was waiting.

Black lightning tangled through me, waiting too.

I walked back toward the water.

31

NOAH

The ghosts were gone, and in the cave at the bottom of the ocean, I was alone.

"I will find you, Beast. You can't stop this."

Almost alone.

The water warped around me with the endless pulling sensation of whatever Judge Engle had become, draining the magic around me. I braced my hands on the wall of the cave, cursing silently. The rocky surface scraped at my palms till it felt like they should bleed. Without the ghosts to help me hold in place, I was skidding closer and closer to the narrow gap at the other end of the cave, and thus out into the open water.

Where that bastard would try to kill me.

I closed my eyes. I could barely feel a trace of the Beast in me now. Just a distant whimper, like a wounded animal hiding from a predator. And this wasn't how I wanted to end, cowering in some cave at the bottom of the ocean, nearly human but not quite, without a single power of the Beast at my disposal.

Where no one would ever know what happened to me.

My fingers crushed into the rock wall. That *wasn't* how this would go. I just needed to hold out for a little while, and somehow, Baylie would help me. I'd picked up on what the ghosts told her, for all that it hadn't made much sense. My stepsister's new abilities could breach the trap imprisoning me. Hopefully, anyway. But the theory was, I just had to hang on till then.

Unless something had gone wrong.

Gritting my teeth, I pushed the thought aside. It'd be fine. Baylie had to reach the ocean first, and God knew how far she'd been from it to start. I needed patience, that was all. Patience and—

The water lurched a second time, dragging me toward the opening. A burning sensation on my back followed, like sharp-edged ice cutting at my skin, trying to bleed me dry.

Oh, hell.

I threw a frantic look behind me. In the eerie blue-white light of the glowing water around me, the rough surface of the wall was a mottled texture of shadows. But something about it had changed. Small pockets of black pooled in every tiny crevice, dark as ink, sending shivers through my skin.

I recognized the sight. I'd seen the same thing in the canyon, inside the gaps in the barricade of stones over the top of this place.

The walls of the prison, and they were closing in. Even as I watched, the small, ink-like pools clustering in the deeper crevices of the wall spread farther, as if drawing through the rock toward the amphitheater that formed the center of this hell.

My impossible heart found a way to speed up. I couldn't

stay here. And going out there…

The water warped again, yanking me toward the gap leading out of the cave. The pools of ink spread across the rear wall.

I didn't have a choice.

Snarling curses inside my head, I retreated toward the cave opening. I was out of time. Whatever Baylie was doing, it wasn't happening fast enough. Maybe it hadn't worked at all. So I just needed to make it to the vine. That damned thing had cracked this prison, maybe it could get me out of here before the trap closed entirely.

And then…

A faint whimper rose inside me, like a frightened animal recoiling even farther into the shadows to hide.

I tried to ignore it as I hovered behind the slab of stone shielding the exit from the cave. The judge sounded like he was somewhere to the right, and fairly far off. Maybe, anyway.

The whimper came again.

I bit back a curse. Dammit, I had to get out of here! What other option was there? And if escape meant the Beast died but I ended up with a normal life—assuming I could make it out of the ocean without drowning—then that was just—

"You can't do this forever, Beast."

Goddamn him.

I pushed the distracting thoughts aside. All my debates wouldn't matter if I was killed by that glowing specter of a judge.

I waited a moment longer and then slipped out from hiding. The cave lay at the intersection of two main rifts of the overall canyon structure, with a long stretch of chasm on either side and another leading to the amphitheater up ahead. The water still glowed, and the dust had settled a bit, affording me a clearer view of the destruction. In some places, the canyon walls now looked more like steep hillsides, with so many rocks and ruins sloughed down. In other spots, the walls still stood, though even as I watched, I could see stones tumble into the chasm.

But the darkness was what stopped me.

I shivered. Down the length of the canyon on both sides of me, the water glowed up until a point where it just… stopped. To a point where darkness hung like a curtain, like a wall of its own: thick, black, and impenetrable. But the dark wasn't motionless, wasn't simply waiting. As I watched, it crept forward, inching over the crumbled rocks and pillars, swallowing them into itself while it slid inexorably toward me.

"I'll find you, Beast."

I flinched. I couldn't see the judge, but he still sounded far to the right.

Good enough.

I swam toward the amphitheater.

"You can't hide forever."

No kidding.

I kicked harder in the water. The entrance to the amphitheater was a pile of pale debris, and the majority of the stairs and pillars had crumbled. Nothing but a swath of white rubble remained where the ruins of the complex had been.

Except in the center.

I struggled through the water, trying to swim faster. The heart of the amphitheater was still bizarrely clear, a flat circular space surrounded by mounds of debris. The barricade of stones overhead held as well, with almost no gaps or darkness showing through.

But I couldn't pick up on that vine of magic anymore.

"Do you feel the darkness coming for you, Beast?"

I tossed a quick glance behind me, confirming he still wasn't there, and then swam for the circle of cleared space. The magic in the water seemed to change the closer to the center I got, tingling over my skin with strange, not-unpleasant electricity. Like pop rocks I'd had as a kid, but all around me, sensation and flavor and sweetness alike somehow dancing over my skin. It was faint, though. Diffuse, in a way.

As if nearly all of it was being absorbed before it could even leave the ground.

Understanding sank over me. Of course it was faint. Of course the vine was gone. The thing that was feeding off of it— the *monster* that was feeding off of it—was inside this prison now too.

I cast a swift look around, not seeing the judge. But that might not mean much. I could go invisible too.

Anxiety pounded through me, and I kicked in the water, swimming closer to where the vine had been as quickly as I could. I might still be able to use the magic. The center of the amphitheater was still the source of this power, whether or not the judge was drawing on it.

And if I could take it in, if I could *control* it, then I'd have my life back. Everything I'd ever wanted.

I sank down into the cleared circle. Magic prickled over me, faint but still present. It almost seemed like light now, for all that my eyes still couldn't perceive it. But my mind did, as if a pale radiance shone from the white gravel, the glow filled with shifting wisps of light green and yellow, blue and purple. The power tangled around my fingers as I placed my hand on the seafloor, the magic twisting around me, waiting for me to let it past my skin.

I couldn't make myself let it in.

"This place will destroy you, Beast."

His voice echoed from beyond the amphitheater, but I didn't look away from the cleared space. Deep inside, I could feel remnants of the Beast, so quiet now, it was almost unperceivable. It couldn't fight me. Couldn't stop me. Deep inside me, it huddled, as helpless as I'd been when it ended my greliaran life. But in one moment, I could undo that. I could reset everything to the way it'd been, before I lost my life to a monster who had nearly torn me to shreds.

Except it hadn't.

I pulled my hand away from the seafloor. That was the thing, wasn't it? That was always the thing.

The Beast hadn't wanted to be a killer, not at first.

And I wasn't either. Not when I had a choice, not when I didn't have to. Not when I wasn't acting out of rage or pain or protecting the ones I loved—just like the Beast. I only killed to survive.

We were so different, and yet we weren't different at all. In the end, the Beast hadn't destroyed me, not really. Almost, but then it stopped. Instead, for this entire year, I, the Beast, or whatever I'd become, had only been trying to live.

Every part of me just wanted to live.

The magic tingled over my skin. *Choice,* the ghost woman had called it.

I closed my eyes, focusing on the scrap of the Beast I could still feel, deep down inside. I wouldn't kill it. Me. But maybe we could use this magic and not have either part of us die. *I could.*

Because this time, it was fully my choice.

Join me, I whispered inside my mind.

"Ah, there you are."

My eyes flew open in time only to catch a glimpse of the man behind me, his too-white face split by an inhumanly black grin. He grabbed my shoulder and my arm, ripping me away from the magic, and hurling me back through the water to crash into the amphitheater debris.

"Is this it?" The judge chuckled as he floated across the floor after me. "You come to the end and face me as… what? A *child?*"

I struggled up from the rubble, glaring, but then my eyes caught on the ruins of the walls.

The darkness hovered on them like a cloak draped around the amphitheater. I couldn't see the canyon anymore.

"Is that what you wanted to be, Beast? A boy? To pretend to be human?"

In a heartbeat, he was across the amphitheater, his hands

slamming into me and throwing me back farther. I crashed into the wreckage of a stairway and caught myself, my hands crushing into the white stone in a desperate attempt to keep from tumbling back into the darkness.

The prison wall shifted like a curtain of oil only a few feet from my side.

I scrambled away from the ravenous shadows.

"Afraid of the dark, Beast?" The judge appeared in the rubble of an archway above the stairs. His eyes were black pits in his white face, and crackles of black lightning flashed around them. He reached up, leisurely swiping his hand through the darkness and then drawing it back toward himself. The shadows stretched like tendrils of molasses, tangling around his pale hand. "Afraid of what they made to destroy you?"

He lashed his hand out, and black lances shot through the water at me. I kicked hard, scrabbling and twisting to get out of the way, but I couldn't move fast enough. A needle of shadows slashed across my forearm, and I cried out, pain screaming up from the gash. It felt like a burn, like ice, like my skin couldn't decide whether hot or cold had just happened.

And I was bleeding.

I couldn't stop myself from staring. Small clouds of blood were drifting up from the wound on my arm.

I hadn't seen my own blood in a year.

The judge scoffed, incredulity heavy in the tone. "You *bleed?*"

I didn't know what to think. I hadn't taken in that power yet, hadn't chosen to be human or greliaran or to kill the Beast side of myself.

But then, I'd chosen to be alive. Maybe that was enough. Maybe it wasn't an illusion of a heartbeat I'd been feeling.

And now…

As I watched, the wound on my arm sealed over, healing completely. My blood faded from the water.

Deep inside, the Beast growled.

"What a fool you are. All that power, and you choose a human body. A human life." He shook his head. "And a human death."

Quickly, the judge swept his hand through the darkness again and flung more shadowy spears at me. I twisted, trying to get out of the way, but I couldn't move fast enough. A blade slashed me, tearing a deep gash across my thigh, and I choked on the pain. On instinct, my hand grabbed the wound.

I looked back up at him as he laughed. For all that it hurt like hell, there wasn't much blood this time, simply because I didn't want there to be. Shivers began in my middle, quivering deep inside my core like a distant warning, spreading outward. A darkness I knew, returning, merging with every reborn molecule of me, every cell, but different than before.

It wasn't taking my life. It was part of it. A force and a power, but I was its core. I held it to life, *real* life, all it'd ever wanted. Home and safety and love. A truth that had been ripped away so long ago, it had almost forgotten it ever dreamed of such a thing.

The word came back to me, the word that had flitted through my mind when I'd been so terrified, when this place first tried to kill me. The word that had been a plea, only I hadn't understood.

I was the anchor.

And inside me, the Beast growled louder.

"Give up and die, *child*," the judge scoffed.

More blades flew at me. I kicked in the water, willing myself wide of the attack, and the water swirled around me, carrying me out of the way. At even that brief display of power, the prison walls rumbled, hungry and closing in.

"I can do this for eternity, Beast. Do you think you have that kind of time?"

Of course not.

The judge flung his hand toward the middle of the amphitheater, and the water around me lurched as the magic there surged toward him. I grabbed at the remains of a pillar, my fingers crunching into the white stone, and hung on as the power at the heart of this place poured into the judge.

And the darkness followed.

I threw a quick look around and then released my grip, letting the impossible current drag me a few yards farther from the prison walls before I grabbed another chunk of debris. The darkness was farther inside the amphitheater now. The glowing water around me was a sphere barely fifty yards across.

And shrinking.

"I don't think you have any time left at all," the judge said.

I looked back toward him. I didn't stand a chance against that darkness. I knew it'd devour me whole. But the judge wasn't the same. The judge wasn't the prison; he was just using it.

And he was feeding from the power that might set me free.

I let go of the debris.

The current caught me immediately, dragging me toward him. Slashing a hand through the shadows, the judge snarled as he sent spears flying at me. I willed myself out of the way, just a flicker of strength that nevertheless made the prison walls close in faster. But the spears flew past me, harmless, even as the current drew me onward.

Straight toward the judge.

His eyes went wide, and suddenly, the pull on the magic stopped. But it wasn't enough to halt my momentum.

The judge lashed out with a burst of lightning, aiming right at me. The blast struck my chest, shoving me away from him, tangling over me.

Absorbing into my skin.

I sank gently in the water, my feet coming to rest on the gravel, while I stared at the electricity slipping into my body like it'd come home. A slow breath entered my lungs, made of water but as effortless as air, before drifting back out again in a sigh.

My eyes lifted to his, and I saw it. Just for a heartbeat. Just a flash.

Fear.

Understanding spread through me. This was why he'd used the prison as a weapon rather than attack me himself. This was why the Judiciary had wanted me dead. Over and over, they'd wanted me dead.

Because I took in magic. Because I could take this, and they didn't have a chance in hell of stopping me.

And suddenly, I knew why.

They couldn't use the pure form of this energy and simultaneously keep me from taking it from them. All their tweaks and changes and protections for themselves couldn't defeat one simple fact. They fed from this power.

I was born of it.

This magic was me.

I stretched my hands out, feeling for the bright, pop-rocks sensation of power filtering through the water. It was faint, so faint, but thanks to the judge, it was everywhere.

A smile lifted the edges of my mouth, and the Beast smiled through me. With a thought, I could feel the magic drifting into my skin.

I was both Beast and greliaran, and so much more.

And I always would be.

The judge snarled, swiping his hands at the shadows, sending spear after spear slicing at me in a rapid barrage. I didn't move, but the water did, the faint tangle of magic inside it shifting ever so slightly, diverting the blades, sending them around me.

Fury twisted the judge's face. The drag on the magic in the water picked up again, harder and more desperate. The prison walls surged toward me.

I let the current carry me toward him. The pull stopped. He retreated.

The prison walls hovered around us, only a few feet away

now.

"You think this little standoff means anything, Beast? You think you've *won*? I can survive this prison. You can't." He grinned. "You're all alone."

The magic around us began to change, prickling with the same pop-rocks feeling as before, but stronger. But the power didn't rush toward him. Instead, the glow around us grew brighter, like a lightbulb on overload. The water began to shake, and through the cracks in the prison, a new-old, so-familiar magic poured.

I smiled again. "No, I'm not."

I lunged forward as the darkness began to fragment. Light flooded through the cracks, blinding, brilliant, and I could feel the truth in the magic surging all around me.

Enough like me to reach the prison, different enough to shatter it all, and connected to me through happenstance and life and deep love.

Pure Baylie.

I grabbed the judge, my own power answering my call. Through my skin, his magic rushed into me, and he couldn't hope to break my grip. The stark white tone of his skin melted back to a pale Caucasian shade, and the black pits of his eye sockets became normal human flesh while the smoke and lightning inside him roared into me. All around us, the darkness crumbled and burned like water evaporating beneath a blazing sun.

Till the prison was gone.

I drew a breath and let it out slowly. The man in my grip

wasn't dead; he had just enough of that magic left in him to keep him alive down here. I wouldn't kill him if I didn't have to.

But that didn't mean he wouldn't pay for all he'd done.

"I know some strakirin and ruanir who are going to want to talk to you," I said.

My gaze rose, taking in the ruins and the canyon beyond. They looked different now, and it took me a moment to realize why.

The glow in the water had dissipated. The ancient magic was still present around me, filtering out into the world now, unfettered by long-forgotten traps and destruction. But what I could see was just me, just my own eyes, with the ability to see in the dark that I'd had for the past year.

Baylie's magic faded from the water like a storm that had passed. *Thanks,* I thought.

In the distance, I felt her smile.

And then more impressions reached me, unhindered by the prison at last. Ari, but she wasn't alone. A host of minds and presences hovered around her. The whispers I'd heard this entire time. They were connected to her, *part* of her, but more than that. I could feel them all through her.

They were scared. So was she. Fear pounded inside her, bringing adrenaline and yet courage.

So much courage.

But something was coming. Something dark.

Logan.

Inside me, the Beast snarled.

With the judge in my grip, I surged up from the canyon and left the ruins behind.

32

ARI

The black cloud let me go, sending me crashing onto the dirt. Pain shot through my hands and knees, and then my shoulder too while I tumbled on the ground.

My gaze darted around. I was on a mountaintop. An actual *mountaintop*, though there wasn't much of it. A few dozen yards of windswept gravel and frost, and then sheer edges of rock and ice where the drop down began. The air was bitterly cold, making a mockery of my tank top and shorts. A shiver coursed through me, and my skin took on a green shimmer as my strakirin abilities worked to compensate for the possibility of freezing to death.

And then my eyes registered the curve of the earth in the distance and the itty-bitty threads that were actually roads far below. Vertigo stirred my stomach and quivering adrenaline surged through my veins, instinctively making me crawl backward and search for the nearest stable object I could find.

It was a *long* way down.

But there wasn't anyone with me. Not a strakirin, not

anyone from the resistance. I was alone.

Or almost.

The clouds above me drew in on themselves, condensing and swirling and finally taking on the shape of a human, though that's where the similarity ended. A body formed of a black storm walked toward me. He folded his hands behind him, a casual posture like he had all the time in the world.

And inhuman or not, I could still see his smirk.

"Well, well, Ariabella Moreau. Long time, no see." Logan chuckled. "Or close enough."

I pushed away from the ground.

A crackle of lightning whipped from him, jolting me back down.

"Uh-uh. I think I like you kneeling for now."

Shivers thrummed through my muscles from the blast despite the fact it hadn't been stronger than a small jolt from an electrical socket. Enough to shake me. Not enough to kill.

Yet.

"What do you want?" I said.

"Hmm, what *don't* I want?" Logan strolled along the edge of the sheer drop, surveying the vista like it was all his kingdom. "Seems like it's all pretty much mine for the taking. The Judiciary... yeah, that'll be mine once that bastard Engle is dead. The ruanir... they'll all serve me soon. The dehaians... oh, they're so going to die. The humans are irrelevant, except maybe for entertainment, and what does that leave?" He turned back to me, grinning. "You. Just you."

I inched backward on the gravel. "Me?"

My awareness stretched out, searching. The hive—my hive, the hive of the broken ones—was still alive, but only for now. Fear and pain whispered over the distance, carrying from them to me.

But their fear wasn't just about the Judiciary or escaping. The hive knew they couldn't reach me in time to help anything.

"Poor little Ariabella Moreau," Logan said. "You don't have a clue, do you?"

"About what?" My gaze twitched over the mountainside. There wasn't much hope of scaling down there, not before Logan caught me.

After all, only one of us could fly.

"Of what you are. Of what's going to happen." He chuckled again. "Of why I'm going to kill you."

My gaze snapped back to him.

"What's the line from that cheesy old Highlander franchise?" he mused. "'There can be only one'?"

Confusion flickered through me, enough that it must have touched my face. He laughed. "God, you're such an idiot."

A chill wind rushed past, carrying a magic like the scent of salt on the air.

My breath caught. I knew that magic, that power.
Noah.

I didn't dare look to the west, but I could feel him more than I had in what seemed like an eternity. He was rising past the horizon, far in the distance but closing fast, heading straight for me.

He was free.

My heart began pounding harder while a desperate plan formed in my mind. Logan could fly, but Noah could too. All I needed to do was get as far from Logan as I could, buy Noah some time to reach me, and then we could get out of here.

As fast as possible, because the thing in front of me would definitely try to kill us both.

Again.

"Only one what?" I prompted, pulling my defenses around me as tightly as possible. My eyes saw a storm monster. My mind was a different story. I felt the drone behind his words, like a single-minded and invisible entity answerable only to him. He'd grown that hive since last I'd seen him. The strength of it crawled over my skin like ants made of electricity.

Thousands of them.

"What do you think?" Logan replied. "Those morons knew they couldn't leave the hive as just a mindless collective. It'd go insane. They needed a genius at the heart of it. A mind that so far surpassed any paltry ruanir, that it could be the stabilizing core. One strong enough to hold their creation together. And so, of course, they chose me."

I inched backward, not taking my eyes from him.

"But they screwed up," he continued, his voice growing heated. "They thought they'd controlled the whole process. They thought there was no risk. That, even if you'd taken in the old Beast's magic, even if you'd spent a few days running around free, they'd cleansed their template of any 'errors.' After all, they tested their creation, and it said you were gone. They ran countless tests, certain that if any trace of you remained, you'd fight them. But you never did. You never *could*. And they never considered checking whether you were hiding in the dark, far below where their little zombie strakirin could perceive. They never thought to ask if you were *powerless*."

His hand slashed toward me as if in a fit of rage. Lightning snapped over the distance between us, driving me back to the ground.

Ari? Noah called.

A ragged gasp left me. His voice in my mind was like a rush of air when I'd desperately needed to breathe. It'd been so long, *too* long, since I'd heard him. An image flashed through my mind—the coast surging closer, Judge Engle plummeting to the sand, dehaians staring skyward as Noah shot past—and then there was only the blur of the landscape beneath him as he raced north to reach me.

I'm okay, I replied.

My fingers dug into the grit and frost. I pushed myself up from the dirt, my arms trembling.

"And then they threw you into the ocean, like the *idiots* they are." Logan was pacing now. "Those dimwits honestly trusted you were gone." He laughed incredulously. "But of course you weren't, were you? No, you were still lurking in there, so changed by that magic you shared with the Beast that it gave you delusions of grandeur. So changed that it made you unlike any of my strakirin, the *right* kind of strakirin, who knew they needed to listen to *me*. No, you were just biding your time, imagining you could take this hive for yourself, imagining you could interfere with *me*."

He was across the space between us in a heartbeat. His hand wrapped around my throat, and I kicked, hitting nothing while he hefted me into the air.

A cold grin showed in the black storm of his face. "Imagining you could *matter*."

My fingers scrambled at Logan's grip. I felt Noah's panic past my own, and the way the air tore around him as he fought for more speed.

Logan tossed me down. Pain flashed through my knees and palms as I tumbled across the rough ground.

"Don't fret, Ariabella, I'm not going to kill you. Not yet. I've got a show to put on first. *Death of the Dehaians*, one night only. I wouldn't want you to miss it."

Ari? Noah's worry pressed on me.

Okay… I'm okay.

For now.

Logan glanced to the west. Rage twitched over his face. "That Judiciary bastard," he muttered. "Coming back to enslave me again, huh?"

"What do you mean?" I rasped, hoping to distract him, even if I didn't have a clue who he meant. But it didn't really matter. I just needed to buy time, because Noah would be here in minutes now. Maybe less. "What show?"

Logan glanced back at me, his irritation fading into cruel amusement. "Oh, just a little weapon I found with one of your friends. A spell, really. Designed to wipe out the judges, I think, though that's not nearly as fun as what I've got planned."

My stomach turned to lead. Declan's weapon. Oh my God,

he'd gotten his hands on Declan's weapon.

"Magic is like putty to me," he said. "Moldable, change-able, and oh, what I've done to change this." He grinned. "The judges believe the Beast altered the magic of the dehaians and landwalkers last year, taking the way that king's girlfriend could go inland and giving it to all the dehaians out there. But that Beast was weak. It had nothing on what I can do."

He lifted his hands. The buzzing on my skin changed. Twin tornadoes of dark magic swirled up from his palms. "Dehaians made this. It was child's play to shift it around to kill them all instead."

My head shook. "You need them, Logan. The magic the dehaians generate from going back and forth between land and—"

He let out a laugh. "You still believe that old lie? Oh, I'm so far ahead of you, Ariabella. The judges never meant us to depend on the dehaians to survive. Why would they? Seems kind of foolish to leave your super-weapon dependent upon magic from someone else, wouldn't you say? They intended me to wipe out the dehaians all along—admittedly, they also meant for me to leave the Judiciary in charge, but what's life with-out a little regime change every now and then?" He grinned. "The weapon will take the closest dehaian, then the closest after that, and on and on. It'll rip through those silly little mermaids like the Black Plague on steroids, and if any manage to hide from it, then maybe, *maybe* I'll let them beg me to live. But until then…" He extended his palms toward the sky and then paused theatrically, as if another thought had just occurred to him. "By the way, I'm guessing your brother is still with some dehaians. He was, last time I saw him." Logan winked at me. "Let's say I start with those ones first."

The tornadoes of magic erupted upward.

"No!" I shouted.

Black clouds swept around us, engulfing the magic and the mountaintop.

Noah was here.

Pain roared through my connection to him, and the sky reflected his agony. The wind snarled. The dark clouds churned, towering above us like a closing fist preparing to crash down. Inside the storm, purple lightning flared, leaving eerie red afterimages like a throbbing heart. The magic fought him, thrashing inside him, resisting his efforts to absorb it, change it, stop it from killing the entire dehaian world. Like acid, it burned. Like a living creature, it twisted, cutting and slicing at everything it could reach.

And past his roar of agony, another sound reached my ears. Logan.

Laughing.

On my hands and knees, I dragged my gaze from the clouds. Across the flat expanse of the mountaintop stood Logan, a storm in human shape with his hands extended to the sky. The threads of magic twisted around his fingers, connecting him to the spell. They twitched at his will, as if the massive weapon was a marionette and he was its puppeteer. His power poured through the threads, feeding the weapon, fighting Noah to a standstill.

And he never stopped laughing.

I couldn't let the real monster win.

Shoving away from the rough gravel, I tore across the open space. I felt Noah's alarm. Saw Logan glance away from the fight.

And then I collided with him.

Logan staggered slightly, one hand breaking away from the threads of magic to grab me. Amused shock crossed his face even as the drone swelled, ready to devour me just as it always had been.

But then, that hadn't happened with my hive.

"What the hell did you think you were—" Logan began.

I love you, I said to Noah.

Ari, no!

I plunged my hands into the storm of Logan's body, dropped my defenses, and let the drone pour in.

A wave of darkness crashed over me. Utter blackness swept across my mind, my memories, intent on crushing everything I'd been. And in it, there was only Logan. Because he was the drone, because they were him. A thousand strakirin bound to his will, his desires, pouring down on me like the ocean itself.

But I'd been made never to drown.

Oblivion engulfed my world, wrapping me in black, hungry tentacles. I could feel the rage of it in my mind, the need to own me, to smother me once and for all, to prove that it was the strongest, the best.

Even if that had always been a lie.

Inside myself, I slipped past the tentacles to sink through the darkness, farther and farther down, like the deepest trench of the ocean lived within me. And Logan couldn't follow me. His power was in façade, in *seeming,* and brute force control. But that wasn't the truth of the hive, because far beyond his roar and fury, beyond his black oblivion that raged on the surface and sought desperately to retain control, a thousand minds also whispered. A thousand minds lay deep within the dark, waiting for the heart of their magic to set them free.

Their key.

"Like this," I whispered.

I reached for the power of the ocean inside myself, through my connection to a deep, dark magic that had always been there, because of Noah, the one they'd stolen from, just to make me.

But they'd never had the final say.

Through the air and the ground, the breath of the ocean's energy reached me. They'd taken living magic to make me, and thought they could control it. Kill it and fashion what they wanted from the corpse. But Noah had stolen me away from them, and we'd shared power for days, weeks even, back and forth.

Choosing to love each other instead.

To make each other free.

Magic from the ocean poured out of me, through the

darkness and into the deepest reaches of the hive. The mindless drone died as each of the strakirin rose from behind the walls of their defenses, riding the wave of the ocean's power back to me, through me, to join the other hive. *My* hive. The broken ones.

The ones who'd never been broken.

Warmth spread through me as my hive grew stronger, driving back the darkness and the empty, soulless drone of Logan's paltry, childish will. The magic that made me surged through my blood, muscles, and bones, engulfing everything in pure, endless, immortal light.

I opened my eyes.

Logan stood in front of me, a tableau of willful destruction, and only a moment had passed. His hands still stretched up, pouring poison into the tumultuous sky. His storm-cloud face remained twisted between rage and shock. And my hands were in his chest, immersed in shadows.

But I was different now.

Mist and magic, glowing silver-white like the moon on the waves, my body was a summer storm, eternal as the ocean, immortal as the Beast above me. My fingers twisted inside Logan, wrapping around the invisible, magical root of what the judges had done, what they'd chosen for him to be without ever asking us what we wanted.

I ripped the core of his power from him.

Logan staggered. The spell pouring from him died as he stumbled backward and crashed to his knees on the mountaintop, one hand clutching his chest. Overhead, thunder rumbled as Noah absorbed the rest of the spell, turning it to nothing.

But the storm of Logan's body melted in fits and starts, finally vanishing back into skin and scales like a strakirin on land.

Horror spread over Logan's face. "What…" He gave a rough gasp, his gaze darting from me to the dark clouds of Noah above us and then back again. "No… *No!*"

Memories flickered in me of sharing magic with Noah, of learning from him even as he learned from me. My ruanir form returned as I walked toward Logan, and he scrambled back, shaking, his eyes locked on me like I was his nightmare. The hive swelled like an invisible host of angels, flanking me, waiting for me.

The hive queen.

And their minds were like a song.

Logan's horrified expression deepened. He could feel them. He was still linked to us, a lonely, angry, entitled whisper, clinging to the fringes now.

"What's it going to be, Logan?" I asked. "You can live. You can remain joined with us, or not. It's your choice." I felt the lightning crackle in my eyes. "But you're never going to hurt anyone ever again."

Logan stared at me. His face twitched as his horror turned to confusion, turned to offense.

Turned to rage.

Screaming, he lunged up from the ground to charge at me.

The hive rushed through me. All the minds of which I was a part, all the voices and the memories and the people who didn't know what we would be now, only that they would never let this monster, this child, this broken thing hurt us again.

They surged from me, tearing into him at the same moment my magic struck.

He flew backward, slamming into the side of the mountain. Limp, he crumpled to the ground, unconscious, still breathing.

But no longer with a trace of magic inside him. No longer part of the hive.

The storm clouds above me swirled and evaporated as Noah drew down into his human form. For a moment, he stood there, staring at me, and even with our connection, even with everything we had, I couldn't read the tumult of emotions inside him.

He rushed across the distance between us, taking my face in his hands, and kissed me.

I closed my eyes, sinking into his kiss, into his arms, into the pure perfection of having him back and here with me.

Alive.

He pulled back, his gaze running over me as if to drink in every inch of me. "I'm never leaving you again. *Never.*"

A smile pulled at my lips. "Me either." I reached up, my hand tracing the warmth of his cheek. "You're… you're breathing. For real. And you—" My fingers brushed his neck, and then I froze, feeling his pulse beating strong and sure beneath his skin. I drew back, looking up at him. "You…"

His palm cupped my cheek, the magic that formed me tingling in response to his touch. "Yeah."

A breeze drifted past, still dancing with the magic I'd felt when Noah broke free. I blinked, drawn to the sensation. "Something's different."

The joy in Noah's face faded, and he paused before giving a small nod. "The power coming from the canyon, it…" Hesitancy filled him while he searched for words. "Ari, it could change you back. If you wanted, if *any* of the strakirin wanted. It could take this away."

I stared at him. He didn't move, but his thoughts retreated from the link between us, as if he was bracing himself for what I would say.

And for the first time, I couldn't even imagine it. Going back now, walking away from everything that'd happened. No, it hadn't been my choice, not any of this.

But good had still come from it. So much good, and to change now would be to turn my back on all of that too.

"No." My hands took his. "Never."

Shivers surged up inside my skin, the power in me rising up to meet the energy in him. A small gasp left him as he felt it.

"We stay together," I said softly.

He nodded. "Together."

 EPILOGUE

ARI

Two weeks later

The smell of salt filled the air, and the touch of magic did too. People on rollerblades swept past us, weaving between tourists and food stands and little shops set up along the boardwalk. Sunlight warmed my hair and skin, while in the distance, the sound of the surf rolling in undercut the rising and falling waves of conversation all around us.

It'd only been two weeks since I took the hive from Logan. Two weeks since the war with the Judiciary ended. Noah and I had returned to the research facility to find that Dhanya and others from the resistance had already broken in. They'd come to rescue us, and to stop Declan. Instead, they discovered the strakirin holding Judge Davenport and the enforcers prisoner.

And they'd found Declan too.

He was alive, barely. Halfway through the change to a strakirin, it was a miracle he hadn't been killed. But now, like the hive of the never-broken, like the strakirin Logan had made who'd wandered in to find us over the past week, Declan was one of us too.

He hadn't seemed to mind. Not once he'd laid eyes on his daughter.

From the song in the background of my mind, their voices rose briefly. He and Jennifer were with Ellie and a few other landwalker elders in what remained of one of Declan's laboratories, trying to piece it back together. They were discussing further research into what we were, though their tests had already shown that my lifespan was seemingly endless, like Noah's, and that the rest of the strakirin would live easily as long as any ruanir. But they wanted to know how they could use what we'd become to change any landwalkers or ruanir who wanted to go beneath the waves too.

And Declan was laughing.

"You like this?"

I glanced over at Noah as he lifted a beaded bracelet from the display rack of a stall selling jewelry. Blue beads the color of ocean waves glistened in the bright sun.

"It's beautiful," I agreed.

He smiled and retrieved his wallet from his back pocket. I grinned.

Logan was in the hands of the resistance now. Judge Engle, Judge Davenport, and a slew of others too. With the help of the strakirin, the resistance tracked down more of the Judiciary's research centers, taking the judges prisoner in the process. The television stations and communication relays that the Judiciary used to reach all the ruanir belonged to the resistance now, and slowly, word was getting out that the dehaians hadn't been behind the newly declared war, the slaughter of the ruanir neighborhoods or, really, much of anything at all.

Besides helping save all our lives.

Over the past few days, calls for Logan and the judges to be tried as criminals had begun among the regular ruanir. There were countless charges to bring against them, countless lives they'd ruined over the years. In their research centers and various headquarters, Miguel and the resistance had uncovered storehouses of records going back centuries. As meticulous as they were cruel, the Judiciary had documented everything, from their plans to create the strakirin to plots they'd never had the opportunity to hatch.

Including their involvement with the death of my father.

I bit my lip, turning away to watch the kids playing in the waves as the ocean rolled in. Before he died, my dad had learned that the Judiciary intended to use Jace and me once my father's own conversion to a judge was done. As Osias had said, the Judiciary had had their eyes on us for years, and they'd planned for decades to create something like the strakirin—as a test run, basically, in case the Beast ever returned. To a real judge, the sacrifice of his children wouldn't have mattered. A real judge would have offered us up and not cared. Instead, my dad had immediately raced to find us, planning to take both me and Jace and run like hell for the resistance, knowing we would have their protection.

He never got the chance.

On a lonely stretch of highway, they'd run him off the road, staging the scene to look like a drunk driver had been to blame. He never could warn us, warn Miguel, any of it. And then we were handed off to Mom, who was only too happy to follow through on the Judiciary's plan once they finally presented it to her.

My mother left Chicago the moment word reached her that the resistance had taken control. She was still out there somewhere, probably carrying on like the Judiciary had never died. Lots of the elite were doing that now, trying to set up their own counter-resistance movements, as if they could return the ruanir to their "glory days" when money was everything and the Judiciary ruled.

They didn't stand a chance, though. Not when the "rabble," as some of the elites once dismissed them, finally had power. The so-called *common* ruanir had spent a millennium under the thumb of leaders who'd destroyed families and lives, and if any of the elites tried to reestablish the Judiciary or take back the reins of the government, they'd face an opposition one thousand years in the making.

Miguel, Veronique, Willa, and all the others would make sure of it. And as for Mom, I knew we'd find her eventually.

"You okay?" Noah asked, coming up to me.

I took a deep breath. "Yeah."

He eyed me with concern before slipping the bracelet onto my wrist. I turned my arm, watching the beads catch the sunlight, and then gave Noah a kiss on his cheek. "Thank you."

We stepped out of the way as a young couple pushing a baby carriage strolled by, all of them looking totally human.

The dehaians were mostly gone for the time being; they'd returned home within days of me taking the hive. Since the war was more or less over, they had matters to attend to beneath the sea—not the least of which was rebuilding their cities and towns. Damerion kept us apprised of how things were going, though, including the fact that Ezio was healing well from his injuries. The Vetorian was apparently enjoying the excuse the wounds gave him to stick around Nyciena for a while, spending time with the commander before either of them needed to get back to work again.

Meanwhile, Osias and the surviving Driecaran spies were scheduled to be tried in Yvarian court for their crimes. To offset any fears that Zeke would be like his father, the king had even brought in special consultants from among refugee Driecarans, asking them to advise on sentencing and show the dehaian world that the trials would be fair.

That strange guy, Wyatt, was back at the hospital where Olivia and the others had found him. Apparently he had his own sentence to carry out, though no one seemed inclined to discuss the details. I heard he'd saved Baylie's life, and possibly others too. Olivia said that Baylie and Ellie planned to put in a good word for him once he was up for parole.

In the end, only a few strakirin decided to let the magic of the canyon change them back to ruanir. Most chose instead to stay part of the hive. Luna and Leo went with the Yvarians, bringing with them the other strakirin who had no home to go back to, or who weren't ready to face their ruanir family after what they'd become. Zeke passed a decree within moments of their arrival, mandating that they were guests of the throne and not to be harmed. Now, with Chloe's help, the king was working with Kreyus to find them a home beneath the waves.

"There's a slushee place down the boardwalk," Noah suggested, lacing his fingers through mine. "You want to try it?"

I chuckled. Food felt like a new thing to both of us, even if, in reality, it wasn't. With the changes brought about by the magic he'd freed from the canyon, we could eat now if we wanted, sleep if we chose, or go without either if we didn't want to bother.

I was still getting used to those things being optional.

We started down the sidewalk, past shops selling "I Heart Santa Lucina" bumper stickers and t-shirts.

"I never understood those," Noah said. "Why advertise your own city, or a city you visited?"

I shook my head, grinning. "Just for the memories, I guess."

He made a considering noise. We kept walking.

Maia and Dhanya were home in Chicago again, putting their lives back together after this summer. They were both still helping the resistance although most of their work had become remote and handled with simple, quick phone calls. Their wedding plans were back on as well; I was still the maid of honor.

I tightened my grip on Noah's hand. And I had a date to the wedding.

Baylie was back in Kansas, though she'd stayed with the ruanir for a while, working on ways to explore her new powers safely, and on ways to help the greliarans as well. Last I'd heard, the greliarans were coming out of the woodwork now, curious to see whether Baylie could heal the cravings within them too.

So far, things looked good.

For Baylie's part, she seemed to be growing more comfortable with her magic every day even if the news that Declan and the others thought she'd go through the adjustment soon had thrown her. And while there was a chance that the power in the canyon could change her back, she'd only greeted that news with silence. Well, silence and a quick look to my brother that wasn't hard to read.

Changing back would mean giving up the power I'd heard they shared. Maybe more than that, in the long run. After all, she might have a life span like the rest of the ruanir now—but only if she kept her new abilities.

So she'd said no.

Learning she might live for hundreds of years still hit Baylie hard, though. Within a couple of days of hearing that, she'd suddenly told the others she needed to get back home. Miguel and the resistance hadn't argued, but instead, arranged a first-class ticket for her under a fake identity, just in case any remaining Judiciary operatives hadn't gotten the memo to stay away from us all.

For every step of the way, my brother stayed right beside her. Jace really cared about her and seemed to fit with her in a way that made both me and Noah smile, especially since someone would have to be blind to miss the feelings growing between the two of them. So of course, Jace went with her to Kansas—though only after I reassured him about a thousand times that I'd be fine here.

I wasn't alone. I didn't want him to be either.

With Jace at her side and her stepmom there too, Baylie finally told her father what she was, what Noah and Chloe and all of us were, everything. The news that neither his kid nor his stepkids were human had understandably been a shock, but from what I gathered from my brother, overall it had gone well.

They were planning a cookout before the weather got too cold. All of us were invited.

"So what's your favorite flavor?" Noah asked as we neared the slushee place.

I made a thoughtful noise. "Blue raspberry."

"Really?"

"What?"

He chuckled. "Nothing. It'll just be cute to see your mouth turn blue."

I bumped my shoulder against his, laughing. "What's yours, then?"

"Grape, but if I get cherry, then maybe we'll both turn purple when I kiss—"

His cell phone buzzed, and his smile faltered, nervousness spiking through him.

"It's okay," I urged when he didn't move to answer it.

He nodded as if steadying himself and then took out the phone. I turned away, watching a little boy run up to the slushee shop, the string to a mermaid-shaped balloon clutched in his fist. I didn't try to listen to the call. Noah's thoughts were sequestered away like they were sealed inside a shuttered house, but regardless, eavesdropping would've been rude. The privacy of our own thoughts, unless invited, had become something of an unspoken rule among the strakirin. As an honorary member, that rule extended to Noah too.

Noah hung up, hesitating a second before returning the phone to his pocket.

"Everything okay?" I asked.

"Yeah." His answer was quick. Strained, too. "Olivia says they, uh… they pulled up a minute ago."

He didn't move.

"You want me to stay with you?" I offered. "Or I could wait here…?"

His head shook. "No. No, that's…" He caught sight of the slushee place again. "You, uh, you still want to get…" He motioned with his free hand.

I hesitated. "If you want."

He faltered for a minute, blinking fast. "Uh, yeah, sure."

"Noah."

He looked to me, but then his gaze darted away. "Or, you know, we could keep walking for a bit—"

"You're stalling."

He froze. Emotions flickered over his face, reflecting the tumult I could feel inside him. "I know," he acknowledged quietly.

I watched him for a moment and then wrapped my other hand over where his fingers were interlaced with mine. "It's going to be fine."

He nodded.

In silence, we walked back the way we'd come. The boardwalk

fell behind us, turning into a sidewalk that curved to trace the edge of a long, gentle slope of grass. Up ahead, a line of trees and bushes shielded a neighborhood, and when we reached the greenery, Noah's steps slowed.

He didn't look at me, but his grip tightened on my own.

We continued past the foliage, and up a circle drive toward a two-story mansion with off-white walls and a tile roof. No one appeared at any of the windows, nor at the door when we reached the front porch.

"It's going to be okay," I promised. "No matter what."

Noah looked over at me, so much more than understanding in his eyes. Love. Trust.

And he lifted his hand, letting it hang in the air for a moment before knocking on the door.

Moments passed. I strained my ears, praying they hadn't left so soon after arriving. But Olivia had called only minutes ago. Surely they wouldn't—

The door opened. An older man stood there, dark-haired with a trace of gray. Beyond him, a short, brunette woman came around the corner only to freeze, the dish towel in her hands forgotten.

A tight noise came from the man, and tears brimmed in his eyes. I glanced at Noah.

"Hey, Dad," he said, his voice choked. "I'm home."

The End.

Want more to read?
Explore the Kindling Trilogy!
Action, suspense, magic, and more await you in this thrilling
YA urban fantasy series!

Love the book?
Please leave a review on BookBub, Goodreads, and your
favorite retailers and book-related websites!

Other titles by Skye Malone
The Awakened Fate Series
The Demon Guardians Series
The Kindling Trilogy

About the author
Skye Malone is a fantasy and paranormal romance author,
which means she spends most of her time not-quite-convinced
that the magical things she imagines couldn't actually exist.

Born and raised in the Midwest of the United States, she
dreams someday of traveling the world – though in the meantime she'll take any story that whisks her off to a place where
the fantastic lives inside the everyday. She loves strong and pas-
sionate characters, complex villains, and satisfying endings that
stay with you long after the book is done. An inveterate writer,
she can't go a day without getting her hands on a keyboard, and
can usually be found typing away while she listens to all the
adventures unfolding in her head.

Connect with Skye Malone

Website: www.skyemalone.com

BookBub: www.bookbub.com/authors/skye-malone

Amazon: www.amazon.com/author/skyemalone

Facebook: www.facebook.com/authorskyemalone

Instagram: www.instagram.com/authorskyemalone

ACKNOWLEDGMENTS

Of every book in the Awakened Fate series, I think DESTINY was the most complex to write. From the technical standpoint, the multiple points of view in separate locations presented an interesting challenge, but beyond that, this series has been a part of my life for so long that saying goodbye to these characters was incredibly difficult. I love them all.

In the creation of this series, there have been so many people who helped me. My mother and sister are two of my biggest supporters, and it's no stretch to say I wouldn't be where I am today without them. Thank you, Mom. Thank you, Keri. I love you.

My friend Robin Augsburg has also been indispensable to me. Her care, her attention to detail, and her support are invaluable, both with these books and in my life. Thank you, Robin. I'm so grateful to know you.

Author JC Lillis is not only incredibly talented (seriously, go check out her books), but also a huge support to me in beta-reading. Her sharp eye caught more than a few missing details, and her input made the books better. Thank you, JC.

When speaking of sharp eyes, I would be remiss not to thank Monica Bogza for her detailed proofreading. In addition to being a knowledgeable and talented proofreader, she also went above and beyond for me, reading every title in the series in order to be thoroughly prepared to proofread the latter books, and I appreciate that effort more than I can say. Thank you, Monica.

Every cover for the Awakened Fate series was crafted by the gifted artist, Karri Klawiter. Karri's beautiful work has inspired more than a few details in my stories, including the fact that the ruanir use jewelry to store magic. For your incredible designs and for the inspiration you provide, Karri, thank you.

Lastly, none of these books would be where they are today without you, the one reading these words. For buying this book, for reading it, for sharing what you loved about it with others (and me!), and for all your support, you have my deepest gratitude. Thank you, thank you, thank you.